Keyboard

A Paninaro Imprint

www.paninaropublishing.co.uk
info@paninaropublishing.co.uk

www.paninaropublishing.co.uk

Contact - info@paninaropublishing.co.uk

A catalogue record for this book is available from the British Library.

ISBN - 13: 978 - 1916088566

Front cover image by A. Bund

A special thank you to Graham Cawsey for all his help in the run up to release day.

Any references to real people, living or dead, real events, business, organisations and localities are intended only to give the fiction a sense of reality and authenticity. All names, characters and incidents are either the product of the authors imagination, real life experiences or are used fictitiously, and their resemblance, if any, to real - life counterparts are entirely coincidental.

Socials;

Twitter @johnnyroc73

Instagram @johnnyproctor90

For Brad

Rest In Power

Chapter 1

Nora

'And see, in a bar room brawl type of setting, I will refer you all to the famous Rudyard Kipling poem, *If*'

Pippo looked up from over the laptop at me with a confused - almost worried - look about him, over where I was going with this. Then again, with all of the lighting that he'd strategically placed in my direction, it wasn't the easiest of things to see any-fucking-thing other than those strong blinding bulbs of light.

If you were looking for a bit of poetry then I'd have probably been the very last person that you should come looking for any but, I don't know. Something from one of the books - I'd read on the inside - must've stuck, because there I was. Spraffing on about Rudyard Kipling, for whoever the fuck was interested.

'If you can keep your head when all about you are losing theirs. Yours in the earth and everything's that's in it. And - which is more - you'll be a man, my son. And apart from that, you'll not only just be a man but will be *the* one cunt inside the establishment who will be primed for cashing in their opportunity to inflict as much damage to their opponents, and in as little time possible, before the police arrive to lift every cunt in their line of vision'

I could just about make out Pippo's facial expression change from concerned to relief, although the fact that for the best part of me being stood there with the spotlight shining down, he'd sat there with a mini - nuclear like - mushroom cloud of Cannabis reek hovering above him, I'm not sure where he found the concern from in the first place. Only concern that fucking wee stoner normally ever showed was where his next poke of Churros was going to come from, or if his local dealer was out of Sour Diesel.

And it wasn't like he already didn't know that once he pressed that *record* button, no cunt was ever going to be able to predict what was going to come out of my mouth, let alone myself. But, I'd been told, this was primarily the key to the success of it all, that I wasn't like any of the others out there and, because of that, it was an accidental USP, of sorts.

A man of extreme emotions.

Aye, that's what that Dr Erskine told me during one of my sessions with her when I was on the inside, back in the day. I admit, I only went for that first session with her because word on the wing was that she was quite tidy and I'd thought that, if anything, sitting down with her might've seen a few deposits paid into my wank bank. Wasn't fucking tidy at all - maybe a five on her very best day but even then I'm maybe being generous - and was more a reflection on how a man's sense of taste, in a woman, seriously drops off a fucking cliff if they've been inside for too long.

Probably helped that there wasn't any attraction though as it meant that I'd been able to sit, listen and fully take in what she was saying to me, rather than be sat imagining riding her.

'You speak from the heart, regardless of if your intentions are for good, bad or indifferent'

Another observation that the good doctor had made about me. These cunts don't get paid the big bucks for fuck all, eh, because she had me nailed, if not in the 'nailing' way that I'd maybe been hoping for when I'd first went to see her.

Life's too short for any fannying about though, eh? Why take half a day, week, month, year to tell someone something when you can leave them in under no uncertain terms about it in under half a minute? And in that respect I'd found myself in the perfect city to accommodate such an abrasive and blunt individual, like myself. Mainly because every second cunt that I ever seemed to bump into or be introduced to were of the same nature. And I guess that was why things took off. Exactly like Pippo - or *Super* Pippo as I would call him in what was both a wee nod to the Italian striker and an in-joke between me and the teenager where whenever he said something positive I'd reply 'super, Pippo' - had told me they would.

Once I'd managed to establish that him and the rest of his young team weren't taking the pish out of me and getting a good laugh at my expense, I was up for it. Plus, as Pippo had enthused, if it was going to get more people to come in and visit and use the gym then there really was no down side to it.

'Now when things kick off inside the boozer and the fuse has been lit the only rule that you need to follow is that there are NO fucking rules. Table completely clear with fuck all left on it, my friends. Go into a sit-u like that looking for 'fair' and you'll be coming out of it on a stretcher getting rushed to your closest accident and emergency. And remember, in a jungle that is your average bar fight'

'Props. Will. Be. Your. Friend'

The more I got into this section the more worked up I found myself getting. All those pub fights that I"d had back in Scotland over the years and how truly alive you feel when you're in an environment that requires half a dozen pairs of eyes to be able to protect you from the madness that's going on around you at any one of the three hundred and sixty degrees, they all came flooding back. The absolute best of times and the kind of days that I'd long since accepted that I would always miss. Days never to return. Well, if I was smart, anyway. Try escaping from prison, fleeing your country, setting up camp somewhere else and cutting about wrecking pubs, and heads, and see how far your 'freedom' extends to.

You've got to find an outlet to let out that radgness that's inside you though otherwise you'll just boil over sooner or later and some poor unsuspecting cunt, or cunts, will be the one who have to take the bullet.

The videos seemed to provide that in some way. As in talking about - and in a lot of examples *encouraging it* from others, - violence had proved to be an ideal way to *prevent* me from *being* violent. I suppose I'd have needed a few more sessions with that prison doctor to get to the bottom of my attraction for being in situations which would lead to me dishing out some bodily harm to someone but it was what it was and, to me anyway, it really was not too much of a problem.

Just say, back in those days where I led the Dundee Utility firm home and away every Saturday, there hadn't *been* a Utility, or something such as a "soccer casual." Let's say that it had been the sport of snooker that had gained an element of supporters who were there for the kicking fuck out of the opposite fans then I'd have been right there in my element rolling around the floor of the fucking Crucible with some Alex Higgins or Jimmy White fan, live on the BBC.

Didn't get beaten as a kid from dad, never had any paedo Scoutmasters trying to fiddle with me, wasn't one of those weird wee kids that liked tearing the wings off butterflies. None of that F.B.I profiler shite that would throw me into the serial killer bracket, because I was violent. I just really, really liked hitting people and those sweet, sweet endorphins that it all came along with. And in my new life, a reformed man who, if at all possible, needed to live out the rest of his days free from *any* police attention, then the ultra-violent side of me had to be suffocated at all costs. But by fuck did I miss it though.

'Now always be aware of your surroundings, ya cunts. Like I said. Props are your friends. If you can see it within reaching distance of you, and it's not nailed to the floor or bar, then the chances are it is going to make an ideal make-shift weapon. And don't make the mistake in assuming that props are exclusively inanimate objects. Let me give you all an example of this'

Pippo stood up from behind the laptop and, remaining silent so as to not fuck with the audio side of things, lifted one arm in the air and tapped his invisible watch - like he would do every week - to signal that I had five minutes left to wrap up this weeks show.

'You've got some fucking wideo stood in front of you. Had a few too many and think that they can make out the big man to you in front of the rest of the patrons of the boozer. Well that's not a fucking option, is it? And aye, we both know that there's that empty pint glass sitting on the bar that's just fucking begging to be smashed over his head, and many would take up that option. But here's an alternative that still involves using the empty glass but with a lot more decisiveness and impact that will add an element of panache for how to deal directly with such matters'

I proceeded to tell the viewer that to maximise the damage that they may want to inflict. A pint glass over the head of someone is but a graze that most won't even bother visiting the hospital over.

'But they fucking *will be* when you've taken one hand and grabbed their collar tight and pulled them towards you. As long as you keep that grip tight on their collar they're not going fucking anywhere and then *right* when you've got them where you want them'

I smashed the side of the pint glass - that I'd had sitting there from my fresh orange and lemonade that I'd been drinking earlier on in the recording - which all most likely looked like it was all planned when it was anything but.

'And you fucking hold them there, on your terms, and plunge, jab and twist what's left of the glass right into their fucking face. The only annoyance they'll be to you after that will be their screams. Props, people. With props *always* follow the Adapt, React and Attack method that I have urged you to follow. Mind now, ARA'

'*Adapt.React.Attack*'

'Simple but by fuck is it effective. Ok then, cuntos that's your self defence tips for another week. Same place and same time next week and if you've not already hit that subscribe button, then sort your fucking life out, eh?'

The video coming to a close with me looking menacingly at the camera while holding out the jagged pint glass out in front of me. Pippo, along with Jeroen, breaking into a round of spontaneous applause for our latest production. This also signalling that I was done until next time. Looking at that broken glass in my hand and trying to comprehend the animal that had taken over me in that moment and who was now responsible for me now missing the only fucking pint glass that I even had at the gym.

Might've looked good on camera - then again, might've looked stupid because I'm fucked if I know as I never watched myself -

but still meant I was fucked for having a pint of orange or water, when needing my thirst quenched as I worked out.

'Bravo, broooo. The part where you smashed the glass? The subscribers will *love* it. I upload tonight and will be on our channel tomorrow. We get those views and that leads to the paper. Cash rules everything around me cream get the money, Dolla dolla bills yaall'

He stood there in his Umbro Ajax shell suit flicking imaginary bank notes in my direction until the smoke - emitting from the joint wedged firmly into his mouth - started to burn his eyes.

He wasn't that far wrong though, Pippo. Somehow over the years there had appeared to have been some seismic shift in the world that had altered peoples view of it. An outlook that had enabled a complete fucking radgey like myself, to have been looked upon as *entertaining*. And that I'd receive money from *being* a radge?

I didn't believe it myself until I received the money into my bank account but the proof was in the deposit that I saw sitting there, paid to me.

And with each deposit growing exponentially month to month.

Well, you can see why it all kind of snowballed from there, eh?

Chapter 2

Nora

It would've been fair to say that it took some adjusting for me to become rehabilitated, with regards to being on the outside of H.M.P Barlinnie. Especially when, technically, I should've fucking still been inside there though, mind. I'd always heard about how those that were inside for years found it a head-fuck when they were eventually released and let back out into civilisation. Aye, I fucking hear you, mate but just try attempting it when every cunt and their dug are looking for you and the great outdoors can seem a wee bit downgraded from *great*.

Every knock on your door, any cunt that you pass in the street that gives you even the most casual of glances as they pass you, and the persistent feeling of paranoia that these moments bring. All those small - but important - rules that you need to follow in your daily life just to make sure that you don't show up on whatever radar that the coppers must all look at. Still, better than being back in that pokey wee cell in the *Big Hoose* where the irony that if I'd just been patient and hung on for a wee bit I'd have been able to see out the rest of my time and be free to live my life doing whatever I chose to? Aye, irony wasn't lost on me, like.

What's done is done though and you can't change the past unless you're keeping some time travel portal on the down low from every cunt else. Was pretty mad to find how quick the years began to fly in though, mind? One minute you're hiding out in your studio flat that you were able to hire from the first unscrupulous cunt that wasn't looking for references, ID and was happy enough to see me turn up with hard cash. Scared to even go out onto the street for fear of being grabbed by the Dutch bizzies (Politie, to you and me) and shoved on the first fucking EasyJet flight back to Edinburgh. The next you're walking around the place like you fucking own the gaff. An actual *tax* payer and part of the Dutch 'system.' Well, Matthijs de Groot - Dutch entrepreneur and city centre gym owner - is anyway. Norman Fulton, aye not so much although for all intents and purposes that boy was forced into retirement the moment he walked casually out of the front door of the prison that was taking care of him, on a day that wasn't his release date. After that. It was felt that he should be withdrawn from society, for everyone's benefit. Most notably my own.

I'd chosen *de Groot* for my Christian name once I'd been made aware of this thing that the Dutch have for their names where each second name literally means something profound like, for example, Baas which means 'the boss.' One that I was sorely tempted to go for myself but thought that it would maybe clash with Bruce Springsteen as two cunts can't be cutting about calling themselves *The Boss*. In the end, though, I found the perfect one for myself when I came across "de Groot"and learned that its translation was literally "The Great" and, I don't know like, maybe it was just self confidence on my part but I felt there couldn't have been a better name to give me so stopped searching after that. Knew that the former king of Macedonia, Eck, was also called "The Great" - more stuff I learned on the inside - but that cunt's been brown bread for hundreds of years so it lessened the chances of any image rights clashes, like with Springsteen, eh?

'OH MY GOD, IT'S REALLY YOU, ISN'T IT?'

A boy in a matching Patagonia jacket and bobble hat shouted over from the counter as he stood there waiting on his order being rung up. This pulling me out of my own wee world that I was in. Sitting there alone at the window table looking out onto bustling Handboogstraat, having a latte while going through all that needed done over the day. Coffee first, as always, and then the rest can follow. Despite it being relatively early morning, the Dampkring was filled with the multi scented smell of weed, from the early morning wake and bakers that had already walked through the door since opening.

As much as I enjoyed those various smells - Indica, Sativa, Hash - that you'd find inside there, or any other of the city's coffee shops, that stuff wasn't for me so early in the morning and would be something that I'd return to later on in the day. My policy of no drugs before lunch time had proved to be a winning one for me so, like a football manager who wont change his starting eleven when they're playing well and winning, I'd felt that there was no point messing with a winning formula and had adopted this approach on a full time basis.

'Well, that all depends on who you mean by *you*, I suppose, eh?'

I said coyly, trying to have a laugh with him even though I knew exactly what he was getting at, since this had started to become an occasional thing when going about my business in the city centre. It's fucking mad though how things can change as time goes by. There I was, in a town that, on arrival, the very *last* thing I wanted was for anyone to recognise my coupon where now, when they do my first instinct isn't to act like a cornered rat, panel the cunt and then do a runner to another country.

Human beings are amazing things, though. The way that they adapt to their surroundings, whatever they are. Did I enjoy prison? Well I escaped from the fucking place if you're in any kind of doubt as to the answer to that question but still, though. I *managed*. I adapted to it and it felt a completely different place

- along with my mentality to go with it - near the end, compared to when I'd walked in the door for my first day.

Being on the run - after a prison escape - is without a shadow of a doubt an assault on your mental health. Can see how cunts go to pieces and end up handing themselves back in, or being so slack with their movements and what trails they leave that it looks like they almost *want* to get themselves caught. The first year is the hardest, by far, and I can see why most cunts get themselves huckled again. Once you get past that first year though. You begin to handle things that bit better and before you know it you're barely even thinking about the fact that you *are* an escaped convict. Almost like that it never even happened in the first place.

And before you know it? You can find yourself so at one with things that - despite being a wanted man - when a complete stranger points at you in recognition when you're out in public you find yourself completely chill about things and the first thought you have *isn't* that they've recognised you from fucking Crimewatch!

'THE DUDE FROM YOUTUBE! UTILITY DEFENCE GYM, MOTHERFUCKER!'

Ronald - the regular day time budtender - laughed at this as he handed a small clear ziplocked bag of grass over to the guy stood shouting excitedly across the room to me.

'Love, your videos, bro. Sometimes I cannot understand which words you say as you can speak too quick but I never miss them. My friend at college told me about them'

For the benefit of all inside the small coffee shop he lowered his tone a little, now across and standing over me as I sat there at the table looking up at him.

'I appreciate the support from everyone' I said, giving him a fist bump, which I'd found - once getting myself out and about in the city - that a lot of the young Amsterdammers had shifted to and I'd decided to change along with them all.

'Haven't seen you at the gym, though?' I tried to have a wee laugh with him, teasing like. Kind of backfired though through the kid's need to give me a detailed explanation for *why* he hadn't poked his nose into the gym, despite being local and a big fan of the videos. Proper felt like the lad was bricking it over the fact that I'd asked him such a simple question and was something that I'd put down to him taking the boy - me - in the video, and his ever projection of violence in all ways, a wee bit too literally.

The short version, which would've been more than acceptable, was that he was skint and couldn't afford gyms. Told the boy that I offered a free session on Thursday nights and to get his fucking arse down which he seemed well chuffed over, saying he'd bring his mate down with him as well.

'Aye, mate. More the merrier, like' I says back to him while hoping to bring an end to this wee exchange. Don't get me wrong or fuck all. I don't mind anyone recognising me and stopping for a wee chat and that but you know how it is, first thing in the morning? You can't normally be arsed talking to any cunt, never mind over enthusiastic members of the public that you've never met in your puff. I had a busy week ahead in terms of the gym and had been quite enjoying my wee moment of calm before it all kicked off for the week and found people watching - outside in the street - while drinking my latte, therapeutic.

Fuck know's if I can give off a scent, vibe or maybe just my general aura, but it felt like the wee cunt had picked up on this. Not that it stopped him from asking one final thing before leaving. Coming across as almost scared to ask but having went too far to go back, he hesitantly asked if he could get a photo with me. Already with iPhone in his hand in preparation.

'Aye, ok, pal. No worries, eh' I said but without trying to hide my irritation to the request. Hey! If you're going to approach the psychopath from the YouTube videos then you should be prepared to roll the dice on how he's going to *be* with you, eh?

'Great, bro' He smiled before adding if he could have one where it looked like I was carrying out one of my self defence tactics that I show on my videos, on him.

Fast forward a couple of minutes and we've got Ronald out from behind the counter to take the picture, or as I'd suggested, series of pictures. Everyone else sitting around in there all watching on as first of all I grabbed the poor cunt's arms, near on pulling them out of the their sockets, and yanked them behind his back, enough to make him allow a few involuntary expressions of pain.

'Right, Ronny. Take one like this' I shouted. Hoping that, if taken at the right moment, he was going to capture the *genuine* look of pain on the boy's coupon.

While still holding his arms behind him tight, I came up close behind him and whispered in his ear.

'Ken what'll make it a bit more authentic, mate? If Ronny catches the full execution of how I perform the actual move, rather than just a picture or two.

'Switch it to video, pal' I told the budtender.

Once he'd done this I sank into my whole YouTube persona and began to explain what I was doing, for the benefit of the video.

'Now with their arms trapped behind their back, with a swift movement, you can easily make the switch to a firm grip of their wrists with one of your hands which frees up your other hand to grab the back of their collar - or in this unfortunate bastard's case, his ponytail - and SLAM their head down onto the table repeatedly. Now hitting the edge of the table is not an easy thing to pull off and you may miss the table completely which will only make you look like a fanny but that aside, hit that edge, or even better the corner and the rewards will be there for you to reap'

This spiel delivered all while he groaned in pain at how extreme this selfie was now turning out to be. Ronald, capturing this as I took a grip of his pony tail, twisting my hand around it twice until there was no twisting left in it, before proceeding to slam his face down to within a bawhair of connecting with the table, then back up again, and down towards the table. Repeat to fade.

Inevitably, and by that I mean intentionally, one of the times I threw his head down at the table it ended up connecting - his cheekbone - with the edge of the small brown table. That dull sound of bone connecting with wood. How I'd missed it. It was like hearing one of your favourite songs on the radio for the first time in ages.

If the sounds that the boy had been coming out with previously had been nothing more than some mild expressions of unsettlement. *Now* was nothing less than screams of extreme pain.

'Oh, shit, pal. I'm so fucking sorry about that. Obviously didn't mean to do that. Fuck, looks like you've already got a shiner coming up, eh? It's not broken, is it?' I went to touch the area that looked affected, then thought better of it. Figuring a feather gently brushing against it at that moment would probably cause it pain, never mind one of my fingers pressing and prodding it. Fucking Doctor de Groot, eh? Actually, wee bit of a ring to that, like.

Aye, he'd caught a bit of a sore one, like, but what could he do about it, eh? It was an accident, after all. Just an innocent mistake, for all he knew. He could've only been late teens, early twenties, but in that moment could've just as easily been a five year old as he stood there stifling back the tears that were forming in his eyes.

He seemed a bit stunned also and not really capable of replying back to anything that was said to him.

'You realise how lucky you are, my friend?'

Ronald asked, as he handed over the kid's phone to him.

'You actually have a real live video of *the* Matthijs de Groot from Utility Defence Gym performing one of his self defence tips, on you!'

With a fractured, broken or simply just really badly knocked cheekbone, you could have forgiven him for not exactly feeling like he was on the luckiest of streaks that morning.

Through enough gaslighting from Ronald and myself he was soon on his way without too much of a fuss.

'Mind and drop by the gym, Thursday night, eh?' I shouted after him as he left. He never looked back.

'Do you think you will see him visit at the gym?' Ronald asked. His own face seeming to question this possibility.

'The chances of that happening are slimmer than one of these fucking things' My own personal feelings on things, as I laughed and picked up one of the complimentary rolling papers that were sat on the table alongside roaches.

Why a gym in the first place, though? Well the short answer to that is that just picking things up and getting yourself back into the narcotics caper is a hard thing to do at the best of times. Hardly any cunt stays on top and on the occasions that they're top, and get knocked off it, they're never getting themselves back up there again. And that applies to when you're in your *own* native country. Try putting together a start up when you're in a foreign one with absolutely ride all in the way of contacts and - despite the fact that they *can* - a lot of people working in the "industry" maintain on talking in Dutch.

While it had been the obvious choice for me when starting out again in life - especially with the war chest that Peter Duncan had so very kindly thrown my way, minutes before he was carted off by the bizzies back in that bar that night - actually getting something off the ground, I'd found, had been a non starter. With money not exactly a problem - at the time, for the foreseeable, - I hadn't rushed into anything and had chosen to just do the basics and keep my head down, while receiving the occasional updates from back home with regards to news on the hunt for me.

After I reached the couple of months mark and with no sign of anyone coming looking for me. Police or any of the gangsters that Montoya had employed back in Rotterdam, and who had been left with the task of ending me, while Montoya - the fucking rat - bid me a less than fond farewell. I decided to venture out and see what there was for me, while trying to work out if I was going to be moving on somewhere else entirely, or stay right there in Amsterdam.

Finding out that trying to get myself into the drug game was a non starter - trying to talk to those North African cunts that punt their council about the Red Light District and trying to get myself a leg up to who their distro was, like trying talking to a brick wall - I kind of accidentally stumbled into my new vocation.

When I was back in The Big Hoose, one of the things that kept my mental health in tip top condition was working out. Feeling the burn and riding the zone, all of that. Because of this, I think it was natural that I gravitated towards using a gym, local to me, in a basement on Vredenburgersteeg.

I think the place's biggest problem was half the cunts passing it didn't even notice that it was there, in amongst all of the hookers in the windows and the multitude of sex shops and churro parlours. Amount of times that I'd been on a city break to the place, most of the time stuck firmly in the Red Light District and I'd never noticed the Actief-8 Gym and even following the directions of the helpful Amsterdammer who had told me where the gym was, I still struggled a wee bit.

Still, back then. Privacy was exactly what I was after so the ambience of the gym was precisely what I was looking for. Plus, didn't really ever have to find myself waiting to use any of the machines or weights, not that there was a king's ransom worth of either though, mind.

Barry, the gadge that ran the place, not really appearing too arsed about the either running the gym or the fact that hardly any cunt ever even *used* it. This all became much clearer years later when - after the pair of us had become good friends, through us seeing each other on a weekly basis - Barry confessed to me that the place was nothing other than a money laundering exercise. This, coincidental timing or not, coming not too far before he asked me if I'd be up for him signing over the deeds to the place to me, so as to ensure that the fucking Feds didn't take it from him.

Closing up the gym behind me after my session was over - despite the fact that the gym was still meant to be open for several hours yet - Barry took me out for a couple of drinks. Saying he could do with a loan of a pair of ears. I quite liked the boy and he'd been the nearest that I could've ever come close to describing as a 'friend' there in the city, so took him up on the offer.

He explained to me that he was part of a network of "business owners" who had been employed by a cartel from Belgium who needed properties to wash their money for them. Barry himself absolutely nothing to do with the actual drug side of things at all. He'd told me that, following a police operation, some of the other owners - that were cleaning money for the Turks in Liege - had been lifted and charged with money laundering, and the fear was that eventually they would get around to Barry.

Telling me that he'd taken legal advice and while there would be no getting around the crime of money laundering - if charged with it - he would still be able to save his property, if he signed it over to someone else to safe keep for him. And this was where I came in.

As his oldest and most regular customer, in addition to someone who obviously held a passion for keeping in good shape. He'd felt that I would be the ideal person to take the wheel and keep it on the road while he was "away for a while."

The daft cunt didn't bargain on the Sahin family stitching him up like a right kipper, by pinning some of the actual drugs activity on him, which led to the slap on the wrist six month to a year sentence that he'd speculated on receiving turning into a near ten stretch.

Leaving me in charge of a fucking gym with my name on the door. Well, Matthijs de Groot, at least. And while Barry Bleecker hadn't really appeared overly arsed over attracting visitors to his establishment, due to the richer rewards that he was receiving from Liege, I was. The more of a success I could make of the place, the more profitable it was going to be for me and it was more through my personal knowledge of the streets than any kind of marketing genius that saw me welcoming in some of the Ajax F-Side boys.

Unlike your British casuals who would need to put their pint and pie down before having a swedge with you, some of these Europeans took pride in their work. Take your Russians and Poles? Setting up fucking training camps to prepare for big tournaments as if they were fucking *playing* in them. So, with that mindset, these types of boys were no stranger to a set of dumbbells.

This, seeing to the lightbulb moment, that summer in twenty eighteen, when I'd got those flyers printed up, specifically targeting the hooligan element of the city of Amsterdam. My sales pitch being that with it being pre season the radge cunts should take the opportunity to get themselves ready for all the battles that would be coming their way in the new season, while offering ten free lifetime memberships and half price for anyone else so long as they presented their F-Side membership card, the deal expiring on the first day of the new season kicking off.

I dropped the flyers off at the known F-Side Clubhouse as well as some of the boozers that some of the F Side boys were known to haunt on match days.

This, bringing me into contact with Pippo for the first time, along with some of his mates who snapped up the free memberships. The ten lifetime memberships disappearing in one day of the word getting out. It was Pippo - who it turned out, happened to live in the same district as myself, along with his sister - out of everyone though who was there on a regular basis and that was what led to him getting the part time gig working for me, and looking after the place. The kid absolutely lapped up my stories from the old days, when I got going. You know what it's like when you're a young casual and you're hearing all the tales from back in the day, especially coming from someone from a completely different country, though? And not only that. Someone from the motherland and *home* of football hooliganism. Not that the Dutch were slow on the uptake there, mind. They just hadn't really bothered about what clothes they were wearing, when they were kicking fuck out of you!

It was through my sheer passion when re-telling Pip those stories, and how much he would crack up over how I would pace around the gym, acting out some of what I was describing on invisible opponents that he came up with the YouTube idea for a page for the gym, which then spawned into my online tutorials.

After him recording me telling of an incident at Haymarket Station, where some delusional cunt from the CSF got too close to me for his own good and ended up being sent clean into the bonnet of an Inter City 125 that was sitting waiting to leave for Aberdeen, knocked clean out the moment the radge connected with that metal. He then went on to show the video to all his boys on the Sunday up at the ArenA at the Ajax game and the feedback he'd got back was, *get that cunt online*. Paraphrasing them there, like.

If you'd asked me to put myself on the internet back in two thousand when I'd arrived in Amsterdam - and I'll fully admit that I barely knew anything *about* the internet, being on the inside until then - I'd have laughed in your face, due to the obvious. As the years fly by though without any hint of cunts coming looking for you, you tend to stop looking over your shoulder as much. Add the fact that with my big fuck off beard, shaved head and even a slight difference to my accent - through having to adapt, otherwise the Dutch wouldn't have been able to understand my Dundee accent - not to mention the Matthijs de Groot moniker, it wasn't even exactly that obvious that it *was* Norman Fulton, of Barlinnie Prison escape fame, who was presenting the self defence tutorials.

From the first video, and the help of Pippo and the rest of the F-Side boys who shared it far and wide, - eventually catching on with *other* European hooligan mobs - things snowballed in a big way from there.

To the point that I was being stopped in public by "fans" looking for selfies, while technically on the run.

If I do say so myself. It really all was a tremendous piece of shithousing.

Chapter 3

Liam

'Awwww man, it's pishing all over my fucking seats. Awww fucking hell, Liam, man'

Percy moaned, while having a quick peek into the back and seeing me grabbing onto and struggling with my four legged friend, only for me to change complete tact the moment that it had started urinating - leaving a stain that didn't look a kick off the arse away from being the shape of Spain - suddenly trying to put as much space between me and the stupid fucking thing as possible.

'You're fucking lucky it's just a pee, lad. You might want to stick some of the windows down though because pretty soon it's going to start to whiff'

Percy receiving none of the sympathy that he was possibly looking for over the fact that a dog, who five minutes before had been happily sitting lazing in its front garden, enjoying the weather, was - now - pishing all over the back seat of his Audi A3.

I'd given him *more* than generous petrol money for this wee trip and, not passing the buck here or anything like, the minute that he knew it involved a dog riding in his motor, then he should've known the risks. I'm sure that's a saying that they use for the TV? Never work with kids or animals, and the upholstery of the poor cunt's pride and joy was now a shining example of that.

'You're fucking paying for the cleaning of the upholstery, by the way. Being left with a pishy car wasn't part of the plan when you asked me what I was up to this afternoon, when you phoned me' He's shouting back at me while - not keeping his eyes on the road - he came about a metre from slamming us into the back of a bus, that had stopped to let people off.

'Aye aye aye, just you worry about not writing off the car, eh? Pishy smell on the seat will be the least of your worries if the fucking thing ends up in Kelbies getting sold off bit by bit for scrap'

Despite his rage over the dog peeing, you could see it all over his face, how close he'd realised that he'd came to taking us into the bus. Which *should've* been enough to calm him down a wee bit but you know how some cunts get with their car? Tam Wilson - that stays a few doors down from me and my mum - spends more time fucking washing and polishing his car than he does *driving* the thing. Even said to him once, like was that all he'd been put on earth to do, clean a fucking car?

Percy wasn't as full on as that but - as I was being reminded that afternoon - was still what I'd have classed as well on the over-protective side.

You can't put the toothpaste back in the tube though, and same rules applies to dogs, and their pish.

'I'm meant to be taking three of my team to a training day in Stirling tomorrow, and I can't with the seats stinking of that wee bastard's piss'

The timing was impeccable but on my mate calling him a bastard - Bannon, and the object of this whole exercise - my dog met this with a series of defensive barks. I thought it more likely a build up of having to put up with Percy's shouting and screaming rather than just taking exception to Percy's name calling.

'That's right, wee man. You fucking tell him, eh' I said to the Colly, helping rile him up even more as he pivoted back and forward between barking at Percy in the front and taking the pets and cuddles I had for him. I'm not sure he knew what the fuck was going on, to be fair. Hadn't seen me for weeks and then finds himself snatched, thrown into the back of a car and kidnapped. Well, kidnap wasn't really the word for it but I'm in no doubt that was what *she* - who was already trying my mobile repeatedly as we were firing down the road - would've told the police had happened.

I was chill about any potential visits from the bizzies over things though, considering it was *my* fucking dog. She was just trying to be a spiteful cow because of the pair of us splitting up. Made it out like wee Bannon was a kid or something and that - like in most cases - should've "stayed with the mum." The fact that I still had the receipt from the day I'd picked him up at his breeders up near Inverness, the year before, something that would kill any kidnap talk stone dead. Splitting up with your bird's hard enough as it is to be fighting about something with emotional ties like a dog so I gave her a couple of weeks to come to her senses, figuring when reality started to bite and it was left to her to do all the walking morning noon and night, that she'd have been on the phone to me fucking begging to come and take him away. That call didn't come from her though, so I'd been kind of forced to take matters into my own hands.

'Don't know why you've even bothered, anyway. Lil's going to be a major headache for you now after what you've done, and apart from that, you think your mum's going to be chuffed to see you coming home with Bannon, either? I mean, she was hardly putting out the bunting at the news that *you* were moving back in with her'

It wasn't like Percy didn't have a point, like. Five missed (ignored) calls from my ex, Lillian, in less than five minutes showed how much of a hassle she was going to be, but that was cool. Wasn't like I was going into this situation thinking that it would all pass off without note in the first place. There was no way that I was getting Bannon back without a song and dance and, fair play to Lil, she took that baton the second she looked out of her living room window and saw me walking out the front garden with Bannon in my arms and into a waiting car. Just as well that my wheelman was quick on the draw in terms of pulling away as she would have one hundred percent started to attack his car, if she couldn't get access to those inside it.

As for mum? Two out of two for Percy because aye, no fucking way was she going to be rolling out the red carpet for the wee man when she learned that he was going to be moving in with her, having only had her relative peace shattered when her one and only son landed up back living with her after discovering that his - ex - girlfriend was a complete and utter fucking lunatic.

'Don't you worry about Lil, lad. She only wants Bannon because *I* do. If I hadn't made such a big thing about taking him with me, when I was moving out, the poor wee cunt would've been at the kennels by the next day. Proper reverse psychology at times when you're dealing with someone who is levels below you in intelligence, like Lillian'

To prove my point I held up my phone as it rang - again - with her name on the screen. I'd long since changed her ring tone to that Star Wars Imperial Death March, safe in the knowledge that she would never hear it as she'd never be beside me when she was calling me. Obviously daft cunt me didn't ever consider that one day I might not be able to find my phone and my "helpful" girlfriend would offer to call my number. Fuck, that was some argument that night. Not enough to get me to *change* the ring tone, mind. Literally left the fucking thing on there, to wind her up even more.

'You're going to have to answer it from her sooner or later' Percy said, not exactly something that I didn't already know but didn't appreciate having it spelled out for me too and making me face reality.

'Aye, I think I'll choose later, like' I laughed - Percy too, lightening up for the first time - as I declined the call once again. A few seconds later a follow up text coming through from her threatening to go to the bizzies about me if I didn't bring Bannon back. As is the case, the medium of text message being such a beautiful facility to conduct business, when you really don't want to fucking deal with it verbally, I didn't have as much reservations in communicating with her in that way, and made things short and clear for her.

MY idea to get a dog.

MY money that paid for it.

Receipt in MY hipper now take yourself to fuck, ya fucking mad boot x

'Anything else from her today is getting ignored' I said as I stuck the phone on silent and put it away.

'If your mum's home you're going to have your hands full for the time being anyway, eh?' Percy helpfully added while turning off onto Finella Gardens, and on the home stretch.

Obviously, the boy wasn't wrong, there. She *did* go fucking tonto, to be fair to him, and her. And don't get me wrong either. Me and mum? Solid as a rock, like that song. If there was one person in life that she'd have been able to say had her back to the absolute letter of the law then I'd have been astonished, as well as disgusted, if she'd said it was anyone other than "her Liam."

Doesn't mean to say that I hadn't driven her up the wall since I'd been able to crawl, though. Taken the poor old dear to hell and back over the years through some of my antics but - all the earache aside - she'd always stuck by me. Know it sounds cheesy as fuck but at times when it felt like we had fuck all, we *always* had each other.

For the year that I'd stayed with Lil, in the flat that the council gave her when her mum and dad kicked her out, it felt like I was missing an arm or a leg, not seeing my mum on a day to day basis. And I know it's not the make or break issue for being with a partner, but there was a major fucking drop off between mum's cooking and Lil's. Lil dished you up a Pot Noodle and she was there expecting you to award her a Michelin Star, for fuck's sake.

I know that she'd expressed an opinion, that said the exact opposite but - when I turned up with a couple of bin liners full of clothes - I knew that she was glad to have me back. When you've got that kind of a bond with a parent they can't hide fuck all from you.

Which was why I didn't take the bollocking I got from her when - after Percy had dropped me and Bannon off - me and him walked through the door and he - being the loveable wee boy that he was - made an immediate dash for mum, sitting reading the paper with a cup of tea, and jumped up onto her, and ripped half of the paper clean off in the process. While standing on her lap, he then secured the double by managing to knock her cup of tea off the wee side table due to his animated jumping about and swishing tail.

Aye, Bannon. This is the person whose roof you're going to be living under so just you crack on and get into their bad books before the front door has even been closed behind you, I thought, as mum held out the partially ripped newspaper with one hand while petting and trying to calm him down. 'Bannon, Jesus?!' She said with irritation but while looking at me as if I was Cesar Millan and had quietly had a wee word with him before we'd arrived and told him to go and destroy her copy of The Courier, and knock over the cup of tea.

Her reaction to this was something that you could've then went on and filed under "you've never had it so good" compared to her mood when she found out that the wee man was now also lodging.

One of her main issues in all of this was that she knew that if Bannon was going to be staying, then this was going to make it *our* dog, despite what I tried to say to the contrary.

'You'll barely know he's even here half the time' I tried to reassure her.

Poor Bannon, tail still wagging a hundred miles per hour while looking up at the two of us. Dogs aren't stupid, so he knew we were talking about him. Just as well he couldn't understand the content though, mind.

'And as for the *other* half the time? The time when you're not even here? Who looks after him then? You think just because you've not been living here, that I don't know about you going away for days at a time? Life's hard enough, Liam. Hard enough without having to look after a dog, son'

Oh now we were skating into territory, that I'd have much rather left alone. The fact that she knew about me going away for a few days - stuck in some afters following a messy night - was something that I'd have rather she hadn't known about but that mouthy cow Lil must've mentioned something to her at some point.

'Awww you know what it's like, mum. You go out with your mates for a night out, end up at an afters in a house you've never been to before in a part of the city that you didn't even know exists, have two or three good attempts at leaving but never quite making it and before you know it you've lost a couple of days, eh?' I tried to make light out of things while steering her away from the whole topic.

'Aye and maybe *that's* why you're turning up with clothes in black bags wanting your room again'

She said, which was a good comeback.

'Nah mum, I missed you too much and it all got too unbearable in the end, eh? What can I say? The better woman won'

And there it was, the break in her face. That smile. The one that no matter how much I did her nut in she still couldn't manage to hide.

'That and the fact that Lilian's an absolute basket case of a human being, obviously'

Chapter 4

Si

Have you seen this radge bastard?

https://youtu.be/b2TttALDVLc

A text - along with a couple of laughing emojis - being my introduction to *Utility Defence*.

Sent to me by a bored Zico, who was stuck in Barcelona, waiting on a delayed flight back to Schipol. Completely disregarding the fact that, while he makes a living at alternative times and hours of the day compared to your average man in the street, they have shit they need to get accomplished in their day. All taking place while he's sitting around airports counting whatever bag he'd earned the night before.

He hadn't said as much, and I'd been too busy to answer his three phone calls that he'd made inside half an hour, but all signs pointed to either drug abuse or sleep depravity, due to the bombardment of shit that he was sending me. Links to songs, online articles and amusing videos. A head that was all over the place, if the variation of stuff that he was sending me was anything to go by. Whilst I've always got time for my best mate, I didn't that afternoon. He was actually doing my nut in a wee bit and was being fuck all other than an unnecessary distraction, and at a crucial moment in my day.

I was standing there haggling like fuck with Henk, at his usual pitch at the flea market - on Waterlooplein - over an Eighty One to Eighty Three Le coq Sportif Saint Etienne shirt. Sized large and a garment of clothing that was never going to fit me in my lifetime, as much as I'd have wished it to. Its hencher size compared to my more svelte frame, not really an issue. The moment I seen it I knew I wanted it, to add to the rest of my stock for going online, and that, even before arriving at an agreement with Henk - on the final price - there would *still* be a decent bit of profit to be had on it.

Henke wasn't a mug though and - unlike a lot over in Europe when it came to the old vintage gear, and something that I exploited to the fullest - knew the value of everything, no matter how old, obscure and insignificant it, to the untrained eye, appeared to be, like this Saint Etienne shirt. Another seller, six stalls down - if in possession of it - would have been likely to have - obliviously - sold it for ten euros. But they weren't Henk. Which was why dealing with him, when trying to procure stock to sell on - mostly back to Britain - was always never nothing less than a pain in the fucking arse.

Multiply that with an attention seeking and bored out of his skull Stevie "DJ Selecao" Duncan sitting in a Barcelona airport with time to kill. It wasn't an ideal mix.

Due to the random nonsense, in general, that he could - and subsequently would - send you. When you see him asking in a text - complete with YouTube link - *Have you seen this radge bastard?* And how the internet is with everyone all sharing the unhinged stuff that's going on in their backyard, to the rest of the world.

When you, *eventually* in my case, hit that link, though and with how big the internet really is. You never expect to *know* the "radge bastard" in the video. Even if I hadn't found them instantly recognisable at first. He'd changed, as in *everything* about him. The only piece of him that remained - and for me the clincher when it came to making an ID on him - was the psychopathic tone and feel to him. Maybe I'd have clocked it all straight away if Zico had actually mentioned him by name inside his text but, instead, left me to find out for myself.

My first impression wasn't regarding who or what was *on* the video. More one of 'Zico's working his fucking ticket if he thinks I'm sitting down and watching a forty five minute video that he's randomly sent me.' With my attention span I'd rarely ever been able to concentrate on films, even when the will was there from me. So forty five minutes of some random YouTube link sent over? Aye, fuck that, I thought.

In reality, however. I watched every single fucking minute of it. Once I realised what it was that I was watching, I was engrossed.

The first few frames of it, a combination of some Dutch (maybe Belgian) techno and graphics. The words then coming flying onto the screen from the side like the wind had blown it in that direction. The letters swirling around and around until they came to a rest in the centre of the screen. A large U and D with a much smaller "nite' sandwiched in between and the name *Utility Defence* spread out underneath that. Gave me a wee smile when I saw the Utility part, thinking back to those action packed days with the Dundee Utility.

Days that I wouldn't have swapped for the world and, at the very worst, they were most definitely character building.

The video cut to some boy who looked like he was standing in a gym, with items like treadmills, weights and punchbags all in the background. Some carpet carrying cunt with a big bushy beard and a beanie hat on his napper.

The fuck's Zico sending me this? I thought to myself, already assuming that it was just some usual pish from someone - like that Mr Motivator boy that used to wear the leotard, from back in the day - who was going to try and teach *you* how to look like *them*.

Aye, as if I'd have wanted to look like that this motorcycle club member, Glastonbury going, squat in a tree to stop a runway from being built, looking prick.

Literally took me a few minutes to suss out who it was on the screen but once I did, I couldn't stop pishing myself. Some fucking balls on the boy, you really have to hand it to him. Balls were never really one of his problems from when I'd last seen him, but still. Being in the same position as him the very fucking last thing I'd be doing would be advertising myself - right down to providing an address for where to go and collect him - to anyone who might be looking for him, like the police.

Each to their own though, I suppose. Wouldn't be me, like.

'What the fuck is this mad bastard doing?'

I said out loud, almost subconsciously, as I sat there back in the flat with a hard earned Heineken in my hand, after a day of trawling the city's charity shops and flea markets and only then going through the list of texts that Zeek had sent me. By that point he had dropped off the face of the earth and was now as quiet as he hadn't been earlier on in the day.

'Welcome back, Cuntos. Matthijs is the name and PAIN is ma fucking game and welcome back to Utility Defence for some more life hacks that will make your shit more secure, whatever that shit is. I see you all out there'

Matthijs? Life hacks? The fucking weird accent?

No, really, I asked no one in particular.

'What the fuck is this mad bastard doing?'

I watched, completely transfixed, the full forty five minutes that the video ran for. I laughed - with him, but mainly *at* him - I slagged him off for being such a cheesy as fuck fanny, and winced at the memories of the days where that same man led me and the rest of the boys into battle. Those memories brought right on at the sight of him re-enacting some of his moments from back in the day, while dressing them up as standard self defence advice. The man wasn't no self defence expert with tips to share. No, he was just a fucking psychopath that was telling you what *he* would do, if placed in a certain situation. No fucking guarantees that someone out there watching his channel could go on and actually replicate it when the time came, though. He was a rare breed.

I hadn't thought of him in years and it had been even longer since I'd set eyes on the boy. Apparently, and according to the video, he was still based in Dam though, and working for a gym. Amsterdam, I'd found, to be the perfect city to set yourself up in. Small enough to get yourself around easily enough but yet still big enough to not be able to bump into Nora on a regular basis. I hadn't even considered the fact that he would've stuck around in Amsterdam, neither did Zeek. We both reckoned that he would either have ended up doing something fucking stupid and getting himself lifted and, in doing so, bringing his whole runaway act to an abrupt end. Either that or a case of him moving on after a while, to keep ahead of the police.

The day I bumped into him, when I was walking through Nieuwmarkt, at first I didn't believe that it was him and that he was still cutting about the city. Due to his own predicament he looked as put out to see me as I did, on the inside, at coming across him and - putting our history over the years - it was a strange small talk filled exchange we shared before going on our separate ways again.

No plans of meeting up and having a drink to talk about the good times, like some would when both on foreign territory. The only part of him that really reminded me of the old Nora - that day - was the last words that he said as he walked away.

'Mind now, any cunt comes and asks you if you've seen me, you seen fuck all, eh?'

I told him that no one had asked in the two years since he'd escaped so I couldn't imagine anyone asking me by that point, which seemed to put him a wee bit at ease as he skulked away again.

Being at ease didn't look too much of an issue to him all of those years later as he stood there with a table leg in his hand while telling the viewers to follow up with this to the head, *directly* after having booted their adversary in the bollocks.

'Trust me. The cunt'll be too busy worrying about the shooting pain to his scrotum area to even think about or see the cosh that's going to be caving fuck out of their skull'

He said, with, I had to concede, a bit of authority as it hadn't exactly been a rare sight to see the man with a weapon in his hand and battering it against some poor bastard's nut with the kind of exuberance that Keith Moon battered a drum skin.

Eventually I began to find it all a wee bit nauseating, watching him give it the big one like he was. I "got it" as well, mind. I never missed the point that this was seemingly the reason for all of the views and comments, his presenting skills. When you already know the cunt though, you've already missed out on the novelty factor that a Lars from Gothenburg or a Piotr from Warsaw would enjoy, when watching.

When you're already "mates" with him and have experienced years of being under his rule. Seeing the guy who would fuck you up more than the other side would if you didn't stand and fight, amongst his other intimidating traits that he'd displayed while ruling a mob of casuals. Something that he achieved through fear more than respect which, as far as I'm concerned, isn't much of a leader if that's all you've got. Easy saying all of that now, I suppose because it literally took him being banged up in the first place before I had even *thought* about leaving the firm. Fuck, you just have to ask Zico how things turn out when you went against the man's word. Poor cunt was like the fucking blueprint towards *not* leaving Dundee Utility under Nora's tenure as top boy!

Once I'd managed to let what was on the video sink in. Clocking just how many subscribers he had. How many likes there were compared to the *dis*likes. The rows of comments from what was verging on fucking fanboys of his?! I can't say it was jealousy from me. I had *fuck all* to to be jealous of the man about. I'd screwed the head - well, a wee bit, I suppose - the bit and had carved out a nice wee life, existing in the Dam with my vintage retro clobber hustle that I'd made something out of. Like I needed scores of VLs hanging on my every word or swing at the air. Aye, wasn't jealousy but, I don't know. I felt it a wee bit off that a horrible cunt like Norman Fullerton was, kind of famous. That all of these people who subscribed to him and left comments for the boy had no idea just what he was capable of. Who the man actually was because I'd already taken the leap of assuming that most viewers had already taken it that this was some "internet persona" and that in real life the cunt probably enjoyed walks on the beach and reading books in his spare time.

Due to the complete safe haven of hiding behind a made up name on the internet, I felt that I should bring him down a peg or two. Maybe let all of his fans know a few Nora - sorry, Matthijs - stories from back in the day, which might give them a more *balanced* view of this maniac whose video, out of the millions that they could've been sitting watching on the whole of the internet, they were looking at?

I almost fucking blew it though by leaving a comment on the video from my *own* "Si_Milne_DUFC" YouTube account which would've had *me* hiding in Amsterdam, and not Nora. Literally had the whole comment typed out and was about to confirm it when that last ditch panic kicked in. Thank fuck too, like.

Instead, I went off and created a completely new account, so I could leave the comment on the video. Oh aye, the levels of pettiness that this man has at times, I assure you. Thinking that it would be a good idea to throw Nora off the scent with my comment, by having something football related in the name, but *not* in connection with our own team. Plumping for "GGTTH1875" I thought this would be subtle enough to have him taking the leap that he had some Hibee giving him grief.

Even then, though. I had no idea just how things would spiral out of control, from the one comment. If I had known what it would have led to. Given the chance all over again, would I have left that comment?

Absolutely too fucking right I would have.

Chapter 5

Nora

'I've just about fucking had it with this GGTTH1875 prick,' I shouted at Pippo - with the kind of rage that it was almost as if *he* was the mystery keyboard warrior who had been winding me up for the past month - straight after I'd typed out, and sent, an all capitals reply comment to this internet hardman's one that they'd left on my most recent video that Pippo had put online.

FUCKING SQUARE GO. CHARITY, LIKE. YOU CAN EVEN NAME WHICH ONE. BET YOU FUCKING DINNAE THOUGH. SHITEBAG!!!

'Chill, chill, Matthijs. I keep telling you. *That's* what the block button is for, bro'

'And *I* keep fucking telling *you* that the block option is for pussies. It's like, when someone is trying to come the cunt with you on the internet, and you block them. Well, it's pretty much the equivalent of someone knocking on your door, with the intentions of being wide with you, and what? You don't answer the door, pretend that they're not there, outside giving you grief? Don't you know how that looks? Makes me look like a total shitebag and I can't be having that. Nah, mate. The block button's for cunt's that cannae handle confrontation, and you already fucking know, that's not me, eh?'

'Pffft, you make life too hard for yourself, Matty'

Pippo's reply, spoken like a true Dutchman.

The kid's laid back and easy going have a schmoke and a stroopwafel attitude didn't mean that I was wrong, though.

'Life, pip? Life is but a dream, ma man. I just need to subtract this fucking Hibs fanny from it and I'm golden'

I don't know why I'd let them get to me, to the levels that they did. Need to have tough skin to stick yourself online - and I kept telling myself that - but the thought of some cunt out there giving me lip - and even worse than that - and that they thought that they were free to do so. Well that's not the world that I come from. Cheques and balances, eh?

It had almost felt like a parent talking to their kid - the way Pippo had told me to just ignore it - that first comment I'd noticed from the person with the Hibernian FC username. Wasn't even that bad a comment - compared to how things escalated - but when it's a negative one, sitting inside scores of positive ones, that stuff tends to stick out.

Chances are if I *had* just ignored it and let it pass it probably would've been the end of things before they'd even went anywhere. I couldn't, though. Most people probably wouldn't have noticed it, stuck there beside rows and rows of comments from people all over the world. But I *did,* and that really was all that mattered. The comment of

GGTTH1875
Fugazi hard man

Sending me into fucking orbit. Well, once I'd looked up what the word *fugazi* meant, like. Could've been a compliment for all I knew because how am I meant to know all the words that exist in the world? When I saw that the cunt was calling me a fucking fake, though. Laptop was fucking lucky it never got launched against the wall, when I sat reading that page from dictionary.com.

Fucking fake? Who the fuck do they think they are, calling me fake? A fucking anonymous YouTube account ran by whoever, from where the fuck ever, calling *me* fake?

Pippo, being my internet guru as such, had told me to leave it. Saying that in all corners of the internet there were cunts that acted like that. Trolls - he called them - which I thought was a stupid fucking name for them to begin with because all I could think of were those radge looking ugly things that had the coloured hair. Pip, telling me that these types absolutely lived for the attention that they'd receive, just through being cunts to people online. Classic mum didn't hug them enough when they were wee kind of stuff. My young assistant explained that I just needed to ignore the comment and they'd soon move on to someone else and that the comment they'd left on my video was possibly one of hundreds they'd left across YouTube that day on people's videos.

I listened to the wee man as well, at first. Kept gnawing away at me though, knowing that comment was there and that cunts could read it for themselves. Away from the whole principle of someone giving you lip and not being held accountable for their actions, I also had my brand to think about. Can't help but feel a bit of a wanker to even be talking about *brands* and shite like that but facts are facts. If I've built up a wee following for myself - accidental or not - and am known online for being a hard man and someone that you would go to for tips to keep yourself safe from other cunts, then having someone casting dispersions over who and what I am. Can't be good for business, like. Never mind reputation.

Hours later though and back at the flat, I was still thinking about that one wee stupid comment. Pulled up the video on my phone to re read it, even though those three words had never really left my mind from the moment I'd read them. The thing is, no cunt can say that I acted in the heat of the moment. That it had been just an act of foolishness. I *knew* that responding was going to make me - and by extension - the gym look unprofessional. You're meant to rise above that stuff, aren't you? Nah, not me. Fuck that.

He was a man of extreme emotions.

That Doctor Erskine popped into my head - as if she was talking about me to someone else - as the inevitable happened, I typed out a reply to the comment.

Utility_Defence_AMS
Fake, aye? How's about you stop by the gym and find out, big man?

If I'd typed what I'd *really* wanted to I'd have had a ban handed down to my page, which would've been even worse for business than an internet gangster. I thought, if anything, my reply comment had been authoritative but mature enough to avoid any name calling or direct threats. Firm but measured and enough to at least allow me to start thinking of other things for what was left of the day.

I was happy to live and let live after that. Any cunt remotely interested in reading the comments on any of my videos from then until the end of time, they would've come across the one time that a viewer thought they'd be wide with me and there, for all to see, would be my response, and an example of how things would work if they tried to make an arse out of me.

But they just had to try and have the last word, eh?

It had actually been a few days since I'd posted my reply - and was actually already in the process of planning out my next video, scheduled for going up - but while I was sat in my office going through my emails, leaving Pippo to look after the members that were through in the hall, I noticed, out of the rows and rows of them, an email from YouTube telling me that I had a comment from a familiar account.

Now I don't want to come across as a dick, when it came to the YouTube attention, but after a while I stopped bothering to even open the emails that they sent because once you'd read one you'd read them all. Such and such has subscribed to your page, that cunt has commented on your video, this fanny has posted a video response, and so on. Seeing that GGTTH1875 in the subject line fairly got my attention though, mind.

GGTTH1875
You think I'm flying to Amsterdam just to see you getting your arse handed to you? Seen you get leathered enough times before, lad :)

Fucking slipped up there though, didn't they? In one comment they told me that they didn't live in Holland - I suppose it was signposted with the username but you can't be assuming things, eh? - *and* that they were suggesting that they knew me, personally. This, ruling out Pippo's theory about the trolls that spend all day online being weird to everyone they come across, and that the person who had left the original comment wouldn't have even known me from Adam.

Whoever they were, they were fucking at it with the implication that I was someone who was always on the receiving end of things. Don't get me wrong every now and again you might not been at the top of your form, or even some cunt just gets lucky. You can't be on top *all* of the time. Even yer Bayern Munich's and Real Madrid's don't win the league every season, eh? One thing I can guaran-fucking-tee to you though is that if someone seen me getting put on my arse in their lifetime then that shite was the stuff of Haley's Comet because they wouldn't have ever been treated to a repeat performance again.

As angry as this, frankly, libellous comment had made me on reading it. It had also left me a wee bit uneasy, the feeling that there was someone in Scotland, who *knew* me. I didn't think anyone would watch the videos in the first place, never mind other countries.

He's trying it on, I tried to calm myself by telling. He hadn't given any actual specific details with his comment. Aye, he's fishing, I said to myself as I talked myself down from the frenzy that this was all driving me into.

Maybe it was a case of "gone fishin" but if it was then I don't think they could've got an easier catch for themselves. Reeled me right fucking in. This time I didn't sit and dwell on things and work myself up only to cave and end up replying. I just acted on instinct. Fuck being measured or mature. Fuck them. You watch my videos you're going to see someone who's "meant" to be teaching you self defence but, in reality, around ninety percent of what they're showing you is more a case of *them* instigating a fight out of something that could easily have remained at a few strong words being exchanged between two people. Why then should I have needed to act any different in print?

Utility_Defence_AMS
Now now, pal. We both know that isn't true now, is it? Maybe it is in your pathetic wee dream world that you live in though, ya wanky wee keyboard warrior. Take yourself to Falkirk and get a ride or something, and let the adults do their grown up stuff.

It really was very much a case of game on from then.

With each reply from me - and I didn't see it at the time - he would reel me in even further with a loaded comment that would have my mind going in all directions as I tried to narrow in on *who* it was. He - and doing away with all of that political correctness shite once and for all because it was obviously a he - was almost behaving like one of those American serial killers, the way that they would send letters to the coppers, dropping wee clues as to who they were but deliberately leaving it short of them actually being caught. Had me on fucking strings, this.

GGTTH1875
Three words for you, pal. BRIDGE OF DOOM. I'll leave it at that. Wouldn't want to say anymore in front of your fanboys and embarrass you, yet ;)

His response back at me, publicly, doubting what he'd said about seeing me get leathered. Now while the majority of my subscribers wouldn't have had a scoob what he was talking about by Bridge of Doom, I did. Sounding like something that came right out of a fucking Lord of the Rings book, the Bridge of Doom was what - as an away supporter - you would often find yourself crossing on your way to Easter Road when your team was there. I'd always felt that the name - obviously chosen by the locals - had always been a case of its bark being worse than its bite. No doubt, though. It seen - and probably always will - its fair share of action back it was hardly like trying to cross it had been the equivalent of going into the gates of hell at the other side. If you'd been to a few away matches against Hibs though, you knew of it.

Utility_Defence_AMS
Only thing that's embarrassing here is you, ya scudbook.

I kept things short while trying to keep my cards close to my chest because, once again, he'd said something in particular that "might've" had something behind it, rather than this being stranger simply trying to wind up another one out of nothing other than sheer boredom.

Because there *was* something in me and the Bridge of Doom. The main problem with this being that my memory of that Saturday afternoon wasn't too fresh. It wasn't that fresh hours later on the Saturday evening that day either, mind. And if this prick on YouTube *was* there that day, then, unfortunately, he was going to have the jump on me.

GGTTH1875
I'd say "embarrassing" was being thrown over the side of a bridge by a couple of Blackley's Baby Crew

The absolute fucking snide prick. Going from one comment saying he doesn't want to embarrass me in front of my subscribers and then right to embarrassing me, in front of my followers. Because I couldn't deny - although would there on YouTube - that this had happened. What he had conveniently neglected to leave out had been the part where I had taken a brick to the side of the head by one of the Hibs mob and was slipping out of consciousness as I was thrown over the side of the bridge. When I came to, in the ambulance, I couldn't remember fuck all about it. Boy in the back of the ambulance was telling me that I was lucky to be alive while I was asking him what the Hibs - United score was, realising that I had a bit of short term memory loss and couldn't remember the score of the match I'd just been to.

Utility_Defence_AMS
Fantasist

While I took exception to being doubted as to my capabilities when it came to gratuitous and mindless violence, he was the same when having his word called into question.

And so it went on. Each video I posted, there he was. With some wideo comment. Probably sitting there with an erection posting it and getting his fucking cheapies. It wasn't just that, though. Other cunts were starting to clock by then and I was starting to get replies to *his* comments, from other subscribers. Asking me if it was true what he was saying and while I'm saying no to them in the replies, GGTTH1875 is jumping in and saying that I'm talking pish and that I'm gaslighting all my subscribers. This then leading to a broad section of comments in response to *that* comment. Some of my fans defending me, others questioning me while others jumping the shark and siding with some person they don't even know by accusing me of being a fraud.

Nope, not good for business Like I said, though. He kept dropping wee clues for me. Wee breadcrumbs that was helping me slowly decipher where the trail would lead.

I hated myself for the way that he had me biting at every turn. Wanted to be the bigger man and just ignore him, but that just wasn't - and neither ever likely to be - in my DNA. If I'd just done as Pippo had suggested I'd have seen the last of him long before and been getting on with life. Aye, and have some cunt sitting in a boozer somewhere in the world telling their mates that I'd ran away from him when he'd started giving me grief? Not in this life, or the life of Matthijs de Groot, for that matter.

When he'd left a comment - on another video - about how the fresh air that I was performing my instructions into was just about an equal opponent for me. What did I do? I stepped things up and used a participant - Pippo - for performing my techniques on. Breaking one of Pip's ribs when I'd got too carried away with things, led to this being a short lived feature. He got one of his mates, Stefan, to fill in for him the next week but he hadn't taken too kindly to, and I'll quote him here, being thrown around like an old Action Man. I tried to turn this into a positive by telling my subscribers that the tutorials were *so* intense that I could no longer get any volunteers to *be* in them with me. I'd tried to turn this into a positive by offering open invites to any of my subscribers who lived locally that fancied being in the videos. Apart from the cranks and the shitebags - who expressed an interest only to back out at the last minute - there was no takers.

This all taking me up to my most recent video that Pippo had upped and, as sure as tourists would walk out the front door of Centraal Station seeking recreational drugs and hookers, *GGTTH1875* left his obligatory comment. And it really was all a case of the straw and the camel's back.

The video - 'The secret to successful bar room brawling' - showed me taking the subscriber through the potential exchanges that you might come across in your average boozer with other piss heads, and how you "negotiate" your way through them.

HenreeHill
Matty de Groot. Showing the internet how to knock over someone's drink, and put them in hospital for their trouble!!

King_Kang
I've watched this video three times in a row, today.

Dijon_mama
Lol I love how grabbing a chair comes across as instructional.

Handofgawd86

'You tried to come the cunt with me, fannybaws so now I must reciprocate' :)

GGTTH1875
Secrets? Oh I've got a secret about "Matthijs de Groot" anybody want to know what it is?

Captcha_Killa79
This shit is SO not self defence and will ABSOLUTELY POSITIVELY land you in the cells if you repeat it on someone ... and I'm totally here for it!!

PenguinsCANfly
Funniest guy on the internet.

Scrolling through the scores of comments that greeted the week's new video the GGTTH1875 comment was the one that stuck out at me over the others although I think, by that point, I was subconsciously *looking* for their comment.

Their trolling, while an inconvenience at first, was really starting to affect things. He was taking the focus away from my videos itself, which all kind of defeated the purpose of making the fucking things in the first place. Worse than that, though. All I'd ever seen had been a rise in views, subscribers, likes and so on. After over a month of him and I biting back at each other. I had started to see a difference with my account. For the first time ever. Instead of my subscribers increasing, they'd *decreased.*

And it didn't take a Countdown champion to tell you that less subscribers equalled less views equalling less ads being clicked which all gave a a final sum of ... less money for me. And this was something that could not and would not stand. Fuck with a man's paper and you better be ready for his reaction.

I was already in the early planning of what reaction I was going to come back with to save both my name and the Utility Defence brand because I was fucked if I was going to stand back and let some fucking wee dick take it all apart, sat behind a computer.

Now he was coming on YouTube talking about "secrets" that there might be about me. By this point. It was clear that he knew me from the past. Too many snide comments had been left that confirmed as much. He'd already brought my page the lies - well, some - about me being leathered on match days so any secret that he was referring to was, as far as I was concerned, going to be my *big* secret. The one that had far greater implications - if let out - than having people question how hard I was or wasn't on the internet. The "secret" that if left in the wrong hands would lead to my cushy wee life in Holland being brought to an immediate end.

Now the stakes were bigger than ever before.

It was time I dealt with this fucking spoon burner once and for all.

Going to be a wee bit difficult to type your wideo comments when all of your fucking fingers are broken, I said out loud, looking at that last comment from him before telling Pippo to put those fucking skins down and that we were going to be making a quick wee video for the subscribers.

Actually, singular, not plural.

Anyone was going to be free to watch it, but I only really needed the one to take *notice* of it.

Chapter 6

Liam

'If you get me there on time there'll be a wee tip in it for you'

I said to the driver, who I'd been enforced to employ due to sleeping in. Mum was already away out for the day to work and the one day that Bannon didn't wake me up by licking my face and standing on my balls, being the *one* day that I could've been doing with him doing so.

'You know? The tip is already a kind of unwritten rule' The man said.

'See that's probably why you don't get tips all the time then, eh? Maybe need to get it *written*?' I joked back although fuck knows what I had to be laughing about.

There was no if, buts or mibbes about it. I *needed* to be on the 10.31 train to Edinburgh. I miss it and life isn't going to be worth living. My own fucking fault too. Should've well been in my bed earlier than half three the night before but that Modern Warfare two can be a demanding mistress. Went through "one more game" syndrome for a good hour and a half. Aye, you can cry about it the next morning but the truth is when you're running around the Favela blasting fuck out of anyone daft enough to pop their heads out, the furthest thing from your mind is what time it is, or that you've got work the next day.

It was a harsh and unforgiving environment - work, not Call of Duty - though and didn't allow for cunts being slack because they were playing X-Box the night before. All the good work that I'd put in over the years would've counted for nothing if I was to miss that Scotrail to Waverley.

'Did you see the United game last night?'

Stewart Fraser - according to his Hackney that was attached to the vents on the front of his dashboard - asked, as he came to a stop at some traffic lights as we neared the city centre. At that moment in time I wasn't really ready for any real conversation as all I could think of was what was going to happen to me if I missed that train.

'Gomis and Bauben were different gravy, eh? Stopped the Aberdeen midfield from even getting a kick of the ball. Aye, was maybe Goodie and Daly that scored the goals but that side would be nothing without those two running things in the middle of the park. Still can't believe wee Jimmy was playing at Cowdenbeath until we picked him up'

Any other morning and my driver would've found me willing to sit and give my opinion on things, just not that one. Any time I'd seen the Senegalese and Ghanaian in a United shirt they'd stuck out like a sore thumb but had no appetite for talking about it. Hadn't even been to Tannadice for a couple of years, personally. Looking back, I think it was more to do with the fact that I hadn't been to bed for around thirty six hours and had just went out to the match but I proper took the cream puff the last game I was at. St Mirren in the cup. We got beat one nil which is alright as that stuff can happen but it was more the fact that we were the home team - and favourites - but that negative cunt Levein set us out to play with one striker. Maybe I wouldn't have spat the dummy in the way that I did but, to be fair to myself, I wasn't the only one giving him grief about his less than ambitious approach to getting his team through to the quarter finals.

Maybe I took things too far but said I wouldn't be back until Levein was gone. *Then* when Levein left to inject some *flair* into the Scottish National Team, life had shifted a wee bit for me, and I wasn't exactly the first fan outside the stadium on match day. That's maybe how pay at the gate fans end up being lost to clubs, though? Entertainment business, is it not? Aye, someone needs to tell that to fucking Craig Levein then, like.

I chose not to bother answering him and hoped that he'd drop the attempt at small talk, instead playing dumb by just scrolling on my phone at nothing in particular. Either he picked up on this from me or couldn't be arsed in repeating what he'd said. Plus, I wanted him focussed on getting me to the train station - just beside the harbour - on time. Although that was looking extremely dicey as we drove down West Marketgait. The train was due in four minutes time while technically a car could've made it to the station in that time. That doesn't take into account that the car in question is driving from A to B in a busy city centre.

'Just about there, mate' The driver said, breaking the silence that had been in the car following his attempt to talk about Dundee United's midfield while I had sat there bricking it over whether we were going to get there on time. We were just around the corner now so technically he was correct. We *were* just about there. "Just about" was no good to me. All, or fuck all, the only parameters.

Being told "just about there" while you're looking at the time and your train is now one minute away from its departing time is the equivalent of that old show I watched once on UK Gold, the one where they had cunts playing darts for prizes. Was well poor form but the boys that were playing for the prizes were shite and couldn't manage it but the TV people *still* brought the star prize out at the end to show the two of them what they could've - but didn't - win! I'd have asked the presenter boy in the glasses if he was taking the fucking pish if I was in that position.

Whatever happened. It was going to be a photo finish, whether I would catch the train or not, and really was all out of my control by then. As we were driving - train station now in line of vision we were a minute after the departure time, but I could see that the train was still sat there.

'I might just make this fucking thing, mate' I said to him. Aye, wee bit positivity and *now* I was happy to speak to him, eh?

I already had my seatbelt off - filling the car with a super nippy noise that the driver wasn't that impressed with but when we drew to a stop outside the station - passengers side door open before the car had even stopped - and he was telling me that it was six pounds and seventy five pence and I was throwing him a twenty pound note and telling him to keep the change I'm sure he was a wee bit more impressed with that.

It hadn't been a token of my goodwill - a near thirteen pounds tip - but was a case of me knowing that if I was going to catch the train every single second was going to count and the difference in me waiting on me getting my change back from him *then* sorting him out with a tip could well have been the difference in me making it or not.

Now normally, if I'm in a hurry for the bus or train, I tend to err on the side of caution and won't make a commotion in trying to catch either just in case I miss it by seconds and am left standing there on the platform - or at the bus stop - looking like a fanny. The risk of the embarrassment proving more influential than actually going and making sure that I caught my mode of transport.

Not that day. It wasn't exactly a few mad seconds that I'm particularly proud of but from the taxi to the platform for southbound trains I managed to knock over some big cardboard display that had flyers for Dundee University, bump shoulders and almost knock some mum on the ground but making up for this by volleying her wee boy - when looking back at the mum - who was a metre or two in front of her. Her scream being enough to draw everyone's attention, which I wasn't hanging about for. Instead, shouting a pretty poor 'I'm sorry, I need to catch ma train' as I ran. When I hit the platform it was empty, but the train was still there. The wee man in the hat giving off heavy vibes of everyone now being on the train and all that was left was for him to step back onto the carriage and get going again.

'OH, MATE, HOLD THE TRAIN'

I shouted at the kind of decibel that anyone in the vicinity of the platform would have heard, never mind the boy from Scotrail. Someone at the top of the Hilltoon would have heard my scream, never mind the boy from Scotrail.

All came down to wherever he was going to be a dick or not, and you never quite know which way that wind is going to blow when it comes to cunts that work on the buses or trains. Amount of times I've been metres away from the bus stop, waving my arm out to the driver and he just sits there with a smug and satisfied wee smile, as he drives on past.

My shout being enough to stop him, just as he was getting on. He turned and looked towards me and pointed at his watch.

Oh aye, here we go, jobsworth time, I presumed.

Instead, though he smiled and waved his arm in a "come on then, but you better be quick" kind of way.

'You just saved ma life, pal' I thanked him as he stood to the side to let me on.

'Not all heroes wear capes, son' The old boy chirpily replied back, giving his whistle a wee blow before following me behind, with the train starting to move afterwards.

In my rush to simply catch the thing I hadn't noticed that it was a smaller service than you'd normally get to Edinburgh. Once I got on though I discovered that the reduced amount of carriages were already seeing to it that I wasn't going to be getting a seat. That was fine. To ensure that I travelled on that particular train and got to my meeting in time I'd have walked up and down for the whole journey checking people's tickets.

A seat, in the general scheme of things, I couldn't have given a flying one about. It was only after the train had slowly began to set off though that I reached for my earbuds and discovered that in my rush to get out the house I hadn't lifted them, which was going to make for a long journey to Edinburgh and back. I'd downloaded a couple of DJ Premier mixtapes from underground hip-hop dot com and had barely had my earbuds out of my ears for the past week since sticking the mixes on my phone. Instead, I was going to have to sit - well, stand - and listen to everyone else's pish. Businessmen who don't realise - or maybe just don't give a fuck - how loud they're talking to colleagues on the phone, bairns crying, weirdos who think just because they're on public transport that it makes it acceptable to just start talking away to cunts that they don't know. All of that stuff.

Which meant that I was treated to an absolute topper of some businessman - who took and made multiple calls all the way to Edinburgh - who, from what I could hear was having the worst day possible for someone to experience. Anyone with a brain would've proper dingeyd the calls when in a public space but you know what some cunts are like, eh? Seem to hold this fantasy that when they're using their mobile phone, no one around them can hear them on it. Like they have some invisible radiation filled force field that surrounds them and cuts off any noise. Maybe the radiation part is correct though?

From what I could make out - didn't really have much choice *not* to make any of it out due to how loud he was talking - over the course of the journey from Dundee to Waverley he was juggling between the fact that one of his clients had cancelled a big order on him, and now his gaffer was demanding to know what went wrong. Throw in the additional content which involved his wife giving him grief because she'd just been looking at their phone bills and found a recurring number on his itemised bill, she'd phoned it and discovered that he'd been shagging someone else behind her back.

Honestly, if it wasn't for the fact that I'd had somewhere that I needed to be I'd have been happy as fuck to have travelled all the way to Kings Cross listening to him. Normally I'd have found this kind of scenario well nippy, but not this. This was like fucking Eastenders or something. I was riveted. Didn't even *need* my buds, like.

The train pulled into the last stop at Waverley a few minutes after its planned arrival time, leaving me something like eight minutes to get myself off the carriage, through and out of the station and up to the top of Calton Hill. Doable, but I would have to get a move on, especially with the emphasis very much being placed on "to the top," with those stairs that you had to tackle to get yourself up there.

If anything, with all that had went on that morning it had given me a wee chance to not be dwelling on *why* I was due in Edinburgh in the first place.

A boy's got to eat, ken? Sometimes though it's the acquiring the funds required for putting food in your belly that can be the right bastard. Sometimes, a boy ends up doing work that has him a paranoid filled wreck until he clocks out for the day again, like I did.

Halfway up the stairs I came across a pair of Japanese tourists who were stood taking photos of everything, and I'm not just going down the route that the TV always tries to make you think of Japanese tourists either, they really *were* taking photos of everything. When the man - out of the couple - spied me about to walk past him he stopped me and asked if I would take a photo of him and his bird.

'Can't, mate. I'm in a hurry' I said as, once passed the two of them, I broke into a mini jog up the stairs. Not quite Rocky or fuck all but the same idea. Felt a bit of a dick for not stopping to to take their picture. All they'd have heard would've been how welcoming the Scots were and yet they get here and find cunts that don't even have the time to take a photo for them? Then again. They ask someone to take their photo in another part of Edinburgh and they'd be *very* fucking lucky to get their camera back again, never mind a picture of them taken.

Who I was meeting though was someone that you didn't keep waiting. They turn up and find that you're not there waiting on them, then they just get back in their car and drive away again.

I made it to the bench - that looked down onto the St James Centre - one minute before the agreed time. The finest of margins. He was five minutes late, which was his right to do so, knowing that I was hardly going to be in a position to say a word about it. I was glad for a few minutes to stop my panting, having literally ran all the way from Princes Street. Sitting catching my breath as I looked out across the city centre and then over in the direction of Leith. While the meeting place - up there - had obviously been chosen strategically I'd always liked the view when I was up there. Same with when you're up Dundee Law. There's just something about being up high in a city, and getting a chance to see everything below that gives you a chance to appreciate just how wee you really are. I'd never even known just how cool Edinburgh looked - as a city - until I'd went up to the top of Calton Hill that first time as a fifteen year old. Having got lost two times along the way, despite it being right next to the station. I thought it was all just tourist pish about Edinburgh, or "Edinboro" like they all seem to call it.

I was still staring at Leith Docks when I heard the footsteps approaching on the gravel.

'Aye aye, kiddo'

Thank fuck it's a Scottish voice, my immediate thought. The other boy - the Polish one, who had only been sent on occasion in the past year or so - scared me. Unlike the Scottish one, there wasn't anything close to a hint of friendliness whenever he was sent to meet me. Just a gruff threat, letting me know what would happen if I didn't do my job while his eyes were making threats of their own. Tried to tell him that we were all on the same team and to be chill - that first time he threatened me - and the mad bastard almost fucking pistol whipped me for my trouble so I never made that mistake again. Never spoke a single word to him more than was needed after that day, which I don't think anyone could blame me over either. The other one, though. He was actually quite sound and sometimes we'd have a fag with each other, while sitting on the bench chatting before he'd jump back into his black Range Rover, leaving me with the bag at my feet and me on my way back to Waverley for a Dundee train.

'Alright, aye?' I said back, relieved that it was him.

Realising that I was sat directly in the middle of the bench I moved over to one side to let him on it.

'No it's fine, pal. I can't stop. Need to be somewhere, like as in ten minutes ago' He said while taking out his packet of fags and throwing one over to me. Initially he looked like he was about to just go ahead and give me the bag but an old man walking his Spaniel came around right as he was about to and he aborted and, instead, crashed the fags for a moment.

Once the two of them were past us - my guy in the suit holding the bag, following the old man with his eyes all the way until he was well past us - I had the bag more or less thrown beside me onto the bench before he then went into the inside of his suit jacket and pulled out that familiar white envelope - 'that's for yourself, pal and, as always, if you get stopped with it, you found it' - and handing it to me with a wee wink and piece of advice, the same advice I'd been getting told when I was fifteen / sixteen and, as far as I'm concerned, was more plausible an excuse when I was that age than me at twenty.

'Hope you're good though, wee man? I'll maybe see you next time you're over, eh? Take care'

I hadn't even had the chance to light the Lambert and Butler that he'd thrown at me before he was on his way.

As I always did, I sat there on the bench with the bag between my feet and took a few moments of pause before getting on my way. I had the feeling when I had turned up to the top of that hill for the first time - years before - that if I stayed up there I'd be safe, but that the moment I walked down those steps and got myself onto Princes Street, or down into the station. I'd be immediately lifted by some plain clothed officers.

Just a stupid wee feeling that I got the first time and, as a result, ended up *always* getting, whenever I was at the top of Calton Hill in possession of one of those sports holdalls on my occasional trips to the capital city.

Buying a few minutes by telling myself that I would start my journey back down to Waverley once I pinged my fag. As much as I'd have liked to have stayed up in the safety of that Edinburgh vantage point. One thing was for sure, with what I had in the bag. If I didn't get myself down the hill, sooner or later cunts would be marching *up* it looking for me.

Grand old Duke of York style.

Chapter 7

Si

The girl from the bar, as she was putting my Heineken down on the table, admitted that she'd been hesitant to approach me. This due to the look that I'd had on my face. Telling me that she thought that she might have been interrupting me during 'a moment.' Fuck know's what my coupon must've been like, mind?

I'd clocked her out of the corner of my eye. Doing this almost hovering dance of sorts with my pint in her hand, looking like she didn't know whether to stick or twist. The smile only appearing on her face once I'd looked around at her - sensed her trepidation - and flashed her my own trademark one in her direction while ushering her over with a welcoming

'Mon over, it's fine. You don't want me to die in your place of thirst, eh? Imagine the paperwork for one thing, plus your tips would take a proper battering I imagine'

'I, I thought that you were possibly receiving bad news and did not want to intrude'

She replied - one of the table service girls inside Belushi's on Warmoesstraat - in a beautifully innocent way that was rare of the city of Amsterdam, or the Amsterdam that *I'd* always known, since making it my home.

Before this wee moment I'd just sat there with my mouth open with one hand holding my phone and the other placed on top of my head in a sort of disbelief as I watched him. I mean, what else was I *meant* to do at this spectacle that he was putting on for the whole world, and without even knowing it, specifically for *me*. Now I'd never - or are ever likely to - put a video onto the internet but I assume that there are various steps that need taken before it finds itself uploaded for everyone to view. All of those steps to take and yet at no point did he, or whoever he classed as friends, think that he was going to come across as an absolute fucking maniac.

Then again, when you *are* one I guess the concern over the visuals that you give everyone must dip a few levels to the average non psychopathic man or woman in the street.

I'd found myself stopping in at Belushi's on the way back to my pad. Over the afternoon I'd pulled off the unthinkable in finding a seven out of ten pair of Amsterdams, from a used sportswear seller who had recently started to pitch up a few days a week. Sat there amongst about another thirty or so pairs of used trainers. Adidas, Nike, Puma, New Balance. Pretty much all the brands that you could think of and pretty much every pair sitting there you wouldn't have touched them with a barge pole. The Amsterdams being what you could only have ever described as a diamond in the dirt.

I'd actually passed the boy's stall before that wee voice in my head spoke up. No chance they'll be what you thought they were, I told myself, but thought for the sake of a few seconds out of my day, I better check.

Fucking *was* them, too. Had to actually go for a wee walk to compose myself before going back to enter negotiations on what kind of funds the boy would be looking for. Seeing them sitting there I knew that I'd have told him what he had - and that's they were worth a lot of coin - without actually telling him if I'd started speaking straight away, so cooled myself down a wee bit before going back to get them.

Needn't have bothered my arse as - when I returned - and asked him how much he was wanting for "those brown Adidas" the clueless cunt told me that they were twenty euros or I could have two pairs from his stock for thirty.

I was already counting the money in my bank account that they would bring in while I was handing the twenty euro note over to him and wishing him a *goedemiddag* before heading off on my merry way. Thing is, this had marked an extraordinary turn of events for the week.

Only two days before - and after a couple of weeks of protracted talks - I'd taken a trip to Eindhoven to pick up, what was until then a complete unicorn as far as I'd been concerned, a pair of *Rotterdams*, also in a nine. Couldn't make it fucking up, like. Like the ones named after the capital city, I'd only ever seen pictures of them - never in the flesh, as such - and had it not been for the photographs online I wouldn't have been able to tell you *what* they had looked like.

Knew they were sought after though. Spoken about in hushed tones by some. And that's why I was taking no fucking chances with the Dutch postal service, couriers or anyone who fancied trying to take the package from Eindhoven to Amsterdam. Only way I knew they'd be safe from harm was going to be if the seller kept hold of them and I paid him a visit.

Hadn't even got around to listing them for sale when the Amsterdams then fell into my lap. Sometimes your luck's just in, you know?

With that entrepreneurial spirit which had ensured that I could self sustain in a city like the Dam. I was soon sitting there in the boozer dreaming up a special collectors Adidas Dutch city series twin pack of the Amsterdams *and* Rotterdams together. Market them in a Ajax versus Feyenoord slash play on the polarisation of the two cities which, despite being so close to each other, were completely different from one another and how, like both cities, each trainer stood out for themselves. I'd learned a lot about the culture of where I'd decided to call home and one of the sayings that I'd been told had always resonated with me when it came to the divide between both places.

While Amsterdam dreams, Rotterdam works.

Obviously used by Rotterdammers rather than those on the other side of the A4 I embraced it, rather than took it as the insult that it was intended as.

I'd rather be a dreamer than a worker. Any fucking day of the week. Plus, you can still earn a crust. You can just do it on your own terms, when you're a dreamer.

I had them out at my table in Belushi's to give them a bit better inspection to see just how much love they'd need before going out to market. The suede in remarkable condition for a trainer that had originally had its tags popped a long time before. Even the sole wasn't wearing any signs of any major usage.

Twenty euros, I laughed to myself while already knowing that they - combined with the Rotterdams - would probably pay for my rent for a couple of months alone.

I was putting them back into the bag - no box unfortunately but when you come across a unicorn you don't turn it away because its horn is a wee bit squint - when this American couple, on their way out of the boozer, asked me if I knew where the Rijks Museum was. The short answer would have been yes I did and that it was a good fucking stretch from where they currently were but while I had been sat there having a drink I'd overheard them at their table talking about what they were going to do next. The husband had said that they should take a walk around the Red Light District. His missus wasn't impressed by this suggestion, though. Questioning him on why he wanted to look at women in windows. Proper tried to shame the boy, eh? *Everyone* has a wee wander around that part of town when they visit. Just the rules of how things go, eh? She was having none of that, though. Saying how seedy it all was and that there were plenty of other attractions that they would be able to cram in on their trip, without the need for any Red Light Districts.

The husband looked well gutted, to be fair. Not gutted enough to put up any kind of debate, though. You could see who wore the trousers like because fuck flying all the way from America and *not* cutting about Oudezijds Voorburgwal.

When they were getting their coats on and on their way out, the woman stopped to ask me if I could help the two of them with directions.

'Aye, of course I can'

I assured the two of them once she'd asked me if I was Irish which - for an American was decent enough guess I suppose - that I lived in the city so would help them out. The *real* irony for me was that she'd made such a big thing about not being in the Red Light District, when she was literally right fucking *beside* it.

Thinking that I'd give her the wee push that she needed, and sort her husband out at the same time, I gave her a series of directions for to remember while safe in the knowledge that after following the first few that they'd then be ... well, not the fucking Rijks Museum, anyway. I can't lie. The thought of the two of them landing up walking along the street and coming face to face with some woman standing there in her stocking and sussies who is not giving a single flying fuck about the fact that the woman with her man stood out on the street is currently looking like she's seen a ghost, while she raps gently on her window to try and bring in some business, it was all too much to resist.

'Thank you so much. You have a great day'

The woman said to me with a warm smile as she started to walk on.

'Aye, you too, both of you'

I replied back but - catching eyes with the husband - I gave him a wee knowing wink that he wasn't going to realise *was* knowing. He soon would, though. That's all that mattered.

Having only went in for a celebratory pint to toast the success of finding something that ranked high on the grail list of many I got the taste for it so decided to stay for another. Since I'd walked in, the place had filled up quite a bit. A collection of all shapes and sizes of mainly tourists which you would see every time you popped in for a drink. The wee pocket of - what looked like - Spartak Moscow fans who weren't the quietest were ones to keep an eye no doubt but as long as none of them messed with me then I definitely wasn't going to mess with them. Ajax - who they were in town to play in the Europa League - and F Side would take care of that side of things the day of the match as sure as the sun rising.

I'd just ordered another pint to the table - while taking care of what was left of my first one - when the notification popped up on my phone. Having been so taken away with the trainers my phone hadn't even made it out of my pocket yet. The short vibration in my jeans pocket sending me fishing it out to see what in the wheel of fortune of nonsense that you can find sent to your phone was waiting for me.

It was an email, from YouTube informing that Utility Defence had just uploaded a new video. No doubt another one of his psychotic rants that if taken to the trades description people over it's marketing as "self defence" would probably see him banned from the website or something, I thought to myself, as I clicked on the link.

Straight off before it had really got underway I could tell that there was something different about it to the others. It was the time that I noticed first of all. It wasn't the usual hour long offering and, instead, was well short of that, by about fifty seven minutes. Then I noticed the angle the video was being shot at. If Nora was standing in the gym - like the other videos - then you wouldn't have known, due to how close he was to the camera.

Hola, cuntos. Apologies to those of you out there who have been waiting on the new Utility Defence video dropping on the page, but I've got something even better lined up for you. You're just going to have to be a wee bit more patient. You're maybe familiar with the expression about poking bears with sticks or even, possibly, the one about where you let a sleeping dog lie? Well there's some cunt out there who fucking doesn't and they're about to learn a lesson that they're going to regret for the rest of their - soon to expire - pathetic shitey life.

I knew he was talking about myself, but where was he going with this? Outside his vicious and threatening - and at times *very* funny, mostly unintentional - replies to me inside the comments of his videos he hadn't acknowledged me. Now here he was, on video.

Things had well escalated since I'd posted that very first comment upon discovering what the fucking radge was now up to. If he hadn't bit to that video comment of mines, that would have been the end of it. He did though which set the tone from there on. I can't even explain it because it wasn't something that had been pre planned in any way but I'd elevated things from what could have just been a fishing expedition from a stranger on the internet to making it clear to Nora that no, the person behind the YouTube account *knew* him. Was from the same world as him and - crucially, as part of the wind up - had "seen" things that all of Nora's subscribers *hadn't*.

While I had ramped things in that area - with each comment - his manic and unhinged replies ramped up in their own way. Due to the fact that Nora was not someone that you saw taking a doing too often, but that I had, *twice*, against Hibs, to maintain as much authenticity as possible. I steered things - and keep them there - in the direction of being related to Hibs. The "glory glory to the Hibees" named account probably didn't harm things either, mind. This, it seems had led to him playing detective. Thinking he was narrowing down the field in terms of potential names of who was behind the YouTube account giving him grief.

Apart from offering up deliberately vague descriptions of events that he one hundred percent knew he'd been involved in, and incidents that had taken place in wider crowd scenes, I hadn't said anything more specific than that. And if I *had* then that would've been purely coincidental but my guess was that this was more to do with Nora having been driven out of his mind by this level of disrespect that he had never known before, and had went so deep with it that he was now seeing things that weren't there.

He stopped for a moment, not sure if it was for deliberate dramatic purposes or if he hadn't worked out what he was going to say next but with such good timing, looked away from the camera for a moment before setting his eyes right back to - what felt like - staring right at you.

Oh, aye? You thought you were safe sat behind your keyboard, eh? Thought that you could say any old shite to me and there be no accountability for you? You're about to find out that you are DEAD wrong. Thing is, pal. You fucked up, left one too many clues, eh? And I figured out the puzzle, and now I'm coming for you.

This had now become a literal address from him, directly to me. I felt seen as I watched it and for a few hairy seconds I genuinely thought that I'd gone too far and that, somehow, he'd found a way to establish where all of my comments to his videos had been coming from.

The sigh of relief that I breathed - as he continued to talk and absolve me of any potential blame - was a pretty good indicator in terms of the mini fright that the mad bastard had given me, even if only for a few seconds.

Think just because you live in another country it'll be enough to save you? Those KLM flights will be worth EVERY. FUCKING. PENNY, when I'm bouncing up and down on your head.

He was becoming more and more animated with every syllable never mind actual word. Still, was nice of him to confirm to my good self that I wasn't on his radar, while the rage started to take over him.

He went off on rant that was all over the place but his loose theme to it was that everyone on the internet should be careful about who they troll because while they do it looking for a reaction, they should think about the different ways a person might respond to *them*. In Nora's case, handing down a death sentence which, aye, is maybe a wee bit extreme a punishment for some cunt being a wideo on YouTube, but this was Nora that we're talking about, here.

I was too shocked at how far the man had been pushed - all through a few simple comments on a screen, that had only been posted in jest - for me to truly be able to enjoy the fruits of my work. It had worked out *way* better than I could have ever possibly imagined. Don't get me twisted, though. I *knew* it would have wound the cunt up. It was literally my prime motivation for committing such an act in the first place. I just didn't realise *how much* it would've done so. Zico was going to piss himself when he found out that through my trolling, Nora was heading to Scotland to find, me! No doubt about it. The boy was going to be pissed off at himself for not thinking of it first when he heard about the current events that had been set in motion, the day that he had sent me that first link to YouTube.

You said that you'd snap me in two, aye? Couldn't snap a fucking Kit Kat, ya cunt.

At that, he seemed to have a moment where he realised that the video was going a bit sideways. From the surface, it looked like it had been meant to be a wee info video for his subscribers to keep them abreast of matters but he couldn't help himself. He never, ever could, though.

The video being nothing other than him dishing threats out to whoever - in his radge mind - his object of desire was.

To all my subscribers, though. Stay frosty. The next video is going to be one with a difference. Isn't that right, GGTTH1875? We'll be seeing each other real soon, eh pal? You sleep tight for now though.

The video ending with the most unsettling of smirks on his face. Fuck knows what was in his head in that moment but it looked dark.

I felt a wee bit shit, like, that someone out there had potentially now been landed with a target on their back, through me doing fuck all other than try to have a wee laugh but, you know? Rather it was them than me, and no mistake.

Plus, the fact that - through fuck all other than a few comments on the internet - Nora had apparently been driven so mental over it all that he was now willing to cross international waters to seek out an invisible man was very, *very* funny.

Chapter 8

Nora

'Keep it the fuck together, now'

I lectured myself, as I walked from the taxi into departures. A Head sports hold-all - slung over my shoulder as I walked through the light drizzle that had started on our approach to Schipol - enough to hold what I needed for my flying visit to the motherland. No need for any of that suitcase pish, and that's before the airlines even start with their nonsense about wanting coin from you to *store* your case on the fucking plane. The same plane that you've already booked to fly on. *Clearly* cunts want to take their case with them if they've bought a ticket for the plane. Airlines have got you over the barrel from there the money grabbing bastards. Not, though, if you're travelling light on nothing other than a wee spot of "business."

Three pairs of socks and boxers. Three t shirts, couple'ay pairs of jeans, single pair of trainers and the Reebok tracksuit I had on for travelling, throw in your toiletries and Bob's the cunt that rides your auntie. Took me fucking longer to choose which passport to use, than it took me to pack my bag.

In the end, plumping for Frank van der Hoorn which - at the point of having all my fake documents made up - had been a wee nod to a Dutch Dundee United player of old, that I'd thought of when choosing the names and had been asked if I had any preference, while also being reminded that it would make sense if my names had been believable for a kick off. Hadn't really had *that* much of a chance to see the original van der Hoorn (Freddy) in a United strip before I got banged up but

I'd liked what I'd seen. One hard bastard that didn't take any shite off any cunt. Type of player that every team wants having their backs out on the pitch. Just like how someone would want a boy like a Norman Fulton having their backs, *off* of it. The 'Frank' element to it was a tip of the hat to my old man, Frankie. So, aye. The whole name - in full - was an amalgamation of two radgeys.

I'd been careful not to nail all my colours to the mast, when it came to who exactly I was, as far as the authorities were concerned. I'd told myself back at the start of the decade - when I'd escaped - that the only fucking way I was going to *stay* escaped would be if I done everything right. Even the tiniest of slips ups could've been enough to be the difference between sleeping in a jail cell or in a pokey Amsterdam flat that isn't that much bigger than a cell and while doesn't come with all mod cons at least comes with your freedom.

I had passports - plural - for travelling purposes, while I had another identity (Matthijs de Groot) for the person that was based in Amsterdam and ran a city centre gym. If it all sounds a wee bit confusing then that is kind of offset, to a degree, when in almost ten years you'd never *needed* the fake passports, due to being too shit scared to attempt to leave the country for fear of what would happen when passing through the security checks. When you buy a fake passport, and as genuine as it might look, there's only really one way to confirm if it's the real deal or not. And a man in my position really could not be finding out that the passport that he'd had knocked up by an Algerian philosophy student called Farid from Westerpark, was nothing other than - in the eyes of customs and airport security - a poor imitation.

As a result, while I'd bought them specifically for the reasons of being able to travel. I'd avoided using them at all costs.

And there I was, loitering outside those big revolving doors to the airport. Hesitant to go the whole hog and move inside the place.

Get that paranoia away to fuck, there's cunts bringing kilos of Ching from South America into the place every single day. I should've been flattered that any cunt even knew who I was, never mind having a unit in place ready for me rocking up to the place after ten years on the run.

Can't blame a boy one wee bit for any para caper, all things considering, though.

I decided to have one last fag before going and checking in for the flight. Standing there puffing away while I thought it an appropriate time to have a last minute check over my Dutch passport, just in case there had been anything I'd not picked up on years before when I bought it but had consciously known that I wouldn't be using it any time soon and, instead, had just stored it away someplace safe.

I felt a wee bit shameful, like. When I looked at it, realising how many years I'd held it for, without actually deploying it. Both mum and dad's birthday parties to mark turning seventy. Some of the more mouth watering United matches that had taken place, on and *off* the pitch. Probably the most shameful of all? Knowing that I had a son out there - one that my ex, Abigail, had refused to bring to Bar L to see me for the first ten years of his life and then, with my escape, me *relocating* for the next ten years - and that I hadn't taken the opportunity to ensure that I was a part of his life. All of the stuff that *really* matters in life had been deemed by me as nothing worth using a fake passport to bridge the gap.

Yet some fucking wideo prick on the internet can mouth off at me, and I can't get to the airport quick enough?

Sucking the life out of the last part of my reek - before pinging it, unfortunately, in the direction of a couple who were sitting at one of the nearby benches. The fag hitting the side of their case without any of them clocking it - I told myself that I was going to book some therapy when I returned to Amsterdam even though I already knew myself that I wouldn't.

Being able to *recognise* some of your flaws is at least a start. Probably saved myself a few hundred euro for a kick off through having that ability. Still, recognising where you're going wrong - like I did there outside the airport - but still going ahead with things anyway, as was the case that lunch time a few hours before my flight, showed me that I wasn't quite there yet.

I'd loved to have said that I was making a wee trip over to spend some quality time with my family in their later years, and after such a large gap since last seeing them. Same with the kid. Being able to spend some time to get to know him. None of that was my motivation for risking it all and getting on that KLM flight, though. It was all about the violent tendencies that had been stirred up by that mouthy spoon burning cunt from Edinburgh. After being away from my country for so long I should've been buzzing about seeing everyone that meant something to me in my previous life. Getting to see the only and only true love of my life, Dundee United Football Club. What was giving me the buzz - and I'm talking hairs up the back of the neck when I pictured it all, like - was the thought of me booting that internet hard man all over fucking Leith, when I caught up with him.

He'd replied to my latest video with a cocky

'Well, you know where I drink. where I've always drank'

Clearly he had thought that I'd been bluffing and not accounted for me having already bought my flight tickets before recording the video. It was the only explanation for him narrowing things down even further for me by telling me which boozer I'd find him in. Aye, he didn't say *which* pub, but he didn't need to. I knew which one it was. The one that if you were in town on match day and had somehow been kept apart from the CCS from Waverley to Leith, you headed in its direction.

Making the decision to travel to Scotland to find him already, this latest comment from him hadn't even been met with a response from me. Instead, I'd told myself, that it was now past time for correspondence, and time for action. Going dark on my YouTube account until I had popped up in Edinburgh to make sure GGTTH1875 was in for a *very* bad fucking day. If I was going to be catching up with him inside the boozer then all the better as there wouldn't be a shortage of jakeys willing to film our encounter in return for me shoving a few notes behind the bar for to keep them topped up.

I'd have taken a personal and private one to one with him. That would've been enough to satisfy the urges that he'd been inciting but that aside, though. If I could grab the chance to shut the boy's puss right up - and in a public way, such as on YouTube - with added embarrassment to him, then I'd have been all over that.

That, it was assumed, was if I hadn't ended up killing the cunt, once I'd got started, mind. A lot of years worth of pent up aggression that had been built up over the years. Working out at the gym could only help you so far, there. Aye, you get the release of pushing your body and make it feel alive but where's the endorphins that hearing some poor cunt scream out in excruciating pain and knowing that you caused it brings, I ask? Because of that, I didn't know where this was all going to end. I'd tried to look ahead and one element that was to be decided was going to be this other cunt's attitude, when I finally caught up with him. I wasn't wanting to be shifting the decision onto other cunts or fuck all but in a funny way it was kind of down to him on whether he was going to walk and talk a wee bit funny for the rest of his life, or if he wasn't going to be walking and talking, at all.

Knowing I couldn't put it off any longer, I told myself once again to keep it together before heading inside. It had been so long - more than twenty years - since I'd been in an airport and the first thing that struck me was just how big the place was, and bright. Never had a migraine in my life before but if I'd had one come on - there in the terminal - I wouldn't have been surprised.

Was more like a fucking shopping centre than an airport, if I'm giving it my honest assessment. Somehow though, I managed to find my check in desk. There was only about half a dozen travellers standing waiting in front of me which was a bit of a blessing and a curse as it gave me a wee bit of time to get my game face on before attempting to put the wheels in motion to me travelling on fraudulent documents, but also giving me adequate time to start to overthink everything.

The woman at the desk will recognise you from the mention in the Sebastian Montoya episode in the narcos documentary that was on the Discovery Channel.

*The name Frank van der Hoorn - being fake - will not be registered on some national database, linked to the passport system, and as soon as you hand it over for her to check you in she's going to know so if she delays getting that flight ticket handed over to you, you get the fuck **out** of there.*

What's your face looking like right now as you're thinking about all of that? There's probably cunts sitting in a room looking at your coupon and body language on CCTV, and sussing out that you're up to something shady.

Keep the interaction simple and don't talk too much, say the absolute minimum.

My mind was flooded with all kinds of paranoid thoughts mixed with some self help tips to try and get me through the next hour or so and onto that plane.

The beads of sweat began when I was only one person away from being up. I took the chance to wipe it quickly before I was called while hoping that by the time the next beads appeared I'd have done the business and would not be wiping it while being chased around an airport terminal by the police.

'Hello, sir'

The blonde haired KLM agent greeted me with a friendly face which can't be fucking easy when all you do throughout a day is greet people with a friendly face and do the exact same time and time again. She was pretty tidy too but that's kind of par for the course for airports and airplanes. Seems like you don't get a look in for a job there if you don't look like one of those women who work in the cosmetics section in Boots.

'Hi, do you need this?'

I said to her while holding up the flight details that I'd printed off the day before at the gym. Just in case, I kept my passport hidden and focussed on the flight tickets.

'Ah, yes, thank you'

She said as she looked at the reference number, typing it into her computer.

'And now we just require your passport for one moment and you will be all set, sir'

Aye well, I thought, least you tried, eh?

I handed the passport over the counter to her and hoped for the best. I knew that the next minute was going to be the most important of my whole life. And I treated it as such. Normally I'd have just let her crack on with it. Looked at my phone or around the airport. Anything other than looking *right* at her. I needed to, though. She was only human so there would be a tell on her face, if she saw something on her screen that wasn't right, even if it only showed on her coupon for a split second. If I was looking somewhere else then I wasn't going to see any of this.

Felt a wee bit creepy what I was doing, though. Of course, I couldn't tell her though that she shouldn't be worried - or feel uneasy in any way - and that I wasn't some creepy pervert leering at her but instead a quite harmless escaped prisoner known internationally by police for extreme violence and drug dealing.

'Ok then Mr van der Hoorn. That is you ready for take off as we say'

With her Dutch accent she pronounced my name streets ahead of any possible way that I could have managed. That way of pronunciation with the letter *h* that whenever I attempted it there would be the real danger of it coming out wrong and me spitting right in someone's face.

'Is it business or pleasure you're flying?'

She asked, as she handed over my passport and ticket. A grateful, not to mention a seriously relieved, me taking it from her as gracefully as I could manage while trying not to go the other way by snatching right out of her immaculately manicured right hand. Taking a moment to think about her question, and picturing what I'd envisaged the trip involving, I answered her back with the first smile I'd managed to raise since I'd joined her at the desk, since I'd left for the airport, in fact.

'Ehhhh, wee bit of both I suppose. You've got to love what you do, eh?'

She couldn't have known what I was referring to, and if she had - and the sick and brutal injuries I'd just been imagining in that moment - then she definitely wouldn't have given me one final smile before I moved on and she was calling for the next passengers after me.

Fucking hell, either she's the best poker player that I've come across in my puff, or I've just managed to bluff my way onto an international flight, I tried to decide while I walked away from the check in desks in a kind of disbelief that I wasn't in handcuffs and, instead, free to stroll around Amsterdam Schipol with a fully legit flight ticket in my back pocket with a much less on the level passport in the other one.

There was only around forty five minutes until the flight boarded so I headed straight for security. Weirdly, despite security at an airport being a lot more interested in scrutinising you than the airline rep at the check in desk, I was more chilled about going through, having passed the first test. If my passport had worked with her then there wasn't any reason for it not to work up the stairs at security, my assumption.

Of course, I hadn't really bargained on just how fucking space age the security area was going to be, all those years after I'd last passed through them. All the new tech that they had. Hand held metal and drug detectors. The machine that spins around you while you stand with your hand in the air that they say shows your knob to the security cunts on the other side of the screen. Wasn't prepared for all of that. Neither was I ready for setting the alarm off when I was inside the spinning booth, leaving one of their security boys wanting to take me to the side for further inspection.

Knew I didn't have anything dodgy on me or fuck all but when you're attempting to take your first flight in over twenty years - and in such circumstances - you really just want to waltz through without anyone barely even noticing you. Fucking daft cunt, I cursed myself as he swiped his detector over me, and the high pitched beeping starting to go mental right about at my belt.

'Schoolboy error, eh'

I said to him trying to laugh it off but in reality the boy probably spent half his day at work doing the same thing because cunts were too stupid - or lazy - to perform a simple task, like taking their belt off for a few moments. He wasn't done, though. Clearly it had been the belt that had set the alarm off, and now it was removed. That really was just the start of his search, though. Cunt ended up putting his hand held detector down on a table so he could get both his hands on me, wrapping them around my legs and moving all the way up from top to bottom, same with my arms. Fair enough, if there was anything there to find, he was going to find it. Other than my hidden identity, eh?

Ran me close with that for a moment, mind. During this lengthy time being detained to the side - while it felt like half of the fucking airport were breezing past me and into the departure lounge - he asked to see my passport. Handing it over. He opened it straight to the page with my name and photo. Taking a look at the photo and then back at me, then back to the photo. To be fair, I had grown the beard since the photo had been taken years before. Same with the difference in hair, or lack of as I was now going. I could see why he'd want to look twice. That was kind of my point, though. To look as different as humanly possible to what I did to back then.

'van der Hoorn, huh? With a Scottish accent?'

He said with a bit of suspicion behind it, or was that just para fucking jock here? If he *was* trying to question my name - and how unlikely it was for someone with my accent to have a second name like that - then I was incredibly fucked, if my very first response back wasn't convincing enough. Those bastards get fucking trained on how to read cunts when they're lying to them, I was screaming at myself inside while hoping my eyes weren't grassing me up.

'Aye, ma mum and da split up when ah wis wee so I grew up in Scoatland, eh. Still goat ma da's name, mind. Stay oer here now though, ken. Jist headin back hame to visit ma mum and the rest o the famuly, like'

I elected to take the bullshit baffles brains approach. If the point of this was that I sounded Scottish then, I thought, I should make myself as Scottish as possible. An extension of English that had no place in Amsterdam - if I'd ever wanted to be understood by anyone - but, in that moment, I'd slipped effortlessly into.

He looked at me for a second, following this, seemingly digesting what I'd just said and weighing up how to play it next. Bit of a curious face to him, like. All until he couldn't resist being wide with me.

'Now I know *that* was some kind of English, even if I only understood around two words of it. I swear, some of you Scots make *Jamaicans* seem easy to understand'

'Ah, dinnae ken, lad. Nivir met a Jim Aitken before, eh?'

I replied while inside was bricking it and questioning if he was just doing that whole toying with me stuff before eventually taking me away. If it had been better circumstances I'd have told him my "which Scottish international captain's dad was Jamaican" joke but knew it wasn't the time nor the place for any fucking about.

'Yes, I made out Jamaican that time. Who know's, maybe if I spent a day trying to master the accent I'd be able to understand a whole sentence by the end of it, huh?'

He started laughing at this. Absolute terrible patter, like, but without any shame, I sycophantically joined in, hoping that it would help things.

'Ok, Mr van der Hoorn,' he said bringing a serious setting back onto his face, while closing my passport.

'You enjoy your trip back to Scotland and I hope for your mother's sake that she can understand you better than I can'

Handing me my passport back.

'Aye, nae sweat, gadge. Cheers ma man, eh' I replied, reaching out to take it from him. Probably the least relevant thing that I could've chosen to say to him because there had been fucking *loads* of sweat during the whole exchange between the two of us. Thankfully it had stayed internally and away from his suspicious eyes, that it was practically his job to look through.

And that was it, as easy as that, aye? Escaping from a prison - along with a well known South American cartel operative - and being on fuck know's how many watch lists, counting for absolutely *ride all*, because some cunt wasn't able to understand what you'd said, and couldn't be arsed asking you to repeat yourself?

Hey, I was through security and that was all that really mattered, whatever and however it was achieved.

I'd pulled it off. Checking the TV screen for details on my flight I clocked that it was on time and boarding in about twenty five minutes. Seizing the wee window of opportunity to grab a couple of quick doubles to calm the pre flight nerves of someone who barely even knew what he was nervous about, so long since he'd been up in the air.

It was more a 'nervous excitement' kind of nervous, though. Now that I'd got the more obvious nervy part over and done with, I could now - realistically - visualise going to Scotland. When I was sinking my second Jackie D and coke I got that Dougie Maclean song - Caledonia - in my head. Almost left me with wet eyes, the combination of the lyrics to the song, alongside the prospect of me returning back to the country of my birth. This, absolute pish, of course. The lyrics not exactly being akin to me, a Scotsman abroad.

That I think about you all the time.

Aye, maybe thought about the place now and again while trying to exist *away* from it. Nothing obsessive though, like.

Caledonia you're calling me. And now I'm going home.

Caledonia never called me at all and if it had then it would've done so a lot earlier than ten years. Truth be told, if that keyboard warrior had lived in say North Dakota or Addis Ababa, I'd have been getting on a completely different plane that day.

But regardless of that. *Hame* or not to me anymore. I was going to be there in around an hour and a half.

Chapter 9

Liam

I'd only popped my head into The Nether for a quick pint, before heading for the bus home. Honestly wished I'd just swerved the whole fucking thing and went straight home and walked Bannon.

I'd taken a wee trip down to the town to get one or two pieces from Manifesto. You could always tell when I'd not long done a wee trip through to Edinburgh for work because shortly after that I'd be walking through the door of Manifesto, saying 'Audi' to all the lads in there before setting about helping fill up their til with used bank notes.

Not that I pished *all* the money that I earned down the drain, either. Was actually quite smart with that and the majority I'd started to store away, in a safe place. Still, though. Can't be doing that working thing without being able to treat yourself now and again. No point getting out your bed if that was the case.

Not that I went too mad inside Tayside's finest clothes emporium, like. Got change back off five hundred pounds - after copping a sweatshirt, tee and pair of trainers - and it's not always the case that I'd have been able to say that when walking back out the place.

I was walking down Commercial Street when Watto had sent me a text asking what I was up to. Him out for a couple of lunch time drinks down in the city centre with wee Rico McNeil. Not exactly a million miles from where they were sat scooping, I dingeyd replying back to him and, instead, walked the short distance over to The Nether Inn to join them.

Rico - who we all joked had to get his jeans from Mothercare, so wee that he was - was in the middle of, struggling, to position himself adequately on the pool table to get his shot away when I'd walked in.

'You wanting me to lift you up, wee man, aye?'

I shouted over to the table, this, enough to have the pair of them looking over my way. Didn't even get a chance to offer any of them a drink before Watto had replied

'While you're over there, lad. Pint of Tennents'

'Aye no worries, Watto. Just a short for you, Rico, aye?'

I couldn't resist it.

'Get yourself to fuck, wide prick' Rico shouted back, not exactly entering into the spirit of things but I suppose when you have to endure the ripping that he got from everyone, it *must've* got old pretty fucking quick.

'You're only about five nine yourself, by the way, ya cunt' He went right on the defensive.

'Aye, which, compared to you, Rico, makes me Kevin fucking James'

A few strangers, getting the reference, joined in laughing along with me as they sat at the bar drinking.

Grabbing the three pints from off the bar I'd ordered for myself and the rest of the boys, I carefully walked across to them.

Having a wee scan around the room to see if there was any other faces I recognised in there for the afternoon but, on the whole, the place was as quiet as you'd have expected on a Tuesday afternoon. Apart from the mannies that were sat at the bar there was a couple of lone wolfs sat at their own tables, minding their own business. And other than that, Watto and wee Rico.

'Pint there for you, as well' I said to Rico as he sunk another of the stripes that was on the table. Not because I'd been slagging him about his height, remember? Nah, just the rules of the pub. Don't take a pint over to your mate while having an empty hand for your other one. Just good manners, like.

'Cheers, L. I'll get it in a minute. Right after I clean this table'

Another stripe rattled into a pocket and down on into the insides of the antiquated looking pool table. I sat down beside Watto, telling him that he may as well sit and talk to me because it didn't look like Rico was going to be letting him up off his arse to take a shot any time soon.

'Hope you're not playing for coin today, lad. That cunt looks like he's … well, technically I don't know the name of any famous pool player so that's my analogy fucked before it's started. You know what I'm meaning though, eh?'

'Maybe we *are* playing for money and this is all part of the plan, eh?'

Watto replied back in what was nothing other than a poor attempt to cover up the fact that he was getting rinsed by someone who could barely even look over the table.

'Aye, ok then, Paul Newman,' I just said back to him, insulted that he had even bothered to say it.

We sat there talking about the previous weekend, filling in some of the blanks that we'd both had left over from our trip to Perth to The Ice Factory, and that poorly planned afters in fucking Invergowrie which had been the predictable pain in the arse getting home from that any cunt with a brain would've been able to predict, had they not been full of MDMA. I showed him what I'd got at Manifesto. He told me the horse that he had on that was running in half an hour. Basically anything that didn't involve Watto having to get up and take a single shot for the rest of the game.

'Check you out, eh? Fucking green baize demon, there' I stopped to give Rico a standing ovation.

'I'd have been as well playing R.A.F Stan, the amount of competition that I just got there, from that cunt sat beside you'

Rico replied, lapping up the applause with some applied arrogance. Referencing one of the old boys that drank in The Nether who only had one arm. Lost it in the war, or so he told everyone.

Watto wasn't happy, like.

'Mon then, ya wee fanny. Rack them up'

'You sure you can take another portion of embarrassment in public, aye?' Rico kept it going while reaching down to the coin slot to sort out the rest of the balls that were sitting inside the machine.

'Sure enough to make it interesting, if you're game?'

Maybe this *had* been Watto's plan all along, I was made to think twice before, knowing Watto as long as I'd had, seeing that all he was doing here was reacting to wee Rico.

'What you thinking, like?' Rico asked, not exactly against this suggestion.

'Loser has to pay the other's drinks for the rest of the night'

Rico thought about this for a wee moment. Like the wee man was trying to work out the percentage of probability against the cost of footing Watto's drinks for the rest of the night would be, if his percentages were off.

'Fuck it, you're on'

Rico agreed, followed by the sound of the remaining balls all rolling out into the tray of the table. While I didn't have any skin in the game, I was intrigued to see how it was going to turn out. You had to say that, logically, out of the two, the biggest loser would've been Rico. Because Rico could barely drink worth a fuck. So whichever way you wanted to look at it, the prize wasn't *equal* to them. If Rico won then he wasn't really going to make the most out of what would have been handed to him. Watto? Well *that* was a totally different teapot full of cod. The boy could fucking drink. An absolute bomb scare when it came to Class A's but aye, alcohol was his drug of choice. And if somehow he *was* hustling wee Rico, then I hope the boy had enough money in his bank account left over from the weekend, because he was going to fucking need it.

Seen as some kind of independent adjudicator, Watto asked me to flip the coin to see who got to break. This leading to Watto - who won - standing up for the first time since I'd arrived, despite the fact he'd - technically - been playing pool for the whole of it. Rico - who had already racked up the balls with the table set for battle, left his place at the foot of the table and came over to stand beside me, while saying that it was only going to be a flying visit as he'd be back at the table soon enough.

Watto - with his first shot - crashing the white into the balls with as much power possible. The fucking noise as the ball connected, sending every single one flying in all directions. *Two solids managing to drop into separate pockets*, in amongst all of the madness that was going on all over the table.

Watts, looking over at the pair of us and raising an eyebrow like he was that old James Bond that you'd sometimes see on the telly at Christmas. Same guy that always had the big goon with the teeth chasing after him. Certainly had Rico thinking twice, though, that one shot.

Watto was just in the middle of eying up which ball he was going to sink next when all of a sudden.

'Woah, woah woah, what the fuck is this, eh?'

The shout from behind him, breaking his concentration.

It was one of the randoms who had been sitting there having a drink on their own. I'd noticed him when I'd walked in. Just sitting there with a pint, not checking his phone or talking to anyone else inside the place. Just sat staring into space with his pint. Being the friendly type, I'd looked his way when I was passing as was going to give him a wee 'alright?' But if he'd known I was there then he clearly wasn't interested in any small talk, even if it was only going to be the smallest example you could ever provide of small talk.

Now he was interested in talking, though. Just not to me.

'This here is what's called a pool table, some call it American Pool, mainly Americans I imagine. Any other questions, pal?'

An irritated Watto replied - with some strong sarcasm - to the guy, clearly annoyed that with such high stakes at play, he was being distracted from the prize ahead.

'The fuck you think it is?' He followed up with, muttering under his breath.

'Aye, I'm perfectly aware that it's a pool table, cunto. That's why there's a fucking twenty pence piece of mines sitting there *on* it. Goes for a pish, only away for a minute and you sneaky bastards go and just rack up the balls to play another game, like you own the table and fuck the pub etiquette, eh?'

'How were we to know that you were playing? You could've left the pub for all we knew'

Rico - ever someone to pounce upon a chance to display some of that wee man syndrome that he had flowing inside of him - protested, while walking over towards Watto and the guy. This agitator who - now that he was over by Watts - looked a wee bit tasty. I couldn't tell if he was naturally taller than Watto or if it was a false impression due to the way he was wearing his North Face tammy. Full tracky on as well - the guy - which I remember thinking at the time that you don't see that too often. Big beard on him as well, the kind that's you'd often link to those American Hell's Angels bikers who ride around on Harley Davidsons cooking shite drugs and getting into gang wars and that.

'No cunt fucking asked you, Frodo Baggins. Away and sit yourself down and drink your Fruit Shoots before you end up making a mischief of yourself'

'Cunto?'

'Who the fuck do you think you're talking to ya weird beard wanker'

Both Watto and Rico shouted at him, pretty much at the same time. This only inflaming a situation that could and should have been sorted with an apology from Watto, possibly saying something about how he thought the guy had possibly left The Nether, due to no longer being at his table, when they'd racked up the balls for another game.

It was much too late for that now. To begin with, this guy was well over the top when it came to starting it all. It was only a game of pool, for fuck's sake. So if he was like that *before* Watts and Rico had even opened their mouths then it was highly unlikely that his mood was going to improve once they *did*.

'Can't say you weren't fucking warned'

The guy kind of wearily sighed while he reached out and grabbed hold of Rico - someone who weighed nine stone if he was lucky - and lifted him up off the ground and shoved him onto the table. Rico's head crashing into one of the balls - weirdly deflecting it to within a bawhair of going right into the centre pocket but, instead, unluckily for Rico it headed back towards his head, mashing into it - as it was smashed down onto the baize. Pinning him by the throat, he reached for one of the other balls and began trying to force it into the wee man's mouth.

Watts instantly jumped in. While trying to pull the boy off Rico he took an elbow to the jaw, proper dull one. Fair play to Watts, though. Went right back for more, just as I started getting involved. Watto's couple of spears that he gave the man with his pool cue to the ribs, enough to have him taking his hand away from Rico's throat, so he could turn all attention to Watto.

Wee Rico was still lying back on the table wheezing and desperately trying to catch some kind of normality to his breath. While Watto's on the ground with this guy in the tracksuit laying the boot - well, black Stan Smith, - into him.

It was the speed that the man had operated at. It all sounds like I'd done fuck all, other than stand back and watch my mate's taking a doing, but it wasn't like that. Rico was lying half dead and Watto curled up into a ball like a hedgehog, all within seconds.

On instinct, I grabbed hold of one of the spare cues that was lying around and ran over and swung it at him. Hitting the scary cunt on the side of his head, just over the eyebrow. Him, with the most unfortunate of timing, managing to look up and to the side, *right* as I was in mid swing, making it a much better connection than I had originally planned, when aimlessly slicing the air with it. It had been just enough of a distraction to stop the kicks from flying in on Watts.

'You fucking wanting it as well, aye?'

He said, touching the side of his head and finding out that I'd drawn blood, leaving a cut to the side of his head.

'The only thing I want, mate is to go home and walk my fucking dug'

I knew that the only thing keeping the two of us from each other was the pool cue that I was continually swinging. He didn't exactly look like he was too worried about the situation, but also - wisely - knew not to stick his head in front of the end of the cue, when it was flying back and forward in front of him.

'What's your walk like? The terrain? Wheelchair friendly, aye?' He said menacingly, with a smile that didn't quite suit the moment. Rico and Watts were quite evidently out of the game by now. It really was just me and him and - considering I'd only jumped in to help my mates who were coming off second best - seeing how effortlessly he'd taken care of the pair of them, I didn't fancy my chances.

'The fucking second the chance arrives I'm going to take that cue off you and shove it right up that fucking wee flapping arse of yours'

He said with creepy confidence, edging himself a wee bit further towards me, looking for his moment to lunge and do away with my advantage of the pool cue.

Thank fuck Craig - behind the bar - shouted out that he'd called the coppers - and that they were on their way - when he did, like. It had been like a dug whistle to this guy. The look that he had in his eyes while surveying me, sizing me up. It was maybe just my imagination like but I'd felt that the way he'd looked at me, I could see the dark thoughts taking place in his mind over what way he was going to hurt me. You could see his eyes and whole facial expression change, over those few seconds following me hitting him on the head with the cue.

The second he heard that the police were on their way, though? Was like some kind of switch had been flicked.

'I guess maybe some other time then, kiddo' He said, giving me a wee wink - while to the side of the same eye he had blood trickling down the side of his face - before turning around and taking the opportunity to give Watto one more kick. One to the face of the poor cunt who was just in the process of trying to get himself up to his feet for the first time, only to be sent flying back to the ground with what was the hardest and most brutal boot that he'd taken out of them all.

'Maybe fucking next time let cunts have their turn on the table, eh?' He crouched down to say to a Watto who was no longer in the mood for any disagreements.

The guy in the tracksuit then, casually walking over to his table - by the main entrance - picking up his pint and sinking what was left of it before slamming the glass down on the table, picking up the black sports bag that was sitting beside it on the floor and disappearing out the front door.

'That's probably not a bad idea actually, like' I said, nodding towards the door. Not remotely interested in the prospect of having to sit and talk to bizzies over a fight I'd just been in. Copying the man who had come so close to making me his hat trick, there inside the pub, I sank what had still been my first pint and one I'd only managed half of up until then.

Grabbing my shopping bags and leaving Watts and Rico to it. I done a disappearing act that Harry Houdini would've been proud of, hoping that I'd be sat on the number thirty two, by the time the bizzies were walking through the door of The Nether.

Chapter 10

Nora

'Surprise'

I shouted out to her when the door crept open to me, shoving the flowers that I'd bought from the Shell when on route. Fucking "surprised" her, right enough. Near on had her on the way to Ninewells with the fright that I'd given her. Can't really blame her, mind. The son that you've never seen in over a decade, and the same one who was famous across the United Kingdom through escaping from a prison, leading to his handsome bastard features being plastered all over the TV and papers, at your door? Probably the fucking *last* cunt that she'd have been expecting standing at her back door that late afternoon on the Tuesday that I'd arrived.

Back door, like, because I wasn't as fucking stupid as to sashay my way up to the front door, like I didn't have a care in the world, was I? Aye, the bizzies would've lost interest in staking out mum and dad's house years before so I wasn't so much worried about any of them sitting waiting on me walking down the road. It's the neighbours that you have to worry about. Some right curtain twitching grassing bastards that you find yourself living next to, mind? Knew it had been a while but you wouldn't have been surprised if some nosey cunt was to spy you at your parent's front door and they couldn't get on the blower to the Crimestoppers fast enough. Probably on the recon to see if there was any reward money kicking about.

I'd never really seen it as some great homecoming in any case but it wasn't until I was on the train from Inverkeithing to

Dundee when I started to think about how lightly I should've been treading, when back on home turf. Edinburgh - where I was planning on spending on most of my time in - wasn't so much a worry for me but Dundee's an awful small city at times, so I already knew that the sensible thing for me would've been to keep my head down when there. Because it went without saying, I couldn't come back to Scotland and *not* take the chance to go and see my mum and dad, even if it increased the chances of me getting myself huckled, ten fold.

Wouldn't have been able to live with myself if I didn't go and see them, especially at their age. When you reach that point in life you start to recognise how little time you've got left with your parentals.

Imagine how you're going to feel if one of them croaks - after you've been to Scotland and then went back to Holland again - and you never took the chance to see them, when you had it, and were only about an hour away in the train, I asked myself.

And there really only was one answer to the question.

I'd just need to be smart when going about it. As much as I'd have liked to have walked around and caught up with all my old mates. Have a few scoops, go to see United while I was back. It wasn't going to be possible. Like I said, Dundee's a small city, and it's not like I could say that I got on with everyone inside of it. You can't make an omelette without breaking a few eggs and - as far as I was concerned - you don't make yourself a reputation, without breaking a few heads.

If word was to get out around Fintry that I was in town then *every* cunt would ken before I'd even managed to have myself a post flight bath at my mum and dad's.

That's why I'd drank in a strange city centre pub - on arrival to Dundee - and also why I'd chosen to take a bus up to Fintry Drive, as opposed to jumping into a taxi. If there's more grassing cunts on this earth than taxi drivers then I've never come across them. Even if I didn't know the driver, you could guarantee that they'd have known *me*.

Next thing you know, whoever jumps into his car next it's a case of

'Here, you'll never guess who I just had in my car ten minutes ago'

And that's all it would take. Word of my presence in the City of Discovery would spread through the town like some bad virus.

Nah, it was going to be incog-fucking-nito. Proper Milk Tray man, stuff. No cunt knows he's been there, until it's too late and he's gone. Need to know basis, ken? Couldn't even be telling my old mates from back in the day, as much as I'd like to have done as had felt that they'd have come in handy for some of my planned activities in Leith but nah, had to be a solo job, this. Really just wanted to slip into the city, see mum and dad and spend a few hours with them, track down Abigail and address the elephant in the room and within forty eight hours I'd have been out of the city again with no plans on returning before heading back to Amsterdam on the Saturday night.

It had been the stuff of Special Air Services, getting to the back door of their house. Instead of getting off the bus at the stop nearest, I deliberately stayed on it so I could drive past, getting a wee look out at the surroundings, while trying to establish a way in and out. Got off about five minutes down the road and made my way back in the direction the bus had just come. Once I got around six houses away I quickly transferred myself from main road to the more discreet back garden route. This in itself a strategy that had its own pitfalls because it would've just taken one person to notice someone flying past their back window while vaulting their fence to blow the whole gig for you.

Absolutely fucking shat myself when - three houses away from mum and dad's - I went to climb a garden fence and it completely collapsed beneath me, falling into the next garden. While picking myself up off the ground, I was anticipating the inevitable, some cunt coming flying out their house wondering what had just happened outside their house. Obviously I didn't know which house the fence belonged to but one of them were going to find one fucked fence when they *did* look outside their back.

Nothing came, though. You could hear the dog barking inside the house, going absolutely fucking radge, you could see the shape of it through the frosted glass of the back door. The house was in darkness though, which told me that no cunt was going to be following the frenzied barks of the dog. Managing the next couple of fences with a lot more smoothness than the previous one, I eventually reached the back door.

I don't think she'd actually recognised me when she opened the door. She was probably a wee bit freaked out anyway because you know what old folk are like when it comes to some cunt knocking on their door in the first place? Conditioned into them that most of the cunts knocking on their door are after their money in some way or other, so multiply that by someone knocking on their *back* door. Before I'd even got a chance to hand her the flowers I could hear my dad shouting through from the living room

'Who is it, Pauline?'

That lazy bastard hasn't changed by the looks of things, I thought to myself. Keenly interested to know who's at the door but not interested enough to get up himself up to find out. What's the point in getting up? You'll only have to sit yourself down again, his standard justification that was generally used for everything, minus going to the toilet or bed.

It was maybe the beard but she didn't show it on her face that she immediately knew who I was. You never forget a voice though.

'NORMAN! Oh my goodness'

She stood there holding onto the edge of the door with one hand while covering her mouth with her other one.

'These are for you' I offered the six ninety nine bouquet of flowers that was a mix of three different flowers. They looked like what I thought my mum would think were pretty. I didn't get bogged down by the details of them. There was tulips in there, only ones I recognised, like.

'Oh, flowers? For me. Oh that is so nice of you, son. I can't even remember the last time someone got me flowers'

She looked all a bit overwhelmed. Fuck knows what was going through her head but she looked super happy, and didn't really know how to respond to it all. Picking up on this I thought I should drive.

'So, is it alright to come in, aye?'

I asked. A question that should've felt daft even asking, considering it was the house that I grew up in and had lived at right up until the evening I was arrested in that Glaswegian housing scheme and stuck right on remand. In that moment, though. It felt a pretty appropriate question to ask. It had been a long time since I'd last seen the place and it had felt like a lot had taken place, and that life had moved on from the days that I'd last lived there.

The question - in itself - enough to bring my mum to her senses because *of course* it was ok for me to come inside.

'Oh god, what is your old mum like? Standing talking to you at the door like you're a Jehovah's Witness. Mon in son, of course you can come in. You staying? You've still got your bedroom, mind. Oh, your head? What did you do to it? It's split open, Norman, you're going to have to go to hospital to get stitches'

'Ach, it's just a wee scratch mum. I knocked my head when I was standing up on the bus on the way up from the city centre. It'll heal up in a few days. I've not got time for any of that Ninewells pish. You know what it's like with A and E, eh? Like the Bermuda Triangle, there. You go in there and fuck knows if and when you're ever coming back out. Only here for a few days and, if possible, it would be sound to spend some of it outside a hospital'

All over the place, she ushered me in, attempted to touch the side of my head before thinking better of it, already taking my bag off me and then moving onto combining looking for her wee box of first aid products, while asking if I'd like a cup of tea.

I told her that we'd sit down and have a cuppa and get a catch up on everything, or as much as you really could do to cover a decade in one short sitting. While waiting on the kettle boiling - and having sorted out a large plaster to stick over the open wound on the side of my head - she said I should pop my head through and say hiya to my dad - which I was going to do anyway - but preferred to stand talking in the kitchen with her, until she was ready to go back through to the living room.

When you're in jail for around ten year and out of all of that time only one of your parents ever comes to visit you, you tend to remember that shite when you're back on the outside. Make no mistake, I was here to see my mum, dad just came with the package.

'Oh aye, here he is, Doctor Richard Kimble, that you doing house calls now, eh?'

My dad said in what was his way of greeting a son he'd not seen in such a long time.

'Alright, dad. How you doing?' I felt no need to reply to his attempt at sarcasm and, in fact, had actually felt a wee bit emotional over seeing him for the first time since nineteen ninety, and how old he'd become.

'Oh, you know son. I could complain but who'd listen, eh?'

Making sure he stayed sat in his seat I gave him a wee hug. Probably held onto him for a wee bit longer than socially acceptable but well, it had been a long time, and when I wrapped my arms around him, I felt it.

'So, sit yourself down, son and tell us your news'

Mum said, sitting down with her cup of tea, anxiously waiting on finding out why I'd suddenly appeared out of the blue at her door.

Clearly I wasn't going to be telling her the *real* reason why I was back in Scotland but, instead, providing her and dad with something quite different that would be enough to have the topic seem plausible and not worth further examination by any of them. Completely on the spot I'd said that there was a gym closing down in Edinburgh and - as part of the fire sale to go with - the equipment was said to be going for an absolute song, so I'd popped back to Scotland on a flying visit to try and secure it, and have it flown back to Holland.

Considering so many years had passed - without me ever coming home - even telling them this lie didn't exactly leave me looking good out of things. Because if the lie *was* to be believed then I was someone who wouldn't bother coming back to Scotland to visit his parents in ten years but *would* fly there at the drop of a hat to get a cheap treadmill or rowing machine? While talking about that I'd felt the need to justify over my visit, or lack of previously.

Explaining to mum and dad that in the early days of my escape it would've been nothing other than bait for me to be around them. Then, adding that it took a while to secure some fake documents to allow me any kind of movement from country to country. Throw in a bit of 'oh where does the time go' and that pretty much explained away the previous ten years.

Dad had told me that in the weeks and months following my escape there had been an undercover car parked near the house, regular visits from the C.I.D to ask if I'd been in touch. Then the cars parked outside were only there every other day, until they stopped coming around at all.

'Boys in blue haven't been around here looking for you in, what would you say, Pauline? Six, seven years now?'

Dad said while looking at mum for some kind of agreement.

'Maybe even more than that, Frank. Long time, though. I think, in the end, they realised that if you weren't in Scotland then that was

probably better for them, so just stopped worrying about finding you as it meant you'd be someone else's problem'

It was music to my ears and - in my more confident moments - had been what I'd thought would be the case. The amount of things that must've happened in the years since I checked out of the Big Hoose, that the police must've had to deal with. Once you drop off their radar then it's normally all down to what you're going to do yourself to *stay* off it. While they were no longer interested in looking for me. All it would take would've been a phone call into them with a wee tip and that would soon change. You know what those bastards are like at the best of times, eh?

Told the pair of them that they weren't to tell anyone - and by that not a single fucking soul - that I was here. Showed them my passport which gave them a laugh at the name that I was travelling under, but had shown them to illustrate how serious it all was, and why no one could know that I was in Dundee.

'Fucking beard like that, I wouldn't have any concerns about being recognised. Look like you've got lost on your way to the bloody soup kitchen'

My dad tried to offer me some words of reassurance.

'Too many enemies, dad. All it takes is that one phone call to the bizzies, and mind now. Two of you are now accessories because I'm in your house so for your sake as well as mine we don't want anyone knowing about my appearance'

I mean, it wasn't not true to say that to him but that wasn't really my reason for saying it. I just wanted the pair of them to take on board the gravity of things.

Those few hours with them meant more to me than I could ever have imagined spending time with my mum and dad could've ever been. You don't know what you've got until it's gone - as they say - and I'd went twenty years without the simple daily occurrence of sitting talking to the people that gave life to me, and it was only through sitting down with them that I fully realised how much I'd missed the two of them. I'd missed out on twenty years of their life and - not even taking into account what they felt *I* looked like, and how I'd aged - seeing them after so long, you could literally see how much of a gap there'd been since we'd all last been together.

You shouldn't live your life looking back and holding onto regrets, but it was hard not to regret getting caught in that house with the gear, probably wasn't wise to hold one of the coppers hostage at knife point either, mind. That one evening had shaped the rest of my life, and taken it in a direction that I'd much rather it hadn't. I didn't want it all and in fact was happy enough making a wee bit of money - enough to be comfortable - from punting the narcotics. Add that to getting away on a Saturday to see my team, while gleefully snatching the opportunity to smash fuck out of a few people across the day. I didn't want the moon and the stars, eh?

It was all fucked though, once my postcode was changed to one in Glasgow at Barlinnie. And after that - however my original life had been meant to work out - there was a whole new butterfly effect to contend with, which, via prison escapes and planned double crosses that were meant to end me, eventually took me to Amsterdam.

I had the nagging feeling that - for all I knew - this reunification of mother, father and son could well have been the first in decades, and the last at the same time. I think that was what made it so emotional. The feeling of loss - of all the years - pressed up against the real facts that they both looked so old now. Mix that with me and my circumstances, someone who was hardly in a position to run mum to Asda ever week to get her shopping, and it all brought a heavy sense of uncertainty about things.

Just enjoy the time you've got right now, my rarely shown sensible side tried to impress on me, while attempting to get shot of the more depressing thoughts.

After sitting for a while and exchanging all of our recent, and in some cases not so recent news, I took myself for a shower and get changed before going out - to see Abigail - for a while. When mum had said that she'd kept my room exactly how it had been before, she wasn't fucking joking. When walking through that door it had looked like I'd been in it the day before.

My fucking United season ticket for ninety ninety one season was still sitting there on my bedside table, for fuck's sake. Pure Marie Celeste activity, like. Thing is, the place was clean so you could tell that she'd gave it a bit of Mr Sheen now and again, but had left everything as was. It was comforting but also pretty fucking weird at the same time.

Running the shower for me, she left me to it and went back to sit down with dad.

My fucking clothes! I suddenly thought to myself. Now realising that I hadn't been in this room in so long and where I'd been in that time I hadn't exactly required the usage of any of them. Some expensive gear inside that wardrobe, though. I thought to myself safe in the knowledge that a lot of it would've kept its value over the years as well, maybe even worth *more,* due to the whole vintage factor.

If you were to have put me on the spot and actually *asked* me what was inside the wardrobe - before I'd opened it up - I'd have probably struggled to have even be able to name you three pieces. Out of sight, out of mind, eh? Moment I flung the doors open though it all came back to me. Stone Island jackets, Burberry shirts, Best Company sweatshirts. A veritable treasure trove of eighties casual clobber.

And *all* destroyed by some little cunt of a moth - or alternative flying insect - with fuck all better to do than munch away on some poor cunts' Italian designer clothes.

The first t shirt I pulled out I thought it was a cigarette burn on it which was a bit of a blow as it had been a nice tee back in the day. A crisp white CP Company with the nice wee understated logo on the chest. Further inspection, however found that it *wasn't* cigarette related, because there was another four similar sized holes elsewhere on the front.

Stone Island hoody that followed the t shirt didn't fare any better. Fucking *six* holes gnawed away on that. After the third item - an early eighties Boca Juniors top - and having the false dawn of finding no holes on the front only to discover three waiting on the back, I didn't bother checking any more. I guess the moral of the story is don't go leaving your clothes lying around for twenty years, without looking at them, eh? Still shite though, mind?

Telling myself that whilst there was probably no point, I'd check the rest of what was hanging up in there later in the hope that there was at least one or two pieces that were salvageable. For now, though. I had business to be taking care of, and something that had been a *very* long time in the coming.

Not that I'd have ever admitted it to any cunt, like, but getting myself changed into some fresh gear for going out again, I could begin to feel the nerves starting to kick in.

Absolutely no fucking idea what *I* had to be nervy about, mind? If anyone that should've been anxious about matters it would've been that vindictive boot of my ex.

Then again, though. She didn't know who was going to be soon chapping on her door so never really had the chance for any anxiety on her part.

Chapter 11

Liam

Heavy. As. Fuck

There wasn't any other way that it could've possibly have ever been described as. Fucking telling you, man. See those Nobel Peace Prize candidates? Them? You could've shoved them in a room with somebody up at the front of the room taking them all through a Powerpoint presentation detailing every single piece - in relation to my experience - of evidence and *that's* what their final findings would've clocked in at. That what I'd been hit with that tea time was, indeed, heavy, *as* fuck.

I'd just walked through the front door and was bending down to take Bannon's coat off - the fallen off the back of the lorry Burberry one that it appeared I was more happy about Bannon wearing, than Bannon was himself. That dramatic show that he'd make of the *freedom* he was being treated to, whenever I removed it from him again, rolling all over the floor and that - when I noticed that mum was talking to someone through in the living room.

'That should be him back now'

I could just about make out from the hall but had sounded like I was the topic of conversation.

With his lead and jacket free from him, the dog bolted through to the living room to see mum - like he'd always do the second he got the chance, post walk - while I got my coat off and hung it up before following a wee bit behind him.

'What's for tea tonight, mum? I'm absolutely sta ...'

I was already in the process of shouting before even entering the room, having effortlessly slipped into the comfort of having your mum cooking your meals for you, now that I was back home again. Once I'd set foot through the door though and into the warmth of the living room, I never quite made it to the end of my sentence. And there's not a living and breathing creature that could have blamed me for being put off my stroke.

Sitting there on the sofa having a cup of tea with mum - and now dealing with an over excitable dug who had jumped up from the floor onto them - was a man. Both him and mum looking towards the door in my direction. The two of them smiling at me although, looking from one of them to the other, I could see that while his *appeared* to be sincere, mum's looked more a case of her smile masking something else that was troubling her. You can smile at someone all you like but if the eyes don't back it up then you're just wasting yours and everyone else's time. Plus, you don't grow up with someone and go through thick and thin - like me and mum - and not know them like the back of your hand.

'Aww you're a handsome wee boy, aren't you, eh? No, now. No licking ma face, pal. I know where you put that tongue of yours, eh'

Why was this 'heavy as fuck' though?

Well the main part of it was probably the bit that involved this stranger sitting there on the sofa - sat there as casual and relaxed as you like - was the *same* fucking mad man that - only hours earlier - I'd taken a pool cue to his napper in The Nether. The plaster stuck to the side of his head not really required to give me any confirmation as to who it was, but was there all the same.

I don't think that I'd have forgotten *those* eyes for the rest of my life, if I was to never bump into him again. So to see them looking right at me, only a few hours after *last* seeing them?

Fessing right up to you, here. I was in plunged into the depths of Nam. Didn't know what to say or how to react. Did I speak, did I say fuck all? Did I need to be scanning the room for any potential weapon?

How did he find me?

Why was there a need to find me, it was only a wee scuffle in a pub. The kind of thing that happens every day in every town and city.

What did he want? A straightener? He must've known that it would've taken him ten seconds and it would've been over. Why go to all the hassle?

Why come to a parent's house about this instead of just going through the normal ways, in the pub?

Mum had looked frightened, had he said or done something to her, before me and Bannon had got back?

Like some fitba team that's one up with twenty five minutes to go, I didn't know whether to attack - probably not a good idea with this guy who had struck me, back in the pub, as kind of dangerous looking, something Rico and Watto would most likely agree on - or try and go on the defensive. My initial thought had been to ask why *he* was in our house, and in doing so confirming that me and him had already crossed paths. Didn't want mum to know that I'd been fighting in pubs though - even if this cunt had possibly already *told* her about it - so just about managed to resist the urge to start mouthing off about things.

The logical side though - even if none of this was coming close to making any sense, in any way - was that someone who, depending on your viewpoint I suppose, had instigated a fight in a pub over a game of pool - and assaulted two people in the process was hardly likely to then be taking any kind of moral high ground, going around to speak to parents and that. What was I? Fourteen? Not like I'd broken some cunt's window with my ball, eh? This was grown up stuff, involving mums didn't make sense.

Looking over at him, I done that 'alright?' thing that you do with someone you don't know but can't exactly avoid since you're only a few metres from each other, and in an enclosed space. Ironically, the very same kind of *alright* that I'd tried to give him back in the pub, before relations turned sour.

'Alright, Liam. Really good to meet you, pal'

He nodded in my direction.

Now *this* was interesting. I was positive that this hadn't been a slip of the tongue from him, and that he'd purposely said what he had to ensure that I picked up what he was dropping down, and that there was going to be no need for me on my side to be bringing up events from down in the city centre.

So just what was this cunt's game then?

I was completely fucking baffled, but didn't have long before getting hit with the biggest bomb to go off in my life in the twenty years that I'd been gifted. Almost as if the moment me and Bannon had left the house, some cunts had snuck in and strapped the living room - wall to wall - with C4, ready for me to trip it, when I walked into the living room.

The man - getting Bannon from up off his lap - started to get himself together to stand up.

'I'm ...'

'Aye, can you come and sit down for a wee minute, Liam? I need to talk to you about something'

Mum, cutting him off before he said anything else, motioned for me to take a seat in the second armchair, mum already sat in the other and leaving the whole sofa to this stranger.

Fuck all *ever* comes out of someone asking you to take a seat, or if they say they want a word with you. Normal every day stuff, people just come out and *say* it. When they tell you that they want to speak to you about something, it always tells you that they're trying to work out how they're going to say it to you, and also to give you a bit of advance warning that something unpleasant is in the pipeline for you.

I couldn't escape the feeling that he never took his eyes off me, while I walked across the living room and took a seat. I'd had a quick look in his direction and had been met with that same smile he'd had since I walked in. Having seen him in action back in The Nether, the smile just seemed weird. Not that psychopaths aren't allowed to smile, obviously, but it just doesn't ever seem to sit well on them. Like their faces are almost meant to have a sinister default setting to them and something like a smile seems like nothing other than an unauthorised modification.

'Liam, this is Norman'

Mum says to me. Now that I was sitting facing her I could see that her eyes were red and that there had been tears shed, while I was out walking the dug. It wasn't just the tears, though. She looked all anxious. Bit of a nervous wreck, like. The puffs that she was taking from her fag wasn't the kind of leisurely draw that you'd see someone who's casually smoking a cigarette. No, this more resembled someone who smokes sixty a day and have just walked off a plane to Australia and hasn't had a smoke in sixteen hours. The suction every time she brought it to her lips, giving me the impression that if it wasn't for the fact that she needed to stop for air she'd have been able to finish one with a single draw.

'Alright, Norman. Pleased to meet you, eh?'

I turned and said to him, trying on my side to let him know that what had happened earlier was in the past and forgotten about, as long as my mum was concerned.

'Never seen you before. You a pal of my mum's, aye?'

I asked *hoping* for that to have been the reason he was sat there in the house. Could've been shagging my mum or a debt collector - that she'd hidden from me - for all I'd have known although, preferably, he'd have been neither.

'Well, aye, you could say that, pal. We go back a long time, me and her and I've not been back in Scotland for a wee while so I thought I'd ... I live abroad normally, ken?'

Aye and that's why my mum's been crying and looks like she needs a vallie to stop her from shaking, I thought to myself. Old pals looking up each other normally leaves one of them as nervous wrecks, eh?

'That right, mum?' I asked, wanting to hear *her* version rather than the one coming from the man who - had it not been for a shout from behind the bar of The Nether - looked like he was moments away from causing me grievous bodily harm, minimum.

'Aye, son. We went out with each other the last few years of the eighties and start of the nineties'

She confirmed, without any smiles which didn't exactly suggest that she was looking back on those days with any kind of fondness to them.

'Seems like a lifetime ago now, though, eh?' *Norman* added, while looking like he was taking his mind back to then for a wee moment.

This kick starting a wee bout of reminiscing, driven by mum's pal on the sofa where it felt like Mum was being dragged along with it, on account of her being the other person that was part of the memories that were being brought up. There really was no need for me to even be there. No disrespect to either of them but I really wasn't bothered in hearing about the night that mum had tripped up inside the cinema - five minutes after Coming to America had already started - and spilled her popcorn and juice all over some poor cunt sitting there in the aisle seat minding their own business, watching the start of the film.

It was during this stroll down memory lane that he finally ran out of something to say, mum's only contributions had been in response to him, none of her own. So when he came to a stop, she matched him. Leaving the three of us sitting there with an uncomfortable silence. Uncomfortable enough to persuade me that I should leave them both to it. I never quite managed to squeeze in the chance to make my excuses, leave and go through to my room.

'So are you going to tell him, or me?'

This Norman said to mum, breaking the silence. Almost coming across as if I wasn't even in the room when he'd said it.

I looked at him and then mum and then back to him again.

What was there to tell me? Never seen this cunt before in my life until earlier that day, and within ten minutes I'd been forced to smack a pool cue over his head due to the doing he was giving my pals, and now he's in my house talking all cryptically with my mum *about* me. None of this was close to being classed as fucking normal.

Whether it was my mum who wanted to tell me - whatever secret that they had - or not, by saying what he had, it kind of forced her hand, making her take over from there.

'Look, Liam' She said, reaching for another fag while struggling to make any kind of meaningful eye contact with me.

This isn't going to be good, I remember thinking to myself as I hung on to see what was going to come out of her mouth next.

'There's not really going to be any easy way to say this - and don't worry, son we'll have our time to talk about it later, and as much as you need - but …. '

She held back from finishing what she'd set out to do. Almost as if something was preventing the last words from leaving her mouth.

'Mum, what is it?'

Now she had me scared. Was she ill? Had this cunt came to tell her that he'd had aids when they were together or something? My mind was going off in all kinds of directions due to just how out of character she was being, along with the crying that she'd been doing before I'd got back.

'Norman here is ….. he's ….'

She just couldn't bring herself to come out with it. And to the side of her, eventually, he got tired waiting on her. You could tell that he'd become a wee bit impatient with her, but was trying - badly - to hide it behind that smile.

'Look, what your mum is trying to say to you, Liam, is that I'm your dad'

My fucking *dad*? What kind of Luke Skywalker Darth Vadar shite was this? Only a couple of hours before, we were trying to fucking kill each other, and now we're face to face again, as father and son?

What the actual fuck was going on? My head was heavy scrambled in ways that I could never have thought possible through one single sentence from someone. Proper what, who, where and how scenario, like. Thank fuck I was sitting like because I fucking *needed* one at such a bombshell to be hit with. I genuinely didn't know whether to be happy or sad, angry or relieved. Didn't know what *or* how to feel in that moment but, if anything, I felt like a bit of a fanny. Something as important as who your dad is, and I'd been kept out of the loop on it. Level clearance not high enough for that intel, apparently?

Mum sat there, now crying her eyes out as she watched for my reaction. And so she *should've* been fucking crying, having let me grow up thinking that my dad had been killed in a tragic accident on the oil rigs when I was a toddler.

Once the shock of it all had been fully absorbed by me, evidently, questions were going to have to be asked of the pair of them.

Both mum *and* "dad."

Chapter 12

Abigail

He was never meant to come back into my life - never mind Liam's - and as far as I'd been concerned, his prison escape had been the absolute best case scenario, way better than I'd ever imagined for an outcome. Because, if he had served his time and been released from Barlinnie - in the way that the judge had intended when handing him his sentence, back at the beginning of the nineties - then he'd have been back around darkening my door the minute that he was back in Dundee.

If there's one thing I'll never forget, it's the day that I saw his face popping up on the screen of the BBC Scotland news, as part of the lead story involving the escape of two inmates from prison, the other, some drug lord from South America. The way that my first instinct of horror had turned quickly to glee, once it had sunk in what this was now going to mean. Truth be told, I'd been worried sick for the previous couple of years because - in my mind - he had to have been nearing to his release date.

I'd cut off communication with him years before that but even so, I knew all I was doing was burying my head in the sand, and that I'd have to face up to things at some point down the line. Ignorance is bliss and so I'd chosen the path of the ignorant, trying to get on with life while raising a kid all by myself, which I assure you, is not the easiest thing to take on all by yourself.

When Norrie escaped from prison, it had given me the feeling of someone who'd been told that they'd just bagged the top prize from Camelot, without even buying a ticket.

It wasn't difficult to work out that - with him being on the run - the very *last* place he was going to surface would've been Fintry. While my ex could have been guilty of accusations of being a psychopath, he wasn't stupid, either. When I saw an update on the story of his escape, that speculated Police had reckoned that him - and the other man he escaped with - had fled to Holland, that improved things further.

Putting myself in his shoes, giving me grief was going to be something that had to have ranked low on his list of things to do. Any other circumstances, however? I'd have thought that my door would've been the *first* place he'd headed for.

Could you have even believed my luck? I'd been trying to deal with the facts that our relationship was dead as a dodo for around half a year, leading up to his arrest. Norrie wasn't going to be an easy person to break up with though, and I knew it, which explained how slow I was in trying to actually make the break from him. I just didn't love him anymore, probably hadn't done so for a couple of years but the combination of fear and hope was what kept me hanging on. Fear, over what his reaction was going to be, and how much of my life he was going to make a hell, following the split. Then there was the hope that things were going to improve between us. Hope can cloud your judgement though, cant it? He spoke to me like I was a piece of shit on his shoes half the time. The other half I never seen him, and the sex? Like a one way street. As long as *he* was happy, then to hell with me. Not that I'd have ever told him but thank god for my rabbit because if it wasn't for that I wouldn't have been climaxing *at all*.

The irony being though that the last time we'd had sex with each other - the week before his arrest - it had been the one that the condom had split. I'd noticed this at the time but thought it would be fine if I'd taken a morning after pill, which I had.

Who knows, though? Faulty batch of medicine, super strong semen or act of god. By the time he was getting himself comfy through in Glasgow on remand, I was starting to be sick in the morning. It wasn't even just the red flag of the morning sickness. I just felt *different*. It's not something that I can even explain but I just *knew* that I was up the duff. Cried my eyes out for days, before summoning up the courage to take a test and make it official.

I'd always wanted to be a mum, just not with him as the dad. Why would you want to have a child with a person that you'd already decided that you weren't going to be spending the rest of your life with? That, in addition to them being a vicious, violent and highly dangerous individual, known for their unpredictable behaviour. Hardly father of the year material. You have a kid with someone though and - regardless of how it works out for the two of you - whether you like it or not, you're going to have a link with them for the rest of your life. Splitting with Norman was going to be a challenge in itself. The *last* thing I needed was a reason to be forever linked to the man.

Before eventually telling him, I'd toyed with the idea of getting rid of it, almost did too. I just couldn't go through with it in the end. Had the appointment booked at the clinic, the lot. Cancelled it with about an hour to spare, telling the woman that I'd had second thoughts on it. I remember her telling me that I'd made the correct decision and that I had to be a full one hundred percent before taking a decision like that.

Once I told Norrie that I was pregnant though, there was no going back after that.

I was going to tell him in a letter but decided that news as big as that would've been better given face to face, so had left it until my next visit.

It had actually been quite touching to see how delighted the news had made him that day, even if it was in the most bitter sweet of ways, with him effectively scheduled to miss out on the first ten years of his child's life. That fact alone, as real for me as it was for him.

It's no joy to not even reach the three month mark and already know that you're going to be responsible for raising, clothing and feeding this baby inside of you, all on your own, for a decade.

Once the baby came, so did the arguments.

I took Liam through to Glasgow - so Norrie could meet his son for the first time a few weeks after I'd given birth to him - but it had been a nightmare. He screamed his head off practically the whole time that we were in there, and effectively ruined everyone's visiting time. Norrie couldn't even take much enjoyment out of the visit due to the racket the wee man was making, *especially* when he was in Norrie's hands.

It had been the right thing to do - taking him in to see his father - but I'd been upfront with him when I'd said that I would not be bringing Liam to visit, once he reached the toddler stage. No way was my son going to be growing up with prison visits making up parts of his memories as a kid. Like going to places such as prisons would be deemed as a normal thing for him. I wasn't letting that happen. Norrie wasn't happy but I hadn't expected anything less from him. Obviously he'd thought of things from a selfish point of view, not his son's.

I tried my best to bridge the gap by sending pictures and telling Norrie some of the latest news, but he had to ruin it all by telling me in *his* letters what was going to happen to me if I didn't start bringing his son in to see him. Maybe he was just trying to call my bluff but telling me that all the Max Factor in the world wouldn't be able to hide the damage he was going to do to my face when he got out - and me knowing just how capable he was of this - only pushed me and his kid away from him further, until I broke off contact with him. Stopped opening the letters from him through fear of what I was going to see inside them. Whenever I'd get that reverse charge phone call from the prison that would play the recorded message informing you where the call was from - and that you would be responsible for paying for the call - and that if you wished to proceed stay on the line, I would always hang up.

All I'd really been doing had been kicking the can down the road but I'd simply panicked, and people can make the strangest decisions when they're under pressure.

Liam had first asked the question about 'if he had a daddy' when he was four. You know how kids start to notice stuff? I think he'd noticed dads coming to pick up some of the other kids at the playgroup and eventually pieced things together enough to ask me. Thankfully he was young enough to swallow any old lie that I'd have been free to hit him with, without questioning things.

I'd have done the same thing again if I'd had to but my instinct had been that I wanted the little guy to have a chance in life, and what chance was he ever going to have if he was universally recognised as *Nora's son?* Talk about having your card marked?

Deep down I knew it was wrong but when the time came I chose to tell my son that his dad was with the angels and that he'd been killed working in another country while working on an oil rig. He was too wee to really be upset over this news but it had been enough of a cover story for him to swallow and - growing up - take as having happened.

I'd told myself that while yeah, I was going to have to deal with Norrie when he got back out, I'd already assumed that he was going to revert to his psychopathic type, and in doing so, which would help me make my point to Liam over *why* I'd taken the decision to keep us both away from his dad. I know myself just how much of a scheming bitch that makes me sound but the truth was, with Norrie. You gave him enough rope, he would always find a way to hang himself with it.

Him getting out of jail, though? In the funniest of ways it had felt like *I'd* got myself out of jail because - I'd told myself - it would mean that we would never see each other again. I'd scanned the news - in the days following his escape - to see if he'd been picked up anywhere but as each day passed, and with no more news to report, the story soon dropped off the radar again.

Every now and again I thought of him. Where in the world he was, and if he was alive or dead. I'd heard nothing from him, which was exactly how I wanted it.

Which is why my entire world crashed that night, when that knock on the door came when I was sitting having a cup of tea. Having not long got home from work and trying to muster up the energy to make a start on tea for Liam and me. I'd arrived home to an empty house and figured that him and Bannon were both out for a walk. The dog, who I'd been against having in the house to begin with, had started to grow on me the longer he'd been in the house and Liam - to my surprise - had been keeping up to his part of the bargain by taking care of everything dog related, like the walks and feeds.

You could've given me one hundred guesses over who was at the door that night. I just wouldn't have guessed that my ex would be standing there looking back at me with that passive aggressive smile that he'd always had for anyone that was in his sights.

'Alright, Abi. Guess who's back?'

I'd carried my cup of tea to the door with me, when it had went, and subconsciously dropped it to the floor the second I saw that face staring back at me.

'Fucking hell, darling. You look like you've just seen a ghost, eh?'

I still hadn't been able to speak a word to him, but he already looked like he'd got a kick out of the shock that was apparently written all over my face.

'Norrie ...'

Able only to say his name in what was a state of disbelief. I wasn't sure that this was actually happening. I hoped to hell that it wasn't. No, the force that he brushed against my shoulder when he decided to 'let himself in' felt too real for this to be a dream, or more relevantly, a nightmare.

'Me and you have got some talking to do, eh?'

He said crossing the threshold and knocking me to the side as he entered. To be fair, in that moment I think a feather could have knocked me sideways, never mind someone with the bulk that he had. He was even *bigger* than I remembered. It had been a long, long time, though.

I closed the door reluctantly - for a few seconds I had thought of going in the *opposite* direction and running from the house to the nearest police station to get him lifted but knew I didn't have the nerve to go through with it - and followed him into the living room, where he'd already made his way to.

'A wee cuppa wouldn't go amiss either, Abs. Couldn't help but notice that you need another one yourself, like'

He said as I walked in to see him making himself at home by sitting down on the sofa.

It scared me how after twenty years he could've just strolled right into the house, like that. How does anyone feel that they can do that, after such a long time passing? Norrie was a man apart, though. He'd always been so, rightly or wrongly, more often wrongly than not.

I could've been married by then for all that he knew of, with my husband sitting through in the living room blissfully unaware of the storm of shite that was about to enter his life, but yet he still felt that it was within his rights to just walk straight in.

Suddenly it occurred to me that - despite the thousands of cups of tea I'd made him - I'd forgotten how he took his tea and had to ask him. This giving him a chance to announce to me that he now no longer took sugar in his tea and that he was looking after himself these days. Standing up for a second to lift up the front of his top to show me the six pack that he had, and one that he most definitely hadn't had when we'd been together. All proud of himself he was with it. Looking down and appearing to admire it himself, while showing it to me.

Standing there in the kitchen I was literally wishing the kettle not to boil. To make those cups of tea would mean that I was going to be back through in the living room with him again, having the conversation that - over the years - I'd lulled myself into the false sense of security that I'd never find myself taking part in.

I couldn't escape my fate though and within minutes was sat down - facing him - in one of the armchairs, opposite the sofa that he was lounging in.

'Look, Norrie. I only did what I did for the boy's own good. You *do* realise that? Prison is no place for a kid to be going to ...'

I made an attempt at starting to explain to him - again - why I'd broken off contact with him, and why he hadn't seen his son from a few months old onwards, but all he did was put his index finger up to his lips and shoosh me.

'Shhhhh'

I wasn't sure if it was done through confidence, arrogance or maybe even a bit of both but he must've known how scared I was, sitting there beside him, and he looked like he was enjoying it. Revelling in the terror that I imagined myself projecting, when confronted with my biggest fear, him. Considering some of the threats he had aimed at me all those years before, I had a *right* to be frightened of him, and what he was capable of.

All of those years that he'd had to build up all of his anger and resentment towards me, all leading up to the day that we were once again in the same room as each other, and he could finally exact revenge on me for what I'd done to him.

I wanted to hear the door going - and Liam and Bannon coming through it - to provide me with a bit of security, but at the same time I wasn't sure if Liam walking in right then on us was going to be the wisest thing to happen.

Whether he did or didn't come home, clearly Norrie was going to be looking for him, now that he was back in Scotland.

'Now now, there's no need for any of that pish, hen. Karma will look after you, for taking the decision that you did to exclude that wee boy from having his dad ... for now, though, tell me where he is'

Surprised as much as I was relieved that he appeared to have been holding a lot less anger inside of him - regarding matters - than I'd have imagined, I complied with his question with the vague 'out with the dog' answer.

I'd hoped that this might've been enough to send him out on the hunt for Liam but, instead, on hearing this Norrie done this kind of theatrical stretch, while telling me that if he was out with the dog then whatever the deal he'd be coming back with it, plus it was approaching tea time, so he said that he'd just sit tight until they came back.

It wasn't like I could have told him to leave and come back another time. Well, I could've *tried*. It just wouldn't have washed with him, though.

Over the course of the time, that we were left there sitting together. As each minute passed, his mask began to slip and slip until we reached the point where he just unloaded a volley of abuse at me for all the sins that I had committed against him.

What a *traitorous little fucking cow* I'd been by turning my back on him, leaving him to rot inside Bar L.

How I'd spent the past twenty years poisoning Liam's mind and turning our son against him. Something that couldn't have been further from the truth, and how Norrie really didn't understand that the most freaked out of *everyone* was going to be Liam when he found out that he actually *did* have a father, and that it was *this* maniac of a human being.

'Don't you fucking start with the crocodile tears, either. This is all on you, cunt'

He'd shouted unsympathetically from the sofa when I finally cracked and started to cry under the verbal abuse that he was giving me.

Life hadn't ever been perfect and in fact it had been the hardest of struggles at various points but you know what? Me and Liam had been happy, and I'd always recognised how lucky you were, if you had happiness in your life. In a series of moments, though. He brought it all crashing down.

Aye, a lot of it my fault, well, most of it. That didn't make it any easier to deal with when it was all on top of me. Sitting taking such cutting and vicious abuse inside my own living room from an escaped convict ex boyfriend while my son - for all I knew - was minutes away from walking in on the two of us, and finding out that his mum had lied to him, on one of the biggest subjects you could *ever* lie to your child about.

I just wanted to walk right out the house - and leave Norrie sitting there waiting on Liam's return - and go right down to the Tay and walk into it until it was above head height.

Somehow I'd managed to survive the next hour which had taken in Liam coming back home to - first of all - find a stranger sitting with me and - secondly - that it was his dad.

And now I was just sitting there, in silence, in the empty living room, alone. Norrie having suggested - where to class it as a suggestion would've been to engage in using figure of speeches

- that him and Liam go out for a couple of drinks, and get to know each other.

'Mon, son. I've been waiting on having a drink with you since you were hanging on to your mum's tit, eh?'

Norrie, either one to never know his own strength or knowing *exactly* what it was, putting Liam into a 'playful' headlock while pulling him towards the exit.

Following them leaving - Norrie making it very clear that I wasn't invited - I'd just sat there, unable to stop replaying the stark polar opposite that the two of them had looked like when leaving the house. Norrie, with chest puffed out, looking like he'd reclaimed what was rightfully his, while Liam just looked confused, and a wee bit hurt at having his whole life pulled from underneath him like some Persian rug.

There was obviously going to be a lot of talking getting done - and for the foreseeable - but I was already fearing that the look of disappointment that Liam given me before he walked out the door was one that was going to haunt me for the rest of my days.

To try and end the torture I was putting myself through simply by being awake, I took myself to bed early for the night, making an exception by allowing Bannon to sleep at the foot of my bed. It was a night where sleep just wouldn't take hold and I reckon I'd seen every hour on the clock.

Eventually I gave up with the tossing and turning around seven in the morning, deciding to get up - ahead of my alarm for work - and make myself a cup of coffee. On my way to the kitchen I popped my head inside Liam's room to make sure he'd survived the night out with his dad, many hadn't in the past.

Instantly I was left with the most horrible sinking feeling in my stomach. Liam wasn't *in* his bed, and with it being just gone seven in the morning the chances of him having been up, changed and out for the day were absolutely zero.

Which all meant that he hadn't actually come home yet, from being out with Norrie.

I knew that Liam was no angel but - by comparison - he had went for "a couple of drinks" with the *devil,* and never returned.

My three attempts in a row to call him going straight to voicemail, this not exactly putting me at ease.

Where were they? What had they been up to since leaving the house? Were they even still together or had they started fighting with each other on their first drink?

I had a lot of worries, and as many questions to go alongside.

Regardless of any of it - single mum and all - I needed to be ready and out the house in time for the bus at eight twenty seven.

If there was no sign of Liam by the time I reached the end of my day, and back home, maybe *then* I would have to start thinking about filing missing persons reports.

Chapter 13

Nora

'You know what, son? I don't know whether to be in awe of you or down right *disgusted* over the fact that the social circles that you move in can entail finding an afters, on a fucking *Tuesday* night'

I was just taking the pish out of the wee man, like. Felt good to say the word 'son' to someone, and it actually *mean* that they're your son, though.

Vewy, vewy pwoud, as Fergie used to say. Used to fucking hate the man - back in the day - with a passion, when it was United and Aberdeen, but that was only because he was your rival, and you knew how he had the capabilities to hurt you. When it's someone that's not worth worrying about, you don't have the emotional capacity to find hate towards them. Fair play though, he turned out to be one of the greatest managers in the history of football and all I have for the man now is complete respect and nothing but understanding over every single piece of shithousery that he ever pulled off as a gaffer. Mad how the world works and how you can end up seeing people through a different lens, when you mature a wee bit, eh?

Didn't have the first fucking clue what it was going to be between Liam and me, on our first introduction. Let's face it, eh? It's not exactly the best of circumstances when you're meeting your kid for the first time, and they're no longer a kid. Lot of water's run under the bridge by that point and I'm talking as much water as could fill the fucking Tay. I was perfectly aware that at twenty, the boy was pretty much a man, and that he'd have grown into himself as a person by that point, his own *man*, as they say. Knew that there might well have been a wee bit of resistance - on his part - when it came to me coming along and gatecrashing his life. Had already told myself that I was going to have to show patience in the way that I'd never offered anyone else in my fucking puff. Hadn't ever really taken too kind to cunt's mouthing off at me - and generally things had never really went well for any daftie that had tried - but knew that, on this occasion, even if it was just a one off, I was going to have to be the bigger man.

Abigail had been given a twenty year head start on things, so who the fuck knew what she had or hadn't told him when he'd been growing up and me otherwise indisposed?

For what it was worth, I just wanted him to give me a bit of his time, hear me out with what I'd wanted to say to him, while I was going to be an open book for anything that he - on his side - might've wanted to know about me.

Over the years, especially the last five or so, I'd wondered just what a young adult he was starting to turn out. Was he going to be a cool cunt that all the girls wanted to ride, a complete fucking radge that was destined for a life inside, a promising sportsman, or even some nerd that was brainy as fuck and top of their classes at school? Nothing was ruled out by me.

As we were leaving the house to go for a couple of drinks - and him telling me that a drink would be cool but that we'd have to go into town a bit as he was banned from all of the local pubs - I got an entry into what my son was like. Almost swelled with pride when he'd told me about being banned from all the boozers near by. Couldn't help but feel that it was a case of a chip coming from the old block. Myself, not exactly a stranger to incurring bans from those same boozers in my youth.

There would be a time over the night where I'd be giving him full disclosure over my own situation but at the time - even though it was going to be my own suggestion, if for a different reason - I just agreed that we'd go into town and left it as we were going that far so that he could get into a pub, instead of me hiding from all of the local known faces, closer to home.

'No wonder you're fucking banned from all the pubs, if you're running around them, skelping cunts with pool cues, eh?'

I tried to joke, while pointing at the plaster on my head but I think everything was too soon for him to be light heartedly laughing about *anything*. Plus, it's been said before that my tone, at times, needs working on, when it comes to me trying to have a joke with someone. That it can come across as serious, when I'm trying to be the opposite.

'Ach, I'm just joking with you, pal'

I patted him hard on the shoulder before giving it a big squeeze as we walked along towards the bus stop.

'I honestly didn't ken that …. I mean, if someone had told me it was my dad …'

'Hey, Liam. You backed your fucking mates up. I can't even tell you how impressed I am with you. If I had to have a chunk of my head removed as part of the process then, cest la fucking veeeee, eh?'

I assured him. And it was the truth, for what it was worth. Can't be many dad's who are introduced to their flesh and blood via such a medium, that sees pool cues getting taken off people's heads and that but aye, he showed me what he was made off. His mates had taken a couple of sore ones and it would've been easy enough for Liam to have seen what had happened to them, and figured that he wasn't too into getting some himself. Choosing to come at someone like me - in the way that he had - told me a lot about what kind of a person he was. Chilled me to the bone, the thought of what would've happened, had I actually *laid hands* on him because, make no mistake about it. Some cunt pops me with the butt of a pool cue then - under any other circumstances - they better fucking hope they knock me out long enough to allow them a safe passage out of the place before I wake. And as such, I'd very much intended on hurting that third kid that had weighed in on things, and he came seconds away from finding out.

Like I said, it's funny how the world works out, eh?

When out on the street I soon became aware that - since leaving the house - I had done almost all of the talking, to the point where it was almost coming across like I was doing that whole talking for the sake of it thing, that someone will do when they're shit scared of reaching an uncomfortable silence so they just keep fucking prattling on.

I could never have expected him to just start blethering away with me like he'd known me all his life. *That's* why I'd suggested alcohol as that was always going to aid things between us - although I could never have ruled out the drink being counter productive once a few had been sunk - and help loosen the tongue a wee bit.

Standing at the bus stop - or on the bus itself - was never going to be the place to be holding deep conversations, so I kept things as middle of the road as I could, Liam contributing very little back and answering any questions from me with as little words as possible. To be fair to the lad - and the look he'd had on his coupon since walking into the house and finding me there - he *did* have the look of some cunt that had been plunged into the jungles of Nam, after a five minute warning.

He needed a wee bit time to get his head around everything, and I was prepared to give him as much as he needed. Preferably though, it was going to be at some point over the night because my plans had been to get myself back out of Dundee the next day, and wouldn't be back again before flying home to Amsterdam.

'Fuck it, fancy going to The Trades? Not been there since the day we knocked fuck out of the Saturday Service when Motherwell were in town for a game at Dens, but aye, that's another story altogether'

I suggested the watering hole while we were stepping off the bus, fresh from a journey that had been largely silent between the two of us. I hadn't meant to mention the part about the Motherwell hoolies but - in the moment - had been taken over by a cherished memory from what was now a previous life.

Liam just shrugged his shoulders in approval of going to The Trades although I'd been left with the impression that *whatever* pub I'd suggested, he'd have went along with.

Once we'd had our first pint though, he started to open up a wee bit to me. I knew I wasn't going to fucking get anywhere if I was to sit there and bad mouth that boot of a mum that he had, so had to sit there and gaslight him a wee bit by telling him - once we got sat down and started to talk - I had no idea what his mum had told him about me but that I believed that whatever she'd done, that it had all been for Liam's benefit. Let him know that I hadn't always made the correct decisions and anything his mum had said or done in the past had been as a reaction to whatever shite I'd put myself - and us - in. The words almost sticking in my mouth as I sat there and defended her, the fucking *last* person that I'd have ever wanted to have sat there and spoke up for.

'She told me that you'd died?'

He said to me with a face that looked like he was questioning everything that he'd ever been told in his life.

'I was too wee to question any of it and by the time I got a wee bit older it was just one of those things, eh? Some of my pals had dads, some didn't. I was one of the ones that didn't. It all felt, normal'

While there had been many possibilities of which story the wee man would've had fed to him - when he was younger - I'd have never have thought that she'd have been as fucking stupid as to say that I was brown fucking bread, when she *must've* known that one day, somewhere and somehow, I was going to come looking for my son?

I laughed - self depreciatingly - while telling him that while quite a few had *tried* to kill me over the years, I was very much alive.

'Like I said, son. I don't blame Abigail for what she did but it's really important that you know that I at least *tried* to be in touch with you, to be involved in your life and for you to know who your dad was. Now don't go holding it against her or fuck all but it was your mum that cut off the communication. I went out my mind for a wee bit - in the jail - when the penny dropped that she was no longer replying to my letters, and had stop visiting, thinking of you growing up, going through all those wee stages that a kid does, and me missing out on every single bit of it'

'I thought you were dead'

He just repeated again to me. He had absolutely ride all to be sorry about but it felt that by emphasising this it kind of absolved him of anything, when it came to missing out on knowing me.

'Well, look, son. You don't have to tell me how much of a complete head fuck this all is, but I'm alive and, now that you know it, I was hoping that we could make up for lost time, you and me. I know we've missed out on first bikes and taking you for a kick around the park and all that shite, but it doesn't mean to say we can't get to know each other from this point'

'Aye, you're not wrong about the head fuck part, like'

He laughed - sincerely - for the first time since I'd met him.

'I know that I should be pissed off at mum, for not telling me about you, but she fucking raised me on her own, eh? Provided everything for me, went without things herself so that I could, fitba boots and that. I'm just proper confused here, like'

Nothing would've pleased me more if Liam was to take a sudden dislike towards his mum, and she'd have deserved it if he'd had. But encouraging any of this - as much as I was tempted to - wasn't going to help things so I told him that he should try and give his mum a pass on things, giving him a wee bit of context towards what and who his father was, and vitally, his current status when it came to him being sitting in the city of Dundee.

Considering he'd been told that I had died years ago, I pretty much had been handed a blank canvas to work with, when it came to telling him about myself. Fuck? I could've invented up a whole new exciting life for what I'd done since he'd been born. I wanted to give him full disclosure, though. Plus - now that he knew I existed - it was probably only going to be a matter of time before cunts started filling him in on me so I felt it would've been better coming straight from the Ruud van Nistelrooy's mouth, so to speak.

Some sons or daughters you'd have sat down and told them the story of why you'd been jailed, then the escape, and the subsequent life of ducking and diving hoping never to be caught, they'd have headed for the door. Liam was engrossed, though. Once we'd got ourselves past that very real awkwardness that was felt between us, we actually found ourselves starting to get on. The fact that he was still sat there when I reached the whole me turning over a new leaf and settling down to run an Amsterdam gym part of the tale told me a lot about the boy. Understandably, some kids might not be too cool to meet someone - and be told that despite what they'd believed all their life, *this* was their father - and be told that they were an internationally wanted criminal, Liam took it all in his stride and had almost been begging for more of the story, like some toddler at bed time, when they want a wee bit more of their book read to them.

I suppose it was a bit of a novel meeting of a father and son because a lot of the questions I'd have loved to have asked all involved when he was wee, and wouldn't be able to fucking remember anything about. Once we dealt with the initial head fuck - and with nothing of any kind of note when it came to shared memories to talk about - we kind of just went directly to more random stuff while doing so finding out a bit about each other. Both of us sitting there talking as grown ups, as equals.

Fuck knows what he'd been making of me but the fact that he was still willing to sit there by pint number three was big for me. In my worst case scenario we weren't even going to be getting on the bus to the city centre with each other with us, instead, having a heated chat - away from Abigail - before going off on our separate ways.

I couldn't have dreamed of us reaching the opposite end of the scale and that we'd be sitting there - almost like a couple of mates - losing track of time, sitting having a scoop together.

When I'd come back from the bar, with our pints, Liam was just coming back from the bogs. It wasn't hard to spot the change in him and, after all I'd sat there and told him, I'm not even sure who the fuck he was trying to kid. From the moment he sat down he was instantly a lot more *talkative*.

I just let him go on for a few minutes while he jumped from how cool it must be to living in Amsterdam to asking if I go to see Ajax before then jumping to a completely different subject in how cold his latest pint of lager was.

'Alright, ya cunt. Slide the fucking ching over this way. Where's your manners anyway? You been fucking dragged up or what, eh?'

I sat and joked with him. He just sat there, a wee bit sheepish, looking at being busted and a wee bit pissed off with himself that I'd been able to clock him as easy as he'd made it for me.

'You know how awkward it would've been, for me to, like, ask? Who asks their dad if he fancies a wee Patsy?'

He reached into his jacket pocket and - first of all, looking around the pub - slid over a wee baggie across the table to me.

'Some cunt who has *me* for a dad'

I said - picking up the wee see thru bag - getting up and giving him another one of those shoulder squeezes as I made my way to the toilets.

By the time I returned - feeling like I had nitro shooting out of my erse, propelling me back towards my son - it was a case of up up and away. I know Cocaine is a drug that is not without its problems, but as a kind of *breakthrough* drug, when it came to a father and son trying to get to know each other after being kept apart for so long, it was a fucking revelation.

We sat there and talked the biggest amount of pish towards each other for the next couple of hours. Aye, a lot of it was pish, but, for me, that was kind of the point. To be able to sit there, with your son, and just talk about all sorts of things that came to mind? Priceless.

What team did he choose, in my absence? Telling me what name his dog had and me getting my answer.

He told me all about the girl that he'd just broken up with, allowing me the chance to give some man of the world advice from dad to his younger.

We started on plans to have him coming over to visit. Me making an open invitation to him to have stayed as little or as long as he liked. Mi casa su casa, regardless of us only knowing each other for a few hours.

I'd wanted to know what exam results he'd got, and wished I'd hadn't, and he was pretty fucking lucky that him and I were in a judgement free zone for the night, I can tell you. Was more frustrated with him and his incredibly bad results than anything else because from a few hours talking to him, you could tell that he was smart.

He'd wanted to know more about my Utility days, telling me that he knew a couple of boys who were currently running with the crew. I asked - more out of the routine than anything else as I'd already taken it as assumed that all of the old Utility boys that I ran with would've sacked it all long before - who they were but wasn't surprised to find I didn't know any of the two of them, although he'd unintentionally warmed my heart a wee bit by telling me that one of them was called Taylor and me making the leap that there was a good chance that he could've possibly been the son of Gary Taylor, who ran with us back in the late eighties and early nineties. The thought of a father passing the torch onto his son in such a way, something that gave me a warm glow to think of.

I'd enquired about how he went about earning money for himself and had been able to detect an unwillingness to tell me in any kind of detail *what* he did other than "this and that." Like any of the other subjects that we discussed that night, though. Anything that I heard that I didn't like, I kept my mouth shut, other than when offering support.

We tore through the subjects - as fast as we did the wee man's gear - until approaching near to chucking out time. Liam had been sitting there fiddling with his phone before eventually putting it away and asking if I wanted to go to Fat Sam's.

'Fucking Fatties? Haven't been there in over twenty years' I said to him while trying to remember when the last time I'd actually been there had been but my memory bank was not up to the task.

'Why's it open on a Tuesday night, though?'

Liam told me it was open on one of the more traditionally quieter nights of the week because some DJ was on a tour and - most likely - they hadn't been able to sort out any weekend dates for him and Dundee, so they'd just scheduled a middle of the week night and hoped for the best.

It wasn't my scene, like. That house music, thump thump thump and all those bleepy noises and all of the other stuff. Maybe I'd have been into it - back in the day when it first came out - but with me getting myself banged up for the whole of the nineties, I'd had the sense that I'd missed the boat with it all. Didn't really like or understand the music but then again, maybe if I was able to *understand* it I'd have had a chance of liking it, eh?

I'd been more into bands like The Fall, Velvet Underground, cunts like that and nothing remotely close to *Louie Vega*, who I'd made a complete arse of myself in front of Liam, after he'd mentioned his name and that he was playing over at Fatties, when replying

'Is that the Mambo number five boy, aye?'

Liam finding this a source of great amusement before telling me that I was way off. Aye, I wasn't much interested in going to Fat Sam's to extend the night but - with the taste for the pints and the rocket fuel that I'd put up my hooter over the night - at the same time, wasn't quite ready to call it a night either.

Telling Liam that as long as he wasn't embarrassed - going out with his old man to a club - that I'd come along with him, thrusting some money into his hand and telling him that the next gram was on me, if he knew where to get us some. Hadn't fucking had Ching in years, as well. It's that kind of a drug, though. You can take years off it but once you find yourself back *on* it you're reminded just how fucking moreish it really is, straight away.

Liam telling me that there was no worries on that score, and that he'd sort it out.

I couldn't believe how busy the place was, once we'd got ourselves inside, having had to queue for a wee bit outside in the cold. I had a wee moment where - looking around at the crowd waiting to get in - I could see just how older I was than everyone else, and now that we were away from the small pub I could see, once again, that we very much looked like a father and son together, rather than the "mates" vibe, that I'd felt when we were inside the boozer.

Once we got in I just found myself a seat and - other than to go and get drinks or pop to the bogs for a cheeky Patsy with the kid - pretty much stayed there all night. Liam - who had met up with a big group of pals inside - coming back to sit with me for a wee while to have a breather before heading back into the crowd again to join his mates, them all dancing. Once again, a concept that I completely could not grasp. The thought of dancing with my pals when I was his age, too much to even comprehend.

The music was giving me a fucking sore head, like. All of that shite just sounds the same after a while, though. Deejay turns up and plays thirty different songs, and you wouldn't fucking know it because it sounds like one long song that just never ends. The crowd loved it though, mind. It looking very much like not a single soul had left the place by the time this wee man in a hat had played the last record, and the lights had been put on.

Liam coming over to me at this with a couple of his pals to introduce to me. It was probably just all the drink and drugs but I'd felt that - when introducing me - Liam was telling people who I was, with a bit of pride behind it.

He hadn't yet managed to find it within himself to call me 'dad' but was at least managing to refer to me - to others - *as* his father. Which I guess was some kind of progress, eh?

'Listen, we're going back to Wullie's flat in Lochee for a wee bit. He's got cans, and I've sorted us for some more Ching, you fancy coming?'

Obviously, the sensible thing to have done would've been to thank him for the offer but that he should just head with his mates, and that I was calling it a night. I wanted to squeeze as much time in his company as I could, though. Knowing I'd be leaving Dundee the next day, I didn't know when I'd see him again, so wanted to at least take advantage of time with him, while it was there.

We sat there for hours until the sun came up - with that same House and Techno music playing incessantly - and the longer that I sat with them all, the more I saw that me and them were on completely different wavelengths, and that I wasn't really meant to be there. I felt welcome enough, mind. That didn't stop the feeling of not *belonging*, though.

This completely summed up by another one of my 'misunderstandings' when one of the group, Alice, the girlfriend of Liam's mate Wilkie, said she wanted to hear *Bits and Pieces* and could someone stick it on for her. Hearing this, my ears pricked up.

'Now you're fucking talking, eh. A bit Dave Clark Five sounds fucking Barry. Give that electronic shite a rest for a while, this lass knows her fucking stuff'

Everyone looking in my direction - some in what looked like horror, others in amusement - as I broke out into song

'I'm in pieces, bits and pieces. You went away and left me misery. I'm in pieces, bits and pieces'

First of all there was a wee snigger from someone. The type that on any other day would have seen the ashtray that was sitting right in front of them being wedged into their fucking head. Then - following that - there was the sound of someone trying to hold in their laugh, but part of it escaping. This being enough to see that everyone else were now joining in, without trying to hide it.

I looked around the room - at everyone laughing and pointing at me - and felt a complete fanny. With the exception of Liam - who was also laughing at me - I wanted to kill every single person in the room, in that moment.

'Aye, I think you might be talking about a different song, *pops*'

Wilkie shouted across the room at me, everyone giving him the laugh that he'd clearly been looking for, especially with the remark that was pointing at the age difference I had to the rest of them.

I'd done so well all night long but with that remark from him I dropped my guard for a few seconds, and had felt that the look I'd given him to greet his wideness had possibly been enough to let him know that he probably shouldn't try it again with me.

It kind of soured things and I never quite managed to shake things off from then. When I looked at my watch and saw that it was now past nine in the morning - the small rays of light that the curtains would allow streaming into the living room - and had a wee look around the room, I had myself a wee moment of clarity. Almost like I'd been able to have the ability to see myself - sat there - from a separate angle. A man in his fifties, sitting in a house absolutely fucking wired with a bunch of teenagers and early twenties, all also wired.

The moment that I started to feel a wee bit pathetic and sad - to be reaching a Wednesday morning, having been out all night - I left soon after.

The night before - and the personal time spent with Liam - had been invaluable but it was without question now - for me, at least - the point of the afters where it all had started to feel depraved and wrong. In that exact moment, knowing that the normal people in the country were now all up having had a night's sleep and now getting ready for work, sitting there in a Lochee flat, sinking beers and sniffing Patsies, it all had the feeling of me having failed at life.

I didn't want to say my goodbye to Liam in front of the rest of them so I told him to walk me out to the door, where we had a few words stood there. After a full night of being on it you would say that the pair of us were a wee bit worse for wear but - combined - we just about managed to find a way to sum up the defining night that it had been.

'I don't think I'll manage to get back to Dundee before I fly home but if I do I'll obviously give you a shout, and if not then the next time I see you will be over in the Dam'

Liam smiled at the thought of that which when you've been on a drink and drugs session all night and some cunt broaches the prospect of you going to Amsterdam, aye, you may well smile.

'Look, I'm not going to say that I'm used to all of this after us having one night out together, and it's probably going to take me weeks to get my head around it all, but it was good to meet you all the same'

He said as he came in for a handshake and to bring our shoulders up against each other, a wee bit unsteady on his feet which saw him giving me a head butt on the same side as he'd smacked me with the cue. The sharp shooting pain that this brought me a simple reminder that while I'd spent all night feeling invincible due to the combination of lager and Cocaine, I wasn't.

'And remember, now? I know the score and that you're going to want to tell cunts about me and that but try not to tell any one that I've been about, until I'm back home again'

I whispered in his ear. Possibly the come down of the Ching kicking in but suddenly I'd - for the first time all night - remembered about my need to display an instinct for survival.

I was heading back for a few hours kip at my mum and dad's and then I would be getting out of Dundee again. Still wouldn't have wanted any Dundee coppers knowing that I'd *been* in the city, though. That kind of intel and before you'd have known it it would've been fucking APBs across the country, which really would not have been that cool. Apart from the obvious issues such heat would bring, it would also make life difficult, when it came to the actual *reason* that I was in the motherland.

Because, I wasn't in town to buy gym equipment and nor was I there to build bridges with the son I'd never had and despite how emotional and, frankly fucking massive my first few hours of being back in Scotland had been - seeing mum and dad after so long and then getting a chance to know Liam - I never once took my eye off the prize. That GGTTH1875 prick.

And after I got myself a couple of hours kip it was going to be time that I went out and started to look for him.

Chapter 14

Nora

I definitely knew that I'd been out the night before - and up most of the morning - when I finally woke up around the back of one. Didn't feel fighting fit never mind ready for any kind of fighting, which I'd been hoping to find - wherever and whenever it fancied appearing - across the Wednesday at some point.

Not hanging like I was when I surfaced for the day, though. The previous night's excesses seeing to it that I was set back a few hours, as far as my plans had meant to have been.

Fuck it, get your head together and just head straight for Motherwell later on, I told myself while I gingerly moved through the house trying to sort out a cup of tea to go with my first L and B of the day, stood outside the back door.

Once I'd pinged my fag - as per fucking always, misjudging things by sending it into the next door neighbour's garden - I went through and had a wee blether with my dad - who was sitting watching a repeat of an episode of The Sweeney, some radgey on screen with the most primitive of shotguns in his hand, with a pair of his bird's tights pulled down over his face - before heading back to bed for another couple of hours kip.

Taking one look at the nick of me, he could do fuck all other than shake his head.

'You look like you've been hit by a lorry, and then dragged along underneath it for about forty miles'

'Fucking *feel* like it, as well!' I replied, taking a big swig from my mug, now that it was finally in the ballpark of drinking temperature for a big swig like that.

'I hope you behaved yourself, mind, son? Last thing I want is the police coming around here again looking for you. You've no idea just how much they tried to turn the screw on me and your mum, after your escape. They had a way of trying to make out that we'd had a hand in it, for god's sake'

'Aye, you ken what the filth are like though, dad. Suspect you of fucking everything, until given a reason not to. Imagine trying to be pals with someone who's like that, eh? Would be scared to fucking tell them anything'

I replied before stopping to take a think to myself over how much I'd behaved myself. The only part where I'd maybe slipped up over the evening had been due to being completely mad with it at certain points of the night, where the last thing I was thinking about had been to keep a low profile. The pub had been quiet, though, and then after that I'd spent the rest of the night in a dark club. And as for half of those clueless cunts that were in the Lochee flat, at the afters? I doubt they'd even *remember* me and the ones that did - if Liam hadn't said who I was - they'd have probably put me down to the laws of the afters that dictate that there is *always* going to be one or two cunts that have found their way there, that no one else seems to know.

'Nah, kept my head down. You'll not be seeing any coppers around here, well not for me, like. Can't speak for any of *your* capers. Mum told me about the *conversion* you'd had made to the camper van, eh?'

'Oh she did, did she?'

He laughed but it was more a case of he hadn't expected me to have known about this.

'Aye, she did. Tell you what? Fit a *lot* of cheap fags into that vehicle now, eh?'

I said, making a direct reference to the fact that he'd had the kitchen - inside of the VW camper - completely hollowed out and had been using it for fag runs over to Europe. Hey, I wasn't judging, like, but *did* enjoy the fact that my dad had his own wee occasional hustles, even at that age. Something that removed a wee bit of any moral high ground that he might've thought about taking. Obviously there's a massive fucking drop off between someone sneaking a few hundred cartons of fags over the border and some cunt breaking out of a prison and fleeing the country but still, though. He who is without sin can lob the first brick so just you put it back down again dad and don't waste your fucking time.

'Aye well don't be getting any ideas for using it for smuggling drugs'

The thought had not even entertained my mind but I suppose, once a drug dealer in some people's eyes.

'I was more thinking you could smuggle *me* back across to Europe - if this trip was to go Pete Tong - inside of it, rather than any narcotics, dad'

I could've sat there all afternoon just blethering shite with him - and really should've done to make up for all the time where we didn't get that kind of interaction with each other - but couldn't deny the fact that I was absolutely fucking hanging, and needed to be in better form for heading to the football later on.

Telling my dad as much and that I was going to grab a wee bit more sleep before getting ready to leave for the game.

'United game's not on until tomorrow, ya dafty. It's because of Sky Sports'

'Aye, I fucking *know* that, what do you take me for?'

Doesn't matter if it's my father or not. When some cunt tries to tell me something that is patently obvious, while trying to make out that I don't know it myself, it winds me up all kinds of the wrong way. Cunt's thinking I'm stupid, eh?

'I'm going through to Motherwell tonight'

I says to him, finishing off my cup and making to take the empty mug through to the kitchen.

'Who are they playing?'

He asked but you could tell that he was trying to remember for himself, before I was able to answer.

'Hibs is it not? What you going to Motherwell and Hibs for?'

'I'm catching up with an Edinburgh mate of mines, who's going through to the match, Hibee, like, eh?'

I left it as ambiguously as that and my dad - being my dad - didn't bother asking anything further. I left him to it and went back to bed again and was sleeping within minutes of putting my head back onto the pillow.

Since before deciding to buy those KLM tickets, I'd already worked out *who* it was that I was looking for. You think I'd come all the way to Scotland without knowing my fucking facts, like? Nah, through some of the comments that GGTTH1875 had left on my videos, put alongside my own intelligence for figuring shite out, I'd pieced it together. Had had to eat a wee bit of humble pie along the way, mind, by speaking to people from my past that it would've been better if I'd never seen nor spoke to ever again.

You want to know how fucking serious I was about things? I even had a couple of "regressive therapy" sessions with some hippy woman - in the Jordaan District - to help me recall that day, back when I'd been thrown off the Bridge of Doom, just so I could remember the faces, and what was being shouted, of the two cunts that had been closest to me before it had all went dark, and me waking up after the event. A few of the comments that had been left on YouTube had practically screamed that it had been posted by one of those two CCS boys that had teamed up on me.

It had taken me a few weeks but my job had been made a whole lot easier when I'd found out that one of them - Adrian "Adi" Fraser - had been, unfortunately, for him, knocked down and killed by a taxi when on a night out in the town which - when you've got a short list of two people that you're looking at - massively made my search a lot easier. With Adi Fraser being hardly in a position to be getting wide with any cunt on the internet, that could only mean it was one person, Mikey "Swanny" Swanson.

Fuck me, though, because that hippy woman - despite coming across as fucking mental as a sackful of badgers - must've known her stuff because out of the two faces that I had come away being able to recall, when I had some of the Facebook pictures sent to me - from Swanson's locked account - I recognised him straight away from my regression session. Aye, obviously a wee bit more filled out and less hair, but you could tell it was the same person.

While the randomly selected Facebook photos - that I'd had sent to me - were more ones that pointed towards a family man, who proudly was telling the world that he loved his wife and two kids, there was the one, from a night game at Easter Road, which confirmed that I'd got the right boy, one hundred. There were other tell tale signs like some of the clobber that he was wearing in the pictures. Him, still sporting the usual labels whereas I'd long before given up on worrying about having to be seen with a fucking compass on my left arm. I was left in no doubt that I'd got my man, though.

I'd been given a wee nod in the right direction from one of the old boys, from The Utility, Watson. This coming via one of the boys - Cherry - that was one of the CSF main boys, back in the day and someone that I'd went into battle against on more than a few occasions - either in Edinburgh or on more home turf when Hearts were in Dundee - but was one of the lads from back then that I'd carried a bit of a grudging respect for, even though, back then, I'd have put him through a plate glass window in a fucking heartbeat, if given a chance.

It had been Cherry too that had dished the news on Adi Fraser's untimely death but - telling Watson that he'd always wanted a chance to get back at Swanny, after a snide move he'd pulled in eighty nine before the derby, when he'd smashed a half brick against his head while Cherry was looking in a totally different direction - he'd told Watson that Swanny had it coming to him, and that he hoped I'd have a ball.

I'd told Watson that I would update him - so he could pass anything back to Cherry in Edinburgh - as and when, but that I was grateful for the help and was due him a favour if he ever wanted to cash it in. It was one of those occasions where you're giving someone a favour but already know that it's all a bit hollow as they're never going to fucking use it anyway. Still, looked good though, mind.

Before leaving for Scotland, I'd had the pictures of him, printed off - to bring over with me, to potentially show others when going about trying to find him - but myself, personally, had so much of an erection for him that his face was practically ingrained in my mind. If - and hopefully more a case of when - I seen him, in the flesh, make no fucking errors, my friend, I wasn't going to be needing to consult the pictures, for quality checking, before knocking the cunt right into his afterlife.

On the way to Motherwell - having chosen the rail route of via Waverley, in the hope of bumping into some old faces on the way through to the 'Steeltown' - I'd found myself surrounded by an almost full carriage's worth of Hibees. Proper Christmas trees, though. The lot of them. Fucking train carriage looked like St Paddy's day, the amount of green that was running through it. Same with the amount of drink that was being tanned on the way through. Cans, cider, Bucky and Mad Dog. I thought it funny that despite how the years passed, and how everyone's team's were barely recognisable from every few years, that the drink of choice of their fans remained the same.

I can't say it's not nippy - when you find yourself stuck in a carriage full of fitba fans all having a scoop, especially *pre* game when they're full of drink *and* hope of getting a result out of things, before your team turns around and gives you a few boots to the balls and mutes your whole day to an extent - because it is, having to sit there and fucking listen to them all go through the songbook and their excited chatter, but they weren't doing anything I hadn't done hundreds of times before myself, travelling across Scotlands railway, and probably being as loud and carefree as all of those Hibernian fans around me.

I hadn't sat there the whole journey with them, anyway. Once the train had passed through Haymarket - and letting on any additional Edinburgh based Hibees, hoping to get themselves to Motherwell on that train - I thought it a good idea to have a wee snoop around the full five carriages of the train, to see if I could spy him. Navigating your way through a train, rammed with fitba fans all having a peeve, was as challenging as it sounds. Almost felt like I was only getting to the final carriage and every cunt were sparking into life, preparing for the train pulling in at Motherwell.

Most of the aisles had been blocked - one of those journeys where the ticket collector takes one look at the train and says 'aye, fuck that' and doesn't even bother *trying* to walk through it, asking for any tickets. Normally you just sit tight in that scenario but I thought it daft to not have a wee scan of the surroundings. Small world and that, eh?

Mainly it was just Christmas trees - on their way through for the game - who were travelling in their own wee individual pockets but - on the train - coming together as a group with the whole train, at times, belting out Hibs songs, or half the time more a case of anti *Hearts* songs, than pro Hibs ones.

There *was* that wee group - sitting at a couple of banks of four, with the table in between - that I'd seen up ahead, on the third carriage down, and had clocked the concentrated amount of Stone Island patches and CP Company Goggles that was on show in their group, and absence of Hibs strips or scarfs. A false dawn, though. I'd stealthily made my way up the carriage towards them while trying to get a proper look at them all. Clearly they weren't the same as the rest of the Hibees on there, and I'd have been amazed if they *hadn't* belonged to the Capital City Service. They weren't old guard, though. Not even close. The majority of them more closer to Liam's age then me.

In another life it would've been practically impossible for me to walk past their table, without something being said and things kicking off. That was then, though. Due to my choice of clothes - all those years later - and different mindset to go with, I was able to just slink past them without any of them even noticing me. One of them holding court to the rest of them, telling them about the girl from Granton that they'd pulled in town at the weekend.

'Now I'm not saying that my performance wasn't one for the ages or fuck all but she's been calling me morning noon and fucking night, ganting on a repeat performance. Telt her, dinnae be fucking greedy now n that she'd had her fun n how she'd just have to wait her turn again, ken?'

Probably a lot of pish, anyway, but his story was enough to allow me a proper look at them all, without anyone sussing out that I had done.

By the time I reached the last carriage of the train - according to the time - we were only minutes out from Motherwell so I just sat tight, or to be exact, stood crammed against one of the bicycle racks by a group of fans, that were stood near the door, first to get off.

You'd have normally had an announcement from someone on the train to give you a bit advance notice of the next stop but with all the singing that was going on in my carriage, if they had announced it then no cunt was going to be hearing it.

'If you hate the fucking Jambos, hate the fucking Jambos, hate the fucking Jambos clap your hands'

The applause carrying its way through the train, almost as if everyone was giving a bit respect to one of their players who had ran his heart out and was now being substituted for fresh legs.

As the train began to slow itself down to pull into Motherwell station, the fans, becoming aware of this, started to get themselves together for leaving. The scenes looking something not too different to five minutes before a boozer's shutting its doors for the night. Cunts sinking their drinks all over the place, as if they were going to have them confiscated if they didn't. Not ruling out the police presence that might be hanging around at the station, they'd maybe have been as well to.

That Scotland England match in eighty nine? Fuck me, that was a brutal day all round but had started off on the wrong note altogether when I stepped off the train at Queen Street - with half a can in my hand - and was grabbed by a bizzie before my other foot had even hit the platform and issued with a spot fine for drinking in public. Shooting fish in a barrel, eh? Grabbing cunts for having a wee scoop in public, the day Scotland played England, in Glasgow? Tell you what, though? Hit a man where it hurts - apart from his baws - and he'll not make that same mistake again. Proper deterrent, as far as I viewed things through in the weeg. Wouldn't even fucking hold a *mate's* can for him, while he was tying his shoelace, after that, like.

With it being just after five - and the match not kicking off until quarter to eight - I had a wee bit of time to spare, before getting myself into the ground. Just really done a bit of surveillance, like. Tried a few of the pubs nearest to Fir Park to see what I could find. Predictably, though it was a case of, more of the same of what was on the train. Just traditional fans, away to see their team. No moody cunts, conspicuously sticking out from the crowd. I'd actually had to shake my head in disbelief at one of the pubs - The New Century - which had a decent fifty fifty split of Motherwell and Hibs fans sitting in it, with no aggro between them, whatsoever. Where did fitba fans go wrong? I asked myself as I left the place - half a dozen Hibs fans going in the opposite direction, passing me singing *Glory Glory to the Hibees* as they walked into the place. Their choice of song, almost a taunt, with it being the famous song that had clearly inspired the GGTTH1875 account - and, having checked all the usual pubs that there was to pop a head into, began looking around the streets that were now beginning to fill up with fans, arriving for the match. From a wee look at the season so far both teams had been doing not too bad and - as always - that shows, with the amount of paying punters wanting to go see them.

Cunts sometimes class it as glory hunting but the truth is, it's a lot more enjoyable an experience - going to watch your team - when they're playing well and putting the ball in the net and getting you off your seat. Build it and they will come? Same with fitba. Play well and they will come. You go out to the game with a wee spring in your step, pure buzzing for days leading up to your match, instead of the feeling of dread when the thought of going to see them depresses the fuck out of you.

Not the case for Motherwell and Hibernian FCs, respectively, and - away from the obvious reason for being there - I'd thought that, as a neutral, it might've been a decent match to watch.

I was hanging about outside the primary school, behind the East Stand - just doing a wee bit of spotting - when I saw a wee group of either Hibs or Well casuals walking past. Was like the fucking terminator, scanning as many faces as I could when they were passing by. Didn't recognise anyone, anyway - and due to not even hearing a single one of them speak wasn't even sure if they were from the East or West coast - but from the different age groups that they were all made up from they were definitely *a* mob, whichever side they were on.

Also - before running out of time before the match - I'd overheard a couple of Well fans saying that they'd seen fighting between two sets of casuals outside the Jack Daniels pub after one set had tried to force their way in, leading to the other mob getting themselves out. *This* was at least promising to hear even if there was absolute ride all point in heading to the boozer for a look because it would've been too late and every cunt would've well nashed before any of the filth showed up.

While, ideally, I'd wanted to have got a ticket for the away end - and give me ninety minutes to try and find the prick - due to how well Hibs had been going in recent weeks, the away allocation had been a complete sellout. Because of that I'd been left with no choice than to get a home end ticket, thinking that if I at least got myself near to the segregation I'd have a chance of being able to see any wise guys in the Hibs end who had also made it a focal point of getting a standing position for the game that could involve some banter with the rival fans in the other stand.

Apart from the actual violence before or after the matches, the segregation at Tannadice was absolute fucking class. Where the other fans and casuals were so close to you that you could see the whites of their eyes, and could smell the beer and fags from their breath as they shouted at you. How fucking good it felt when United scored - and scored they would in those days - and you could just turn to that cunt who had spent half an hour nipping your head and just going proper radge, right in front of them.

Technically my ticket *wasn't* for the corner of the East Stand but well, I sat there anyway and when that fucking wet wipe came up and tried to tell me that I was in his seat, I just got him fucking told.

'Sorry, pal. You'll just have to find another one because I'm not fucking moving now, like'

Let him know under no uncertain terms to not push this any further with me. Maybe it was the look I gave him, or he was just a shitebag, but he never contested things any further. You could tell he was about to go to one of the stadium security to get them to move but then saw that she was only some young girl - who looked out of her depth as it was - that was never going to be getting me to move, so he left it, altogether.

There was only around five minutes until kick off - teams had now went back down the tunnel to get themselves stripped and ready - and I'd just sat there watching the Hibs end fill up since I'd got in. As the minutes passed - and with more and more filling the stadium - the atmosphere began to build with singing from both the home and the away ends. Felt like an imposter, like. Being in a part of a stadium where everyone's singing, and I'm having to keep quiet because I don't even fucking support the team. It's one thing being in an away end - with your mates - intent on smashing fuck out of a few of who's inside there, but when you're on your jack, you feel a wee bit weird, like you don't belong.

Talking of not belonging, though. It only took the first five minutes of the match for me to clock that the boy stood beside me wasn't a Motherwell fan either.

Maybe around late forties, maybe earlier and had just had a hard paper round. With everyone else having refused to sit down yet - due to an exciting opening couple of minutes - he was stood beside me swaying a wee bit back and forward, definitely had a few before coming into the game. I could smell it off him too, in that way where if you're not drinking yourself, you can smell alcohol off some cunt from fifty yards.

He wasn't wearing any team colours but with his body language - reacting to passages of play - it was looking like he wasn't just not supporting Motherwell, like myself, but was actually *supporting* Hibernian, and not doing too good a job of hiding it. Wasn't exactly standing in the middle of the Well fans singing 'Ooh to ooh to be ooh to be a HIBEE' but with the way he was getting excited during the moments that, technically, he should've been bricking it, he wasn't exactly flying under the radar, either. Well, not from me, anyway. And I reckoned that if I'd clocked him, then it was probably only going to be a matter of time before some of the home fans did as well.

Thought I'd do the boy a favour and let him know, before I found myself in the middle of it all. Sometimes I like to do a favour for the humans, not a lot but catch me on a good day and you never know, eh?

'You need to keep it together lad or you're going to get us both thrown out'

I said to him - discreetly - cupping my hand and saying to him, giving him a wee knowing wink.

He looked at me for a moment - bit of a glazed look which suggested six pint minimum - before finally getting what I was saying to him. His face lighting up as he replied

'Awww, mate. Nice one. Up the fucking cabbages, eh?'

I definitely wasn't getting into explaining to him that I was neither, so let him continue to think that I was one of his crowd, under enemy lines.

It had been a frantic opening ten minutes where Hibs had gone ahead with an Anthony Stokes individual effort, having megged one of the Well midfielders before putting a defender on his arse as he took the ball past him, finding the keeper's near post, top shelf. A beautiful goal that had I watched on the telly I'd have been out my chair applauding. Not so much standing with the Motherwell fans.

I'd cringed when seeing the ball hit the net as I had expected the guy beside me to start losing it but, instead, I felt a tight squeeze on my arm which had apparently been his attempt at an outlet to greet the joy of seeing his team go a goal up. Whatever joy he'd experienced I hoped he'd made the most out it because - from the centre - Motherwell went right up the pitch, won a corner and big John Sutton took it from there with a glancing header that soared into the net, over the Hibs defender on the line who had seemed to attempt to stop it with his hand only to think better of it and let it go past him.

After those two goals, things began to quieten down on the pitch, with not much in the way of goalmouth action. This, in turn, led to me and the Hibs fan starting to have a blether. With the drink that he'd put away - pre match - he was proper chatty as fuck, one of those cunts that end up telling you their life story, if you let them. He was sound enough, though. Quite funny at times and was decent craic as far as who you'd find yourself next to at the fitba because some other weeks you can be beside a complete fucking weapon which makes it a long ninety minutes. I say that with enough self awareness that *I* a lot of the times may well have been the fucking weapon, who made it a long ninety minutes, for *others*.

His name was Joe and he'd told me that he was from the Muirhouse part of Edinburgh. Muirhouse was never a place that we in the Utility got to sample, due to it being off the beaten track as far as Easter Road or Tynecastle, but its reputation had always went before it. After calling him Joe - at one point in the first half - he'd amended this by telling me that everyone who knew him just called him Strings. The irony that I'd been scanning the Hibs crowd for Mikey Swanson and coming up with fuck all while Strings was telling me to look at the boy in the white baseball cap and green puffs jacket, right on the aisle. Him explaining to me that this was his mate Benji who he'd travelled through from Edinburgh with. Benji having assured Strings that they'd get an away end ticket for him, when they hit the boozers in Motherwell.

'Clearly that went without a hitch, eh?'

I laughed over him telling me this story, while standing in the *home* end.

By the time we reached the break, I'd already settled that - unless there was anything that came my way on the journey home - I'd had a good look but it probably wasn't going to be my night. Being honest, the away match had been just a punt, and I'd placed my hopes way more on the home game on the Saturday. When it's a home game it's a lot more easier to predict the movement of fans or mobs of casuals. Away games? A bit of a lottery at times where - once you reach the town or city you're away to - you just have to live from one moment to the next, without any real plan of action. It had been fuck all other than a punt but wasn't to be my night.

While talking further with Strings - by this point into the second half with Motherwell winning two one and Hibs not exactly looking like they were putting on any pressure to get an equaliser - he told me about the interesting line of work he was in. Either he was really drunk, naively trusting, or had actually felt the bond that had kind of formed between the pair of us across the match, but you really wouldn't go boasting to practical strangers that your line of work was illegal, and as likely to get you put in jail as it was the hospital. Had some scam that involved lifting money from puggies. At first I'd actually thought I had been an official job, like.

'So what is it that you do, Strings?'

I'd asked him, having already told him about my gym and how he'd be welcome to pop in if he was ever in Amsterdam.

He'd looked a wee bit sheepish at the question but, regardless, had had no issue in telling me.

'Aye, I empty fruit machines'

'Oh aye, work at the amusement arcade, like?'

'Aye, something like that'

With the laugh that followed I could tell that there was more to it, and it didn't take him long to fill me in. He'd been a proper character, anyway, so I wasn't exactly surprised to find that he wasn't an accountant or surveyor.

Like how cunts can be like, when they've had a good scoop, they can bum themselves up with what they're talking about, Strings was no different. Telling me about how he had his bandit hustle going on, but that he had some links to the Edinburgh underworld as well and how he would do the occasional job, here and there.

'Fucking underworld, aye?'

I says to him, making out I was more impressed on hearing this than I actually was. I'd already assumed that he was talking things up in any case.

'Oh aye, mate. Heavy people. Fucking Barry White heavy, ma man'

'Who we talking, like?'

I asked, figuring that there was fucking zero chance of him not telling me. The conversation was, by then, infinitely more entertaining than the final quarter of the match, by a distance. Motherwell had appeared to have settled on their one goal lead and had decided to try and hold what they had while, on the other hand, Hibs looked to have chucked it for the night.

As "merry" that he'd been over the match, he took a wee look around him at the Motherwell fans that had surrounded us since taking our seats - Something he'd never appeared to feel the need to do for the whole of the match, despite being there in an away fan in the home end capacity - before bringing himself a wee bit closer to me and saying

'Davey McKenna, not sure if you've heard of him or not but, aye, he pretty much runs the city'

Now I only had a few seconds to digest this, and give him my reaction. I mean, there was no way I'd have thought that I'd ever be stood inside Fir Park, talking about the man who had engineered me being put away years before, with a Hibs fan, in the Motherwell end, during a midweek match. And not only that, though. Talking about him, with someone who fucking knew him. Not knew *of* him, fucking *knew* him.

Aye, I could've immediately went on to tell Strings that his gaffer was a fucking snake of a man, who wasn't against feeding tips to his contacts in the police force, when it suited him. Go on to tell him *my* story, having been touched by the indirect hand of McKenna's, and the rest of my life going into free fall as a result. What good would that have done, though? I'm pretty fucking sure that Strings - if he actually *did* work for Davey McKenna - was already well aware what a cunt his boss was, *king* cunt, actually. Telling him that I had a major grudge against McKenna would've done fuck all other than soured things between him and me, and him likely clamming up on the whole subject of who he worked for.

Straight away - from the moment I'd heard the man's name spoken - I sensed an opportunity out of this. They can say whatever the fuck they want about me - and plenty have - but they, you, *any* cunt, can never, ever say that I'm not resourceful and quick on my feet.

'Awwww *Davey?* Fucking hell! Me and the big man go way back. How's he doing, anyway? The fact that he's still alive, in the game he's in, has got to be a good thing. I thought he'd have retired by now, not like he's short of a bob or two, eh?'

As sound as Strings had been, I played him without a moment's hesitation. Professing to be some old pal of McKenna from back in the day - telling Strings that I used to be in the drug game myself - I left him feeling at ease, while talking about someone who enjoyed such a reputation.

'Aye, he's still the same old Davey, just a bit older and nastier, eh?'

'Listen, Strings. I'm going to be in Edinburgh up until Sunday. It would be brilliant to catch up with him before I fly back'

I was interrupted by the Motherwell fans erupting with protests, after seeing the referee pointing to the spot, with only a couple of minutes left to go. This delaying things between Strings and myself, while we watched Stokes blaze the gift horse that his side had been offered right over the bar and into the upper tier of the away fans behind the goal.

Strings just kind of shrugging his shoulders at this while all the fans around us went off their fucking nuts, the penalty miss being almost the equivalent of Motherwell scoring a third goal to finish the visitors off.

I didn't let the conversation stray, though.

Going back to it while the Motherwell goalkeeper took as long as he possibly could to take the goal kick, ending with a yellow card for time wasting before he'd actually managed to scud the ball up the park.

'Aye, would be sound to catch up with the big man. Is he still in that big house in …'

I deliberately left my question hanging at that, mainly because I didn't have the first fucking clue where the man lived. Could've lived in Timbuktu for all I'd known, like.

'Aye, aye. Still in Silverknowes, mate. That big fucking black and white mock Tudor, cannae miss the thing, eh?'

'Aye nice house though, Strings. Can see why he didn't move'

I said, finessing him further.

'Aye, if I can squeeze in time I'll maybe pop up to see him' I said, in a non committal kind of way while, inside, had *more* than fucking committed towards making time.

'Aye well if you don't catch him at his pad he'll probably be down at the scrapyard in Portie'

'Nice one, Strings, pal. I'll keep that in mind'

I told him, the final whistle going a few moments after that.

Two one to Motherwell. I wasn't arsed either way and - despite being the Hibs fan out the two of us - Strings didn't exactly seem us much arsed himself. Then again, when you support a team like Hibernian or Dundee United you're already someone who knows how to take the rough with the smooth.

'Been a pleasure, mucker. Mind, now. If you're ever in the Dam'

I shook hands at the end of the match with him, as the fans around us applauded their boys off the pitch, three points secured.

'Aye, Franky, ma man. Same back, like. Same back. Have a safe trip back along the road, eh?'

He replied back to me, before we both turned to leave the ground. Becoming separated on the way out, and off on our separate ways from there on.

What was it I'd been saying about it not being my night?

So, I'd maybe not found that prick Swanson. I still had from Thursday to Saturday night to do so, and would.

Now though, I'd just been given some credible intel on where I could find the man who ranked third - Margaret Thatcher and Peter Duncan taking the first and second spots, respectively - in my top three most hated people in life, right on a plate for me.

I headed off in the direction of the station, contemplating how I had now - hopefully - doubled my work load and that between now and Sunday morning's flight I was going to be even busier than I'd even anticipated, before taking off from Schipol.

Chapter 15

Detective Constable Roy van der Elst

When Goosens had buzzed through to tell me that he wanted me in his office straight away, I knew it was going to be the entry point into a major pain in the ass. I'd heard that tone once too often to know that there was only ever going to be some kind of clusterfuck, waiting on me attempt to mop up.

'Ah, Roy the boy, come in, sit down. How *is* my favourite Detective Constable?'

Here it comes, I thought but kept to myself, the old routine. The old lube up and fuck routine. I'd always pitied his wife at home because the man had *no* foreplay game what-so-ever.

'Well, apart from receiving hourly updates from the Liege counter terrorist unit on the movements of Abrak El Masry and his cell, trying to locate the Serbian gang - on the run after the Deutschebank job - who pinged facial recognition leaving Leipzig Hauptbahnhof station on route to Nice, finalising the transfer of Rene Makaay back to Amsterdam from Malaga, I thought that if I could find myself a spare few minutes I would shove a broom up my ass and clean the floor too'

I knew that my words were going to be nothing more than a waste of my time and energy but at the same time I felt it important that - before he was to throw something else onto my pile, and most probably something that was going to go right to the top - the boss knew how busy I was. It's how I like it though and it's the *exact* same reason I wanted to work with Interpol. Sometimes though, you can really do with a bit of time to clear your workload, remove a few of those spinning plates from your repertoire and afford yourself something that resembles a breather, before the next challenge falls your way.

Not with Bert Goosens sitting in the main chair, you wont.

'Quiet week, huh?'

He said, as he opened a drawer from his desk and produced a bottle of Scotch and a couple of glasses. I wasn't sure if he was being serious with the comment which - to someone of a much thinner skin - had been another way of saying that I hadn't been busy.

Whether he was or he wasn't, the Scotch told its own story, and I sure as hell didn't want to stick around for the ending.

I'd had a full - and not to mention weary - day of trying to catch the kind of criminals that have the cojones to crime their asses off while moving around the planet, as if normal rules don't apply to them. Ranging from some real evil pieces of shit to characters who *were* characters. As much as I love the job, I was glad that I could go home for the day.

Jara had texted, asking for me to stop off at Double Luck and Happiness to bring home some takeout for us and the kids, (even if I always said that buying Chinese food for kids aged three and five was the equivalent of throwing your money out the window in a storm) later Ajax were playing Real Madrid in the Champions League on TV - how I missed those European nights at the ArenA, since taking Jara and the kids to Lyon, one sacrifice I'd had to make in the pursuit of career progression, I guess - so what wasn't to look forward to Chinese takeout, quality time with the family and a few bottles of Amstel with my feet up, in the study, watching de Godenzonen?

Even if I didn't have any of that good stuff waiting for me walking out the front door of our headquarters that evening, I still wouldn't have wanted to have hung around, drinking Scotch with Goosens. Not when I knew that the "friendly drink" was nothing other than a precursor to me walking out the office, nursing some throbbing balls from the boot that he was in the process of shaping up to deliver.

'Well, about as quiet as the F Side will be tonight when Christian Eriksen bends one of his free kicks into the top corner later tonight,' I answered him.

Goosens - who had made his name coming through the ranks in the Rotterdam serious crimes unit - was a Feyenoord supporter, and I enjoyed the chance to wind him up. Football, probably the only outlet that allows you to tease your boss, without ending up in the dog house over it, then again, that all depends which team your boss supports, or, sometimes, more importantly, what team *you* do.

'Blah blah blah, pipe down, Jew boy. Ronaldo, Kaka and Benzema will tear you a new asshole tonight'

He playfully waved this away from me as he passed the *generously* poured out glass to me before screwing the cap back onto the bottle and putting it back in the drawer.

'You know, Roy? Technology is a great and wondrous thing, isn't it?'

Fuck, did I just want to yell out at him to just cut the shit and tell me *why* him and I were sitting in his office with a glass of Scotch, when I should have already been on the Metro home.

He was a temperamental fucker, though. You had to just make sure you had a bit of patience about you, *if* you wanted to endure the guy.

'Oh, of course, Bert. I find it funny that decades ago there were experts who were telling the world that literally everything that needed to be invented, had now been invented'

'The tools that we're now in possession of that can be utilised against the bad guys? If any of it had been suggested back in the twenties, when the unit was formed, the person suggesting it would've been burned at the stake for being a witch'

He seemed tickled by this thought as he smiled at the thought of it. It was undeniable, though. The difference in how an early days Interpol Detective Constable would've went about their business, up against a modern day one, would've been quite the contrast.

'One of the key things about tech, one of its most important aspects and, in this case, one of its drawbacks. Is the tendency for how fucked up things get, when there's technical difficulties. We become so reliant *on* the technology that when it experiences some issues, it leaves us knee deep in the shit'

'Well, yeah, things like computers - for example - are amazing items, when they're working'

'And that is a very salient point, Roy'

By a pure fluke, what I'd said back to him had inspired some focus as he flicked through a pile of files in front of him, all separated from each other by their own brown folder. Eventually he came to one that made him stop for a second. Looking up at his face, I could see that he had apparently found what he was looking for.

'I received a call an hour ago from from the head of security at Schipol to inform us that they'd suffered from a recent outage on the facial recognition program, that we have set up there in departures and arrivals'

I'd been more than aware of the fact that there was facial recognition at Schipol. We'd caught enough unsuspecting chumps inside the terminal, who had mistakenly assumed that their fake passport would have been enough to move from A to B. It was one of the most important airports in the world to *have* facial recognition. The Amsterdam airport, undeniably one of the worlds most busiest hubs for international travellers with connections of flights, happening all day every day. If there was an issue with their facial recognition - which would ping any match moving through the airport and alert local police in time to arrest the individuals before they even left the airport - then I'd have wagered my entire years salary that, if the outage had been for a fair amount of time, at least some one would have managed to escape the net and either boarded their flight out of the Netherlands or had been left to leave the airport and out into the city Amsterdam.

And I guess *this* was now why I was sitting being told about it, because, somehow, through someone fucking up in their job, it was now going to impact on *my* job.

'They only realised that it *was* down when they received three alerts, all at once. Three alerts in a day, at Schipol? Yeah, easy enough scenario. Not three unconnected alerts at once, though. Henk - Kerkoff - launched an investigation instantly and, through this, found out that there had been an outage with the system and that, while the cameras were rolling, even identifying any offenders as they remained in operation, they did not flag *up* the travellers at the same time of picking them up on screen'

'And this delay in pinging the targets ... allowed them to'

'BINGO, Roy'

Goosens knocked back his drink while - by comparison - I'd barely touched mines. I didn't like Scotch for one thing and would've much rather preferred a bottle of Coca Cola but when Bert offered you a Scotch, you would be best served to take it and if you refused him the first time, there would not be a guarantee of a second.

'So anyway, skipping to the end. Some dangerous and sought after criminals managed to slip the net - due to the outage - and fly out of Amsterdam. A real messy business, especially with one of them being a known Hamas financier. Political stuff, you know how it is'

Oh for fuck's sake. This was the last thing I wanted, or needed. A case that was going to involve some asshole politician sticking his nose into things and expecting some form of special treatment. Terrorists - and sympathisers - being able to move between cities on public transport wasn't a good look though. Look how that shit worked out for the Americans, eh?

He could've easily spotted the apprehension on my face over what was next due to pass his lips, because I certainly was not trying to hide it from him. Taking a sip of the drink while trying to mask my extreme distaste for the stuff, sitting on the edge of the chair, leaning towards him.

'But like I said, like I *always* say, Roy. You're my favourite Detective that I have at my disposal. I wouldn't have *dreamed* of handing you a case with an asshole politician from Brussels, with an inflated sense of who they actually are, making life more difficult for you than Hamas'

Well that was a major relief to hear. I'd always said that politicians were the *real* crooks and made the people that I chased after - and caught - seem like kindergarten level.

Give Goosens - and his slight of hand trick - credit, though.

I was still focussing on the fact that I'd been spared a pain in the ass case trying to locate a terrorist collaborator who - if he'd been trained to the usual Hamas standards - would've went to ground the moment his plane had touched the tarmac at the other end of his flight, when Goosens told me which part he needed me to play in this whole clean up mission to lock up stable doors while the horse hadn't just run away but boarded an international jet and left the country completely.

'No, Roy. I wouldn't do that to you. I gave that to Ralf Simonsen. Poor fucker is currently on route to Saint Exupery for the first flight out to Istanbul'

'Rather him than me'

I said, truthfully.

'Yes, you're going to Scotland instead'

He slid the folder over the table at me. The brown folder that he'd taken from out of the pile earlier.

Scotland?

What the hell did I know about Scotland? Off the top of my head. Golf, kilts, The Proclaimers, bagpipes, an international football side that hardly ever won. None of this helpful - I assumed - in the pursuit of locking up bad guys.

'Norman Fulton'

Goosens said as I flipped the thin folder open and was alerted to the picture - held onto the page with a paper clip - in the top right hand corner of the man, snapped by the Schipol cameras, going through security. He looked almost like a biker with that long beard and black woollen hat pulled down tight over his head.

'Known for extreme violence and narcotics dealing, and a person with links to the South American drug trade. Someone who has been on the run for approximately ten years, following his escape from prison. He'd dropped off the radar to the point that as far as we were concerned he was either dead or lying in a Peru jail by now. His case file hasn't even had any updates made to it in over five years. According to our records the man's been a ghost since his prison escape with Montoya from the Arizmendi Cartel. Today, though he came back *on* our radar'

Goosens took me through things. Fulton - a Scottish national - had boarded a flight to the capital, Edinburgh and apparently had headed home. He'd arranged for me to link up with one of the local detectives over there, with the intention of making sure that the hunt for the fugitive was taken seriously - Interpol making an appearance generally insured this to be the case - and that he be rounded up, *especially* in his native country which, on the paperwork or *lack* of, would have been worth the trip alone.

My ticket on the seven am Lyon to Edinburgh - via CDG - flight would be available for collection at the Air France desk, I was informed.

I ended up leaving the boss's office around ninety minutes later than anticipated, already having accumulated a series of missed calls and texts from Jara, over the fact that her and the kids were now sitting there starving. And that was *before* I even told her about me going away for a while.

The cry from Goosens ringing behind me. Bellowing out instructions that - with such an early flight on the cards for me - I would be needing to get home, pack and get myself an early night and make sure I was fresh for travelling, telling me that he expected me to hit the ground running when I reached Scotland.

'Oh Roy, Roy. One last thing before you leave'

He called me back, just as I was about to press the button to call the lift.

'Yeah, Bert?'

I shouted across the - now - empty floor.

'I hope you get fucking annihilated tonight by the Spaniards'

He chuckled, heartedly, while giving me two middle fingers that - with us both being Dutch - I knew were not just for show.

When Cristiano Ronaldo made it four nil to Real - there in the Amsterdam ArenA - the image of a gleeful Goosens with that big smile waving those middle fingers around was unavoidable to prevent from popping into my head, thinking of him sitting at home celebrating each of the Real goals as if he was a Madrista, born and bred.

I switched the TV off at that point. The combination of the scoreline, the thoughts of Goosens and the image of a pouting Ronaldo telling all the Ajax fans to sit themselves down, all too much for me.

I quickly made sure that I had everything I needed for the next morning - all ready for grabbing in the inevitable hurry that I was no doubt going to be in the next morning - and joined an already sleeping Jara in bed and set about joining her in that same state with the real facts of the matter being that *whenever* I got off to sleep I was going to be sitting in an Air France business class seat inside eight hours time, on my way to Ecosse.

Chapter 16

Nora

You ken? You really don't realise that you've missed the touch of a woman until you've got one shoving her big arse, right into you. Grinding and rubbing against you until you're ready to blow in your fucking trousers right there, *exactly* like some cunt who haven't had their Nat King in too many years to mention.

'Would you like to go on for longer, baby?'

The tidy Eastern European girl named Saskia - that I'd barely paid any notice to due to never being sure if it's a real name or not, when it comes to sex workers - bent over to give me a good look at her while taking one of her garters and pulling it away from her leg to indicate that she wanted me to top things up before she continued.

'Listen, hen. Give me another fucking one of *those* and you'll have to be offering some in house dry cleaning services to me afterwards, eh?'

She didn't really get what I was saying, which was probably just as well as it couldn't have been something that would've touched her day, not that I was really giving a fuck, like. Over her shift she was surely going to face far worse than a wee snide remark about how close she was to making me shoot ma fucking load.

My body language must've been enough though because she went straight from smoking hot - and someone who had been as near the knuckle as it came to stopping just short of taking your cock out and riding the fuck out of you - to cold as Aberdeen on a midweek match, with a 'be off with you' vibe to things.

Ken what I did as well, just to piss her off, like? Walked straight back *out* into The Western Bar - with her following behind - and walked up to the very first lap dancer - that wasn't Saskia - and gently grabbed their arm - in what was more domineering than rapey - and as loud as I could, started talking about how much would she do *two* dances for me. Her - this dark brown girl in thigh high leather boots and a one piece black fishnet body suit in the same colour as the boots - gleefully snapping up the chance.

I made sure to look for that Saskia as I was being led away by the girl with the African - Nigerian my first thought - accent. Gave her a wee blown kiss across the room, she returned this with the wanker sign.

Fucking *did* cum as well. Fucking telegraphed, like. Something that - following that first dance - it would not have taken that old Nostradamus cunt to have predicted. You could've rubbed a fucking mop against me for a few seconds and it would've done the trick, so it wasn't exactly a challenge for the curvy African to pull off, bouncing that big arse up and down on my groin, then holding it there on top of me as she moved it back and forward while pressing her hands down on my legs for balance.

Couldn't go back on my word, especially with how public I'd made things, but you can imagine just how disinterested I was in that second dance from - who I was to learn was called Adure - her. I almost just told her to take the money and me just skip the second one but thought I'd just plow on with things and at least get my money's worth, but it was more the case of buying two kebabs and really enjoying the first one but being so full up by it that you've got fucking ride all chance of wanting the second one.

Then again, when I left my mum and dad's house that morning - for Edinburgh - I wasn't intending on having one lap dance, never mind fucking *three*. You know how it is though, eh? How easy it is to get into the spirit of games and how - as a result - you can get carried away with things.

I'd woken up to further intel on Swanson, once again from Wattie. I'd never dabbled myself but apparently a lot of the old casuals who had made a habit of smashing fuck out of each other every Saturday now chatted on Facebook and, from what I'd been told, were all very civil about it all, now that they were grown up. Well, it was definitely helping me, when it came to the case I was building.

Cunts will still carry vendettas though. It's easy to throw up the white flags, down weapons and get the fitba out and have a kick about, when you've not got a personal grudge to bear. Get yourself one of those though and fuck knows how long you'll carry it around with you, if you don't get the chance to address things along the way.

Through this CSF boy, Hammond, - who had passed on the intel to Dundee - Watson had been able to tell me that the last known occupation of Swanny had been as security at one of the bars situated inside the Pubic Triangle in Edinburgh, which had sounded a promising lead as I boarded the train at Dundee with a one way ticket to the capital.

The plan being - with the family stuff all taken care of - not to return back home before I took care of business and then got myself the fuck out of the country again, karma delivered and balance of the universe fully restored.

Fucking train was almost empty but even then I managed to find myself sharing a carriage with four cunts on their way to some comic festival or something which they'd been excitedly yapping about, whose autographs they were going to be getting when they got there, the speculation over what kind of merchandise there might be available to pick up, that kind of stuff. All four of them in fancy dress as characters from Star Wars. Complete nerds, like, you know? Had never been that into Star Wars when I was younger. That fucking C-3PO just rubbed me up the wrong way anytime I seen the cunt. Each to their own, like. Have a gay robot in your science fiction film all you want but they don't have to be *that* fucking camp though?

A couple of these fannies were both dressed as Luke Skywalker - which seemed daft as fuck that they'd go somewhere dressed as the same character, as I'm sure that contravenes all kinds of fancy dress by laws - complete with pishy plastic light sabers, the lot. Thought they'd take advantage of their excited states - and the empty train - by re-enacting some fight from one of the films. Firing lines back and forward at each other, while making the sounds to a light saber when swinging it at each other.

Adults, here, mind.

Were well into it, like. Probably would've been quite impressive to the eye of someone who was into that kind of stuff, just not me.

As we were approaching Kirkcaldy I'd had enough of the cunts by this point, and had got them told. Said that the pair of them should grow up and maybe get their hole, with the added piece of advice that they wouldn't be getting a fucking ride anytime soon if they were carrying light sabers about with them, free of charge. Ever see Luke Skywalker, Yoda or Obi wan Kenobi getting their Nat King? I rest my case.

The two of them looked a bit wounded by my criticism - some fucking Jedis, eh? - while sitting their arses back down as their two mates. One, Han Solo - I think - and the other, I didn't have the first fucking clue who he was meant to be, some commander or something. Those two were making sure that they looked in any direction of the carriage other than mines.

When one of the two Jedi Knights lifted up his light saber to collapse it back in on itself - in the tiered way that it was designed - I says to the cunt

'Oh, where's the noise it makes when Luke Skywalker switches it back off again?' Thinking that him - or his mate - would've recreated the noise for me but I reckon my previous tone of how I'd spoken to them had them all on edge.

The train journey - apart from the virgins - on the route from Dundee through Fife and into Edinburgh was a right good trip down memory lane as I sat there looking out at that familiar coastal scenery that had often been the backdrop to a Saturday morning train journey, filled with Dundee Utility, off for a day of mischief in the capital or - if connecting at Waverley - even further afield.

While looking out the window - as we passed through Burntisland and Kinghorn - at the golden sand with the shore so far out it looked like you could almost walk halfway across to Edinburgh, I closed my eyes for a second and was instantly taken back to those days of the mid eighties.

The Fila and Tachini. Forest Hills and Trimm Trabs. The couple of twenty four packs of cans - rarely paid for when acquired at the Dundee end of the journey - sitting around the floor of the carriage, with the whole team getting fired into them. The excited chat mixed with anticipation over what our day ahead was going to entail. The banter, piss takes - but always never less than - and camaraderie. Fuck, those days? When I stopped to think about them, as deeply as in that moment, I couldn't deny how much I missed them, still.

Breaking the illusion, though. Going from those thoughts, I opened my eyes again and - instead of seeing a bunch of Saturday's kids, in tennis gear firing into cans. I had Han fucking Solo, sipping a tin of Tango.

Really couldn't be dealing with a bunch of VLs like that to have to even be acknowledging on the journey. Had way too much other things to be focussing on.

I have to be honest, leaving Dundee had been a wee bit emotional for me. Don't think I was buying a pack of fucking Kleenex for myself from WH Smith at the station or fuck all like but, I don't know? It had been so long since I'd seen the place. Can't be many who go a couple of decades without "going home" but that was the reality that had been forced on me. Getting a chance to return, though. Even for the short amount of time that it had been for. It had given me a wee chance to reflect on things, family and that. I'd gone so long *without* really having a family, I'd almost forgotten what it had felt like to be *part* of one.

Seeing how old mum and dad had got. They say that there's a time when you're older where, over a few years, things change and you *really* start to show your age, and they'd both looked like they'd reached that point, years ago. I didn't want to be on a downer or fuck all - especially with the business I had planned when I reached Edinburgh - but when I gave the two of them a big cuddle and kiss - before going for the bus down to the station - I couldn't shake the feeling that it was most likely the last time that I'd ever be in the same room as the two of them. It was a depressing thought. To counter that, though. There was Liam. It's fair to say, the way that we met wasn't exactly *conventional* but, with me being the father and him coming from the same genes, it was as "on brand" as you could have possibly got. I know that a lot of shite is spoken when cunts are firing into the pints and shoving Patsies up their hooters but - as I began thinking about him - I hoped that he was going to take me up on my offer and come over to the Dam to visit, and give us the chance to get to know each other a bit more. He seemed a good kid, clearly loved his mum and I was quite proud of him to see such qualities. You can't kid a fucking kidder either so I could see from a mile away that he wasn't any angel either, but he definitely wasn't going to be finding any judgement passed from me on that, *especially* when I probably played a part in some way or other.

We'd never really quite covered *how* he made a living either, but due to the uncomfortable position - I was in - of being an absent father for the first twenty years of the boy's life, and someone that he could well have read about on the internet for being a dangerous criminal with links to the drugs trade and is only sitting having a drink in a Dundee boozer with him due to entering Scotland on a fake passport as a result of escaping prison and had never been caught, I was in no position to press him on it, on *anything*. If we got a chance to know each other a bit further, and Liam letting his guard down a bit, though, all of that intel would flow eventually.

It was around half one when I was stepping off the train at Waverley. Couldn't help but notice the wee differences to it from the last time I'd been down there. Obviously, it had received a lick of paint and a few upgrades here and there but what stuck out was the fucking armed police walking around and how no cars could drive down to the wee turn circle, and drop cunts off for their trains. All concreted to fuck to stop anything getting in or out.

Waste of fucking money if you ask me. Those scummy Al Qaeda bastards only ever tried it with the Scots the once before, and it didn't exactly go too well for them, so they never tried again. Fucking mad cunts even trying it in the first place. Obviously didn't do their homework, otherwise they'd have already known that there would be too many random mad cunts that could've been in the wrong place at the wrong time to fuck their plans up. They're trying to fucking bomb our airport while some cunt, who's having a wee skive at his job and a fly smoke, is karate kicking them through the air, when they're on fire. Can't blame them for not coming back for a second attempt, like.

With it being decades since I'd walked through the station I ended up walking in the complete opposite direction as where I'd intended, and only realised when I reached the top of the stairs to take you onto Princes Street. I stopped and threw a couple of quid into the beggar's - who was sitting at the top of the steps with his greyhound - woolly hat that he had on the ground in front of him. Fucking gratitude that he showed me - on account of my donation - while I stood for a minute and clapped his dug while asking what its name was, the look on his face. Considering it was only a couple of quid, it made you want to fucking weep.

Dug was called Gonzalez. Beautiful creature and was loving the attention.

'Fucking bet he's speedy, like, eh. Should get it to Musselburgh, you'll fucking clean up, mate'

I says to the boy as I made my way towards the North Bridge to take myself over to the Old Town, while wondering if I'd made an arse of myself as I began to doubt whether it was dugs or nags that ran at Musselburgh, or if it was even Musselburgh that *held* the meets, then remembered that there had also been

Powderhall races, before putting it all to the side. Fuck it, would've probably beaten a horse anyway if the boy took the dug to a meet and - on account of me and my fucking nonsense that comes out of my mouth at times - found out that he had the wrong animal with him.

I'd put it down to this whole me appreciating things about Scotland because I'd never been there in so long, but Edinburgh? It almost felt like I was looking at it through a completely different set of eyes from any time that I'd ever seen it before.

In my defence, despite being from Scotland and Edinburgh hardly resembling the end of the earth from my home city of Dundee, I'd never really seen too much of it. Hundred fucking percent there would have been American tourists who had only visited the place for a couple of days who would have left again, having seen and learned more about the capital city than I had in all the times I'd ever visited, and there had been many of those occasions.

You don't really get to do the tourist thing - visiting Edinburgh - when you're stepping off the train, alongside another hundred boys where you're either escorted by coppers through the city or are scrapping your way until you get to the stadium for the match. These occasions are not exactly conducive to squeezing in a walk down the Royal Mile or a tour of the underground tunnels to the city.

Living in Amsterdam - and making it my home - I'd found a bit of an appreciation for how unique and beautiful the city was, the architecture and that. Edinburgh was the same, though. Hadn't thought of it that way before but by just how old the city looked, I could see why all the tourists raved about the place. Apart from going to games, I stayed away from the city. For a major city, I'd never felt its clothes shops had been that outstanding, or worth travelling through for so, that wasn't normally a consideration, and neither was nights out, *definitely* nights out.

You never fucking knew who you'd bump into in a club and if it just so happened to be on enemy turf, chances are you're probably going to end up outnumbered. Like what happened to a couple of Utility boys who went through to The Venue in Edinburgh for the Stone Roses gig in Eight Nine and found themselves surrounded by a dozen Hibs for the night, and the subsequent carry on that took place *after* the gig, leading to Westy and Daz heading to Edinburgh Western General for the night, instead of Waverley train station for their train back home to Dundee.

Walking around Edinburgh - in such a casual and stress free way - I'd found almost liberating, of sorts. The thoughts of the sick acts that I was going to commit on Swanny - and in such an imminently short space of time - barely entered my mind as I crossed the busy North Bridge in the direction of the *Pubic triangle,* named - unofficially - on account of all the city's lap dancing bars being in close proximity of each other. Didn't take Floella Benjamin to fucking tell you that it wasn't the shape of a triangle either, but I'm probably splitting hairs with that, like.

The intel Hammond had provided me with was as vague as Swanson working the door at one of the lap dance joints. It wasn't exactly going to be a hardship - even if I'd had to check all of them - walking the metres from one to another. Thank fuck it wasn't Amsterdam with such vagueness, though, I thought to myself. You'd have needed a fucking *week* to go through all the establishments, checking who was on each door, and probably end up swedging with some roided up bouncer way before you even found the right place you were even looking for.

As I arrived at the first out of them - The Burke and Hare - all I found was some boy outside in an old Hearts Inter Milan style away top, loading beer kegs out the back of his lorry to take through a side door and into the cellar, the actual bar itself in darkness, of course it was, it wasn't even fucking two o clock in the afternoon.

If I'd actually stopped and took a thought to myself, I'd have already fucking clocked that places like that weren't going to be open for business and if they were it would've been low key, with no need for door staff.

Stopped and had a few words with the boy, completely disregarding the fact that he didn't actually fucking work for the Burke and Hare.

Asking him what time the place opened while following that up with if he knew any of the door staff that worked the front or inside. The boy - who looked a wee bit irritated that I was getting in his way - holding his hands up as if I was sticking a gun in his face, telling me that he just worked for the brewery and delivered the swally, while taking away the empty kegs with him.

'Aye, nae worries, mate, eh? I'll let you get on with things, cheers anyway' I says to him as he jumped into the back again to produce another keg.

I walked the few steps across the road to *Baby Dolls* but didn't even get as far as I had with the Burke and Hare. The place empty with lights off and doors firmly closed.

The Western Bar - and the final lap dancing bar - I could find - to complete the non triangle - *wasn't* closed. There wasn't anyone on the door either, or girls for that matter. It was simply your average pub setting, the girls putting in an appearance at a much more appropriate time of day, no doubt.

To try and get a wee feel for things, I got myself a pint and tried to see what kind of intel I could squeeze out of the staff, but got nowhere. Two women behind the bar, one Aussie and the other, a Pole, who I'd sat and had a wee laugh with in the otherwise empty bar, got them a drink for themselves as well, so I wasn't drinking by myself. When I'd asked them about who was on the door for security - and specifically Swanson, and if they knew him - they seemed to clam up while shaking their heads to confirm that they didn't know him.

Obviously, a man of the world like myself, I know how dodgy it might look, when a stranger appears asking about security that runs the place. A lot of money to be made in the door business, if you get the contracts across a city centre so it could well have looked shady to them and - for all I knew - they'd maybe already suffered from that side to the underworld. Maybe it was just my paranoia or even just a case of my bullshit detector going off but when they told me that they didn't know who Swanny was, there was something in the way that the Australian girl said it, that made me think otherwise.

I wasn't going to push things, though and, instead, finished my drink and wished the pair of them a good day, with plans already decided that I would go for a few drinks around the city, get a bit of scran somewhere and return back down to The Triangle once the sun had went down and the place started to come alive.

My gut instincts proved bang on the money - when I returned to The Western Bar - about Swanny and the place, even if it wasn't exactly what I'd wanted to hear. Approaching the front door I was greeted with a biggest and warmest of smiles from the gorilla on the door. The boy had never seen me before in my life but from the welcome he gave me, you wouldn't have known it.

Because of this, I took a chance.

'Alright, pal. How you doing?'

I asked as - instead of just walking on past him - I stopped and took my cigarettes out, offering him one while I was at it. You just don't a better fucking icebreaker than a fag, like. The great leveller in life. Something that - as unlikely as may be - a top level European fitba manager and a housing scheme junkie could bond over having. He took one from me, thanked me before getting his lighter out and doing the honours for us both.

'Swanny on tonight?'

I asked, taking a complete punt.

He blew out the reek from the cigarette almost like he was in a hurry to do so because he wanted to laugh at what I'd just said and, obviously, you can't perform both tasks at once without leaving yourself a coughing and spluttering mess.

'Fucking Swanson? Where you been? On the inside or something?'

He laughed back at me.

'Aww, has he moved on from here now?' I asked, already knowing as much from his response but now hoping to see what I could find.

'Aye well, moved on is *one* way of putting it, I suppose'

He said sarcastically while taking another big draw on the Lambert and B, before going on to explaining to me that aye, Swanny *had* been part of the security that worked at The Western Bar. That, though was until he got one of the fucking lap dancers pregnant - seemingly the biggest money earner and one of the pulls that The Western Bar could boast - which put her out of action.

'Dirty bastard got his jotters after that. Cunt went through the fourth wall. We're here *precisely* to make sure that no one lays a hand on any of the girls, not get them up the fucking duff. The boy was lucky he had his casuals connections or he'd have ended up with a lot worse than just his fucking P forty five'

'Daft bastard, that's Swanny for you, eh? Never did have much up top,' I said to the boy, hoping that I might've been pulling off the act of an old mate of Swanson's to a standard that might still pull some prime intel out of the bouncer.

'Aye, I'm over from Amsterdam, where I live, for a few days and thought I'd look him up while I'm here. Haven't seen the radge for years but last I'd heard, he was on the security here. You any idea if he got work anywhere else or where he's known to hang about? Not the end of the world if I don't see him to be honest but I thought, you know? Since I'm here, like'

I cast the rod to see if it might get me anything.

He pulled that face - with additional noises - that you normally get hit with from a tradesman when asking them for the price of some work before offering a few tips.

'Couldn't tell you if or where he got himself other work. If he was on the doors in the city centre I'd probably already have been told as it's a wee community we've got but you could always try the Calton Boxing gym. He must've went there three, four times a week, while he worked the security here. Was fucking militant about going, one of *those* gym cunts, eh. Haven't seen him since he got his jotters from here, personally, though'

'Another place that would be worth checking would be the *Tanfastic* tanning salon on Lothian Road. The boy went religiously every week. Made Jimmy Calderwood look like a bottle of milk half the time, Swanny. Like I said, haven't seen him since he got his cards from here, but I'd be astonished if he had fucked off that sun tan carry on'

'Nice one, pal. I'll maybe try there for him'

I thanked him before completely forgetting about the fact that I now no longer needed to walk *into* The Western Bar, and walked past him to find a completely different vibe to the deserted pub that it was earlier that day.

And it would take two pints, four Morgans and Coke, three lap dances and one premature ejaculation before I was able to leave the place again.

Chapter 17

Detective Constable Roy van der Elst

'Detective Constable, Roy van der Elst - Detective Constable, Colin Samuel'

The top brass Detective Chief superintendent introduced me to *what* was going to be my so called Scottish compatriot although, and without sucking my own dick or believing my own hype, there *is* a major drop off point between a Detective Constable for Interpol, and one of the same title inside Edinburgh an Criminal Investigation Department.

That the top brass had been there to welcome me and virtually stop short of rolling out the red carpet - for their visitor from Lyon - had said it all.

'Pleased to meet you, Roy. You some super cop then, here to show us reprobates how it's done aye?' He said straight off the bat. The use of the word 'aye,' something that I soon found I'd have to get myself used to.

Even through the rough accent, I could still see through it enough to detect the sarcasm and that whole taking umbrage at some "foreigner" coming over to tell them how to do their job. I'd faced such insecurities before during my work, so that in itself was not something that was going to faze me, whichever the country I found myself in.

'Likewise, Colin'

I said reaching out to shake his hand before telling him that no, I was not there in *his* territory to tell him - or anyone else who was watching on and taking in the arrival of this apparent rock and roll European detective - how they were all to do their job and was, in fact, only there because of some computer error.

'Only here to help catch the bad guys'

I attempted a weak as fuck joke to try and break the ice with him but, evidently, he was going to be a tougher nut to crack. Him choosing to ignore what I'd said by looking past me - and straight at his boss, Detective Chief Superintendent Steve Irvine, - and with a bit of a sneer behind it arrogantly said

'The fucking results that I get for this department, and *this* is how I'm treated?'

Pointing at me right as he delivered the word, *this*.

'Huckled with some clog wearer who couldn't find Princes Street, with a Tom Tom strapped to him'

I was more surprised to see a Detective Constable speak to his superior in such a way rather than be offended in the way that I was being spoken about although, on first impressions, it was looking like it was going to be a super fun time of things, once the two of us were left on our own.

I'd already been handed some vague warnings about Samuel (and his general conduct) that made a lot more sense when I met him, as opposed to before he appeared into the office - late - that Thursday morning.

Irvine had arranged for me to be picked up at Edinburgh Airport by a couple of his uniformed officers, the two of them standing by international arrivals and - being semi competent officers - they managed to find their man, without the need for any of those chauffeur style name cards. It had been a nice touch because it was only when I was walking through the airport tunnel - having officially arrived in the U.K - that it had dawned on me that I'd neglected to think of *how* I was going to get myself to the Edinburgh Headquarters, which was apparently square in the centre of the city.

Figuring I would just hop in a taxi outside the airport and put it on expenses, I was in the process of actually walking past both the officers when one of them called me back

'Excuse me, Detective Constable van der Elst?'

He said, a little hesitantly, as if he wasn't a fully behind the words he'd just said. It felt novel as usually it was *me* who was on the look out for someone else, walking through international arrivals at an airport.

The pair of them led me out to a black Mercedes people carrier with blacked out windows, sat directly outside the entrance to the airport. As I walked out of the terminal I couldn't help but notice the massive *Welcome to Scotland* that was sat above a giant picture of one of the city's landmarks, some kind of castle lit up in the night.

I didn't know it at the time, but it was the best welcome that I would receive in the country.

I'd attempted to sit and speak to the two officers - on route to the headquarters - but within minutes of sitting down in the car my cell - now having connected to the now British network - had gone, an update on the Islamic terrorist financier who we had been tracking, which I was just coming off again, as we drove into the car park at the rear of the building. Technically they shouldn't have had access to me taking the call but I'd taken a calculated guess that there couldn't have been too many

Scottish citizens, with the ability to speak French, so carried on with it.

From there I was led up to C.I.D where Steve Irvine was already waiting on me, my would be partner for the duration of my trip, however, was not.

I hadn't sailed down the Amstel yesterday though and could already tell - from the Detective Chief Superintendent's choice of words, when talking about Samuel - that there had been an element of buttering me up and preparing me, *before* meeting him.

Irvine had told me that his Detective Constable was a force of nature at times, a law unto himself and someone who, for the most part, was unmanageable, but got results and had a track record of some big arrests while removing some serious figures from the streets of Edinburgh. The way it had been put across it was almost a parody. Tough, abrasive uncompromising cop who plays by his own rules. I'd seen it all before. Had originally assumed that it had been a characteristic feature of the Dutch psyche, having brushed shoulders with the same types of cops, when I was coming up the ranks with the Amsterdam Police Department. It's been said that a Dutchman could cause an argument in an empty house, something that I'd always found funny because it was near to true. So you can only imagine the *personalities,* in an average Netherlands police department?

Samuel's start time for the day had come and gone, with no sign of him. Irvine looked embarrassed while I - always aware of first impressions - tried to suppress my annoyance that I'd got out of bed at four in the morning so that I could be sitting in that office while someone who could only have lived a number of miles away from his office, could not.

I'm not quite sure why but in my mind, I'd imagined some young hot-shot self confident, suave, arrogant, designer label wearing and completely up his own arsehole Detective to swagger unapologetically into the office, once he arrived.

I was way, way off as I was presented with a lesson on not judging a book by its cover.

'Oh here he is now'

Irvine said, almost with relief, drawing my eyes towards the funny looking unkempt tubby little guy, who had just walked into the large open scale office where someone had stopped to talk to him before turning and pointing in the direction of Irvine's office, where we both sat waiting on him.

Walking up in our direction - already seeing me and his boss through the large panes of glass to Irvine's office - he knocked on the door, more for effect than to give anyone a warning that he was entering, and walked in.

'Look at the bloody state of you, Colin?'

Irvine greeted him by pointing at the front of his shirt - whose buttons were doing some extremely heavy lifting, in their attempts at keeping in the stomach that was trying to bust its way out of the shirt - which had some kind of barbecue sauce splattered down the front of it.

'Fucking McDonald's, eh? Told the daft cunts I wanted a wee bit more broon sauce than they normally stick on the bacon rolls, but you ken what half of them are like in there? Taking direction not exactly their forte. Fucking bites into my roll and, well ...'

He - while not really needing to, we could see fine enough - opened his suit jacket further open to highlight the sauce stains on his white shirt.

With that, Irvine took us through the whole awkward introduction which gave Samuel the chance to mouth off about how much of a personal insult he was taking - for the whole of the Criminal Investigation Department as much as himself - that his bosses felt that he needed outside assistance to catch someone, instead of allowing him to just get on with the job.

'You ken, you only needed to tell me who I was to find, and I'd have went and done it. No need for him to fly over here. No wonder the planet's fucked, carbon footprints and all of that shite, when you've got cunts flying from pillar to post when they don't fucking have to'

'Now wait a minute'

I stood up. I'd sat and tolerated all of what he'd said, and how he'd said it. At times talking like I wasn't in the room, while the other times, like I wasn't in the room!

'I did not fly over here from Lyon to have *him* call me a cunt'

This, to my great surprise, something that both of them found amusing.

'Roy, Roy, sit back down, please. Colin, here, wasn't calling *you* a cunt. It's a Scottish turn of phrase, figure of speech, if you will. And don't get me wrong. While you're here on your visit, depending on who you encounter, you very well may *be* called one by someone but even then, it isn't guaranteed that they will call you one for a negative reason. It's a complex country. I think we have something like twelve different uses for the word'

'I'd say fourteen, you senile cunt'

Colin Samuel interjected, with the two of them bursting out in laughter at this.

What the fuck was going on here? I thought to myself. Had I found myself in some alternate dimension?

We quickly got down to briefing Samuel over *why* he was being asked to team up with me, once he'd aired his whole general grievances for *having to*.

With Fulton being from Dundee, and having been arrested in Nineteen Ninety in Glasgow, Samuel admitted to having never had any brushes with the man but, like most in Scotland, knew *of* him. With how high profile a case it looked, his resistance to everything connected to me appeared to start to thaw a little.

My feeling had been that we had wasted enough time waiting on Samuel arriving, and then the briefing time to bring the Edinburgh Detective up to speed, and it was now time to go out and see what we could dig up.

With how messy - and unprofessional - Samuel looked, I could not have blamed him for wanting to change his shirt, once we left the headquarters and off on our search for Fulton. Colin driving us the five or six miles out of the city centre to his flat, where he left me in the car with the engine still running while he quickly - as quick as someone as rotund as Samuel anyway - ran up to his flat to change into something fresh.

I could, however blame Samuel for then taking us to what he called a "greasy spoon" for breakfast, where we could, as he put it, strategise for the day.

I had no interest in food. I'd had breakfast on the plane and an extra large coffee from the airport on arrival.

'Hang on a second, wasn't the whole point of us going to get you a change of shirt was due to you messing it up while *having* breakfast?' I asked, as we took a seat at a small table in the cafe that had so much wooden panelling on it it would've been an absolute tinderbox. Sat there with two other tables filled with workers in bright yellow vis vests and hard hats, the only other customers inside.

'Aye, those bacon rolls from Macky D's were really more of a *pre* breakfast snack, Franky'

He winked while - for around the sixth time since learning my surname - referring to me as Franky, on account of the Belgian soccer player.

'Two fulls, Janie'

He shouted over to the old woman behind the counter, who took out her small notebook and wrote down his command.

'Couple of teas as well, doll'

'Coming right up, Colin'

I'd barely really acknowledged *what* he had ordered until I was faced with the reality of it sitting there on the table in front of me.

'You know, Colin, I really wasn't that hungry as I'd already had …'

I tried to apologise for the fact that I had no inclination to eat what was in front of me, some of it I literally had no point of reference for what it even was.

'Nonsense, get it down you' He barked, while already - knife and fork in hand - started to get torn into it. Cutting a piece of bacon, sausage, egg and forcing them all onto the fork, dipping into that same coloured sauce - that looked like had ruined his first shirt of the morning - before shoving it all into his mouth.

'That's the problem with all you European cunts and your continental breakfasts and that, you don't know what a fucking proper breakfast even *is*'

He said to me without having fully cleared his mouth off all of the food that was in it and before I'd even - reluctantly - picked up my cutlery.

The meal was an education in itself as he told me what *that circular black piece of meat* was - Black Pudding - and how it included pigs blood in it. You can't say that I'm not adventurous because, well, I tried it, and found it to have a weird metallic taste to it. *Tattie Scones*, now them I liked but when it came to Haggis - after the way that Samuel had explained to me what it was - I would have fought you in the street rather than put a single piece of it in my mouth. I barely touched the breakfast, save for trying the corner of most of the items that were on the plate. Rather than be annoyed at this, Samuel seized the opportunity, scooping up what I'd left, onto his own plate left for himself.

With the way that the man put away food, close proximity car rides were going to be a joy, I thought sarcastically to myself as I watched him tear into what was as good as breakfast number for him, or three if you wanted to look past his alternative view about the 'non' breakfast he'd had on the way to work that morning.

'So why do you think he's come back to Scotland, after all of this time following his escape from prison?'

I asked him, now that he had been fully briefed on things.

With a mouth full of food that even he wasn't prepared to try to speak through, I had to wait a moment for his reply.

'Who's to say that this is his first time? For all I know you doss cunts have been letting him come and go carte blanch?'

A reply that hadn't even been worth waiting on.

'Which would suggest that the average Scottish detective is so inept that a category A criminal - escaped from a Scottish prison - can walk the streets of Scotland, and no one notice? Doesn't matter *which* country you come from. A wanted criminal like that pops his head up, people talk'

'Touché, ya smart cunt. Check oot fucking Interpol boy, there'

He laughed, after taking a moment to think about having his words thrown back at him. I could already see that with this man, to receive anything in the way of respect of kind ship from him, I was going to have to hit him with his own medicine.

'Well, from his file. The cunt has no links to Edinburgh and I'm guessing that the only reason he even flew into here was because Dundee's pissy wee airport can only handle hand gliders at the best of times, so we're going to be wasting our time conducting any investigation in this part of the country. One thing that stuck out in your file, too, was that Fulton's mum and dad are still alive, they're not exactly young though? I wouldn't discount the possibility of one of them maybe being ill. That's the exact type of thing that a son or daughter would come out of the woodwork for. By the time it took to get warrants and a look at both their medical records Fulton could've been and gone - although fuck knows how he now thinks he's going to *travel* home, with a burned passport, that is - so the best policy is for us to take a trip to Dundee, and pay them a visit'

For the first time since meeting him, he sounded pro-active and actually like a fully functioning Detective, as opposed to the clearly hung over, red eyed "broon sauce" stained mess that had walked into Irvine's office hours earlier.

'It's around an hour and a half's drive, we can continue discussing the case on the way' He said before he took a slice of bread and scooped up the combination of egg yolk mixed with brown sauce and shoving it in his mouth, drinking it down with the last of his cup of tea.

As far as I was concerned, it was half past twelve - half past one on my watch which I'd forgotten to change back an hour - and we'd lost half of the day already. The sooner we left for Dundee the better.

With a lot less urgency than I did - before we got on the road out of Edinburgh and on the motorway to the city of Dundee Samuel told me that - figuring we'd be away for the rest of the day - he needed to pop down to London Street - something I had no point of reference of - to speak to an informant. While I thought it pressing that we got on with things I also had to be appreciative of the fact that if I'd had several plates spinning in my day to day role, then so might he have, and I had to respect that so told him that we should go take care of that before we concentrated fully on the hunt for Fulton.

He pulled the car up - on London Street - outside a dingy looking establishment titled "Happy Endings Steam Sauna" that had it not been for the sign outside you would not have been able to guess *what* business was going on inside it's walls.

Taking my seat belt off at the same time as he did, he reacted to this strangely, almost nervously.

'Emmm, you can't come in with me, pal. You know, like, how cagey informants can be, cautious cats, them'

On this away trip I had wanted to sample as much as I could but understood the concept of not burning informants. They see a face that they don't recognise turn up and they'll split on you without even thinking about it. Still, though. Samuel really should've thought about the fact that a detective really cannot kid another detective. I could tell from his reaction that there was more to just protecting a source. I did not bother to question him, however, but it *did* leave me questioning whether I had been handed one of Lothian and Borders' finest, to assist me in apprehending someone whose name was flashing in lights at Interpol HQ. Could I really trust him? This man who had seemed more interested in eating than he was fighting crime. From what I had seen so far, this was not the look of a man who "got results."

'I'll be back in five minutes, Franky. I'll stick the radio on for you, mainly all pish that's on it but it'll still be better than that yodel ya ooh hoo shite that you cunts listen to, eh? Oh and do *not* come in looking for me if I'm a wee bit longer than five, alright?'

He slammed the door and walked the few steps from the car to the front of the sauna, before disappearing through the front door.

Twenty seven fucking minutes later he emerged - tucking a portion of his shirt into his trousers - with some kind of a self satisfied smile on his face that could've powered the whole of the shops and businesses on the busy street.

'Sorry about that, didn't think it would take as long, Franky. Let's go to Dundee, eh. You heard of The Beano, by the way?'

He said as he turned the key of the car and - having a quick look to make sure the traffic was clear - pulled away and down the street.

I neglected to mention to him that during my wait I had googled Happy Feelings Edinburgh, and knew *why* he'd been there, and for so long. That aside, I could smell it, smell that he'd had sex. Just that smell that you can have after fucking someone. I prayed that his triple breakfast was soon going to catch up on him, and he was going to be giving off a completely different scent altogether, something I would have been amazed at the thought of me hoping for, half an hour before.

Whilst inside I was livid that so far - on arrival - I'd been dragged away for a breakfast that I didn't want and then - to follow this - made to wait in a car while my "partner" had sex inside a sauna parlour. For the unity of the two of us and the greater good of trying to track down Norman Fulton, have him detained and me getting myself back to Lyon as soon as I possibly could, I would keep my thoughts to myself.

We exchanged general chit chat on the journey to - what Samuel called - the home of Dennis the Menace. Swapping stories from the job. Samuel expressing an interest in finding out more about Interpol, while also taking the time to remind me that there was fuck all special about any of us, compared to local detectives. Like I'd done since meeting him that morning,

I humoured him. It was clear for anyone to see that there was more insecurity on his part about *not* being an Interpol agent than there had been any superiority on my part about *being* one.

Due to the conversation, it hadn't felt like a ninety minute car ride and we were soon driving past the sign welcoming us to Dundee. We'd already decided that the first port of call - on arrival in the city - would be the home of Fulton's mother and father - Frank and Pauline - where we would enquire if they had received any visits from their son in recent days. An advantage - we'd expressed in planning our next move - was going to be how old his parents were, and how they would not be in the best of positions to be sitting there trying to lie on their son's behalf. If Fulton had been to see them - and who knows, maybe we'd have even caught him living there? - then we'd get the information from them.

That had been the plan. After what had been around fifteen minutes of driving along the outskirts of Dundee, until the signposts started to indicate for *other* towns, I began to get the impression that Samuel had decided to make a change to the plan. This confirmed when I noticed us pass the *thank you for visiting Dundee* sign, with us having never set foot *in* it.

When I'd questioned Samuel where he was going he met this with a small wink while telling me that he was making a slight detour before we visited the Fultons. A 'slight detour' actually proving to be a thirty mile round trip. Not in the pursuit of capturing a dangerous criminal, wanted in several different countries, but, instead, to buy *fish*.

He'd kind of kept things vaguely at a slight diversion until saying to no one in particular

'This'll do'

Stopping beside a small wooden hut with rows of fish hanging from the roof by small pieces of rope tied to their tails.

I watched from the car as he stood there talking to the fishmonger, stood there in his filthy white apron, having a laugh with the guy as if he didn't have a care in the world, while he had the man cut down two of the fish and wrap them up.

When he got back into the car, I was incredulous.

I'd managed to remain patient over the time consuming breakfasts, I'd stayed silent over him having sex with prostitutes during his day, but this was a line crossed. We'd reached our destination - and who knows how time sensitive everything all was - and he had kept on driving in the opposite direction, to purchase some fish.

'Samuel, what the fuck, man?'

I said to him, unable to hide - didn't try, actually - my annoyance with him. This knocking the smile that he'd had on his face returning from the wooden fish shed.

'These are fucking Arbroath Smokies, for fuck's sake, Franky. Arbroath, mind? I'm not expecting you to know what that means but I'm fucked if I'm coming all the way from Edinburgh up to this part of the world and not taking the opportunity to bag a couple of Smokies out of it, ken?'

The man did not give one single flying fuck. We had a very real job to do, but the stance that he was taking with me in the car it suggested that he was the one in the right out of the pair of us.

'*Now* can we go visit Fulton's parents?'

I asked, kind of exasperated.

'Well, time of day it is I was going to say that a couple of pints in The Athletic Bar would be a good shout ... I'M JOKING. Any of you Interpol cunts got a sense of humour, no?'

It had been a good save from him because I was genuinely about to erupt at the mere suggestion that - after everything up to that point - he was hinting at going to the pub.

God, those fish smelled too, where were they when I needed them back when the car was filled with the foul stench of sweaty sex from an overweight man?

Fulton's parents had not bore as much fruit as we'd anticipated. Having already looked over the files from the investigation, that had followed his prison escape, when I was on the flight over to Scotland, their answers had been almost word for word the same as when they had last received a visit from Detectives looking for their son.

'I haven't seen him since the last visit I had to him at Barlinnie, before his escape'

Pauline Fulton's response.

'And I haven't seen him since before he was put on remand in Nineteen Ninety'

Her husband, Frank's input.

The pair of them meeting the news that their son was in the country, with what had appeared as genuine surprise.

'I'll tell you one thing for nothing, boys'

The elderly Frank Fulton, said to Samuel and me, on hearing their news.

'If he's in the country and he doesn't come to visit his mum and dad you'll not need to worry about catching him as I'll catch him and put him six feet under. It'll be fucking *me* that you'll be coming looking for'

He joked with us. Looking like it would me a major task to just get in and out of his armchair, Frank Fulton was not going to be kicking *anyone's* asses, anytime soon.

Inside the living room, I was treated to the other side of Samuel. In the presence of two OAPs, the man could not have been any nicer. The friendly manner that he spoke to the two of them, which was balanced with a cheekiness that I'd felt was a Scottish thing as the two of them lapped him up.

When Samuel asked them if we could check the rest of the house - which I'm sure he was going to be doing whether they allowed it or not - Pauline was happy to escort us around the house, while we checked each room.

Curiously, one of the bedrooms was clearly what you would have assumed to have belonged to Frank and Pauline, while the other bedroom was what had appeared to have been Norman's, when he lived there. A Scottish saltire flag on the wall, only in the colours of orange and black. What was curious about it was the bedroom that would have belonged to Norman had the look about it that someone had been *using* it. The bed looked like it had been slept in that night and hadn't been made and there was a half drunk cup of coffee on the bedside table, with a couple of cigarette butts in an ashtray, along with an empty packet of cigarettes.

While her back was to us, I nudged Samuel and nodded my head towards all of this. He took things from there.

'Now, Pauline. I thought we were pals'

This, enough to have her wheeling around.

'What, what do you mean by that?' She said, looking genuinely hurt by what he'd said to her.

'Well I asked you to tell me the truth and that if you did then you'd be fine'

I'm not sure why but she looked at me, almost for back up, that was never going to come. As far as this small exchange was going, I was fucking Switzerland.

'But, but I have ..'

She answered, nervously.

'Wellllll, why did you not tell us that Norman's been staying here then?'

It was a smart play. He wasn't asking her if her on the run son had been staying the night, he was *telling* her.

'I can't tell you what hasn't happened, son. Well, if you want me to tell you the truth, like you asked me to. The mind's not so sharp at this age so I'd appreciate it if you don't confuse me. Just tell me if you want the truth or if you want me to make something up, to suit what you're looking for?'

It was quite impressive from her and I couldn't help emitting a small smile at this rebuttal. Samuel, though, had only been baited by this and pointed straight at the cup of coffee sitting on the bedside table.

'So I suppose if we take that away to forensics we're not going to find the prints from Norman on them?'

He said as assured as you could get, having secured his smoking gun.

Pauline Fulton, however, was not fazed by this in any shape or form.

'Take it all you like, son. And don't be surprised when you find Norman's fingerprints and DNA all over it, considering he was the last person to drink from it'

A-HA, a confession. My heart leapt at what she said, until she continued.

'Take a look around you? Anything stick out to you?'

We'd already had a good look around - including inside wardrobes, just in case - so there really was no need to do so but did all the same.

Neither of us had an answer for her so she carried on.

'It's been more than twenty years since Norman spent his last night here, in his bedroom, in his home, and I've never been able to move on from that. Have always waited on him, just walking through that door. I've tried to empty that ashtray and take that cup down to the kitchen more times than you've had hot dinners so aye, take it away for your forensics, take the ashtray as well, save me a job that I should've done years before'

I understood, mums can be like that with their sons. Guys that go off to war and are killed and their room is left exactly how it was, before they left for duty. From the look on Samuel's face, he seemed to get it too.

'No, it's fine, Pauline. I was just checking, I hope you understand, hen, I need to be seen to be doing my job, no offence'

He said, getting her back onside again. Her agreeing with him and saying that she understood that he had a job to do but - having nothing to hide - she was happy to help if possible.

Frank - once we rejoined him downstairs - also was full of help and understanding.

Telling Samuel and me that if he was to go looking for his son then Tannadice Park - later on that night - would have been his first destination. Saying how much his son loved the club and that if he really *was* back in Scotland, then there would've been a good chance that he'd have went to see Dundee United, especially with it being a big match against Celtic.

It really wasn't the worst idea in the world. While neither Samuel or myself knew Fulton's motivation for travelling to Scotland in the first place, no one needed to remind me of the emotional pull that a man's soccer team has to them and how - be that causing divorce, heart attacks, loss of jobs, being caught by an Interpol and Edinburgh C.I.D joint operation - it can sometimes be a man's Achilles Heel.

Leaving our cards with the Fultons, with instructions to call us the moment that their son showed his face, the two of us decided that we would act on Frank Fulton's suggestion and try and look for him in attendance in the crowd at the stadium.

Leading up to that - Samuel either working me from the back, or telling me the truth - being told that drinking was a big part of soccer culture in Scotland, it was felt a good idea by Samuel and me that we should try visiting some of the various pubs in the city centre and nearer to the stadium, to see what we could find.

Chapter 18

Liam

Apart from when answering the call and ending it, he spoke, and I listened.

'Alright, I have work for you. Not Edinburgh, further afield, if you dig what I'm saying. Same deal as before, so bring your passport. You leave at six in the morning Sunday. Same place as last time, don't be late. Oh and this time you're taking double to what you did last month so you're getting double the money, is that a problem? Lot of responsibility on your head, remember'

There was too much to think of at the time, but the one dominant thought of all was the double the money part.

'Emmm, no that's sound'

All I could really say back to him.

'Good, good that's what I like to hear. Until then, then'

He hung up, no thanks or fuck all. Then again these types didn't really have to worry about what level of manners they used.

Once I put the phone down onto the table, I immediately remembered about that this was now going to completely mess my Saturday night, and the following morning and beyond.

Fucking, Derrick Carter, too? Playing in town. I'd been looking forward to it since the date had been announced and me and the rest of the boys were going to get absolutely brutally mad with it.

Once in a blue moon stuff, when the boy Carter was behind the decks, when you stayed in Dundee, and I was going to fucking *miss* it. The kind of scenario where if I'd had any normal clock in clock out twenty four days a year holiday plus publics job, I'd have heavily considered pulling a sicky.

Who *I* worked for, though?

They weren't the kind of employers that you phoned in sick to.

Chapter 19

Detective Constable Roy van der Elst

'Wait a minute, you mean to say that one team plays there, and'

I pointed towards one football stadium, before turning to the side of me.

'Another plays, *there*'

I'd already grabbed the concept - having immediately asked Samuel what was up, the moment that I noticed the ridiculously small proximity one was from the other.

'Well, aye. Not on the same day or at the same times, though. Too much on the police resources to worry about four different sets of fans. Have the two Glasgow - or Edinburgh - teams here, at the same time, playing the Dundee sides and you'd be as fucking well calling N.A.T.O in advance and telling them to get prepared for a wee trip to Scotland'

'Oh *that* I understand. If De Kuip and ArenA were side by side, like these two stadiums, well, they wouldn't stay standing for too long. You must be *real* civilised over here'

Samuel found this amusing without going on to elaborate why, or more specifically, how wrong that statement from me had really been.

It was just gone seven in the evening and we had arrived at Tannadice Park, home of Dundee United and the side that

Normal Fulton had been linked with - in a hooligan capacity - in his earlier years. They were scheduled to play Glasgow Celtic with the kick off not until quarter to eight but, even by then, the outer area of the stadium was a hive of activity. Large TV trucks, with staff all running around making their last minute checks that all was in order before they went live. Vendors already pitched up trying to sell their wares, curiously I'd noticed that despite Dundee being the home team, the majority of merchandise on sale was for their rivals on the night. The long line of fans in orange and black lining up to get into the club shop to pick up their tickets while on the same subject, more than a few opposition fans walking the streets either trying to buy a spare from someone, or sell one.

Samuel and me had spent the previous few hours touring some of the more well known pubs that were used on match days. This had become more of a task than I'd been told it would be. This, Samuel reliably informed me, down to the fact that the travelling support A, would be travelling in great numbers and B, a good percentage of them liked to drink before the match.

This had led to all of the pubs - or boozers as Samuel referred to them as - being full to the brim, half of them with drinkers standing outside in the cold early evening night, with their pints of lager. While it had been nothing more than a needle in a haystack, it had been worth looking for him. Even though I'd only known him for half a day, and with how hungover the man had appeared on first impression, when he finally made it into work, I should have known that him and touring drinking establishments would not have mixed well.

By the third pub that we'd walked into - Frews Bar - and me watching Samuel go through the same routine of him having a bit of friendly chit chat with the bartender, this involving him showing a picture of Fulton on his phone - with mixed results but none leading to any hard intel on *where* we could find him -

and it invariably ending with Samuel with a glass of Whisky in his hand, and it quickly down his hatch before we moved on. After watching his sink a third one, and despite being in a strange city in a country where they drove on the wrong side of the road, I had already taken the decision that it would be *me* doing the driving back to Edinburgh, at the end of the night.

An argument that, no doubt, the two of us would be having when the time came but I was fucked if I was going to let an alcoholic drive me anywhere. If he'd been breathalysed when he'd got into work he'd probably have been over the limit. Knocking back the shorts the way he was, while we searched for Fulton, he was *absolutely positively* over the limit for driving, and the night was yet young. If - as I'd suspected - Samuel was one of those drunks that once they'd had the taste for a few there was no stopping them, then it was going to be a challenging night.

The pubs themselves had been an experience for this Dutch copper. Yeah, we like a beer in the Netherlands, of course we do. The Scottish drinking culture before a football match was on another level altogether, though. The pubs that looked like they'd been taken over by visitors from Glasgow - which, being Dutch - I could not puzzle out why opposition fans had not come along and wrecked them, and the pub, but if anything it was refreshing. There were the pubs - like Frews and The Snug, the last bar we visited before heading to the stadium - that were exclusively home fans, even some that - to me, miraculously, - had pockets of *both* fans.

When explaining my amazement to Samuel over this, he remarked that this wasn't always the case, and that as far as getting Rangers and Celtic fans in the same pub before an Old Firm Derby then you could "forget that shite."

The more he told me about Celtic and Rangers, the more parallels I saw between my team and Feyenoord.

As I'd said, though. Showing Fulton's face and mentioning his name to people in and around the pubs *did* bring results and was in no way a case of showing a picture around people and getting a series of blank looks. This, though was on the other end of the scale and, to an extent, almost counter productive. Because - as Samuel had already told me on the drive from Edinburgh - Dundee was not a large city, and as a consequence, pretty much everyone that Samuel asked about Fulton, *knew him*.

Some commented on the fact that they'd never heard his name spoken in years, others reacted in surprise over how he was looking in more recent times with that big beard while you got the occasional - as Samuel had taken to calling them - "wideos" who would hit Samuel with a smart arse answer, just to be seen to be fucking with the police in front of their friends.

Nothing close to concrete although with some of the types that we'd spoken to, I'd been left with the impression that they could easily have just spoken to Fulton five minutes before bumping into us in the pub and we would've been the very last people that they'd have thought of telling. Even Samuel's tactics of buying drinks for "the jakeys" bore no fruit.

After leaving the rammed to capacity *The Snug* whose patrons were all in the middle of singing some song about their city rivals to the same tune as Please Release Me Let Me Go, Samuel nodding his head in the direction of the already lit stadium floodlights, suggesting that we get ourselves down and in place, only then dawning on him that - for something like this - he should have called ahead to the club to inform them that we were coming and would be needing access to their CCTV room.

'Too late for any of that shite now though, so we'll just have to take care of it when we get there'

God how I wished that he *had* called ahead because the drama of just trying to get *into* the stadium was enough to have made you tear your hair out.

Approaching the main entrance, Samuel - led by the smell of a nearby hotdog truck - told me that he would be a minute and that I should carry on to the main entrance, and that he'd catch me up there.

When reaching the front door to the stadium, there were two suits stood there, acting as security to ensure the chosen few were granted entry. When I reached them, one of them stood - blocking the door - with a clipboard in his hand and greeted me with a smile, while I told him that my name was Roy van der Elst and that I was from Interpol, and needed entry for myself and a colleague.

This leading to him scanning the sheet in front of him, which was obviously a waste of time, since no one knew we were coming. This I attempted to tell him but with the noise of the crowd outside singing and entering to the side of us, into one of the bigger areas of the ground, it was futile.

'I'm afraid I'm not seeing your name on the list, Mr van der Elst but my guess is that if you're here scouting for Inter then your comps will be sitting over the road at the ticket office. Tell you what, though. You boys are at the back of a long queue. We've already had Man United, Roma and Bayern Munich looking at young Russell the past month alone'

If I'd got this correctly. I had tried to tell him that I was wishing to gain entry to the stadium, in the name of representing an international crime agency ... and he thought I was there on behalf of a football team, to scout a player?

Once I'd processed this and got my head around how someone could get something so badly wrong such as this and was in the process of fishing out my identity card, a Samuel with a couple of bites left of a hot dog in his hand appeared, and took over.

'What's going on here, problem, Roy?'

He looked at me and then set his glare on the security guard.

'No, no problem, mate'

The security guard in the suit answered.

'I was just explaining to your man here that you collect the tickets for scouts over at the ticket office inside the club shop, just a few metres'

'Aye, and that would be all fine and dandy'

Samuel answered while taking a closer look at the man's official name badge.

'Graham, were we actually fucking here to scout any of your players. We're here on police business'

Samuel produced his card to show the guy, while asking for him to get the head of match day security, down to reception to meet us.

This seemed to confuse the man in the suit.

'B b but, he said that he was from Inter Pol'

Samuel just looked at me and shook his head.

'You believe this cunt, aye?'

'Just out of interest, pal. Which league do you think "Inter Pol" play in?'

The suited man looked completely burned, ashamed at how much of a fool he'd made of himself, once he'd had it explained to him that I, in fact, was not in attendance on behalf of a European super power, scouting United's hot prospect that had been drawing admiring glances from around the continent.

I guess the name *Interpol* carried a lot more weight elsewhere inside the corridors of Tannadice Park because within a few minutes we had a Bill Robertson - big cheery beast of a man with an orange and black striped tie and similar coloured striped lanyard around his neck - down at reception to greet the pair of us, where he would take us away to his office and have things explained further to him.

'Look, Bill. You don't even need to begin telling me that you've already got your work cut out for you tonight, with it being Celtic in town, category A match I assume?'

While I didn't get the exact reference I thought the equivalent would've been something like *De Klassieker* back home where - for that one day at least - things were treated a lot more seriously than they would be when a smaller team with little of an away support would come to town.

Robertson nodded back to Samuel.

'Look, all we're needing is a good look around the crowd with your CCTV. Our man's hardly going to be difficult to spot, if he's here tonight'

Samuel passed his phone over to Robertson to show him Fulton's picture. Robertson, who as it would turn out was an absolute joy to work with, proactively had Samuel send him the picture so that he could get around to speak to all off the turnstile operators on the night to ask if they had he either seen this man come into the stadium, and if not to keep an eye out for them.

Robertson also seeing to it that Samuel and me were given a monitor of our own, to concentrate on the search for Fulton, as well as making sure we were fed, although that was more on Samuel's part than anything else.

'Can I get you chaps something to drink?'

The *actual* question that had been asked to us, which Samuel had managed to turn into.

'Any chance you could get someone to knock us up some hospo sandwiches? A few sausage rolls or pies, too, maybe some cakes just to round things up?'

'I'll see what I can do'

Robertson said but in a tone of voice that pretty much said that all of what Samuel had asked for was coming right up.

When left sitting there alone in the control room, Samuel went on to tell me that he already knew how good the sandwiches were here at the stadium.

'Came here on hospitality, a few seasons back when an associate sponsored the match, and was given the top tier hospitality package. Barry as fuck scran, you want to see the swally that they gave us before and after the match, as well, fill your fucking boots, stuff. We'd all planned to go out in Dundee after we left the stadium but by half five half of the group had fallen by the wayside, no wonder as well. I reckon that Robertson would've probably got us a pint from the bar as well if we'd asked him but you have to watch with some cunts. As nice a boy as he appears I fucking bet wild horses wouldn't have been able to stop him from telling people about our visit and before you know it - with the Chinese whispers - the story had evolved to an Interpol agent coming to Tannadice for the night and getting absolutely fucking mortal'

I loved how - in his mind - he elevated things to the Interpol agent being the drunk one when - in reality - it was the Interpol agent who had remained absolutely teetotal out of the two of them.

Finally getting a proper look at the stadium - pre match with the four sides all beginning to fill up - I found it to be a funny looking but quaint stadium that - in a world of identikit arenas for a lot of teams - in constructional ways - didn't even appear to make sense in some parts but - following Ajax in both the league and Dutch Cup - I'd seen much, much worse in my time as a football fan. Despite knowing barely anything about Scottish football - other than the obvious of the two teams from Glasgow, which I'd always understood were more famous because of the rivalry than being famous modern day world football for them being anything special as footballing teams - I had actually heard of Dundee United, this through me always noticing their name in the UEFA cup each season where - despite being relative unknowns - they had seen off so called superior European teams from leagues such as the German, Spanish, Dutch and French.

Through time, seeing their name in the list of European ties began to dry up to the point that you stopped seeing them altogether, but they were a team I had been *aware* of. Back when they shocked the whole of Europe that night by winning in the

Nou Camp - back when I was just starting out at the police academy in eighty seven - I could never have guessed that I'd actually visit their stadium, and if that had ever been mooted as a possibility I would have one hundred percent have guessed that it would have been Ajax related. As an Interpol Detective? Not even in my wildest dreams.

While Samuel sat there with what resembled a mountain of sandwiches and pastries piled on top of each other - and me receiving a quick tutorial on how to navigate the security camera - I got down to some actual police work, one of us had to, and I had definitely not flown from Lyon to sit and eat tuna and mayonnaise sandwiches and scones.

It hadn't ever been something that I had needed to consider before, but god was it a laborious process, trying to carefully scan a camera over a full to capacity stadium of - what Robertson had told us - around fourteen thousand. The possibility of Fulton being inside the away end with the Celtic fans extremely low so that, at least, cut down the work load.

Being such a big football fan, I was cursing the fact that while concentrating on all the Dundee United support inside the stadium, I was apparently missing out on a classic match. Three goals inside the first half - the home side taking the lead with the last kick of the ball in first half injury time - which saw to it that I was trying to forensically study thousand of fans, with most of them not remotely interested in sitting in their seats and making their identity fully clear to me.

Yeah, Fulton was quite distinctive and would be easy to spot, even inside a packed stadium. But not if, say, he had his back to the camera hugging a friend behind him right at the same moment as my camera was trained on that particular section of the stadium.

On a personal level, while getting the chance to experience the atmosphere of a match in a foreign country, I was impressed. The Celtic fans to a man had sung their hearts out on their side while the United fans were matching their Glasgow counterparts.

Out of a whole half of scanning half of the stadium, however. There had been no sign of Fulton. As far as I was concerned though, football is a game of two halves and that applied the same, when it came to looking for the object of my bosses desire, back at HQ.

Samuel - whether for appearances sake or through genuine desire to help - occasionally would chip in by standing over my shoulder and looking at the screen. Stopping me now and again, when he thought he'd possibly spotted something. Like when he pointed out to me the man who had his United hat pulled down right onto his head as far as it could go until it was almost cover his eyes while he had his orange and black bar scarf wrapped around his face, all the way up past his nose and just sitting *under* his eyes.

'HIM, Get onto the police down at the East Stand to go and get him to take his scarf down from his face, so we can get a look at him'

It made sense. If you were on the run but wanted to go and watch your football side. The smart person would at least make some kind of attempt to go in disguise.

We kept the camera focussed on that section of the stadium, while receiving radio updates from the police that were overseeing things in that part of the stadium. With crystal clear quality we watched the two officers walking down the stairs - of the lower tier behind the goal - until they got to the aisle where our man was sitting - obliviously - in the aisle seat. There we saw a heated exchange between the man - whose face was obscured - and the two officers. From a distance, it definitely looked like the man was putting up some resistance to being asked to reveal his face.

'This is looking promising here, Franky, my man'

Samuel said as he grabbed hold of my arm as we watched on. It *was* promising, I can't deny. We had someone here who had went to great lengths to cover who they were and, - now asked to reveal themselves by police - were resisting being asked to prove their identity.

Then came the pushing and shoving when one of the police officers grabbed his arm, which had him pulling himself in the opposite direction to free himself from his clutches. This producing a reaction from the other United supporters around him who had then all started arguing with the police, a couple of them pulling on the guy with the scarf over his face to make sure that the police couldn't grab him and take him away.

After a few moments of scuffles, there then followed a moment of calm. Our guy in the scarf - during the scuffle having freed himself from the officer's grip - was standing there with a peaceful stance, hands up in the air to both the officers, still standing on the aisle. Him reaching forward to say something to one of the officers before the three of them cordially and paradoxically - considering what had just taken place moments earlier - all walked up the stairs, disappearing into the stadium concourse.

'What the fuck is going on?'

Samuel shouted.

'It didn't have to be that hard. Just get the cunt to take his scarf down for one second, and it would've been cleared up, there and fucking then'

We had a few minutes of waiting to find out if we'd got our man or not before Samuel got the call from Robertson who - god knows what he was like on a normal match day but due to having Interpol requiring his help - since we'd arrived had been like a man possessed, gave us the bad news that it wasn't our man. This backed up by the camera - which had not moved on yet - capturing the still very much face obscured gentleman walking back down the stairs, and taking his seat to a piece of applause from the fans around him.

Despite it being a negative result, Samuel stood there - listening to Robertson fill him in on things - with a smile forming on his face, this coming after an expletive filled rant, on finding that the mystery man hadn't been Fulton.

'To be fair, I'd have done the exact fucking same thing as the fella. No worries, Bill. We'll keep looking and you'll know about it if we find anything. Keep up the good work, pal. Telling you, Bill, you need to get yourself on the force'

Samuel ended the call and went on to explain to me that our guy - that we'd focussed on - was not Norman Fulton but who he *was*, was a random United supporter who should have been at his work and had pulled a sick day, so that he could go to the match. Worried about the match being covered live on TV, he had told the officers that he'd had to cover his face during the match, just in case he was busted by the TV cameras. Apparently he had told both officers from the very off that he would be happy to show his face, but just *not* anywhere that the cameras would be able to spot him. You know how things can escalate, though?

Apart from a few "is it or is it not him?' moments, it had been a waste of a night and I knew that we had officially ran out of ideas when - around the seventy minute mark - Samuel hit upon the idea of having the stadium announcer put out a request for Normal Fulton to report to the nearest steward. *This* tactic most probably wouldn't have worked back in the pre cell phone days, when it was regular to hear such an announcement during a game, but in more recent times? Where our target was probably carrying more than one phone, never mind being someone that if you needed to get in touch you would phone a football club to get hold of him on your behalf, no, it was never going to fly, which it didn't.

Leaving the stadium and while walking back to the car, I decided to broach the subject that maybe I should drive the two of us back to Edinburgh. Something that I felt that he would take offence at, but instead was receptive towards.

'Aye, you're probably right, Franky. No way I'm passing a breathalyser, if stopped. Not that there's a traffic cop that's going to be fucking giving me a test in this life, though. But, aye, better to do the responsible thing and not get behind the wheel'

He said to me, as we made our way through the throngs of people who had all stayed behind right until the final whistle to see United edge the game three to two.

I was surprised that it had been that easy, to literally take the keys off him.

I wasn't so surprised, however, by his follow up suggestion that involved - now that he was no longer driving - us heading back to the pub 'The Snug' for a couple of drinks, while chancing on the possibility of us seeing our man, Fulton.

As we walked up the steep hill - surrounded by animated United fans buzzing from the win and all excitedly discussing moments from the match - in the direction of The Snug, my optimism for how fresh and on his A game Detective Constable Colin Samuel was going to be the next day - when we took another stab at locating Fulton - was not exactly filled to the brim.

Chapter 20

Nora

Oh how I fucking hate that moment, whenever time of day that it pays you a visit. That moment where you pick up your phone, and you see over fifty missed calls, and just as many text messages waiting on you. That exact moment where - at that point, some unknown reason - you already know that something is fucked, somewhere, and that it's going to be impacting you the moment you find out what it's about.

In my case it was really more once my phone - which had been dead from around tea time the day before - had got enough charge into it for it to spring into action, displaying the missed calls and the number of texts that were on there.

With the sickest of feelings in my stomach, I opened it up and faced my fears.

Ninety nine percent of the missed calls and texts were from my mum. The main gist of things.

FUCK

Somehow the fucking bizzies had cottoned onto me being in Scotland. Some fucking grassing bastard, no doubt, but who? I'd tried to keep my network close as I could, basically to *avoid* some cunt sticking me in, but there we go. Barely back two fucking days and my mum's telling me that they're looking for me, one of them from another country which, unless the coppers had went fucking diversity crazy in my time out of the country, meant that one of those Interpol or Europol cunts were looking for me as well.

Once the moment - where I'd felt like wrecking every fucking thing inside that B&B bedroom - passed. I phoned mum to get the Hampden from her. Good girl, hadn't told them fuck all and have to admit - despite how serious things now were - I got a wee laugh at her telling me that dad had sent the two coppers on a wild goose chase to Tannadice for the Celtic match, knowing full fucking well that I wasn't going to the game. What a magnificent bastard of a man.

Who knew what the score was with things, conversations being taped and that shite so I kept it short before hanging up again, and trying to re-strategise. It really is times like that where a man can either sink or he can swim the fuck out of his worries. Those moments where you either think straight, and at least give yourself a fighting chance, or you don't and would be as well phoning the filth, and telling them where to come collect you.

As always, I chose the first option.

The first thing I thought of was that if the bizzies were looking for me, that meant that someone had told them that they'd seen me, which meant descriptions would have been provided.

The beard would have to go, pronto.

There was also the *biggest* issue in that if the police knew I was in Scotland, they'd be looking for me trying to *leave* the country again. I didn't know what they knew and *that* was the fucking problem. Had the police been given a tip off that they'd seen "Nora Fulton" or - with this foreign copper on the case - were they looking for *Frank van der Hoorn*?

Well that would be a question that I'd be daft enough to get the answer from, if I was stupid to try and fly out of Edinburgh airport on the Sunday, I thought to myself. Full disclosure, that Friday morning I didn't have the first fucking clue *how* I was now going to get back out of Scotland. It definitely was a bit of a puzzler, like.

But, if you think any of that was enough to throw a spanner in the plans of *why* I was even in the country in the first place, then you obviously don't fucking know me. Just because the police were running around - in the complete wrong Scottish city - looking for me, that didn't have to mean that I couldn't carry on with my own plans.

First of all, though. The beard had to come off. I popped out of the B&B to the nearest Nisa to grab a packet of cheap BIC razors, along with the first shaving foam that I spied before heading back and - near to emotional - got rid of the beard that I'd spent around the best part of a decade growing.

By the time I was wiping down my face with the towel, I barely recognised the cunt looking back at me. Fuck, it had been *decades* since I'd seen my actual face, free of the beard.

In my mind, now a lot more inconspicuous minus the facial hair, I was ready to hit the street. Coppers on my case or not, I had a full and busy day ahead.

Starting with a visit to Calton Gym.

I'd walked past it twice before I'd even managed to find the place but I would be quicker to put that down to the place having absolutely fucking ride all in the way of signage - from the Main Street to point you up the side street to where the gym was situated - than I would've done for my premises finding abilities.

Walking through the battered green front doors, I was met with a series of steps, indicating that it was one of those upstairs gyms, with not a single sign of life until you get to the top of the stairs and reach where the magic happens.

With it being late morning, I didn't know what to expect in terms of how busy the place would be but it was hardly what you'd have called peak time so I was surprised to see there was quite a few people in there, staff and members. It was all going on. There was a select lone rangers, just doing their own thing, treadmills, lifting the weights, rowing machine. Other than that, though was an instructor taking a group of kids through some exercises - every one of them copying him to the letter of the law as if he was some army drill radge - and apart from that you had the familiar set up of someone - buddy or actual physical instructor - standing over the other person, encouraging them in their own wee mini quest that they looked to be trying to achieve.

With the place being so busy it gave me the perfect chance to get a decent look around before - no doubt - I'd have some cunt from the gym appearing and seeing how they could help me, which if I hadn't been able to identify Swanny - out of everyone in the room - I would most definitely be finding out if they *could* help me. Still, I much preferred to get a decent swatch for myself, before having to engage with anyone else.

I took a walk around the place which, admittedly, showed my place back in Amsterdam to be as wee as it was. This Calton gym had to be two, maybe three, times as big as Utility. Nobody that resembled this Swanny prick, regrettably. Which meant that whether a staff member of the gym was interested in speaking to me - which they still hadn't looked to be - I was now going to have an interest in talking to *them*.

I was walking past two men, one of them sat on the Lat Pulldown machine while the other stood spurring him on. When passing them, I must've distracted the guy who was stood doing the spotting, because he turned to clock me for a moment. Me, meeting that by looking right back at him as I passed.

It was then that we both seemed to realise that we knew each other, but not one of those immediately springing to mind *why* kind of ways. It had been enough, anyway, to see to it that neither of us dropped our stare. Almost like a game of chicken until one of us remembered who the other one was.

Weirdly, we both seemed to peg at the exact same time, with completely different reactions.

'What are *you* doing here?'

He said before checking with his guy on the machine to ask if he'd be ok to be left on his own for a few minutes, indicating that - now that he'd seen me in there - he needed a word with someone. Which was fine, I wasn't against having one or two with him either.

Brett "Banjo" Ireland, one of the main boys with Hibs Capital City Service and someone who - at an early age - had proved his worth to his mob so many times that he commanded the kind of respect that was generally reserved for those - in the firm - much older than he was. Apart from being one of the reasons that the CCS had the reputation that it had, he was also a prized boxer and had represented Scotland in his youth, while at the same time he was doing a lot more *unofficial* fighting out of the ring. One of the main takeaways from this - and had been my thoughts at the time back in the eighties when I learned about his boxing prowess - was the guy just must've really, really liked to fight.

Him and I, like most top boys in a Scottish crew, had enjoyed a few run ins with each other, over the seasons. Clearly, once his memory bank kicked in and he was able to recall the face in front of him, he hadn't forgotten those encounters either because, regardless of them being twenty plus years before, his initial reaction on seeing me had been one of direct hostility.

Walking on with me - and away from earshot of the guy on the machine who, clocking the logo on the T Shirt Ireland had on, I'd assumed was a client of the gym being assisted by Banjo - he repeated his question, all be it a wee bit more forcefully.

'What the fuck are you doing here, eh?'

'Woah, woah, woah, Banjo. Time out, amigo'

I laughed, completely at ease while making a peacemaking letter T with my two hands.

'Well, I'm not here to settle any scores from back in the eighties, mate, if that's what you're thinking. It's twenty ten, for fuck's sake'

I didn't think he appreciated how casual I was being about it, when he'd already been prepared for something more extreme but - at the same time - it *did* allow him to tone down things a bit. Probably wouldn't have been ideal for the boy to be fighting at his work with members of the public either, I thought to myself. Well, until he went on to tell me that he fucking *owned* the place.

Despite being deadly rivals back in the hey days of the casuals, we were able to stand there and laugh at the irony of years later , and the two of us both running a gym.

We engaged in a wee spot of awkward small talk, that only old casuals - who don't even really know each other in the first fucking place - could've found themselves talking about. Whether they're still going to the games while talking about how they eventually got out of the fighting part and had to make an attempt at growing up.

Obviously, though. Ireland would've known that I hadn't stopped by just to say a wee hi to him. I hadn't planned on bumping into any *other* CCS linked or affiliated boys in the gym. Hadn't planned for this as I had been so centred on whether Swanny was going to be there or not and - had it came to it - if I was going to have to speak to one of the staff of the gym to ask them about when Swanny might be back in again, I didn't ever think that the staff member I'd find myself speaking to would be fucking ex Capital City Service, though. Someone who - unlike your run of the mill shop worker - was already going to know that my 'I'm in town for a few days and was trying to catch up with my mate' approach was complete and utter bollocks.

Owner of one business - and specifically the exact same area - to another, I decided to take a chance.

I told him that while I had no business or interest in looking for any old CCS, CSF, ASC or whoever the fuck else I'd danced with in the past, I *did* need to find someone who was linked with the Hibs boys, whether he was still active or, like Banjo and yours truly, fully retired.

Explaining to Ireland that this was in no way a Dundee Utility and Capital City Service thing, and that this was purely down to me trying to protect my business. I knew I was taking a chance by telling him. That - for all I knew - him and Swanny could have went on to become best man at each others' weddings, so tight they were. I took the leap, hoping that with all the decades that had passed, since those naughty Saturdays, Ireland had managed to see life through a different lens, and appreciate the real issues that all of us business owners face in the struggle to make a go of things.

'Fucking Swanny? Haven't seen that radge in a couple of years since that reunion we all had when we went to Magaluf. You sure it's him that you're looking for, aye?'

Ireland asked me as he stood holding my phone in his hand watching one of my videos that I'd pulled up for him, following that by showing him some of the comments.

'Fucking, in there, Nora. That's some big numbers you've got for views, by the way'

Banjo, more interested in the views my video had received than my reason for showing him it.

'Tell you what, though? That's maybe not a bad idea, get a wee video knocked up myself, get a few extra punters through the door, likes'

This, pretty fucking irritating considering I couldn't really have given two fucks about the man's business strategy. I had my own agenda to be worried about.

'And you're totally sure that he doesn't come in here, because , well, that's what I've been told. I just need to speak to him, business, like. Like I said, fuck all to do with the casuals, eh'

I tried to say this in a way that didn't come across as me calling him a liar - from what he'd already told me - but it was kind of unavoidable, really.

'Did you not hear what I just fucking said? I haven't seen the cunt, not since Mallorca a couple of years ago'

He spat at me, while forcing my phone back into my hand, having seen enough.

'Just double checking, Brett, pal. Look around. Busy place you've got, can't expect you to keep track of everyone that comes and goes'

I knew how poor this must've come across. Busy gym or not. If you were the owner, you'd tend to notice if one of its patrons was one of the boys that you went into battle with, week in week out, like Banjo and Swanny did with the CCS.

'Well if you'd seen the *physique* of the cunt in Magaluf, you'd have been surprised if he'd been able to fucking *spell* gym, never mind visit one. Whoever's been whispering into your ear, they've been giving you duff information, mate'

I didn't believe him, but couldn't prove otherwise, plus, to tell him so would have one hundred percent have resulted in the two of us rolling around in his gym, which would have went against my supposedly planned out strict strategy of only popping up to commit an act of extreme violence just the once, to minimise the risk of coming to the attention of the bizzies. Going one to one with Ireland, in a public place, and in Edinburgh City Centre no less, I wasn't sure that it would have been over with - and me having made my excuses and left - before the police got there.

Banjo, with a neck that made Mike Tyson's look like a kid's, and those muscles that were the product of someone who had lived and breathed a gym for years, had always been a worthy adversary if you ever had the fortune or misfortune - that all really depended on how much of a shitebag you were - to go at it with him on a Scottish street. And decades later, he looked every bit as much of a titan. Not that I was scared of the cunt, mind. Sometimes you've just got to pick your battles, ken?

I put the phone back into my pocket and - I guess - from my body language, Ireland noticed that I was shaping up to leave, said.

'And just so I got this right, mate. Some cunt posted a couple of comments on your YouTube videos, and you've flown *all* the way from Holland to sort it out?'

Nobody had really said it to me, in the way that he'd said it, the tone used.

'Well, pretty much, aye?'

All that needed said.

The big lump just laughed at this. Telling me that I was a fucking radge and to never change.

'Bit late for that, eh?'

I said back to him, as I walked out the place, already second guessing myself on whether I had just made an arse of things and - with Ireland sure as fuck on the phone to Swanson straight away to tell him about the visit he'd just had - through sheer bad luck I had just given away the element of surprise, especially for the next day - when Rangers were in town - on an occasion where all the ex Hibs boys - as well as the new breed that were very much active - would surely be out in attendance.

It had always been the main part of the plan, the Saturday of the Hibs Rangers match, and my chance to take advantage of the chaos that would engulf Leith for a few vital hours.

It was just going to now be that wee bit harder, if Swanny knew that I was chasing him down, in the way that I now was.

Chapter 21

Stephen

Visiting dad? I guess the only way to really ever describe the experience - each time I went to see him - was as both joy and pain.

The mutual joy, that we both shared in seeing each other. The way that his - well wearied and worn - face would light up on seeing me, the kind of feeling that money could not possibly have ever purchased. It had been quite a few years that he'd been there but even so, I don't think I could have ever *really* imagined what it must've been like to have stayed there, permanently. How something - that used to be nothing other than routine - like sitting and having a blether with his son could ever reach the heady heights of being the best part of his day?

Like I said, it was mutual though. I went in to see him as much as I could and - apart from Glasgow Rangers Football Club - seeing dad was the only thing that I really had in life that I looked forward to, I didn't have much more than that. As grim as his surroundings undoubtedly were, if they'd have let me I'd have stayed with him, there. As long as I got to watch the Teddy Bears on the telly, of course.

The pain far, far outweighed the joy part, majorly.

The decline - physically and mentally - in the man over the years that had been evident for all to see, and the full impact on the family, over its head's tragic downfall. It's funny but sometimes you never really know just how much one person can be the glue that holds a family together, until they're not there and it all falls away, fast.

When they news came out, making him famous across the whole of the nation - BBC and STV news, the lot - the scandal quite literally ripped the family apart.

Maybe my own loyalties had clouded things, but I'd thought that he'd been made a bit of a scapegoat out of things. One of those examples where the authorities can't catch the *real* criminals, so they bring the hammer down on the patsy that's left standing around when the shit goes down, like dad.

Scapegoat or not, though. His conviction had been enough to put mum in an early grave with a heart attack, see Emily - my sister - emancipate herself from the Craigan family and me losing what - up until then - had looked to be a promising career in the force.

I think that was one of the reasons that the visits meant as much as they did to us. It was because him and I were pretty much all the family that we had.

To keep up his spirits - on his low days when he'd maybe have been less talkative - I would tell him about how much of a team we'd be when he got back out, how he could move in with me and that we'd watch the Bears on Sky, having a couple of cans.

While his appearance had changed drastically over those years, away on the inside, with him ageing before my eyes on an almost week to week basis, he never lost his wicked sense of patter and would have me pissing myself, with some of the tales he'd gathered from in there from my last visit. Due to the sensitive occupation that he'd held - pre sentencing - it had meant that he'd had to go on a wing that was reserved for the more *niche* inmates like your nonces, which couldn't have been nice but, pragmatically, dad knew what the consequences would've been, had he been stuck in a normal prison wing so was cool with it. Told me that - early doors - he'd got everyone in his wing told that he didn't intend fucking with them but if they wanted to try it with him, then they'd take what was coming to them, and that after that day he'd had no problems from anyone in there and had kind of ended up in charge of the place, not that being king of the nonce wing was anything to stick on your CV, as dad had told me that time.

He did have those low days though, he *was* human, after all. The days where - when I got there - he was already deep in reflective mode about *why* he was on the inside, and the regrets that he held of having rolled the dice on risking the last best years of his life, and losing.

Whether I'll ever know the real story or not, it all felt like dad had been hung out to dry. He'd told me that with it involving heavy characters like South American narcos, he'd not really been given the option to say no, when it came to what happened at Barlinnie.

The newspapers all screaming about the "greedy and corrupt prison officer" who had been paid off by gangsters to turn a blind eye to their plans when - in reality - it wasn't anywhere near as simple as that.

Despite the years that had passed since it all going down, on those days that he got thinking about it all, he would bring up their names, on the off chance that any of them had surfaced.

I would always answer him with the standard reply, word for word.

'Dad, the minute either of those bastards surface, trust me, you'll be the *very* first person to know about it'

It had always been for no other reason other than to placate him and help pull him out of the malaise that he'd be in which, given his surroundings, was not exactly the ideal mental state for the old man to find himself in.

While not quite obsessed as my dad about them, I had also continued to keep them in my head over the years, how really could you not, though? The two people that you blamed for losing your dad for ten years of your life, killing your mum and having your sister disown you and the rest of the family. These aren't the kind of offenders that you forget in a hurry and - some nights - I saw the two of their faces in my sleep, knew their faces better than I did my own. Lording it up on the outside, laughing their tits off at my dad as they enjoyed their freedom.

Realistically, though, when it came to any chances of vengeance? Forget it. Because that's what I did, as much as I hated every inch of both their being. I'd never known *hate* until those two. I thought I had, with Celtic fans. But when it came to those two, who were responsible for dad getting the jail?

The dark thoughts that I had when it came to *if* I could be alone with them in a room for an hour, and the pain I would subject them to, for dad. That's all they were ever going to be, thoughts. They'd taken dad's last best years of his life from him, just so that they could skip prison but a lot of time had passed by then and - reluctantly - I'd eventually put it down to a case of not forgiving and not forgetting, but nothing further than that.

One of them - the Peruvian, not exactly someone who was "in hiding" back in South America, having escaped from a

European prison - you'd have needed a small army just to even get close to, and the other one - the Dundonian - who left my dad holding the baby?

He - unlike his co-escapee - had went complete ghost. Dropped off the face of the earth. Maybe a year of dad being on the inside - and the obsession I'd had in trying to prove his innocence - I'd even hired an internet private eye of sorts to check into where he might be in the world, but all searches had come up as blank.

It was almost as if he hadn't existed.

Chapter 22

Nora

'No, mate. He's not been here all day, eh. Normally pops down in the morning, for at least a couple of hours anyway, but haven't seen any sign of him, and I opened the place up this morning'

The oil and dirt covered mechanic at the scrappy - who had been working on removing something from the engine of a two thousand and three Vauxhall Vectra - stopped what he was doing to stop and talk to me while a German Shepherd barked viciously at me but, fortunately, from the relative safety of the iron fence that it was tied up to.

'Ach, no worries, pal. I just needed to see him about a wee spot of business but I'll catch up with him later on. I'll let you get back to things'

I assured him before he went on to tell me about *this bloody alternator* - that he was having a bit of a challenge trying to get off in time for the customer who was coming down to collect.

'The fucking nuts on the fixing bracket are all rusted to fuck'

Almost told him that I hadn't asked for his life story, only where his gaffer was. You can't be a prick with everyone, all of the time, though. I think even most pricks realise that.

Instead, I just nodded to him while saying that I was the last fucking person to look at for mechanical tips. I remember that time I was pretty much expecting an M.B.E from the queen just because I'd managed to change my windscreen wipers on the Escort that I'd had back in the eighties. Not that I'd accept it from the old boot, mind. Be good to get the invite from the palace though, just so you could be given the chance to tell the parasites to go and fucking ram it.

I'd ended up jumping in a taxi to take me out to Portobello, and McKenna's scrapyard. Spur of the moment stuff, like.

Following the visit to the gym - and with no other red hot leads to speak of - I'd jumped on the bus to Leith and headed down to that part of town, on a bit of a reconnaissance mission.

Popped my head into all of the boozers nearest to Easter Road, including the traditional pubs that I'd always known boys from the CCS to have drank in before, keeping in mind the comment that GGTTH1875 had left me - in relation to me coming to track him down - that went something along the lines of me knowing which pub he drank in, where he'd *always* drank in, and that he looked forward to my visit and that he'd get me a pint, once I'd woken back up again.

Wide prick.

I'd played the same role in each and every one of the boozers that I popped into for a drink, the Scot who was back home for a visit and was hoping to catch up with some of his mates when he was over. With me being in Leith I'd added the extra feature of being a Hibby who was going to the Rangers match the next day - which, removing the me being a Hibby part, *did* have its truths to it - something, I'd felt would help ease my integration to my surroundings.

It didn't take long before I found myself sitting blethering with an old jakey - must've been early Seventies and if not then, aye, some life the boy must've had - in The Corinthian, which was one of the two pubs that I'd have always went looking for any heads from the Capital City Service, before any other establishments in the whole of Edinburgh.

He'd already been sat there - near the end of his half pint and whisky - when I walked in and went straight up to the bar to order a drink.

When the barmaid was in the process of pouring out my pint of Tennents, I turned to the side to see the old boy staring at me.

'Alright, pal?'

I asked, kind of laughing at the way he wasn't really trying to hide the way he was staring. Normally cunts would know that not to be the best policy with certain people, and most definitely fucking me.

'Aye, son, aye. Been better and a hell of a lot more worse'

He replied in what sounded a well rehearsed - and used - reply, when asked how one was.

'Here, get this man here another round of whatever he's drinking, and one for yourself'

I upgraded my original order with the barmaid to universal thanks from both her and the jakeball beside me.

Nice to be nice, eh?

'Aww that's very nice indeed of you, son. You're a proper toff, so you are'

He took off his tartan bunnet and quite literally doffed it to me as I sat down beside him. I could've sat anywhere I'd wished in what was a relatively empty pub at that time of day, but to do that would have defeated the complete purpose of the reconnaissance. You don't find out much if you don't open your fucking mouth and talk to cunts, as was highlighted by me buying *Harry* his half pint of heavy and Jamiesons, and the results that it produced.

The drinks, a clear ice breaker that led to the pair of us sitting blethering away, like we'd been old drinking buddies for years. Hearing my story - and how I was over from Amsterdam - he sat there laughing away while telling me that he'd completely obliterate what was left of his pension 'hooring' with the window girls. Dirty old bastard, eh!

It was when we got talking about the Rangers match the next lunch time that I tried my luck, when it came to any info on Swanson.

'Aye, I've got a ticket. Looking forward to it like you wouldn't believe. Not easy getting to Easter Road when you live in the Netherlands, like'

I said, choking on the feigned enthusiasm for a match involving two sides I couldn't have given a flying about.

'Hoping to bump into some old pals, boys I used to go to the games with back when I lived over here, but have lost touch with over the years'

I said, leaning my way into asking the jakey if he knew who Swanny was, without me actually asking him directly.

'Some boys, them. Especially Swanny'

So into my act that I was, when I delivered this line I allowed myself to appear to drift away, with some supposed thoughts of those days of old.

'Who, Michael Swanson, from Niddrie?'

Harry's ears pricked up, sensing the chance to help the friendly stranger who had came in from the cold and topped up his drink.

Now, I'll admit. I hadn't had much interest in Mikey "Swanny" Swanson or what his life revolved around, until he started dropping his comments onto my channel, so he could've been from fucking Mogadishu for all I'd known, never mind Niddrie. But for old Harry to be namedropping someone of the same name of who I was looking for - *without* me having mentioned the first name of the boy - well, that had to have a bit of promise behind it?

'Funnily enough, Harry. Swanny's first name *is* Michael, well, Mikey as we used to call him'

I said, hopefully.

'Well, aye, aye. I suppose that's what the rest of the boys in here call him as well, when they're not calling him Swanny'

Oh now *this* was very fucking promising. Turned out that such a fixture of The Corinthian was Harry that it was almost *his* fucking house, so with that being the case, it was only right that he knew the comings and goings of pretty much everyone that frequented the place. That, in itself, possibly one of the reasons that he was taking a right good look at me when I'd joined him at the bar to order.

'Aw, you ken Swanny, aye?'

However much of what I'd sat and said to him, and the others that I'd ended up speaking to in the other boozers, and as much of it had been an act.

The enthusiasm that I'd said this to the old man was with the utmost of sincerity. Happy that I was speaking to someone who was the type to know every cunt else's business, and more specifically the business of the radge soon to be dead cunt that had provoked me enough to make me board planes and cross international waters to get to him. *Ecstatic* that he had casually made the comment that confirmed that Swanson drank there in The Corinthian.

That hot or cold game that I used to play when I was a bairn? Well *now* we were getting into the boiling scorching hot area.

Apparently - according to this fucking oracle that was sat beside me - Swanny worked for a courier service and drove from Scotland to the Midlands in England and back again each day through the week, but on any Hibs home game at the weekend would be seen there in The Corinthian before and after the match.

I didn't want to get carried away but hearing the words flow from Harry, I felt like I'd struck green and white gold.

'They're a lot more calmed down these days to what they used to be like, Swanny and his mates. They used to be those casuals that went to the fitba and fought with the other teams fans, never seen the point. You're meant to go to support your team, not worry about knocking the living daylights out of the opposition fans, eh?'

'Aye, we've all got a past though, Harry, eh? I bet he's a lot more calmed down now, wife and family and that?'

It felt strange, defending the man that I was going to take out over a month's worth of frustration out on whenever I set eyes on him, until I realised that I wasn't defending him at all and was actually defending myself, up against Harry's take on how pointless that stuff all was.

Knowing that - with the intel given - there wasn't much chance of me bumping into Swanny there in an Edinburgh pub when he was sat in a van on the A seventy four, I didn't think there was much more point to extending any more of my day to trying to find the cunt.

Which was why I landed in Portie, at the scrapyard.

Having that last drink in The Corinthian, I began to think about what I would do for the rest of the day - with me now suddenly being at a loose end - because I sure as fuck wasn't going to spend it getting fucking hammered with an old jakeball. I was just about recovering from the self loathing of that afters in Lochee, and the furthest thing from my personal requirements was more shame.

The boy - Strings - that I'd got speaking to at Fir Park, and what he'd let slip to me about a certain Davey McKenna? Didn't seem like too bad an idea, to take advantage of the free time I'd been granted, by trying to see if I could get some kind of a visit with the man himself. There was *plenty* that I was going to have to fucking say for myself, if given the chance, and under favourable circumstances, which was never going to be a guarantee with the man.

Shit like that - if you didn't take the chance to do, when you had the chance - would haunt you for the rest of your days, long after you'd left Scotland again. Due to that lost decade of the nineties - and from the accounts of those who lived through it - and what a decade it had been, I *owed* it to myself to have that face to face meeting that I'd always dreamed about having, once I'd finally managed to piece everything together over the circumstances of me being trapped in that Weegie housing scheme flat that night with the gear, and my ill advised idea to take a copper hostage.

Not that any of my efforts had got me anywhere, stood there saying my goodbyes to the mechanic as he positioned himself back underneath the Vectra bonnet.

With the bit between my teeth though, I was soon on a bus to the Muirhouse / Silverknowes area of the city. Now while the boy Strings had not exactly drawn me a map, or given me name or number of Casa McKenna, he didn't really need to. That big black and white mock Tudor mansion which was easily four times the size of all the other houses on either side of it and the ones across the road.

Stood outside, I had a wee peek through the gates, following the drive all the way up to the front of the house where a silver Mercedes SLK sat parked outside. There was more CCTV cameras around the place than you'd have found in an airport. Cameras fitted to the front of the house and then another batch of them fixed to the top of the perimeter wall, that stretched around the grounds.

With as many cameras as there appeared to be - and I can only have imagined that there were some I hadn't even clocked - I'd already assumed that if there was any kind of real security to the place, then I'd have already been clocked by someone on the inside.

May as well, eh? ? I thought to myself as I pressed the intercom that was on the outside of the massive electronic gates.

'Yes?'

Came a woman's voice, after quite a bit of a wait, so long, in fact, that I'd impatiently pressed the buzzer again. She seemed irritated and put out by having to come and speak to me, and it showed with how short she was with me.

'Emmmm, Mrs McKenna? I'm an associate of your husband's and I was just wondering if ....'

I didn't get another single word out before she cut me off.

'Wellllll, if you're, as you say you are, an *associate of my husband's* then you would already know *never* to come to this house looking to do business with him'

'Now piss off before I call the police'

'Aye, well, tell your hubby that an old friend from the Nineties was looking to catch up with him, another time, maybe aye?'

I replied but was no longer sure if she was listening to me anymore, having said her piece.

Fuck, that didn't exactly go as planned. There was me thinking that I was going to be fucking running things from the moment someone came to the intercom and, instead, she completely called my bluff and took my pants right down for me.

I wasn't fucking happy, mind. Had never been much a fan of cunts trying to talk to me like that, and wasn't really giving a fuck if it was a woman in her sixties or a boy at sixteen. Talk shit, and shit you will most certainly be handed.

I wasn't fucking around to find out if she was bluffing about calling the police, though. Fuck, as far as I was concerned - there in Scotland - that was the magic words that you only needed to utter if you wanted to turn me into a ghost.

I must admit, though. I was heavily buoyed later on that evening - sat in Dirty Dick's on Rose Street - back in the city centre drinking overpriced lager as I sat contemplating about the likely scenes over at the McKenna household.

It may not have big, wasn't clever and *definitely* did not make up for ten years in jail, but even so. If Mrs McKenna had appeared to be mildly put out at having to find it within herself to actually answer the buzz of her intercom to speak to a stranger, how the fuck was she - and I sincerely hoped, her husband in attendance also - was coping with the shish kebab and garlic bread, white pudding supper, chicken tikka massander with pilau rice, shrimp chow mein, fourteen inch double pepperoni pizza - all ordered from different eateries - that had been "arranged" to be delivered to their mansion, over the course of the same hour.

And then the cherry on top.

The rent boy - whose number I'd found on a card shoved in a city centre phone box - booked for visiting a *Mr McKenna* and strategically timed to arrive *just* as the McKenna household were starting to calm down again from the tsunami of fast food deliveries that had flooded their house a little earlier.

Small victories, eh? Whatever you could call it, the images in my mind of the chaos at their big posh house left me feeling well chuffed in the way that prank calls really should not have been able to do for a man in his fifties.

That, alongside - providing the old geezer at The Corinthian had been gen with me - the knowledge that the next day it was now looking nailed on that I was going to find Swanson at some point over the day down in Leith. With Rangers coming to that part of the city it was sure to be carnage, and oh make no mistake about it, I'd be contributing to it.

The prospect of that *alone,* leaving me sat there in the boozer feeling as if I was a bairn on Christmas Eve.

Chapter 23

Nora

Sitting in that wee cafe on Leith Walk, back of eight in the morning, I was absolutely fucking buzzing. Hyped over the prospect of a game of fitba that didn't involve my own team in a way that I'd never thought possible. Well, outside of anything related to gambling, obviously.

I'd been up for hours, even before that. Saturday being the day that - traditionally, anyway - you've worked hard all week long and - reaching that blessed day - it was almost your birthright, to allow yourself a nice wee bit of extra kip.

Not *that* Saturday, though. I was way, way too excited about what the day's prospects had held in the palm of its hand. I mean, I'd been fucking buzzing the night before just *thinking* about the next morning so aye, now that it had arrived. Take a fucking guess what the boy Nora was like, eh?

You know when you wake up and straight away the good things going on in life pop right into your head, and it has you springing out of bed with a big fuck off smile on your face, ready to face the day. That was me that morning.

Don't get me wrong, either. I wasn't waking up in no fucking garden of roses, mind. Still had the small - *fucking huge* - issue of the bizzies looking for me, and with me having absolutely ride all idea of how well or how pish their search for me was going. It was always something that I couldn't not have hanging over my head. At the same time, though. It's all about priorities, eh?

And when it came to mines, worrying about being caught by those clueless cunts came well down in the list, compared to finding Swanson.

Like I'd said to myself - when first hearing of the coppers at my mum and dad's house looking for me - if gaining a wee bit of attention from law enforcement came through my pursuit of the imminent disembowelling of this Swanson cunt then, so be it. I'd have been happy as fucking Larry to have holed myself up in some Edinburgh rental, for as long as it took for me to get myself another passport to get myself back to the Netherlands, if it came down to it.

Let's just say - that Saturday - that the five o were the very least of my worries.

I sat there in the *Walk in* cafe with a cup of tea and a couple of bacon rolls - that I'd deemed more of a necessity than any real desire to have something to eat at that time of the morning - while thinking about Swanson. Probably just surfacing for the day wherever the fuck he was, buzzing for the lunchtime kick off himself, if in a completely different way to what I was.

The bacon rolls, I'd felt, were an insurance policy because, with the best part of a gram of Ching in my hipper and with plans for me to get fired into it in the not too distant future, there would be no guarantees that any further food would be partaken over the day. A boy's got to keep his strength up when possible, eh?

I had the *best part* of a gram in my pocket because - depending on how you wanted to look at it - I'd either been well behaved the night before - by not fucking tanning the whole lot of it - or badly behaved to have found myself *back down* in the pubic triangle - late on the Friday night - and putting myself in the position of procuring Ching from a random dealer I'd bumped into in the toilets of a pub along the road, funnily enough, prior to heading *into* the triangle. Not that I'm trying to buck pass or fuck all, like. The Ching came *before* the pubic triangle, though, that's all I'm saying.

Even when buying it from him, it was from the strategy of having it for the next day. Couple of Patsies up my nose right before I stormed into The Corinthian and fucking wrecked the joint sounded like just the very dab, the thought had been as I passed him the notes in what was the quickest of exchanges that, once completed, was ended with a warning from me that if the gear was shite then he was going to have me to fucking deal with.

'Best in the city, mate'

He said cocky as fuck while leaving the small bathrooms that could barely handle a two person drug deal, never mind getting to discussing what size of cats that you could swing around.

'Aye, that's what they all say'

I shouted after him, knowing that I'd heard the same patter many times before.

Couple of lines just to test the water, eh? I thought to myself, while in the process of following the dealer back out before backtracking and ducking into a cubicle and quickly chopping out a couple of lines with my Matthijs de Groot ABN AMRO bank card.

'You got lucky, ya cunt'

I smiled to the dealer - sitting at a table with his mates - when I eventually left the bogs - absolutely fucking flying - and departed the boozer altogether.

With a couple of Patsies of - what was clearly high grade - Ching up me, ending up walking deep into the pubic triangle on my own late on a Friday night was as predictable as it was tragic.

Fucking good at the time though, mind, and with that, alongside all of the McKenna stuff from earlier on, Friday had been an absolutely magnificent entry point into what had looked to be shaping up as a weekend for the ages.

Ching makes you do the most stupid of things, though. And by that I'm not talking about going for a couple of lap dances. With thoughts about what the Saturday was about to bring, as I walked back to my hotel from The Western Bar, I thought it would be a good idea to record and upload a wee spur of the moment video, to my Utility Defence channel.

The last video I'd had up on my page had been me when I'd snapped about the trolling from that GGTTH1875. In the video I'd said something like stay tuned for an update, but due to all that I'd had on since getting to Scotland, putting videos onto YouTube hadn't really registered. For all my subscribers had known, I'd just been bullshitting and that I'd had no intention of *actually* coming to seek out the internet hard man who had been leaving the comments.

A wee video walking up one of Edinburgh's most iconic streets would put paid to any of that shite, eh? I thought to myself, as I walked from The Western and towards the colourful Victoria Street. With the swally that I'd put away, mixed with the swagger and arrogance that the Ching always brought out in me, I pulled out my phone and made the recording without a second's thought.

Alright, cuntosssssss

(Throwing a fist towards the camera)

Or specifically, cunt- OH. Did I not fucking tell you that I was coming for you, no?

(Looking at that camera I swear in the moment I'd genuinely thought that the cunt Swanson was actually looking back at me)

Well ...

(Taking the camera away from my face and panning it around to show the sloping curved street)

Recognise anything?

(Bringing the camera right back to show a smirking me)

I'll be seeing you tomorrow.

(At this I'd suddenly remembered that it was quite late on and looked at my watch to see that it was around one in the morning and, looking back up towards the camera again)

Actually, I'll be seeing you *today*.

And to the rest of my subscribers, keep your eyes peeled for my next video, I promise you that it's going to be one that you do *not* want to miss and if you've not already subscribed then you're going to want to hit that button, now.

Stay safe, everyone. Well, apart from, *you*.

(I'd guessed that any subscriber following me would've known who I was specifically talking to)

Fucking governments, Delta Force, Mossad, S.A.S, NATO and international peace treaties could not fucking keep you safe, my friend.

I uploaded it there and then, walking up the hill on my way to my hotel at The Cowgate. Pippo had always spoken about being careful what time of day you uploaded the videos, and to make sure that you upped them at the same time as when most of your followers would be awake and using the internet.

Fuck that, I said, and fuck any of that hashtag shite that everyone had been starting to do on everything.

Instead, I tapped out a simple - but in my mind very much effective - title for the video of

The calm before the storm

With a title like that, I may have overlooked the fact that only really *I* knew the background of what was about to go down in a matter of hours time, and that the title was probably a bit vague for everyone, but just you try telling that to the boy who's flying on Ching, unassisted and in control of the iPhone.

I sat there in the Walk In going through some of the comments that the video had already attracted in the seven plus hours that it had been online for.

The majority of the comments full of well wishes for me to fuck him - whoever this person was that had clearly got to me in a way that I'd been willing to share with the public - up.

JerryThaNerd
I am TOTALLY here for your next video, bruh

Frank_loves_Dank
Gotta respect a man who will fly to another country for a straightener. That's some top, top level commitment to fucking people up. Respect, bro.

Smiler99
Beat that assclown's ass, bruh.

Clipperzzz
Someone best call Inspector Taggart because there bout to be a murderrrrrr!!!

JenJenJo
*LOVE that accent, especially when you swear *love heart eyes emoji**

Johnny-Robbbo
Fucking bury that spoon burner, lad. Mon the fucking Gorgie!

The comments - as always - were a mix of supporting, funny and random. Reaching the end of them - having started from the first ones that had been posted and worked my way up to most recent - that was when I saw that within the last half hour, *he'd* left a comment.

GGTTH1875
Yawwwwwwwwwn

Sleepy, aye? I thought as I looked at his comment.

I'll be fucking putting you to such a deep slumber that Sleeping Beauty will be talking about you behind your back, saying about what a lazy cunt you are, I said under my breath, as I put my phone away and fucked off through to the cafe's wee single bathroom, to get a line or two up my hooter - which meant two then - and get the day's festivities officially kick started.

Having not remotely noticed how long I'd been sat inside the warmth of that wee cafe, when I walked out back onto the street I couldn't help but notice that things were far busier than when I'd ducked into the Walk In. You could tell that there was a game on in a few hours time, the combination of early morning shoppers, walking up the hill towards Princes Street and the St James's Centre, workers still on their way to work, and the splattering of the colours green and blue that was on show.

The occasional solo Hibs fan simply trying to get himself from A to B for whatever his morning's plans were. When it came to the Rangers side of things, bigger pockets and groups of them, no doubt fresh off the train at Waverley and in search of an away friendly boozer that they could hole up in until kick off time. From some of volume of some of them - in that fucking Weegie accent of theirs - it appeared that they'd already got their day's sesh underway. Loud, lairy and funny to absolutely not one single cunt on the street, apart from themselves.

I found myself behind three of them, when I'd stepped out of the cafe. Bumbling down the street, each clutching the obligatory bottle of Buckfast.

'Here to see the Rangers, yer only here to see the Rangers, here to see the Rannnnnnnngers'

The three of them sung as they walked down the street, me a couple of metres behind them.

Shouting and singing into random members of the public's faces, who were walking past them in the opposite direction.

'FUCKING BOOOOOOOO'

One of them crouched down to get in the face of a wee boy - couldn't have been more than ten - who was wearing a Hearts Umbro bench jacket, while holding his mum walking past them. Poor wee bastard fucking shat it, and his mum. Grabbing his hand tighter and pulling him out of the way of the adult who thought it cool to do such a shitey thing to a kid.

Fuck these cunts, I thought to myself, as I deliberately hung back behind them. Was only around ten in the morning and check the fucking nick of them? If ever there were three people who were destined to end the day with a sore face, it was them.

And it goes without saying, if I could've have played even the smallest of parts to this, then I'd have considered it as fuck all other than my basic civic duty.

One of them - the one in the patently obvious snide Stone Island hoodie that not only had its compass on the wrong side but the biggest of "Stone Island" fonts, written across the back that I'd have bet my fucking life that Otsi would have had signed off on only over his dead fucking body, and the same cunt that had scared the wee Jambo kid - was heard telling the others that he was 'bursting for a single fish,' and that he'd catch up with them, breaking off down Dalmeny Street while the other two carried on strolling down the walk.

None of them had clocked me at any point walking behind them, so full of their own shite that they were insisting on treating Edinburgh with. I'd followed on, flying from the Ching - always the most powerful lines of the day, your first - consumed with feelings of wishing great harm on all three of them, even though this was levelled with the confidence that it would come to them soon enough over the day. Wasn't fucking daft as to try and start something on a busy Edinburgh street with three weegies, already halfway into their bottles of Buckfast at ten bells in the morning, though.

Can't be carrying out my prime objective of catching Swanny - sitting having a pre game scoop at the Corinthian - if I was on my way to either the cells or to the Western General to get fragments of Bucky bottles removed from my head.

When he broke off to the side of Leith Walk, sensing an opportunity, I followed a wee bit behind him and be under no illusions, I *did* follow on with the intention of fucking leathering him, he didn't have to make it so easy though.

I stood across the road from him as - undoing the buttons from his jeans - he stood in a doorway to do a pish. Now I wasn't going to fucking attack someone - mid slash - due to the obvious splash back issues that would inevitably present themselves, but the minute I saw him shaking, I was fucking having him. He altered the plan though due to being an even worse cunt than I'd already established him to be.

While standing, urine flowing from him and the dribble already forming a trail on the pavement beside him. I could see it all happening *before* it did but while couldn't stop, it you can be fucking sure that I finished it, and him.

As he was standing doing his pish - on the same side of the street as he was on - there was this young girl, I don't know? Maybe sixteen or something like that, walking along. More paying attention to her phone than the pavement ahead, which meant that she wasn't prepared - in any way - to be met with a man stood there with his cock out.

In fact, it looked more like he'd clocked her before she'd come close to seeing him. This kind of confirmed by the fact that - with a member of the public passing - instead of him turning further away to prevent the lassie seeing anything. He turned *towards* her as the last bit of his piss started to drip out.

'Like what ye see, babe? Since it's already out maybe we dinnae let it go to waste, eh?'

She just kind of instantly screamed, dropping her phone on the ground before reaching down to pick it up and running straight across the road - almost getting herself ran down by a black cab - in my direction and then right past me up Leith Walk.

At this point I 'd already started walking over towards him, who was stood there - definitely half pished already - with a leer on his face, while he unsteadily attempted to button up his jeans, he only made it to button number one before I'd crossed the street.

'Fucking big man, eh? Scaring wee kids and flashing teenage lassies'

I said, feeling that joyful rage beginning to build inside me. That same one that when you felt it coming on, you knew it was only going to go one way from then on.

He seemed surprised by this. I think the whole stepping off the train at Waverley and acting a complete cunt from minute one - and with no accountability to go with it - had lulled him into some false sense of having carte blanch to do whatever the fuck that he wanted, here in the capital city. Wasn't even *my* city so you could hardly have ever given me the benefit of the doubt that I was defending it, in any shape or form.

I guess it could've been anyone that morning because, admittedly, I was hyped up to fuck in the kind of way that I used to get, when it was a Saturday morning and me and the Utility were off on manoeuvres to somewhere with the potential for a proper good scrap, like your Pittodries and Easter Roads. The fact that it had been a pond life piece of shit, like that Rangers fan, only made things a lot easier, as well as more enjoyable.

Don't get me wrong, all teams have got a element of fannies for fans and I'd made a few mates in Bar L who were current buns so it's not like any cunt could say I was anti Rangers. *This cunt* though was your general Scot's stereotypical idea of a Rangers fan, when visiting your town.

'Fuck's it to you, ya fucking weapon. Maybe just you mind your own fucking business, prick'

He arrogantly shooed me away.

'When you make wee bairns cry and expose your fucking Walnut Whip for an excuse of a fucking cock to your girls, I'll *make it* my fucking business'

It was all done in a heartbeat but as I said it to him I had reached down to pick up a triangular "flood" metal road sign, that had been by the side of the road, possibly left from the heavy rain that I'd flown into Edinburgh to on the Tuesday.

Before he even had a chance to reply to this, he found the majority of the sign smacked to his head, first of all sending him crashing back into the doorway, then against the door where he was kind of slumped against it. The door - itself - propping him up and the only real difference between him falling to the ground and remaining upright.

When I took the sign, readjusted it enough so that I could force the side of it right into his windpipe, followed by a boot to his balls so hard that I was surprised I never put a hole in the fucking door *behind* him.

Now he could find the ground, and where he wouldn't be getting up from again any time soon.

He tried to speak - I couldn't tell you if this was through hostility or in an attempt at some peaceful defence - but from the blow to the windpipe it was clear that speaking wasn't going to be too easy for him, not when he could barely fucking breath.

'Shhhh shhhhh, maybe it's better if you don't try to talk for a wee while. Give yourself time to recover, eh?'

I said with the most obvious of fake concern for him, hardly bedside manner stuff.

'And when you're taking that time out maybe use it to learn how to be not as much a *cunt*'

I followed this up with two beautifully connected kicks to his face - the second one with such accuracy you couldn't have done better with a fucking Predator on your foot - that left him with a nose that had exploded with blood as if someone had hit him square in the face with a water balloon, filled with red paint.

I felt king of the world as I walked away from him to re-join Leith Walk again to the soundtrack of his groans and - kind of concerning, for him - wheezing from his windpipe problems. The combination of the two forces of Cocaine and violence such a devastating cocktail but one that, when met with each other, I'd always found to be such a winning combination.

A wee bit down Leith Walk I passed a pub - The Crown - where it had appeared that quite a few Rangers fans has assembled. Strategically it was probably close enough walking distance to get to the ground but not too close enough to Easter Road to encounter struggling getting served, due to wearing away colours.

Stood outside it were the other two out of the group of three that had been in front of me walking down the road. Standing having a smoke I heard one of them saying to the other

'Where's this fucking fanny got to?'

Couldn't help breaking out into a smile as I passed the pair of them, thinking that they'd be waiting a very long fucking time before they would see their pal coming down Leith Walk, judging by the condition that he was last seen in.

Due to the terrible affliction I'd always had of an addictive and compulsive disorder for the finer things in life. The two patsies mixed with the violence had only given me a taste for it. Which sent me popping into a Macky D's bogs to get another line up me as I knew I was going to be on Albion Road soon enough and at The Corinthian, and for that, I wanted to be tip fucking top.

Ended up - predictably - having two Patsies, just to make sure, and fucking marched my way over to Albion road towards the boozer. The closer I got, the more concentrated the streets were full of people in their football colours, admittedly the majority in the green and white of Hibs.

I barely noticed anyone else, so focussed I was on my own personal mission. I'd waited fucking weeks on this moment arriving and oh fuck was I going to savour things. I was going to relish the brutal leathering that he was going to be on the other end of. The pleasure derived from heaping the eternal embarrassment of having this filmed for all my followers to see. My plan had been that it was not going to be much of a challenge to bribe some drinker - inside the boozer - with a few quid, simply to hold an iphone in the direction of me, when I was taking care of business.

Oh it was going to be sweet as a fucking nut, as those Cockneys say.

Which only made it such the anti climax, that it was, when I entered the heaving Corinthian, full of everyone all getting a few scoops in before heading off to the match. While heaving - and it had taken me a good ten minutes to go through what wasn't the largest of boozers - there was no sign of Swanson. Probably due to the self confidence of the Ching - and how things had went with that piece of shit hun bastard on Dalmeny Street - but I'd more or less assumed that it was all going to fall into place and next up was going to be Swanson sitting there like a fucking duck waiting on me.

Even checked the bogs and everything, literally knocked on the doors of each cubicle that was closed to see who was in there. I wasn't fucking about. Every single nook and cranny was getting checked. It made no difference, the elusive Swanson had remained just that.

The old jakey - Harry - from the day before was sat there, though, in the very same seat as he'd been when I'd drank with him, almost like he hadn't even fucking moved.

'Has Swanny been in this morning, Harry?'

I said having squeezed my way through the crowd to get to him. Despite the fact that it had been less than twenty four hours since we'd last spoken, it seemed to take him a moment before he was able to clock who I was, and what I was asking him.

'Alright, pal. How's it gaun the day? Swanny? Think you maybe missed him by about half an hour. Him and his boys, about fifteen of them, were in here earlier on but one of them got a call, telling them that some Rangers fans had been causing a bit of bother up in Rose Street so they all jumped into taxis up to the town. They'll be back in here after the game though as usual on home games, well, if they're not locked up, that is'

This was a blow to hear. I wanted this taken care of A fucking SAP and even a few hours delay was too much in my book. It was what it was though, and I couldn't say that I hadn't ever been in the position of sitting in a boozer with the boys before getting a piece of intel that would see the lot of us piling out in search of the enemy. It was interesting to hear that they'd all fucked off in search of Rangers and their ICF because - considering everyone's ages - I'd been under the impression that cunts like Swanny weren't active anymore. Then again, old habits die hard, I suppose.

Knowing that - on a day like this - there would most definitely be pockets of trouble going on in various boozers and streets in the vicinity of Easter Road, none of it was my fight. Because of this I just chose to stick there inside The Corinthian with all the Hibs fans, until close to kick off before sinking my last pint and - saying I'd see Harry after the game - heading towards the stadium to get myself in there in time for the early kick off.

My first impression - on getting inside - was just how Easter Road had changed from the last time I'd been there, and the terracing, now missing. Even the old segregation was gone which had been some prime real estate for standing in, back in the olden days where C.C.S and The Utility would stand and issue threats at each other all throughout the ninety minutes - most that would indeed be carried out after the match - alongside lording it up to the other side when your team tucked one away.

Second impression, what a fucking seat I'd been given by the Hibs ticket office when calling them up to buy a ticket. They'd placed me right in the corner, front row and as close to the Rangers end that you could now possibly get, inside the new format of the stadium. Their end had almost filled out and were already in full voice. Belting out God save the Queen - in the direction of the home support - which was something I'd always been confused about them. They say that the captain's peg in the dressing room at Ibrox has a framed picture of the queen above it? Don't get me wrong, I'm not one of those unionist cunts myself but each to their own, like.

I just had never been able to work out why the queen came into it. What's the point of worshipping some rich old cow - who is only rich in the first place because she gets handouts in the millions from the public, some who then worship her as a result - who both doesn't know who you are and definitely doesn't give a flying fuck about you. Proper serf like behaviour, if you ask me although a huge part of me had always suspected that the Rangers fans had always sung it *purely* because they knew it wound up the other fans, which it would.

I was so close to them it was almost white of the eyes stuff and you were able to hear each individual insult flying back and forth. Despite having no skin in the game, I couldn't help get involved myself and was soon issuing some carefully inflicted insults, directed at various individuals who had caught my eye. This being counter productive because my whole point had been to get a ticket for one of the areas of the ground that would be close to the Rangers supporters, and a part of the stadium where there would be a far better chance of finding some ex or existing C.C.S, there to get a wee bit of Saturday lunchtime excitement.

By the time the teams had come out onto the pitch - and with the couple of bumps I'd topped myself up with in the Easter

Road toilets - I was that pumped, you'd have thought I'd been a fucking dyed in the wool Hibs fan. Probably clapped the team onto the pitch more fervently than half of the fucking Hibs season ticket holders, sitting inside there.

Hadn't even been given a chance to calm myself down before Rangers had went straight on the attack, which had led to the ball being knocked out of play for a throw in to Rangers, right into my waiting arms. Their number four - Kirk Broadfoot - came sprinting up to the side of the pitch to collect the ball, to try and take a quick throw, only to find me standing there next to the advertisement boards, at the front of the stand. With a bit of impatience on his face urging me to throw the ball back.

'Aye, there you go, mate'

I shouted to him, before taking the ball and throwing it in the complete opposite direction of where he stood, choosing then to remind him that he was a fucking wanker, hand signal, the lot.

The Hibs fans around me absolutely lapping this up.

I was actually enjoying this, despite my neutrality. I'd missed this level of hostility and hatred felt in a public environment like this and the teams involved, for me, was almost irrelevant. I was somewhere with the type of edge to it that I lapped right fucking up. To illustrate this, almost for the first time since arriving in Scotland, I was able to put Swanson at the back of my mind, and concentrate on this beautiful wee cauldron of hate that I was sat in.

Swanson would be there for me, after the fat lady had broke out her voice, in a couple of hours time.

Chapter 24

Liam

'Where the fuck do you think you're going, son? Get you're arse back here, mon, you'

He was leaning against the drivers door lumming a fag with one hand and calling me back with the one finger from the other.

I'd tried to do that thing, you know the thing? Where you already know that it's you that someone's wanting to talk to, but you pretend that you've not clocked this and keep walking, hoping that it'll be enough for to get you out of the situation, like that rarely ever does, to be honest.

I'd had this weird idea that I was being followed - on my walk to the shop to get a few much needed provisions that were of paramount importance to recover me from the hanging state I'd been left in from the night before. A few square sausage rolls and a couple of bottles of Lucozade Orange and I'd be fit as a fiddle again - but on the few times I'd actually looked around, I hadn't been able to see anything out the ordinary.

Walking back out of Ahmed's again - and seeing them both standing outside their car, both completely reeking of a fucking swine abattoir - I just *knew* that they were looking for me.

Having plain clothed - or simple clothed - officers looking for me was always something that had been a possibility. Just pure risk management, like those businessmen talk about. If I'm to manage my way through life, in the way that I choose to, then that would inevitably involve some element of risk attached to it. Dad had called me from a phone box the morning before, though. First of all asking me if I'd had any visits from any law enforcement asking about him and when I'd told him that they hadn't, he then gave me the instructions to carry out for him *when* they eventually caught up with me and, he assured me, that they would and that it was probably more through luck - than anything else - that I'd not bumped into them yet.

This was now, probably, the moment that he'd predicted, the day before to me. Still, with the very much less than legal job I had on my own cards looming the next morning, and it weighing heavily on me, and becoming heavier the closer it got. I really could have done without a paranoid inducing visit from the Federales to have to put up with.

'We'd like a word with you, *Liam*'

The Scottish copper said to me, calling me back. You could tell what he was doing, with the whole use of my name even though we'd never set eyes on each other in his life. If he was Dundee C.I.D then he must've just been promoted because I'd never seen him around town and - at some point or other - I reckon I'd seen them all. I say "Scottish" copper because I was soon to find out that the other one, who was standing beside him, *wasn't*. Dutch or Belgian, something like that, that accent they kind of all have.

Having absolutely nothing on me, apart from a banging sore head, I was able to be a wee bit cocky with them, even though that was possibly straying from my dad's instructions that he'd given me, in preparation of when the visit came.

'And what can I do for you today officers?'

I smiled walking towards them, swinging my grocery bag back and forward.

'All will be revealed, my friend. Now if my intel on you is correct, you'll already be familiar with this process?'

He opened the front door of his Corsa and slid the seat forward, then tilted it.

Aye, I know, in the fucking back, I thought to myself as I made my way into the back of the car without saying a word.

'Good boy'

I heard him condescendingly say from outside the car before he re-adjusted the front seat so that he could get in himself. The passengers door and the other officer following suit.

'I'm Detective Constable Colin Samuel and this here is …'

'Detective Constable, Roy van der Elst, Interpol'

The other one cut in, with not a chance on earth that I was ever going to be prepared, for such an accent to come out of the guy's mouth.

'Interpol, aye? I thought you only existed on the telly, and at the pictures'

I joked with him while inside was breathing a sigh of relief that this visit looked more to do with my mental bastard dad, than it was his son.

'Oh, trust me, they exist'

The Scottish detective said - taking control again - while kind of rolling his eyes for my benefit, knowing that his partner - if that's what he was? - couldn't see him do it.

'So, anyway, you're a smart enough kid, so we're not going to do you the disrespect of having you sit here and explain to you why we want a word with you. Just tell us where he is and we'll be on our way, and so will you'

Now if this was the part where they expected me to come over all innocent while asking them

'Where *who* is?'

Then they were going to be pleasantly - on the face of it - surprised by my reaction.

Because this was the thing, my dad - who must be some kind of advanced chess player - had already told me to play ball with them. Not to be awkward, or to be seen as lying to protect him. Said to me that considering him and I had literally only seen each other once in our life - on what was one fucker of an introduction, both parts one and two that day - that I should play up on that. He wasn't wrong in what he'd said to me about the only thing easier than lying to a copper is telling the truth, which I'd been given license to. Well, my dad being dad,. License, up to a point.

In amongst my instructions to share with them - mainly surrounding the fact that I'd never seen him before in my life until the previous Tuesday, and where we shared some father and son time - he had given me one small white lie that I was to deploy, where needed. As far as he could game it out, I'd tell them so much truth, that when I dropped in the lie, it wouldn't look out of place to them.

'I take it by "him" you mean the person who *technically*, as well as legally, goes by the name of my dad?'

'Hole in one, Seve'

The one called Samuel replied back, appearing to be genuinely surprised at me not attempting to be awkward with him from the very off, something that had I not already been advised not to, I most definitely fucking *would* be. In my book, if you're not putting the bizzies through twenty questions when they try to interrogate you, then you need to be giving your fucking head a wobble.

Before actually telling him his answer which, incidentally, would be the only lie I told him, but according to dad *very* important. I took the two of them through him appearing out of the blue on Tuesday night - I'd felt it probably for the best to leave out the incriminating bar fight from earlier in the day - at me and mum's house to introduce himself to me, and told them how I'd never seen him until that day.

Sat in the back of the car telling them that me and him went out for a drink in the city centre, and that I hadn't seen him again since and - according to what he'd told me on the Wednesday morning when he left the afters - I probably wouldn't be seeing him again.

'Did he tell you *why* he was in Scotland'

The other detective asked, in that funny accent that made me think of that boy out of that Austin Powers film.

'We had twenty years of catching up to do, mate'

I appealed.

'Our talk was more heart to heart, man to man, than other stuff. I wasn't sure if he'd come to Scotland just to see me or not but I'm guessing not cause I'd have thought he'd have come to see me a long time before now, if that was the case. He just said that he was here on business and even that was in the passing when he was saying cheerio to me and that he had business that he needed to take care of over the next two or three days'

All of that - up to then - had been the complete truth. Dad had told me that it hadn't just been Scottish bizzies looking for him, which meant that the authorities had already sussed out that he'd internationally travelled, and that whatever they said I was just to agree with. If they said that he lived abroad then that was the story I was to also go with. I thought my performance had been decent and that had the old man been given a chance to see it, he'd have been well proud of his flesh and blood. And now for the lie, I thought. Because it was sure as shite that the question was going to follow, or be repeated, I suppose.

'Where is he? Where did he say that he was going?

'Look, this guy - apparently my dad - goes missing for twenty years and then appears out the blue, for a single night before disappearing again. Forgive me if I'm not in a position to give you things like his date of birth or shoe size but look ...'

I deliberately left the long pause, following my mini spurned son act.

'I don't know if it'll help you or not but he said that he had someone he had to meet up north. Shit, blanking on the name of where it was, but it's where Ross County play, I'm sure it's the same town as that, *Elgin*, no, it's not that'

The Dutch / Belgian detective looked as clueless as I'd have been if he'd asked me to name the town, village or city that Excelsior plays in.

'Fucking *Dingwall?*'

Samuel said, like he knew the answer anyway but was just saying it out loud because it was a major pain in the arse to take on board, Dingwall being fucking *miles* from Dundee, and even further from Edinburgh.

The strange thing was that it didn't feel weird, covering for my dad, considering the past - or lack of - that we both had. I wouldn't go as far as to say that it was all done through some deep rooted sense of loyalty to him as how the fuck can you achieve loyalty status with someone as quickly as that but, I don't know? That day we met, starting with that mad as fuck coming together we all had in The Nether, because of a game of pool, and then the "quality time" we'd spent hours later, once *officially* introduced. It certainly didn't make up for twenty years of being missing and leaving me and mum to fend for ourselves, but as far as first impressions, he was alright. It hadn't taken me long to learn about his reputation and had heard all the stories about him, but that had been decades before. You know how radgeys can start to mellow as they get older and look back at their antics and begin to realise that those days need to stay in the past. That was what I was getting from off him, when we'd sat speaking in The Trades that evening.

'Dingwall, what is Dingwall? *Where* is Dingwall?'

The Interpol guy turned to the side to the Scottish one and asked. You could tell that - not being from around here - he was feeling left out of the loop, there inside the car.

'*Dingwall* is a bigger pain in the arse than having an Interpol detective *up* your arse'

It wasn't hard to spy that the Scottish copper wasn't exactly too happy about having the other guy partnering with him. He wasn't exactly shy in showing it, anyway.

With me having told them where their man had headed off to, this, inevitably led to a further series of questions about the *whys* of him heading up north, exactly as you'd have expected and it really hadn't taken my dad to offer me any advice on this.

These questions were easy enough to bat back at them, with my whole 'hardly know the cunt' position such a safe landing for me to always look to fall towards, when it came to their lines of enquiry.

'Couldn't tell you, mate. He just said that he had some business to attend to. From what I've heard about him though I'm going to take a punt on it being something dodgy as fuck'

He'd have laughed at that, I thought to myself, sat there in the car - instead of being withdrawn and defensive as coppers are generally used to - as I egged the two of them on and doing anything but cover for the fact that my dad was a wrong un.

'Can you please tell me who else Mr Fulton was in touch with when he was here in the city?'

The guy - van der Elst - asked me, just as his partner's phone started to ring. I attempted to give him that same one track answer based upon me knowing barely fuck all about the person that they were looking for and - factually - that *they* knew more about the man than I did.

I didn't even manage to get the full answer before the Scottish copper - who had done much more listening than he did talking on the call - interrupted, still on the phone, with a loud.

'We're on our way. Keep me updated on the way, ok? Cheers. Remember, now. No arrests until we're back. Just keep tabs on'

Turning first to me.

'Right, you. Out the fucking car, chop chop. Fucking, Dingwall'

He got out with such a rush he smacked his door hard against a Honda CRV that was parked next to the C.I.D Vauxhall Corsa - not that he appeared like he was giving two fucks about it and definitely wasn't searching for a bit of paper and pen to leave his details - and slid the chair forward to let me out.

I think - due to the sudden change around - I was as confused as the Dutch Belgian Detective.

'Samuel, what the fuck?'

He shouted out the car to the other one, while I - just to be a dick - ever so slowly made my way out of the back of the car, to the detectives impatience.

'Mon to fuck, get a move on ya wee fucking reprobate'

I just laughed back at him before remembering that I'd left my carrier bag from Ahmed's there in the back and having to turn round and reach in to get it again.

While doing so, the detective still sat there in the passengers seat repeated his question, if you could call it that.

With a bit of a self satisfying smirk on his face, looking at me but answering his partner he replied.

'We need to be getting ourselves back to Edinburgh, Franky boy, and fucking *pronto*, that's what ze fuck'

He gave me one last look before jumping in the car. The two of them - like the film - literally gone in sixty seconds.

I knew that dad was in Edinburgh, had told me that after he got out of Dundee he'd be there for the duration of his time, before heading back to The Dam.

Seeing the look on that copper's face - having taken that phone call - and how urgently he now wanted - *needed* - to get back to the capital.

I couldn't have imagined that any of this was going to be in any way positive for my dad.

And there wasn't a single thing I could do to warn him, either. During that call he made to me - from the phone box - he'd told me that he was ditching his standard phone - maybe he was too paranoid but I guess when you've got fucking *Interpol* on your case, eh? - and was going to buy a couple of burners for himself, and that he'd give me a call once he'd got them up and running.

That follow up call never came, though. For all I knew, the next time he called me he would be back in Amsterdam again, with his feet up on his coffee table having a smoke and a flapjack. It was all on his terms. Despite having prior knowledge of the police looking like they'd just discovered something in connection with him, I literally had no way of knowing where he was, or how to get in contact with him.

Whatever the mad bastard was up to.

He was on his own.

Chapter 25

Stephen

Hullo, hullo, we are ra Billy Boys, Hullo, hullo, ye'll tell us by oor noise.

I sung alongside my fellow bears, as I marched through from the kitchen with another can. Fucking tell you, lunchtime kick offs? Not good for you, or your liver. I'd sunk three cans of Tennents since getting up - enjoying that early morning buzz that they'd provided - and was going onto numero cuatro as the Sky Sports cameras panned their way around Easter Road. The Rangers fans that were in their end of the stadium already all packed in and in fine voice. Me matching them from the kitchen room and through to the living room.

Fucking belting out The Billy Boys, so they were, Clear as day, as well. Wasn't surprised to see that some quick thinking bod at Sky Sports - anticipating the next line of the song - cut the audio from the Gers fans before viewers started hearing about anyone being up to their knees in Fenian blood, and stuff like that. For the record, Sky Sports can't mute me so the rest of the song was belted out with gusto, there in the living room as I cracked open the can and got myself in position for the game in my seat, even though - as usual during a TV game - I'd hardly be sat *in* it.

You could say that I tended to get a wee bit animated, watching the Teddy Bears. Was the same when I used to go to the games, home and away. Used to go on the Paisley Terry Hurlock Loyal bus to the away matches. Some days, them but - unfortunately -

the price of a season ticket for home matches and the average cost of an away match - ticket, transport, food and the all important peave - did not exactly align itself to the budget of a part time shelf stacker on nights at Asda. Could barely afford the Sky Sports - as it was - but was at least achievable, compared to going to matches.

Would've been a good buzz to be there - Easter Road - though. Was never exactly the kind of place that you ever found a red carpet rolled out for you, on arrival in the Republic of Leith but that only made it all the better when we won, which we normally did. Seeing the pusses - on the Hibs fans close to you - completely dropping when having to put up with three thousand of us lording it over them. Priceless, that stuff.

It was only a few minutes before kick off and the panel were all being put on the spot on their call over how the match would go, while - on the other side of the glass - you could hear the atmosphere ramping up behind them, from both sets of fans. The panel all going with the usual safety answer that it would be tight but that Rangers should just about edge it, rather than answer what they *really* thought, that we would canter to a victory.

Three nil, my prediction. No way were they going to be able to handle the red hot Jelavic who hadn't been able to stop scoring and even then, if they tried to double up on him then they'd be leaving space for others to move in and exploit.

FUCKING COME ON THE RANGERS, INTAE THESE CUNTS

I screamed at the telly as the cameras zeroed in on the two teams, stood in the tunnel, waiting on the ref's call to emerge out onto the pitch and commence battle.

And *intae* them we most certainly did, right from the very off. From the kick off we went straight at them. Tried to initiate an attack - that was intercepted by one of the Hibs midfielders - but we came right back at them again. In an attempt to knock it out wide to Edu, the ball - not quite reaching him - deflected off one of their players head's. The ball going flying into the Hibs fans, towards the front of the stand.

You saw Broadfoot going over to take the throw and him standing there with his hands on his hips in frustration. The camera angle then changing to show a more close up picture of events, which explained Kirk's annoyance. Those Hibs bastards were trying to be funny, by not throwing the ball back for him, obviously had it been one of their own players they wouldn't have been able to throw it back onto the pitch quickly enough.

The camera catching it from the view of behind Broadfoot while he looked towards the Hibs fans, bringing his hands up to the side of him as if to say 'come on, play the game, eh?' It also picked up which one of them, who was holding the ball. Some prick holding it with one hand while gesticulating towards our defender, before eventually throwing the ball back, but as far away as he could from Broadfoot.

The unfortunately placed pitch side microphone picking up his

'Broadfoot, you're a fucking wan ....'

Classic SPL behaviour, when it came to matches on Sky. Unless they train their staff the art of being able to know what someone is going to shout, *before* they shout it, they'll never stop it. I'd always thought it brilliant banter that they'd quickly cut the volume right at the part where you'd pretty much heard most of the insult anyway.

Fucking prick, I shouted at the TV at this random Hibs fan, no doubt Gers fans across the country were shouting something similar about him. The fans around him were all pissing themselves laughing, while also giving Broadfoot grief.

While waiting on the ball being returned back in Broadfoot's direction, Sky showed a slow motion replay of the incident.

And *that* was when it hit me and oh fuck, how it hit me.

Taking a big swig out of my can, while keeping my eyes on the TV, I almost spat the fucking beer out all over the living room when I realised.

YOU, IT'S FUCKING *YOU!*

I stood up, pointing at the screen then reaching for the remote to pause the game. I'd always said that I'd recognise him, if I was to ever see him again. Didn't think I ever *would*, but could never forget the face. I had to be sure, though. Heart racing like someone was chasing me with a chainsaw, I ran through to the bedroom and fished out the newspaper clippings I'd kept from back in the day, and ran back through to the living room again.

Looking at the faded cut out from the Daily Record, with the pictures of the two prisoners who had escaped from Barlinnie. Going from the small picture on the page and up to the TV screen and back again.

It fucking *was* him. Obviously he'd aged a wee bit in the years since he'd escaped - although weirdly looked good for it, as opposed to most people who age ten years - but nowhere near to disguising that it was one hundred and fifty percent fucking him.

Everything that followed? Complete and utter instinct.

I never thought I'd set eyes on the man in my life, who knew if I ever would again?

The game was literally only two minutes into the match, and I lived an hours drive away.

I'd been to Easter Road more than my share of away days and knew the stadium like the back of my hand, and where he was sitting, and where he'd come out.

It felt like the universe had presented me with an opportunity. One I never thought I'd get, but would quite literally have sold my world to be offered. Everything looked like it had all been meant.

I ran back through to the bedroom again, to the wardrobe to find the Nike box - from my Air Max I'd got years before - at the very back of the top shelf. Hadn't seen the box in years and - over time - I had almost assumed that I would never need to go looking for it, as it was almost sat there waiting on a day that I'd never see.

Pulling it down from the shelf and placing it on the bed I quickly opened it up and grabbed the Beretta M9 - the gun that dad had bought as a form of protection for if the cartel was to ever come to the house. Didn't know that *I* knew that he had it but had been glad that I did, having swiped it from his house, before the police took him away - and picked up the spare round of bullets, rushed back through to the living room again.

The fact that - according to the scoreline in the corner of the screen - we'd scored to go a goal up, now resigned to irrelevant.

Before leaving, I stopped to down what was easily three quarters left of the can, some of it dribbling down my chin due to my hurry to get it down me. The thought actually popping into my head that I was about to jump in the car - after four cans - and drink drive, something I'd never done before.

Then again, neither had I shot someone.

Chapter 26

Nora

GGTTH1875
Just wanted to check, mate. When you said that you were coming to leather me, you did mean 2010, aye?

The notification buzzed my phone about halfway through the second half. I'd suffered enough goading over the game - weirdly, considering I wasn't even a Hibs fan - from the Rangers support to the side of me, watching their team coasting through the match, three goals up - and them making sure the home fans fucking knew it - to have *this* cunt trying to antagonise me as well.

By the time I'm done with you after the match you're not going to know *what* fucking year it is, ya cunt, I thought to myself before shoving the phone back in my pocket, resisting the very real urge to bite back at him, publicly. It might have been a quick - but steep - learning curve but putting out your thoughts on the internet, while high on Ching, I'd found, had not been the best of ideas.

With the game being long gone, as a contest, and - as a knock on effect - the home fans somewhat subdued, the only noise coming from the away end, I'd started to lose interest and was beginning to start to think of *post* game plans.

Undoubtedly, it was going to involve heading back to The Corinthian.

That's not to say I hadn't been pro active *during* the match. Taking the chance at half time to have a wee wander around the concourse to see if I could stumble across any familiar faces, in amongst everyone milling around, grabbing a pie or heading for a half time slash, or in my case, another couple of wee bumps to get me up for the second half.

When I was in there - inside the cubicle - with the door locked behind me, while I racked up a couple of wee lines onto the pishy wee toilet roll dispenser that was fixed to the side, I couldn't help but overhear two wee cunts arguing with each other.

'You fucking said you'd do it, as well?'

'Said I *might*'

'Why don't *you* do it then, big man?'

'Hey, wasn't me that was telling every cunt that they were bringing a flare, like all the Ultras in Europe use, to the Rangers game and was going to light it up, eh?'

They were still at it by the time I'd done my two lines - the volume they were going at, the perfect disguise for the noises coming from the cubicle, not that I was too worried about that, mind - and come back out of the cubicle.

Two teenagers - about fourteen, sixteen tops, in matching black North Face jackets - were stood there, one of them with this flare, that they'd been arguing about, in his hands.

'Yer mate bottling out of using it, aye?'

I said, on the wind up. Fuck that Ching was fucking good, like. Mind you, I'd hardly touched the stuff in years so to be attacking it the way I'd been, since buying it the night before, no wonder I was flying.

'I'm no fucking bottling *anything*'

He said, looking a wee bit scolded that this had now escalated to strangers becoming aware of it all.

'He totally fucking is, by the way. Giving it the big one all week, once it arrived through the post'

His pal laughed, sensing a bit of support from me.

'One of those ones with the proper fucking flames shooting out of it, aye? No they pishy smoke ones that smell like some cunt's dropped their guts?'

I asked, mind ticking away.

'Aye, part of me is thinking that I should've waited until a night game. Kind of thinking that it would lose it's effect, being let off at the back of one'

'Aye, excuses excuses, eh?'

His pal laughed but was looking at me for back up.

'Fucking give me it here, ya cunt'

I said to him, taking over the situation from the two of them, as well as the flare.

'Watch out for during the second half, and it going off'

I snatched it out of his hands as I went to leave the bogs. I'm not sure he was that pleased about it, but what really was he going to do about it?

'Well, at least some cunt will be lighting it up today, eh?'

His mate shouted out after me, hardly showing signs of hostility over the fact that his pal had effectively just been stolen from.

When I was on my way through the concourse - heading back towards the stand for the second half - I almost bumped right into Banjo Ireland, and a couple of other recognisable faces, who were all standing getting served at the food kiosk. I had a snap decision to make as had thought I should maybe try and hang back and follow the three of them - to wherever they were sat - to see if they were part of a bigger mob of old CCS boys at the match.

Common sense kicked in, though. Things could've went downhill pretty quickly for me, if I'd been spotted by some of those old acquaintances from back in the day and something had kicked off. Would've just been my fucking luck to end up in a scuffle with some other cunt - that wasn't Swanson - and get myself huckled by one of the bizzies - there on match day duty - and carted off without having even *got* the straightener that I'd put so much time, money and effort into.

And even then, I'd have the fact that the local bizzies would only be moments away from the penny dropping over *who* they had in custody.

Nah, while I went to Easter Road that day looking to see if I could clock some of the older Capital City Service guard, that didn't mean to say that I wanted them to see *me*, if you know what I mean?

After the first half - and the exhilarating high tensioned powder keg atmospheric build up that led up to it - the second half was a bit of an anti climax. Games against the old firm are generally shite, if your team's not in the game. Don't get it twisted, though. When things are going your way, and you're either in a winning position or are still in with the chance of nicking a cheeky three points against them, then they're fucking well barry. This was not one of those occasions and to have lit up a flare - there in the home end - would have been fuck all other than - what the cunts in the away end would've called - a 'riddy.'

While sat there watching the second half action, I wasn't really 'watching' it at the same time. I was too busy peering into the future. I couldn't fucking *wait* to get out of that stand, and back to The Corinthian and get the business done. I looked around the three quarters of the stadium.

Where are you? I thought to myself.

There was maybe around fifteen minutes left to go when you started to see the odd wee group of fans upping and leaving. This wee trickle - as the minutes ticked down - building until, with five minutes left, there was only around half the amount of home fans that had been packed in for kick off. Maybe not a bad idea to get gone too, I thought. Bang a couple of extra large Patsies up my konk and fucking march my way down Albion Road like a man possessed and right into The Corinthian and be ready to shoot on sight, so to speak.

The moment I saw the YouTube user GGTTH1875 aka Mikey "Swanny" Swanson and soon to be seen in the obits of the local newspapers - and I really wasn't giving a fuck whether he'd be with a crew of his boys, standing at the puggie or sitting doing a shite in the bogs. He was getting fucking got.

I took one more look around the - apart from the away end - stadium that was showing more green and white seats than people by this point, as I got up myself to leave, via the bogs for a wee livener. The chances of Swanny being in amongst all those empty seats now well reduced to when I'd had the initial thought as I'd looked around thinking of him.

Doesn't matter a fuck, anyway, my follow up thought.

I'll be seeing you soon enough, cunto.

Chapter 27

Stephen

I made it to Leith. Not sure *how* I'd made it, right enough. I suppose grabbing the last two tins of Tennents - for the drive - that were left of the six pack, that I'd started tanning earlier on in the morning, probably didn't help, either. Driving on four cans, well, six by the time I'd reached my destination - I'd found out - had been more challenging than I thought it would've been, and I'd led a charmed life not to have either smashed into someone, or had anyone behind me grassing me up to the traffic cops.

The Astra that I'd almost went right into the back off as hadn't noticed it up ahead while reaching over to grab that fifth can. That Mitsubishi Lancer that I came within a baw hair of taking its passengers side quarter panel off, when it was going past me and I was trying to overtake myself. The hair-raising tailgating to intimidate whoever it was in front of me in the Punto to move to the side and let the big boys past, when at times you wouldn't have got a Rizla between both car bumpers. The multiple times I either found myself veering into the central reservation - when I was in the right lane - or going right into a ditch, on the left hand lane.

And all of that was just on the M8, to take me towards Edinburgh.

In an ideal world I'd have been one of those druggies. Like how you see them in the films, when they shove a wee bit of that white shite up their nose and before you know it they're all alert wide eyed and talking pish. Not that I'd ever put any of that poison inside me, though. Would've helped the old focus that day although some might say that had I taken a wee bit of that Charlie it might've been the difference between me being fucking daft enough to drive to Edinburgh to kill Norman Fulton, and not.

It was a hellish drive, though, and was relieved when I passed the 'Welcome to Edinburgh' sign - on the motorway - and had done so without wrecking myself, my Golf or anyone else.

So many full beam flashes that I'd seen in my rear view mirror that - most of them - indicated that I'd pulled off some kind of fucked up manoeuvre, that I wasn't even aware I'd done.

I was too far gone to care, and I don't mean with the alcohol although six cans *did* provide a buzz that was the path to inebriation. Who knows? All of my near misses and fuck ups behind the wheel might not have actually all been down to the Tennents. Not when all I could do on that journey was think about *him*. So consumed by the thoughts of killing the man - or one of them, at least - responsible for the downfall of the Craigan family. The nasty piece of shit who helped rob my dad of all those years on the outside.

I listened to the match on Radio Scotland on the journey, and celebrated when the other two goals went in as if I was standing behind the goal at Easter Road with the rest of the bears in attendance. Tooting the horn and flashing my lights, when hearing the high pitched scream of the Sportsound commentator as the second and third goals flew in.

A canter, just like I'd predicted.

Actually, with the scoreline - the way it was by the second half - as I arrived in Leith I was beginning to worry that it might've been a wasted journey because, if I was him, I wouldn't have been sitting inside that fucking shite hole of a stadium a minute longer. If Fulton had the same mentality, then I would be arriving at Easter Road to find him long gone. Had that been the case, I honestly cannot have ruled out me just walking about the streets of Edinburgh looking for him.

Getting near to Easter Road - on the road up to it, inside the space of a few minutes I'd managed to take the car up on to the kerb, making all the commuters standing at the nearby bus stop scatter. Following this up by driving through a red light, at a pedestrian crossing, and almost running over some old boy with a walking stick - from nowhere, it dawned on me that the last time I'd driven to an away game there, I'd found the area an absolute nightmare to get parked, something that others on our bus went on to confirm as being standard stuff for the bigger Hibs matches.

With the mindset I had that afternoon, though. Leaving your car illegally parked in a busy city like Edinburgh, while planning the murder of someone, is not something that you really give much in the way of fucks over.

Parking - abandoning? - it across the front of metal shutters with the

DO NOT PARK - 24 HOUR ACCESS REQUIRED

sign that belonged to a small backstreet garage, just a few minutes away from the stadium.

In such a hurry to get to the stadium, I never even stopped to lock the car, which was always a risky tactic to try in a Scottish city that was in the vicinity of a football stadium on match day. For fuck's sake? The lads at Ibrox that would make a killing "protecting" your car for you, and I left my Volkswagen just there for the taking.

I had other priorities.

It's not the easiest of things to do - running fast, after drinking cans - but I sprinted as fast as I could towards the ground, guided by the sound of the Rangers fans, who sounded like they were enjoying their day out in the capital.

'We can see ye, we can see ye, we can see ye sneaking out weeeeee can see you sneaking out'

I heard them sing, towards the Hibs fans, an indicator that they were now leaving in numbers.

I'm going to just miss this bastard, I bet, I said to myself as I jogged up towards the East Stand, where I'd seen him standing on the TV.

Go to all that fucking trouble, risk getting yourself lifted for drink driving, or a lot worse than that, and you'll get there and he'll have already fucking left.

I'd never wished for my team to be winning so comfortably less in my life at that moment. Reaching the entrance to the East Stand - with it being so close to the final whistle by then - I found the gates already open for the fans to be streaming out of. With there being no security standing around by it, I took the opportunity to sneak into the stadium, and head out into where everyone was sitting.

'Yer a bit late, mate. Game's almost finished'

Some smart arse said to me, as I passed him - and his mate - on the way into the stadium. The two of them laughing their way past me, while I just ignored the pair of them. Getting into the concourse I took a wee second to get my bearings over where I was, and where he'd been seen on Sky. Working this out I headed into the seating area, nearest to the corner flag.

Heart was fucking pumping like I'd never experienced before in my life. The weird feeling of emerging into a football stadium, while the love of my life are out there on the pitch, and me not even stopping to have a glance.

I suppose the scoreline - and how it had evidently dampened the spirits of the Hibees who had now departed the scene of the murder that they'd just watched Glasgow Rangers commit on their team - kind of worked out for me, once inside the place, because it made it a lot easier for me to look around and try to find who I was looking for.

Fucking hell, *that feeling,* when I spied him, still there. Had to stop myself from just pulling the gun out and walking over and executing him right there and then. Of course, I say that like some experienced hitman, instead of the six cans deep and never shot a gun in his life example, that I was that mid afternoon.

There wasn't much logic about the choices that I made that Saturday, but at the very least I'd managed to find some that told me that shooting someone inside a football stadium, during a match being beamed all over the world on Sky Sports, would not have ended well for more than just Norman Fulton. Aye, I was in the kind of a bammed up zone that I had never known to be a part of my whole fabric but I wasn't so far gone as to disregard the one very important part about shooting someone, the getting away with it.

Sitting there - barely taking my eyes off him - from his body language, I could tell that he was shaping up to leave.

Be cool, be fucking cool, I said to myself quietly, something that in the noise of the stadium no one was ever hearing. The heart rate that I had on me did not resemble anything close to *cool*.

While pretending to watch the action out on the pitch - Rangers making a late substitution which was just your usual time wasting and seeing the game out decision that managers in a winning position make every game - I watched him making sure he had everything that he must've took to the game with him, before making his way along the row of seats until he got to the aisle, walking pretty much right past me, in the higher up in the stand aisle seat that I'd sat down in.

He wasn't the only one leaving around this time, which made *me* leaving my seat closely behind him look nothing out of the ordinary. Following behind while enjoying the luxury that I had over him - in that only one of us knew what the other looked like - I watched him pop into the mens.

This could be *the* chance, I thought, following him in.

When I shot him, I just wanted it to be in whatever workable way that would see no witnesses. I wouldn't have been against pulling the trigger right there inside Easter Road, inside the mens, as long as there was no one else inside there when I done it. From the bogs, and back outside onto the street, it would've taken me seconds. By the time anyone had realised what the noise had been, and discovered Fulton lying there dead, I'd have been back on the street and gone.

No such luck. Apart from Fulton - who had popped inside a cubicle - there was another three men in there either in mid pish or washing their hands.

'Who the fuck does that cunt think he is, anyway? Thinks that he can just go and bad mouth you and their be no fucking repercussions to go with? No comebacks? Well he's about to learn the hard way. I'm not giving a fuck who he's with or who he's not. This wide prick fucking DIES, this afternoon'

I - and the rest - heard coming from the cubicle, closely followed by the sound of him sniffing once and then a few seconds later sniffing in a similar way for a second time.

One of the Hibs fans inside there who had just finished blow drying his hands looked at me and pressed the side of his nose with his index finger, to indicate what was going on in the cubicle.

I'd thought - at first - that he was on the phone to someone else before it had became apparent that he was giving himself some kind of pep talk, alongside taking Charlie.

To be honest, I'd never thought that he was ever the friendly and cuddly type, not from what I saw on the news and in the papers about him. Being separated by a few inches of wood in the mens at a football stadium, though? I could hear that the man was quite clearly fucking insane. *No one* talks to themselves like that, well, no one that I'd ever heard speak or met before.

From what he was saying, though. It sounded like he was up to something, hatching some kind of plan. One that didn't sound like it was going to be too pleasant for someone. I thought he'd maybe said Swanny but this was while the blower was in action so it could just as easily have been fanny that he'd said, the way he was getting carried away in there.

In the time I'd been stood in there a few men had come and gone, without Fulton emerging from the cubicle. At no point was there ever just the two of us. I'd pretended to do a pee, washed and dried my hands a couple of times - all for effect -

just to excuse me hanging around in there and not looking like a George Michael. When I heard the sound of the door unlocking I'd just finished washing my hands and was standing there with my hands over the drier when he marched out, and I mean fucking marched. I'm surprised that the man didn't just walk *through* the wooden door, the mission that he came out of that cubicle on. Those sniffs that I'd heard? Well - and whatever the fuck that shite does to you - they must've been some pure uncut Colombian shit.

I have to admit, seeing him, like that, he looked quite fearsome, and even though he hadn't even noticed me when he came bouncing out of the cubicle, I'd felt a wee bit intimidated by his sheer presence. The man looked in some kind of zone, but the look on his face and what was in his eyes. He looked a dangerous bastard up close, but I wasn't too sure how much that was down to what that powder does, when you take it.

A gun, though? What a leveller that can be when pitched up against some drugged up crazed mad man with a look on his face that would keep kids away from the fireplace. Bullets don't care for your mean look that you have on your face.

With him leaving, I ditched drying my hands - those machines never fully really work anyway, always walk away from the fucking things wiping my wet hands on my jeans - so that I could keep close to him. I merged in with the other Hibs fans all walking out through the concourse, while keeping an eye on the back of him, every now and then taking a few faster steps to get myself closer to him. That, in itself, not such an easy thing to do because *he* was walking like a man with some kind of a purpose.

He'd almost had a fight with someone out on the street, due to his lack of comradeship towards his fellow fan. Pushing one fan out of the way as he walked past him, the guy saying something about it. Fulton turning around and pushing him again - harder - landing the guy on his arse with the additional warning to stay down there.

At one point, I got so close to him in the crowd that I could have quite literally pulled out the Beretta and - with the length of my reach - pressed the end of the barrel against his head and ended him.

Not the place, Steph. Not the time. I'd never murdered anyone before and could never see ever being given a reason to do so again, but something inside told me that it would feel *right* when the time came. That it would *feel* the moment when I should do it. As long as I had him in my sights, that moment would arrive.

I just wished I'd known what his intentions were, and where he was going. Had I known this kind of intelligence, it would've possibly helped me know where *I* was going.

My 'intentions' not in question.

Walking down Albion Road he started to veer off in the direction of a boozer, The Corinthian. I hung back a little bit just to see the lay of the land, which I'm glad I did because, instead of walking right into the pub, he stopped outside, pulled out his cigarettes and lit one up, appearing to be on the look out for someone, rather than just someone standing outside a pub having a smoke watching the world go by.

I chose to make my way to the other side of the street, and allow us to be separated by the fans walking down it, with me still able to keep an eye on him.

He finished the smoke - pinging what was left of it indiscriminately out into the crowd of people passing by - and turned around and stormed his way through the doors to the side of him and into the pub.

At this point I would now have to just trust in the fact that whatever it was he had planned, it was going to involve him walking back *out* of the pub again, because he'd have to leave sometime. In my rush to grab the gun and leave for Edinburgh I hadn't grabbed my wallet. Could literally see it - sat there on the kitchen bunker back in my house - while I saw any route to me following him into the pub - to keep my eye on things - shut right down. The possibility of a stranger walking into an Edinburgh pub and opening up a slate, a non starter, especially with a Glaswegian accent.

That was okay.

I'd waited ten years for the man.

Hanging around outside a pub while he had himself a post match ale?

Why, it would almost be a pleasure.

Chapter 28

Nora

Here we fucking go then.

I have to admit, going through those doors felt like being back in the old days with the firm in a way that it hadn't the day before when I'd walked into the almost empty boozer. I had that top, top buzz about me as I bombed into the place. Could've almost felt the hands on the back of my shoulders, the screams in my ears and the breath of some of the other lads behind me as we stormed the place, hoping to catch the Capital City Service on the hop.

Instead? Fucking hell, the circumstances could not have been so at odds with each other.

Aye, maybe some things were the same too, though. It was match day and I was heading into the establishment with unflinching intentions of doing serious harm to someone linked to the Capital City Service. It's just that I didn't have the hundred or so friends behind me for back up.

That single fact should really have been enough to have made me see some kind of sense and stop myself right there and maybe not bother with it.

Aye, and fuck that.

There maybe wasn't a hundred strong team rushing in behind me - as back up - but by fuck, you wouldn't have guessed it from the way I swaggered in.

Cocaine, as they say, however, is a hell of a drug.

And don't take that as if it was only the Ching that was the reason for me going in there. I'd have *always* went in, it's just that I'd have went a completely different way about it, had I not had that top quality powder up me. Let's just say, I'd have been a lot more discreet, in my attempts at finding Swanson.

The place - through what would've been a combination of those that had never left the pub all afternoon and those who had left the match before the final whistle - was almost full to capacity already.

Due to that fucking stupid Ching, instead of having a wee snoop around, in the exact same cautious way that I'd conducted myself since embarking on the hunt for Swanson, I - arrogantly - thought that instead of going looking for him, maybe I could let him see *me*.

Ordering a double scotch for myself and seeing my old guy from the day before a wee bit down at his usual spot. I nodded at him while making the international sign language for me getting him a drink, receiving a thumbs up back from him.

Even in the short time that I'd been stood there - waiting to get served and then downing the double - there had been enough CCS enter to show me that this was where a lot of their boys were going to be popping up at. The very fact that they were there in the pub, instead of fighting with the ICF out in the streets, told me that there was nothing on for the day. It tells its own story when a firm is standing having a drink half an hour after the match, instead of smashing fuck out of their opponents in some side street scrap. When I was having my second double, for the second time of the day, Brett "Banjo" Ireland and his boys were within whispering distance as each other when they entered the boozer and walked past me, without them noticing. The three of them continuing on before joining another younger crowd at the bottom of the bar.

Still no Swanson but, like I said, the arrogance in me decided that it was time to stop looking and time to start being found.

In what some might have classed as a case of Dutch courage - where as me on the other hand would more call it Scottish stupidity - I fucked off through to the bogs. Not even bothering to do any of that clandestine hiding in the cubicle racking up the lines shite. Instead, I just fucking keyed the stuff. Having a couple of wee scoops while the bogs enjoyed a rare moment of quietness. The way I was, at that point. I'm not even sure someone else in there beside me was going to be enough to stop me from just getting wired into it.

I think, this proved by the way I exited the bogs and emerged back into the pub again, with a lit flare held up in the air. Crackling and fizzing away with some kind of green glowing fire shooting out of it.

This'll get these cunts' attention, I thought to myself when I found the flare - that I'd commandeered off one of the young team - in my coat pocket and, without even really questioning, or caring, about the fire and safety regulations of lighting up one of those things in a closed environment, lit the fucker right up.

Attention, I definitely attracted.

Felt like fucking Moses parting the Red Sea, the way I walked through the pub with everyone going out their way to make sure that they didn't end up in the path of the mad cunt holding the piece of fire in his hand.

I think that the only reason that I managed to get as far as I did - and wanted - was because of the colour of the flare. To anyone looking, I was obviously a Hibs fan, possibly defiant after a humping from the Huns or maybe just some cunt who wanted to use up the flare that they had, and had stupidly chosen a boozer to do it. There *was* some in there though that - looking at me holding the flare up, like I was the fucking Olympics - knew this was not the case. Banjo Ireland, for an absolute fact clocking me, me seeing him at the same time. There was no initial hostility from him, though. Just a curious look on his face, towards this unexpected bout of randomness after the game.

Without even stopping to think about things, my direction had taken me up to the pool table that - understandably - was not in use at the time. Jumping right up onto it although almost making a cunt of things and stumbling and dropping the flaming torch onto the baize of the table.

Once up onto that vantage point I was able to get a true appreciation of who in the pub were looking my way, *every cunt*.

And, well, now that I *had* their attention. There would be no better time for it.

I have absolutely no explanation for my actions over those following few minutes but turned into the town crier of Edinburgh. Waving the flare around like the bell those cunts use to tell everyone the news.

The scenes below on the floor were a mixed bag. Amusement, curiosity, fear and, from the point of view of the landlord, well, him? Proper incensed, he was. I already saw him - I assumed landlord anyway, had that whole *I run this place and don't ever forget it* vibe to him. Aborting the pint that he was in the process of pouring out to rush from behind the bar to confront me.

Wasn't quite sure what the fuck he thought he was going to be able to do about it, once he got around the bar and up to the pool table, mind? The zone I was in? Well you don't really have to explain to any cunt what kind of a zone you were in after telling them that you lit up a flare inside a - likely going to be hostile - pub and then proceeded to walk through the place before getting up onto the pool table to shout to everyone in there.

At best he could've got a boot in the coupon from me. At worst? Well I still had that flare in my hand and - having lit it right up without thinking about - well I was going to have to get rid of it at some point so it would've been a good idea not to be coming the cunt with me, when I had it in my hand.

'HERE YEEEEEE HERE YEEEEEE'

I shouted across the room - which was almost stood there silent which you'll be well aware is almost a minor fucking miracle for a place that indiscriminately sells alcohol to members of the public for consumption - while swinging the flare back and forward like that big bell that's normally swung. Sparks flying out into the bar as I flung it around.

I'd never actually used a flare before. Closest I'd come was in Monchengladbach, with United with my dad when we played Borussia over there where getting your hands on things like that were a lot easier in Europe than back home in the U.K. Cunts were being randomly searched on the way into the ground though and muggins here was one of them. Was well pissed off when the copper took the two from me that I'd bought a couple of hours ago in what I'd taken to be the German equivalent of Frank's Army Stores. Would've looked right cool - that bright tangerine glow - inside the stadium that night, but wasn't to be.

Tell you fucking what, though. If you'd told me - that night in Germany where we watched United put in a performance where they had their backs to the wall more than you would do if you went for a night out to the Blue Oyster Bar - what the circumstances leading up to me *actually* lighting up one for the first time, there's absolutely fucking ride all of a chance that I'd have believed you. On the run from prison? YouTube video star? Me going on what would have normally been looked on as a kamikaze mission by going into The Corinthian on match day, by myself. None of it would've made sense, back then. All those decades later, though. Despite most of it - in the cold light of day - *still* not really making sense, it *did* to me, at that moment.

I was a man out of fucks, and full of Ching. Tell me a more dangerous mix and I'll instantly correct things, and tell you that you're talking a lot of fucking pish.

'I VISIT YOU ON A MISSION OF MERCY TODAY AND ...'

'WHAT DO YOU THINK YOU'RE FUCKING DOIN, YA FUCKING MANIAC?'

The landlord screamed up at me, now up at the table subconsciously holding onto the half pint of Guinness that he'd been pouring before clocking my capers.

'Just you shut your fucking mouth and let me speak or else what I *think I'm doing* is going to suddenly be recalibrated to involve you,' I crouched down a wee bit towards him before taking the flare - which because of how much I'd got into things I'd barely noticed that those things were pretty fucking hot to hold - and dropping it into the pint glass, extinguishing it in seconds. I'd made my point - as far as the flare - and now had everyone's attention. The flare's use had expired, plus, it really was only a matter of time before I unintentionally burned me or someone else with it, or ended up setting the boozer on fire.

I stood back up to greet everyone, looking on, and pulled out my wallet. The landlord made an attempt at pulling at my leg and received what I'd have classed as nothing more than a playful boot, as I reminded him that I was getting down again in a minute. I just wanted a moment to say my piece. I wasn't asking for much and I'm sure the place had seen *much* worse than what was taking place that mid Saturday afternoon.

'I'VE GOT FUCK ALL PROBLEMS WITH ANY OF YOU IN HERE AND COME IN PEACE BUT THERE'S SOMEONE - WHO YOU *DO* KNOW, THAT IS TRYING TO DESTROY MY LIVELIHOOD, AND THAT *IS* A FUCKING PROBLEM'

I looked over at Brett Ireland and his boys - both the old guard and a mob of much younger boys - where things seemed to be a bit animated. I couldn't have been completely sure as there was a lot going on but it looked like some of the younger team were wanting to come over and - have a go at - leather me but the older heads were telling them to hang back.

That's the difference between the young heads and the old ones. Experience and maturity. Why team up on me and boot me all over the boozer *before* I'd even got to the point of saying *why* I was even there when you could let me say my piece and then *after that* you could *then* proceed to throw me around The Corinthian like a rag doll. Ah, the exuberance of youth. Something I'd went through myself. Probably never more encapsulated than by Robert Duvall in that film Colors when he's telling the joke about the two bulls fucking the cows to Sean Penn.

'ANYONE IN HERE TODAY CAN TELL ME WHERE I CAN FIND MIKEY SWANSON?'

I stopped for a moment to scan the room just in case I hadn't noticed him from up high but nah, still fuck all, so continued.

'TELL ME WHERE HE IS RIGHT NOW AND I'LL PUT ENOUGH DRINKING MONEY BEHIND THE BAR FOR YOU THAT'LL MAKE SURE YOU DON'T HAVE TO PUT YOUR HAND IN YOUR POCKETS FOR THE NEXT FUCKING WEEK'

The CCS boys stood towards the end of the bar seemed to find this amusing while it looked like a few of the jakeys in there were possibly smelling blood when it came to free booze and whether they were in the position to achieve it.

Wisely - despite trying to keep an eye on the whole room - I kept coming back to the Capital City Service contingent and making sure none of them were about to try something on me. Any confrontation, heated words or full scale hand to hand combat - apart from with irate landlords who go over the top about things - in there was always going to come via whatever hooligan element was in the place, and I had to keep that in mind at all times when I was up there shouting down at everyone.

Never knowing when to say when, a fault that I would readily admit to never having quite being able to overcome as I'd turned from boy to man. I was in the middle of some demented follow up, where I was offering a *month's* worth of swally, if I could get the location of Davey McKenna, when I noticed Banjo signal three of the CCS boys to come over towards the pool table.

Here we fucking go, then. I steeled myself for the attack, looking down at the table hoping to find that the last players had left a cue or two lying on top, which they hadn't.

Crucially, though. The three of them hadn't come over in an overly hostile way. No outstretched arms asking me to "come on" when it was them who was meant to be coming towards *me*. No shouting, swearing and dishing out baseless threats of what's to come. They seemed quite casual about their approach, pun removed and that.

Probably just as well they came across in this chilled manner, to be honest, because if they'd come over aggressive then the nearest one to me was going to be taking a severe boot to the coupon, and then we'd just have to have seen what followed that but even in my most optimistic of moments could've seen it going well.

Was *ever* going into a Hibs pub - in the way that I had, with the intentions I had - something that had ever really stood a chance of going well?

That was how much that fucking GGTTH1875 had got under my skin.

They were some of the younger boys that had been standing on the periphery of Banjo and the rest of the older lads so I wasn't sure if they were bricking it or there was something else to it. It just didn't feel like they were over to take me on and I trusted this by giving away any advantage I'd maybe held over the three of them by crouching down so that one of them could speak to me.

'Mate, Banjo and some of the rest of the boys are wanting a word'

He was maybe around twenty at the very most. Average height and - despite the Stone Island compass on the side of his purple sweater - by no means looking a fucking gladiator.

'Well, only if your wee performance is finished with, like?'

One of the others, maybe mid twenties and similarly dressed, chipped in sarcastically, clearly unable to negotiate this wee exchange without trying to be a wideo, knowing that I wasn't going to do anything about it.

I never really had too many other options than to accept the invitation so - with one of the casuals reaching out to help me down - took a helping hand to get me down on the pub floor again.

'RIGHT, YOU'RE FUCKING **BARRED,** PRICK. OOT YE GO. THINK YE CAN COME INTO MA FUCKING PUB AND ...'

The landlord leapt on the chance to show who was running things, now that I was back on level footing but was shut down by Banjo Ireland instantly. Showing who - when it came down to certain things - *actually* ran The Corinthian, the Capital City Service boys.

'Haw, Kenzo, leave the cunt alone, he's not a bad lad, just clearly a wee bit stressed. Happens to us all, eh? Get him a pint and stick it on ma slate'

Banjo said to him, which had been all that had needed said, to get him off my case.

Now while Banjo had appeared to have been quite relaxed about all that had just taken place. A so called hostile, coming into *their* pub and demanding the head of one of their boys, active or not. People have been eviscerated for far, far less in the confines of a Scottish boozer. Much fucking less. Some of the others - around him - were not so quick to see the funny side of things, if there was actually anything funny about it or not, Banjo's feelings on things, apart.

By the looks on their coupons some of them were just waiting on the moment to just go for it, and with good cause. I recognised some of them from back in the old days while others - despite being ages around me - if I'd seen before they'd long gone from my memory. The one's I *recognised*, though? Well you couldn't have blamed them for not exactly being happy at the sight of this ghost from the past. Shite can linger, I get it. Ask Peter Duncan about that.

If one of them had tried to pull the same trick inside a Dundee boozer - with a few Utility boys inside there - it would have provoked a mirror image. They were standing looking at someone who - in the past - had been prone to trying to inflict as much pain on them as possible in the short amount of time handed down. It was fair to say that we shared a "history" between each other.

'The fucking *nerve* of this cunt'

One of the older ones and someone I swear I'd never seen before in my life said to no one in particular, the main goal being that *I* heard it.

'Tell you fucking what, Nora. You've either got something wrong with you or you've got a death wish coming in here'

Another - who I *did* recall, just not their name - remarked, smiling while shaking his head.

'Fucking see this?'

Another old guard. *Tattie*, someone - despite the long gap - I knew straight away, with good cause. He pointed at a scar underneath his eye.

'Thirty fucking years and it's still there. Doctor at the hospital said that an inch higher, from that chair that you swung at me, and I'd have lost my fucking eye'

He said, like it was the week before that I'd done it. Seeing the scar took me right back to that epic battle we'd had at the top of the stairs at Waverley where it spilled out onto the road on Princes Street and I'd grabbed one of the chairs that were there at that scran place outside the Waverley Centre. Tattie being one of the unfortunate ones who found themselves on the other end of the chair until the police arrived and we were chased down to the platforms at the station.

I think seeing me - and being taken back to *why* he had been scarred for life - was too much for him, and emotions overtook things. Making a lunge towards me, getting as far as grabbing my sweatshirt with a hand, while I grabbed a piece of him back - both of us readying ourselves for what was about to come next - before some of his boys grabbed him and pulled him back from off me.

By the time I'd been handed the pint I'd noticed that I was now in the middle of a complete circle of CCS. Like I was part of a Barca training session rondo.

'Chill, Tattie' Ireland said as he put a playful arm around his mate, who was still looking at me as if he wanted to inflict great harm my way.

'I think anyone who has the balls to come in here on the day of a match, and *especially* someone with a past that this cunt does with us, and do what he just did without being heard out, come on, lets get a table'

Banjo - who had been the top boy back then - clearly showing that he still pulled rank, when required.

And it was through this authority that the man commanded that saw to it that despite there being no free tables inside the place. When he made it known to some that were already sitting down at one, that *he* wanted it. He found them more than happy to give up their place for him, me and another five of the older squad. The rest of the group - which must've been around thirty to forty strong - were left back stood around at the bar.

'Look, Banjo. You know the score, eh? I already bumped into you yesterday. You know this is no Utility and CCS thing. I'm just trying to protect my business, and that boy is fucking things up for me. Simple. I just need to talk to him and sort things out. Not even any need for it to come to blows, like. He probably just thinks that he's having a wee laugh, that it's all harmless and that getting a bite out of me is keeping him going even more but it's not on, like. Destroying the good name I've built up for my business. It's not something that any of you wouldn't do. You protect what's yours, always, eh?'

I went first - on the defensive - hoping that I was going to have them seeing things from a completely non hooligan perspective. Lied my fucking derrière off about there not being any need for things to come to blows between me and Swanny. There was *every* fucking need for it to come to blows. It was literally my focal point of even being there.

If I was looking for empathy or even a shred of understanding, I wan't going to be receiving it from anyone sat there with me at the table.

Now I'm quite a smart cunt. Well clued up, regardless of the exam results I left school with. After my wee entry speech to them, I clocked the wee glances between them, I just didn't know what those looks at each other meant.

'So how's our mate ruining your business then?'

Someone I didn't know - sat there in a dark blue Paul and Shark baseball cap - piped up. This, allowing me to explain to them about my gym and the fact that I'd went viral on YouTube and had gained a following of fans of the videos which - in turn - had grown the business to the point it was literally a brand, and Swanny was making it look bad.

'Look, lads. What we all got up to back in the day. Aye, it was naughty at times and we maybe went a wee bit over the score at times, but it was a long time ago now. You have to leave the past in the past, eh? Not even sure why Swanny is doing it, I know we had a couple of run ins but like I said, it was just what we did back then, eh?'

'So, what? You're like fucking *famous* then?'

One of them - him, I knew his name from years back but was blanking on it, there as I looked at him. Now a lot more rotund than he was back then and with far less hair - started to laugh while he, and another two others all automatically started to fish for their phones from their pockets.

Following me telling them what to type into YouTube, within minutes three of them were crouched around one phone on one side of the table while the other three repeated the same thing on the other side while I had been strategically placed in the middle of them with my back to the wall.

It was a mixed reception, how the videos had been received.

Some sat in silence, others pissed themselves laughing while the rest made wideo comments.

I think - out of them all - only Banjo Ireland seemed to 'get it,' like he'd done the day before when I'd showed a video to him.

'That's some fucking exposure, all those views, like'

Ireland said, looking up at me.

'Aye, like I said. With the greatest of respect of to you and the rest of your boys. I can't have him making a cunt out of me in front of two million viewers, Brett'

The boy in the baseball cap - whose phone it was that some had been looking down at on the table - who had now went into the wee video I'd made the night before when I was walking up Victoria Street from the Pubic Triangle, just looked up and started laughing, the rest joining in with him. Just myself who wasn't in on the joke.

'You're not wanting *Swanny* to make a cunt out of you in front of your fans, aye?'

Felt like asking the beetroot coloured Alan Brazil looking motherfucker if he'd actually been *listening* to what I'd just said but thought it would probably be better if I didn't.

'Aye, look, Nora. Here's the thing …'

Banjo butted in, already seeming to know what his mate was about to go on to say.

'I admire your dedication, commitment and passion that you've clearly got in abundance, to try and rectify this wee situation you're involved in here but the fact is, Swanny hasn't made a cunt out of you'

'*You* on the other hand?'

Baseball cap boy butted in before getting a look from Ireland that shut him up, even managing to stifle the laughter that he'd followed with.

'Well, aye, Nora. It's not easy telling someone that they've made a cunt out of *themselves* but *you* have made an absolutely *epic* royal cunt out of yourself, with this'

Then the laughter came, some with proper tears, so funny they found it.

I didn't follow, but soon did.

When Banjo - who had told me a completely different fucking story, the day before, but who then went on to explain that why the fuck would he give away information to someone like me, which to be fair made sense - went on to tell me that Swanny had been on remand in Strangeways for the past three months, following a bookies job in Manchester that went breasts up and a person not exactly in a position to be sitting browsing the internet, never mind finding a target for some regular trolling.

Well, hearing the *real* truth about Mikey Swanson's location, the *one* thing I had wanted out of my trip to Scotland. Words cannot even begin to come close to describing just what an absolute fucking imbecile I'd felt. The crusade that I had went on. Bringing myself up on the radar of the authorities, all of that time spent obsessing and searching for what?

The wrong fucking person?!

I could've almost glassed my fucking self, for being such a hot headed moron. Now, with reality biting, I had put myself in the position of being nowhere closer to knowing who GGTTH1875 was, having made probably the biggest arse of my life there in that pub in front of everyone, and now a really iffy chance of being able to get myself back home without being pinched, something that I knew I was going to have to deal with sooner or later but had been so focussed on the whole Hibs Rangers early kick off that I had put it to the back of my head.

Ireland telling me that Swanny - and his wee crew - had been down the North of England on a wee bookies tour, of sorts. The Manchester one being the sixth one they'd pulled off inside a week but had been a case of pushing their luck just that wee bit too far, which had led to them being caught and with the fact their crew had used real guns in the robberies they'd all been sent on remand, and weren't going to be seeing daylight for a very long time. I sat there feeling such a fucking fanny, so much that there probably was no hiding it, so I didn't try.

'How stupid do you feel right now, all that flare shite?'

Another - who hadn't spoken up to that point - in an old school Adidas green tracky top spoke up. I chose to ignore the cunt. Had to do more ignoring sat at that table than I'd done the rest of my life but it had to be done. If things were to kick off then I'd take a few of them with me but I knew that if I was to make trouble now with them then I wouldn't be making it out of the pub alive.

I just wanted out of the pub, end of. I was hardly amongst "drinking buddies" after all. I was sitting with just about the *last* fucking cunts that I would choose to sit and have a swally with.

'Ah, fuck it then, eh?'

I shrugged my shoulders and - before getting myself together - said that, what with me being a man of my word and all, I would stick a few quid behind the bar for them to get a few drinks. *Technically*, I'd put out an offer for someone to tell me where I could find Mikey Swanson in exchange for me buying some drinks for them. As much of a fool some in the pub would go on to describe me as that afternoon, I wasn't having any cunt saying I didn't pay my debts.

I asked the question as I made to stand up, only to find Banjo's strong arm grabbing at my wrist and yanking me back down.

'Where do you think you're going?'

Not for the first time since we'd sat down at the table, I didn't follow.

The rest of them - and the faces that were on show - all seemed to know what was going on. Despite how cordial it had been, well, as cordial as I could have ever hoped for and I wouldn't have even been as greedy to think it would've been *that* non hostile, it looked like I'd maybe focussed so much on the Swanson part that I'd disregarded some of the other shite that some of them were more interested in.

'You might be done with us but we are most definitely not done with you'

Tattie said across the table, with the kind of smile that - knowing that the smile is anything but sincere - could've unsettled you due to how dead it was.

'I'm afraid to say, Nora. Some memories run deep. You shouldn't have come here today, pal. Surely, now that you've calmed down from your quest to find Mikey, you must realise that showing your face inside here was *never* going to be a good idea. Sometimes the water never quite makes it under the bridge, ken?'

'Aye, you're fucking telling me, Banjo'

Tattie butted in, pointing at his scar under his aye once again. Don't know what he was so bammed up about anyway, the cunt. It was only a wee scar and - with what age I gave it to him - he'd have probably got his hole many times over, on account of having it. Cunt should've been fucking *thanking* me for all the sex he'd got in his youth, never mind wanting to fight me.

If they wanted to settle old scores then - other than me just take the worst of beatings as they all tossed me around between them - I didn't see how they were going to address things. Wasn't exactly fair to expect me to fight them all at once but then again, you walk into a known pub of a renowned firm of hooligans and start shouting about how you're going to kill one of them, you really need to then prepare for *whatever* the fuck comes after it, because it's going to produce something.

Once again, Banjo - out of them all - seemed to be switched on. Could see that he had several mates who all wanted a straightener with me, for acts committed that half of I couldn't even remember doing. But could also appreciate that I couldn't take them on like I was fucking Steven Seagal or some cunt.

'Right then, Nora. You're not daft so by this point I'm going to assume that you now know that, at this moment in time, the chances of you walking out of this pub are sitting at fucking minus zero, and if you then start to think about the possibilities of being carried out on a stretcher - not being able to walk - then envisage yourself with one of those black zipped up bags over you, while they carry you out'

The others around the table all sat nodding in agreement, enthusiastically.

'Forgetting all of the snide shit you pulled back in the day. Just coming into our pub *today* and trying to pull the shite that you have is pretty much enough to get you ended. You think we're going to have you going about re-telling this story, and it not involving you getting your cunt kicked?'

The beetroot faced boy said, as much of a prick that he'd appeared to be since we'd sat down, I couldn't really disagree with him.

But I was in this now.

'So you'll know why we can't have you just thinking that you can come in here as if you're running the place. I've just watched a video of you on Victoria Street, boasting about what you're going to do to Mikey Swanson. Who's to say that people don't link that video to you being seen in The Corinthian. Next thing you know - you know the internet and all the lies that's on there - cunts are saying that you were in The Corinthian giving it the big one with a flare and threatening the CCS, who done fuck all about it'

Banjo took back control of things. My attempt at reminding him that I wasn't actually threatening the Capital City Service, only one of them in particular, not really helping at all.

'The way I see it. If you walk back out of here, without any kind of response from us? Well, you can see how that would make us look, eh? We've retained a rep after all of these decades and I'm fucked if it's going to get dented due to a fucking clown on a fucking suicide mission, like yourself'

The menacing side to Banjo was now starting to show. Aye, he'd been friendly enough - up to then - but I knew that could well have turned at any point, and now it looked like we were there.

'So what we talking here, then?'

I asked, absolutely fucked if I was going to try and be seen to attempt to talk my way out of things with them. Reputations take years to build and can be obliterated in seconds. I'd rather have drank my meals through a straw for the next six months than plead for - what could have been for all I knew - my life.

Banjo, sitting there and still scrolling through all of the videos on the Utility Defence page, looked up and smiled back at me.

'Oh, you're about to find out, Mr Internet Star'

He then turned to "Scarface."

'Tattie, get the keys for the basement from Kenzo and tell him we're not wanting disturbed, and then get the rest of the boys'

Sending Tattie on his way on his errand, Banjo then turning back to me and in the most unnerving of ways started to sing to me a bit of a Jamiroquai song, or his version, anyway.

'We're going deeper underground, there's too much panic in this town'

With talk of basements and all of those CCS inside it with me, it sounded pretty fucking much like there would be more panic down there than up there in the bar.

From my point of view anyway, like.

Chapter 29

Si

There weren't many things in life that would've been enough to merit me quite literally dropping what I was doing - in this case, me in the middle of trying a pair of jeans on in the G-Star Raw shop, just off Rokin, inside their dressing room - but when I was stood there in my socks and boxers and heard my phone buzz in my pocket of the jeans lying on the floor - and bent down to take it out and have a look - and found the reason a notification informing me that Utility Defence was broadcasting live. Considering the fact that I'd been keeping an extra special eye on the boy Nora. How I had engineered it that he was in Scotland looking for the wrong person, and that, unless I was mistaken, he *never* broadcasted live. This was categorically nailed down as one of those things that *everything* would be dropped for.

I sat down on the wee wooden stool - inside the dressing room - as I hit the link on the screen.

I don't know, like? Following his - evident - Ching and drink fuelled rant, that he'd posted the day before while walking through the streets of Edinburgh. I had sort of expected something similar when the stream began.

I was *way off*.

The Wi-Fi inside the dressing rooms wasn't the best so it took a few moments before actually connecting but I'd already assumed that when the feed began I was going to see Nora making a proper fanny of himself, which I eventually *did*. Just not in the way that I thought he would.

The feed kicking in and the first thing I noticed was the massive green, white and black Union Jack with the words **Capital City Service** stretched across the middle of the flag, attached to the wall, and some kind of primitive looking boxing ring in the middle of the room. Unlike all of the other videos - which had looked like being shot from the same angle which would never change at any point from beginning to end. This style of video, however, was clearly being shot by someone holding the camera, due to how it would pan across the room at different things while the actual camera work looked like it was being taken care of by someone half pissed who couldn't hold the camera still.

As unprofessional as it looked, it was just about enough to do the trick and capture whatever the fuck was going on over in Scotland.

As the camera moved around the room, you were finally able to get a more accurate impression that - wherever this was being shot - this was being filmed from a tiny room with a boxing ring shoved in the middle of it, leaving a wee bit of room for people to stand all the way around it.

Caesar's Palace or Wembley Stadium, this was not.

From what I'd been able to clock from the early minutes of the stream it was obvious that this small room was completely rammed with casuals, some of the labels clearly identifiable and when you see a concentrated group of men *all* decked out in labels like that, then you can draw your own conclusions.

Maybe see someone out on their own, doing their thing, and they're wearing a piece of Stone Island or an equivalent label and you really couldn't just go and assume that they were a football hooligan. Successful fashion houses don't base their whole business strategy on whether Matt from Hull City Psychos buys a coat from them or not, well, you wouldn't think so, anyway. Clock a whole mob of boys all wearing gear like that in close proximity of each other, and that tends to change the perspective of things.

Due to the shaky camerawork the early minutes of the video did not really provide much in the way of clarity. Apart from the confirmation that the video was being streamed from Edinburgh - this coming, via the flag on the wall - there wasn't much explanation of things. None of your cheesy intros that Nora was prone to beginning with. In fact, there wasn't even a fucking Nora, at all.

Whoever it was running the show - shooting the live stream - started to walk around, getting some of the crowd's reaction to things. Unprofessionally, speaking - off camera - to the crowd as he went through them, like some pissed cunt who've been given camcorder duties at a wedding when they're drunk.

'Haw, Tattie. Any words for the You Tube dot com, mate?'

You heard coming from behind the camera while this guy - I vaguely thought I maybe recognised him but fuck, those days had been so long ago and fuck knows how much of my memory the drugs had chipped away at over the years - with a scar under his eye in a - admittedly - really nice Best Company sweatshirt turns to the camera and goes.

'Aye, how about fuck the Hearts, eh?'

The guy laughed while raising up his bottle of Corona that he had in his hands. Hearing him say this, also producing a repeat of "Fuck the Hearts" in unison, from a few of the others standing around him. Had it not been for the boxing ring in the middle of the room you'd have have almost thought that they were all standing in some basement or some secluded location. From the multitude of views that the person shooting had offered there hadn't appeared to be any windows to the place, or bar, despite the fact everyone - captured on screen up to that point - had either pints or bottles of beer in their hand. I suppose, had I not had too much to try and take in as I sat there in that dressing room cubicle, the fact that some had *pints* in their hands should've been a good indicator for where everyone was that afternoon.

As unprofessional as you could possibly get, the cameraman then completely disregarded focusing on anything in particular and - for maybe thirty seconds or so - actually appeared to stop filming and - instead - just walk with the camera in his hand but down by his waist, the camera swinging back and forward.

After a few minutes of fucking about - had I not been so intrigued as to where this was going I'd have ended the stream and continued to go about trying on the pair of jeans - the camera, once it returned to filming the room, now looked higher up, not by much but definitely higher than before. My guess that the cameraman was now standing up on a chair or table. More importantly, they were now no longer walking about - *fucking* about more like - with the camera, and had chosen to stay fixed on the boxing ring, that big CCS flag to the back of it, on the wall.

The more rigid style of filming - I guess - was explained when seconds later you saw someone, first of all putting their bottle of Stella on the edge of the boxing ring before climbing into it themselves. Once in, bending down to pick up their bottle again before making their way into the centre of the ring. Everyone surrounding the ring all appearing to clock this. The loud conversation - that you're always going to find with thirty to forty boys standing having a drink are always going to be making - all of a sudden going down several levels, until you could barely hear a whimper.

The guy with the beer in his hand who - and me always keeping an eye on what clobber someone might be wearing - had a really nice looking La Mille khaki jacket on, and seemed to command a bit of respect from those at ground level beneath him, saw this as the cue to begin as he started to shout out to everyone.

Gentlemen, we're here today for the Lothian and Borders and Tayside cross unification bout for the RSB - Radge Scottish Bastard - title belt. Please give it up for the man, fighting out of Edinburgh's Calton gym, who will tear you apart as if he was fucking Joy Division. Make some fucking noise for the one ... the only ... and YOURRRRRR, Brettttttt... Banjo... IRELAAAAAAAAAND.

At this, the camera moved from the centre of the ring to a door in the corner of the room where there was one of the casuals stood beside and - appearing to take his cue from the music starting to fill the room - opened the door before then standing back.

Seconds later the mean looking figure of a guy in proper boxing gloves, shorts, boots the lot, came walking through the door with an almost guard of honour made to ease his passage from the door and up to the boxing ring.

The sound of Dr Dre and Snoop's 'Next Episode' playing from the speakers as this dangerous looking bastard entered the room. The way he had his breathing going, his nostrils were resembling a bull, moments before it's about to fuck you right up. He had a neck like Mike Tyson's and an even bigger physique to go with. The closer he got to the ring, the more scary he looked.

Then it hit me.

Oh, Brett *Ireland*. I remember who you are, I said out loud, fixed to that wee wooden stool that had clearly not been built in mind for someone with any firm plans to sit on it for more than one single minute of their life.

I had left the casual scene so long before and had - over the years - gradually forgotten about a lot of what had went on in those days, and some of the people whose names were almost the stuff of legend inside the subculture of the hooligan. This only highlighted because when I'd heard the name shouted out by the "master of ceremonies" of Brett Ireland, I should've fucking recognised it straight away. Instead, it took me the combination of hearing the name, then matching it with a face, before I was able to make the connection.

Now *this* was interesting because it all fell into place at once. Never had any hand to hand face to to face combat with the man, and thank fuck for that, but - from memory - something told me that Ireland was quite a decent boxer in his younger years, and I'm not talking about in the stadiums, streets or down in train stations, but in the actual boxing ring. And here he was casually limbering up, rolling his neck around and throwing a few shadow punches. As he moved closer to the ring.

Clearly - from the reaction of the crowd - he was fighting in front of a friendly audience and - the flag fixed to the wall confirming - undoubtedly a home crowd.

I couldn't help but then think that this was Nora's YouTube channel, but up to that point there had been no sign of the man anywhere. Most of his subscribers across the world wouldn't have even had the first fucking clue who Brett Ireland and the Capital City Service were. At least I had the jump on them, when it came to that side of things.

This meaning that I had already convinced myself that the *other* fighter was going to be none other than king radge himself, Norman Fulton, or whatever Dutch made up name that he'd been going by, de Groot, I think?

This is TOO fucking mental, I thought as - with me starting to realise what was potentially about to happen - I found myself so excited, that this pishy wooden stool - that had been so difficult to sit on and had sent my erse cheeks to sleep - was only having the edge of it used by myself. Quite literally a case of 'sitting on the edge of your seat.'

Ireland reached the ring - music still playing away - and climbed his way in and - stopping to take a bottle of Corona through the ropes from someone ringside - before standing in the middle of the ring holding the beer up in the air to rapturous applause before bringing his arm back down and tanning the whole bottle in one go. Not exactly the kind of behaviour that you'd see at a professional boxing match although this - clearly - was not a fight that the British Boxing Board of Control were overseeing.

Banjo! Banjo! Banjo! Banjo! Banjo! Banjo!

The crowd were all chanting, beers being raised in the air by the lads surrounding the ring, spilling lager all over the place, and each other.

Ireland broke away from the centre of the ring and made his way towards one side of it, continuing to limber himself up with some last minute warm ups and stretches. As he went about this, the boy in the La Mille jacket - who was clearly making this shit up as he went along and was no Michael Buffer - started shouting out to the crowd again.

This afternoon's other contender - representing Tayside and fighting out of Utility Defence Gym - please make some noise for the man who runs more than a red sock in a white wash, Norrrrrrrman... Norrrrrrra... FULTONNNNNNN.

Camera pans back over to that same door - that Brett Ireland had walked through - and around about the same time the theme tune to the Benny Hill show started to play out of the speakers. A less than impressed - but somehow mixed with a bit of shame to it - Nora entered through the door.

Decked out in shorts and boxing gloves - I hadn't been able to clock what he had on his feet until he entered the ring and found that, unlike his opponent, he was wearing a pair of ZX 500's which, mixed with boxing shorts, just looked plain bizarre. Obviously, though. I knew nothing of the background to the madness of what was going on over in Edinburgh - walking towards the ring - with the demeaning soundtrack to accompany his walk in - he didn't look to be getting the same respectful guard of honour that Ireland was given.

Jostled and pushed by the crowd, all of them giving him verbals and threats while getting right in his face. One of the crowd throwing the remnants of his pint over Nora as he passed by to the ring. This, almost enough for Nora to begin fighting with him, instead of in the ring with Banjo. Taking a few of the crowd to drag the boy away while another two had grabbed hold of Nora, turned him back in the direction of the ring, and pushed him forwards, towards the grinning Ireland now watching on while waiting to *get* it on.

If it wasn't for the fact that Nora - through life - had been nothing other than a sociopathic, dangerous, nasty wanker of a man I'd have almost felt for the guy because it looked like he'd landed himself in the most hostile of situations, while looking like he didn't have a friend in the world to back him up inside the room. The actual concept of Nora having an *actual* friend - as opposed to someone being on terms with him simply because of him being the type of person you couldn't afford to have on your case - though was something that I couldn't quite wrap my mind around.

Instead of feeling for him, I laughed, lots. I can only have begun to imagine what it must've sounded like - on the outside of the dressing room cubicle - with the sound of the giggling from behind the door, but the introduction that he'd been given - classing him as a runner and just about one of the very worst things that you could ever accuse Nora of being - and how much it would have wanted to make him hurt everything in the world in his line of vision. And then there was the comedy music that had been picked out for his walk in.

How the fuck was I not meant to find this anything other than amusing? From the surface of things - and whatever the fuck was going on over there - part of this stream was with the intention of humiliating Nora, and it didn't miss the spot.

Also, from a personal point of view, I couldn't help but take a wee bit of pride over the part that I had played to engineer all of this coming to pass, even if saying that would be most definitely straying into the territory of someone trying to take credit for something that they hadn't quite earned. Because this would be a true assessment of things. How the fuck could I have ever imagined that from a couple of wee wideo comments on his YouTube videos from me - just because I knew the man and knew how it would wind him up - it would have led to him being in a room full of CCS, and shaping up to have a boxing match? What the fuck did Nora know about boxing? Queensbury rules and that stuff?

For the record, though. I couldn't have been more happy with what little work I'd actually had to put in, to produce a result like *this*.

After the ordeal of the walk in, Nora was then able to get himself into the ring - joining Ireland and the boy in the jacket - and prepare himself for the *real* ordeal of some hand to hand combat with someone who, at schoolboy level, was a Scottish champion boxer.

I really wanted to give Zico a quick text or a call to tell him to get Nora's channel on ASAP, but with how dodgy the Wi-Fi was - inside there - I couldn't have ever guaranteed getting back into the stream again, and - selfishly - I wasn't wanting to miss a single second of what was going on so - for Zico's sake - hoped that this live stream would be transferred over to a permanent video, that could have been watched at any point in the future. Something told me, though, that it probably wasn't going to be likely that Nora was going to let that happen.

The boy in the jacket - trying to retain some sense of reality that this was, in fact, a boxing match that he was overseeing - brought Banjo and Nora up to face each other. I couldn't get over the contrast between Ireland in his boxing boots, and Nora in those Adidas ZX trainers.

With there being no microphone to use but still wanting everyone to hear what was being said to the two boxers stood inches away from him, the guy in the La Mille - grabbing an arm of Banjo and Nora - shouted out.

This afternoon's fight is brought to you by Capital City Service promotions in association with Calton Gym, Fight yourself fit.

Now I'm not going to pretend that I know what I'm meant to officially say at this point but the two of you both know the rules, eh? Twelve three minute rounds. No punching below the belt, gouging, kneeing, kicking, head butting and biting and all of that shite. Knockdown rules apply. You dinnae get up after ten seconds then you're fucking done. Any questions?

(Despite the offer, it seemed like just for show because he didn't give any of them a chance to answer, instead, continuing to speak)

No? Good. Right, no ref so quite literally knock yourself out so no taking the pish. Now touch gloves and have a good clean fight.

The pair of them brought up their gloves to smash into each other. Nora looked pensive, Ireland on the other hand, confident as he swaggered back to his designated side of the ring - there didn't appear to be anything as advanced as a "corner" as such - while Nora kind of just loitered around the centre of the ring, psyching himself up.

Before vacating the ring, the guy in the CP jacket really could not resist it, and there's not a person in the world who would have judged him either.

Let's get ready to rumbllllllllllllllllle

Everyone in the room, going mental to this before breaking into that Banjo song again. Well, if you could *call* it that. Shouting someone's name over and over again is hardly going to leave you with an insider's chance of an Ivor Novello.

Then there was this wee moment where a sort of calm descended on the room - as Ireland and Nora walked up towards each other in the centre of the ring, not taking their eyes off each other - that was quite similar to the moment you get inside a football stadium where you've been awarded a penalty and everyone is going tonto, celebrating the referee's award. Only, once that ball's been placed on the centre spot and you see your player standing there - hands on hips - ready to run up and take it, everyone all seems to hush up at once. This was the same deal.

Everyone knowing that in a second's time these two men were going to start knocking fuck out of each other - and I'm sure those in the room were looking for it being a bit more one way traffic - but for those preceding few seconds, the anticipation of what was to come resulted in a a slice of - almost - tranquility, which would go on to be at complete odds with what then followed.

With no ringside bell to speak of, no ref to guide the two of them. The fight started with a kind of nod of understanding between Ireland and Nora before the first punch was thrown, predictably by Nora. As they shaped up to each other it took a second or two before one of them moved on the other and Nora, being Nora, it was not a surprise to see him go first, even if he got it all wrong and completely fresh aired it, taking a brutal looking punch to the body to go with, winding him enough to back off for a moment.

I was by no means any kind of a boxing expert or aficionado but knew enough to at least know that one of them in the ring *looked* like a boxer with their footwork, positioning and general movement, while the other looked like they'd stepped into a boxing ring for the first time in their life.

Watching Nora try to fight - in the setting which disallowed using his feet and swinging or throwing any inanimate objects - was a sight to see, I'll say that.

While Ireland simply oozed the confidence of someone who was no stranger to this environment. Nora simply looked like someone who *thought* they knew what to do when in a boxing ring. This only reinforced with Ireland landing him on his backside with barely a minute on the clock. At close quarters, Nora trying an uppercut on Banjo - who saw this coming a mile away - who managed to combine ducking from it while performing a right hook to Nora's unprotected side of his jaw, sending him to the canvas.

This was the type of content that should have been on fucking Pornhub, so arousing it was. Watching a dazed and confused Nora sitting there trying to figure out what had just happened, while the crowd all began shouting out the count to ten. Banjo, taking this wee break to have a quick swig of someone's beer, to emphasise just what a stroll this all was for him.

Took Nora all the way up to the count of eight before fully getting back to his feet. With no referees to check each fighter, this was all left down to the boxers' discretion. Which meant that - with the two gladiators that were in the ring - things may get messy, because none of these were the type of people that would give up. One would need to put the other down, and make sure they *stayed* down. And I know which one of them my money would have been on.

Once up on his feet Nora looked both shocked *and* angry. Unless he'd had a lobotomy since that last time I'd crossed paths with him - back in Amsterdam at Nieumarkt - then Nora really only knew one way to react, when it came towards someone showing him aggression.

Our ex leader of the Utility, however, finding that you can be angry all you fucking well want, but it won't stop you from having your arse handed to you, all the same.

Ireland landing Nora on his arse - once more - with a beautifully delivered right and left combination of punches, landing his opponent on the deck for the second time, there inside that first round. It was either going to be a very long fight for Nora, or an extremely *short* one.

As they took a breather at the end of the first three minutes, I just wasn't entirely sure which one out of the two it was going to turn out for him.

Chapter 30

Stephen

What's taking this bastard? I began to get impatient, standing across the road, outside the pub. Having seen some come and go from it in the time that I'd been standing there, but not him.

I'd been happy to hang around outside, knowing that he was *inside*, but had been hoping that it wasn't going to be for any real length of time. It had been well over an hour now since my last drink and you know what it can be like when you've had half a dozen cans, but then things dry up, much like your mouth?

Needed another beer to kick start me again and save me from that wee in between zone that you find yourself in, when you've been buzzing off the drink but then the tap gets switched off and you're no longer as buzzing as you once were, but neither are you what you'd call sober. Some kind of nether zone that's in between the two states.

I didn't want - or need - that state of mind.

Seeing the face of the man who had ruined not just my dad, but my whole family's life had inflamed me so much that there I was. In Edinburgh, packing a gun and ready to unload all of its bullets into someone. Now, though. I was being given time to actually stop and take a pause. I was no longer on the mad dash to Edinburgh, all over the shop in the Golf. The intense period of finding him and then following all the way to the pub had been dealt with.

After this, though? That's when I was able to stop and actually *think* about things. And the more I thought about them, the more my desire to *do it* decreased. The logic of *not* committing murder starting to drip drip drip into my consciousness.

I didn't *want* to see sense or logic, though. I wanted that bastard to fucking pay for what he did. It was this attitude that was the reason for my impatience, that he came out the pub and got what was rightfully his.

Knowing myself, I knew though that the more time I was given to stand and think about things, the less chance there was going to be that I would go through with it.

And this was something that I was not going to allow happen. I had been gifted the chance of doing something I'd dreamed about for ten years, and likely would never get the chance again.

Never live life without regrets - ironically - it had been dad who had told me, back when I was sixteen and Stacey Smart had packed me in. If I was to let this Fulton get away - right when I had the chance - I just knew that it would be something that I *would* regret.

So, feeling like my hand had been forced.

If you're not going to come to me then I'm going to have to come to you, I thought to myself as I reached into my coat and pulled out my Rangers scarf to wrap around my face. I'd never wanted to do it in public, purely through the sheer risk of being recognised and caught. Now, though, I felt like I'd been given no choice, if I'd wanted to actually go through with it, I would just need to go to plan b and - going down that route - with that being the case, with CCTV cameras and all of that technology, I felt that I could at least cover my face, with the scarf that -

fortunately - was only in my pocket because I had grabbed my work coat - the one that I'd wear on that cold walk to work at eleven each night - which had the scarf rolled up inside one of the pockets.

Probably not the most ideal of scarfs to be wearing into the pub that I was heading into, I thought. Then again, this was not the most ideal of situations.

Psyching myself up to walking in, spying where he was, and going up to him and shooting him in the head, and then walking out again. I wrapped the scarf around me multiple times from my chin all the way up to just underneath my eyes and pulled the gun out of the other jacket pocket and began to walk across the street towards The Corinthian.

Picturing Fulton, sat there inside, having a scoop and a laugh with his mates. Blissfully unaware of what was about to come in and wipe that smile from off his face, for ever.

Chapter 31

Nora

Fuck, me. Those first two / three rounds were the harshest of lessons dished out to me by Ireland and I think - if you wanted to flip things around from the perspective of someone having his arse completely felt in front of fuck knows how many people on the internet - that the fact I was still standing, and some might say stupidly, coming back for more was an example of my toughness, both physically and mentally.

Well that's another nice mess you've got me into, I heard my mind tell me in the voice of Oliver Hardy as I - "guarded" front and back by various members of the CCS - headed down into the basement of the boozer. A basement that you would never have guessed had even existed, had you not been a regular. Had to go through this wee trap door behind the bar and down some stairs before you could reach it.

Banjo - ever the entrepreneur - as we'd all sat at the table had - as I'd noticed at the time - had commented on the reach of my videos, how many subscribers and views that they brought in, and in the gym's case, this was all monetised, and in Ireland's case, he wanted a piece of it.

Apart from the very obvious fact that not a single one of those cunts was ever going to allow me to leave without me getting a sore face. Banjo - sitting there at the table while the rest of them pished themselves laughing at me - had come up with a way that would provide a perfect outcome, with numerous permutations that suited him.

Knowing his worth - as a boxer - he was obviously sure that he was going to take me to the cleaners and how that wouldn't look too well on the YouTube page of a self certified hard man, so there would clearly be the embarrassment factor for yours truly. Apart from that, you had the exposure that the live stream was going to give not just the Capital City Service across the world but Banjo - himself - and the gym gig, that he had going on at Calton.

Obviously, to the untrained eye. Someone being taken from the potential of having their cunt kicked right in from a proper bunch of boys to the chance of a one on one fight seemed like a great deal. Which, I suppose it was. Just not when you're fighting some cunt who actually fucking *knows* how to box.

Never really had a choice and, in fact, fronted things big time. Telling Banjo that it would be like old times but - in truth - I wasn't too keen on disappearing into an Edinburgh pub's hidden basement with forty CCS, with their leader telling the owner of the boozer that he wasn't to be disturbed and that he'd be back up, when he was back up. Cunt's go down to basements and don't come back up again, though.

And the way that Ireland had went about dealing with me in those first three rounds there were points where *I* didn't think I'd be coming back up again, either.

I'd actually thought that he'd been having a wee joke with me, at the start, when telling me what I was going to do if I wanted to leave The Corinthian in one piece, myself in no doubt whatsoever just how much some of the boys inside that pub would've relished piling on, if given the nod. Even so, though. When someone tells you that the answer to avoiding that is to step into a boxing ring - gloves and shorts, official, like - that is situated *underneath* an Edinburgh boozer, you *would* tend to think that they were winding you up.

Edinburgh, famed for having lots of shit going on underneath its streets, I shouldn't have been so surprised when we reached the bottom of the stairs which led to a series of rooms. One where, fuck me, there was an actual *boxing ring* inside it while the other a much smaller room where Ireland and me - amicably - stood and got changed for the fight. Ireland looking through a pile of boxing gear that was lying in a box before throwing me a pair of gloves and shorts, telling me that they'd need to do.

We were on completely different wavelengths as we shared the room, up until we had to get one of Brett's boys to come in and do up our gloves for us.

While I was trying to just stand there and come out with patter, inside, I was frantically trying to recall every boxing match I'd ever watched, and how to try and replicate what the professionals do, he was asking me about how much money the Utility Defence YouTube videos made, and if it was good for business in terms of getting people into the gym and signing up. Had he not been sitting in a pair of boxing shorts while looking down tying up a pair of boots - from his whole aura - you really would not have guessed that the man was about to have a fight with a fellow man.

'Oh, aye, Banjo'

'You get the merch started as well. T shirts and that, and you can make a decent bit of cash, like'

I replied back while feeling that the next half hour or so - depending on how it would go - could well turn out to be an event that would be the blame for me experiencing a serious dent into those funds that I was always ever so grateful to find coming in each month.

The bastards took every opportunity to heap as much embarrassment on me as possible, and that was before even getting into the fucking ring. The cunt that pretended to be Michael Buffer telling the world that I was a runner and then them playing the Benny Hill Show theme tune for me walking to the ring. Well you can imagine how much I was raging, eh? Couldn't do a fucking thing about it, either. I'm hearing that stupid tune playing while - as a complete contrast to comedy style music playing - I'm walking to the ring and have someone telling me that even if I last the twelve rounds he's going to stab me there in the ring, and that I wouldn't be the first person it had happened to down there.

Once the whole drama of getting myself into the ring was over and done with, though? The boy Ireland, immediately took charge of things. Running fucking rings around me while - instead of fully focusing on things - I took punch after punch in the coupon and ribs, thinking of that GGTTH1875 - *whoever* the fuck they were, *now* - and if they were sitting watching and pissing themselves laughing at what they'd been the prime cause of.

This was not an environment to be standing there, letting your mind drift but that GGTTH1875 bastard had been living rent free in my head for weeks by then so why would they move out, on the greatest day of their miserable trolling life?

After the revelations of where Mikey Swanson was currently residing, I now had literally no idea who the fuck this internet bastard - who had brought me to Edinburgh looking for them - was. The strongest of leads that I'd - thought - had which had led me to, well, *this*.

They could have been one of the crowd - standing beside the ring - or they could have been some bored kid who had heard a second hand tale of events from back in the day. After the blow that I'd had in being told that I had been way off with my calculations, I'd have been cautious to attempt to pin the tail on another donkey, so to speak.

Whoever they were, though. They must've been absolutely fucking wetting themselves. What an absolute fucking fanny I'd been. The thought off it, understandably, something that I hadn't taken well.

Fuck, was it hostile down there, in the basement, though. Think Galatasaray v Fenerbahce then double it with Partizan and Red Star Belgrade and after that, go and times that by Zamalek v Al Ahly and you'd be just about there, for a point of reference.

Apart from having fucking Rocky Marciano bobbing and weaving around me, connecting with some serious punches into my head and ribs, there was the torrent of abuse and threats from the crowd who, lets face it, had their own agenda. Neutrals they most definitely weren't.

After the shock of the first round - and how many times Ireland knocked me down - I tried to re-strategise, by going into the second with the intentions of hanging onto the cunt as much as I could. I mean, if I was holding onto him there wasn't as much chance of him ghosting around me and inflicting death by a thousand punches, was there?

Despite this being an unofficial and unregulated boxing match, the same rules applied to the official sport. Namely, cunts don't take too kindly when one boxer isn't as into actually boxing as much as the other one. A carefully delivered half can of Tennents lobbed at my head - while I clung onto Ireland - letting me know this kind of caper wasn't going to be acceptable in there. Aye, neither is lobbing fucking cans at someone's head, either. Couldn't resist booting the can - still lying on the canvas, having bounced off my napper - right into the crowd at the end of the second. Almost causing a disturbance, due to the group - who just happened to be standing in the general area of where the can was launched into - taking exception to a whirling lager spraying piece of metal coming whizzing at them. One of them surged forward, trying to get into the ring while I stood there with arms outstretched egging him on. As had been the case more than once since I'd walked into The Corinthian, one stare from Banjo had been enough to stop anything from happening before they even began.

Going into the third round, I tried to go on the offence, as opposed to having a three minute cuddle with the boy. Of course, though. Take whatever the exact wording of what the word *offence* means in the dictionary and forget it because in this environment what "offence" *actually* meant was to leave yourself open for Brett Ireland to take pot shots at you, at his absolute leisure, and pleasure.

With each punch he delivered it seemed to make me more tired, and him more fresh. By the time we found ourselves in the third I was - without a shadow of a doubt - involved in the longest fight of my life. Fights, I'd always found, could've been over in seconds, or a few minutes at best. Yet Banjo was just dancing around assuredly as if he'd just stepped *into* the ring. Without any ring side trainers or doctors to look after you, fuck knows what I must've looked like to him, because I certainly didn't feel like a pillar of health.

Fucking put me on my arse another two times in that third round. That wink he gave me right as I was falling backward - but continuing to look at each other - was one that showed just how in control of things he was, and he clearly knew it.

On that fourth knockdown - and hearing that now familiar count from the crowd - I almost never got back up again. It gets a wee bit old when you're in a boxing ring with someone else and they're connecting with - at least - half a dozen more punches on you, than you are with them. Not that much fun - getting hit in the face - as I had always more derived my pleasures out of *dispensing* the punches.

You know how you hear about people - in times of strife - and how they get a voice in their head? Some call it a guardian angel. Well I'm not saying it was no fucking guardian angel that decided to guide me, there in that third round when I was sat on the deck, - if it had been a cartoon there would've been birds flying around my head by that point - but it was some kind of divine intervention.

As all of the hoolies surrounding the ring began their count to ten. I sat there - trying to get my head together, again - and, just about managing to shut out the noise around me, out of all the things to be thinking about in that moment. I thought about what the people around the world watching this were saying about me. What comments were being left, how many people were hitting the thumbs down icon. No doubt, subscribers deserting my page by the minute.

And *that's* when I had that moment of clarity. Thank fuck because I needed something, from somewhere, and I wasn't too picky about what it was - or where it came from - if it was going to help me last the next nine rounds.

Subscribers?

Comments?

Dislikes?

Just fucking look at you, I said to myself, disgusted with who I saw myself to be in that moment. Looking up at a Banjo -

pacing around the ring while smiling and encouraging the count from the crowd - who was clearly enjoying punching fuck out of me, and I'm fucking thinking about *subscribers?*

And that was where the piece of inspiration kicked in, that voice of mines from no guardian angel, but the radge known as Norman Fulton.

You used to be about the violence, so *be fucking violent*, I told myself as I gradually got myself up, just beating the count by a second.

I think this surprised Banjo, that smile dropping from his face when he saw me up, and coming back towards him.

'You should've stayed down, mate. The next few might hurt that wee bit more than any of the others'

Banjo said to me as we danced around, me doing well in blocking the punches he'd been throwing but - as a consequence - not providing much in the way of threat to him.

'You fucking know the Hampden by now, Banjo. You want me to stay down, you're going to have to make sure I don't get *up* again then, eh?'

I replied while giving him a jab to the ribs with my left and then making a decent connection with my right with the uppercut. To give a clear example of how tough things had been, *that* had been the first time I had landed two punches on him without reply, but it was a start, at least.

This is more like it, lad, I coached myself, taking a wee bit of personal enjoyment out of seeing Banjo visibly *feel* those two punches. He didn't seem much of a fan of them which, inevitably, provoked a series of punches thrown back. With seeing him visibly reel from the two blows that I'd connected with, it - weirdly - allowed me to almost soak in the punches that he replied back with.

'That all you got, Banjo? You should spend more time using the gym yourself, rather than standing over cunts telling them what to do, soft lad'

Now it probably wasn't the best idea to antagonise the guy but, I don't know? Something had shifted in the dynamic.

From that moment where I realised that I wasn't fighting for the benefit of people around the world - that I didn't know and would never meet in my life - but, instead, fighting for me myself and I. *Then* came the focus. Did it make me a better boxer? Of course it didn't, because I wasn't a fucking boxer. What it *did* bring though was belief, but more than that. The nasty and violent streak that I could *never* have found within myself to bring out for the benefit for others. For myself, though? Something that I could flick on like a light switch.

As the countdown from the pissed up - not to mention hyped - crowd, for the end of round three, reverberated around the ring, for the first time since that opening punch, I stood there feeling that this fight was maybe just getting warmed up.

Chapter 32

Detective Constable Roy van der Elst

'Am I fuck giving some other cunt the collar'

Samuel's opinion - as we made our way out of Dundee - on my suggestion that if there had been a positive ID on Fulton back in Edinburgh, then maybe we should've just had him apprehended, while the chance was there, was as strong as it was blunt.

I, personally, could not have cared less if the *Duke* of Edinburgh had been the person to put the handcuffs around our P.O.I, but Samuel had other ideas.

'Why the fuck you wanting to do all the spadework and then let some other cunt just sweep in and take the glory, Franky? Not right in the fucking head, you, pal'

He shook his head at me as he took us around a roundabout and then onto the motorway to Edinburgh, where the intel was now pointing towards our man.

'But, Detective Constable Samuel, since I got here, we haven't had a single firm lead that has allowed us to even know where Fulton *was*. Now we know *exactly* where he is, and you don't want to act on it? This situation is highly unpredictable and, with the greatest of respect, we can't know what is going to happen next'

I 'got' the whole policeman's fixation with being given the credit for the arrest, I was once one - in the conventional sense - myself so was no stranger to the competitive side that would occasionally surface between colleagues. Sometimes, however, there is a bigger picture. A greater good, if you will.

Something like when your local force has a Detective from Interpol fly in specifically seeking your help in finding someone. The kudos that this would all heap on the local department, if successful. That was the main problem, though. Samuel knew this, and wanted the glory for himself.

'Think about it, Franky. We both win, here. *You're* the one that's been sent here to a foreign country to track down a dangerous criminal, fucking, Dog the Bounty Hunter, you, eh? Imagine how the bosses back in Europe are going to react when they find out that not only did you help locate the fugitive, but you *personally* caught him. Probably get a promotion, at the least, eh?'

He said, taking a moment to look at me seriously before looking back ahead at the traffic.

'And I suppose any praise that you might get out of things will all be purely coincidental, huh?'

I laughed, sarcastically at him, completely having the man's number.

'And besides, the eyes that I've got on Fulton right now. We'll not be losing him, don't you worry about that, my clog wearing friend'

He replied, conveniently skipping the part about how this tactic was clearly all being driven through a selfish point of view from him in his desire to be the one taking the pats on the back and - with a story as big as capturing someone who had been on the run from a Scottish prison for a decade - the likely news interviews or press conferences.

'Think of how many goals that ponce, Ronaldo scores every season'

He continued, although I had no idea why - during our debate over the merits of having Fulton arrested before we reached Edinburgh - he was moving on to sports.

'Your point being ...'

'Well, see all of those goals the boy tucks away, that he gets all the adulation for from fans and the media, do you ever remember who lays them on for him, or notice others talking about who *they* were?'

'Me and you are, fucking Ronaldos, Franky'

This defensive line - for why he was willing to put a major police enquiry at risk all so that he could be the golden boy - continued on for most of the journey. I'd almost taken the decision to overrule Samuel - by way of putting in a call back to Lyon, to get something done about it from up high - but figured that by the time anything was fully done about it, we'd have as good as been at Edinburgh. And, of course, had I done as much, the relationship between Samuel and me - for however long it was scheduled to continue - would have been broken beyond repair.

Samuel didn't look the type to take - what I'm positive he'd have seen as - disloyalty from a partner. Selfishly - although from a completely different perspective - I wanted Fulton picked up so I could get myself back home again and never have to spend another single day of partnering up with my

Scottish compatriot. He was rude, abrasive, disgusting, sexist, homophobic, farted and belched constantly and stank up the car. He was more interested in eating than he was working and the days that I'd spent with him had felt like weeks. And *that* was with him *on* your side?

When we weren't arguing about whether to have Fulton apprehended, Samuel was on the phone to his colleagues in Edinburgh, receiving status reports on how things were going.

Fortunately, Fulton had been spotted in an area of high visibility and in a busy public space, which allowed for our colleagues in Edinburgh to keep a close eye on him via closed circuit TV, as well as eyes on the ground from some plain clothed officers.

My issue was that busy public spaces were the *exact* type of environment that - if your target decides to go on the move - you can lose sight of your man, just as easily as you found them.

'Chill, Franky, my man. We're professionals, here. I know that all you Interpol cunts must look down on us unwashed coppers but trust me, we get the job done as well as yous do'

I'd been through this whole insecure act from him every day since meeting him and - by then - it was water off a duck's back.

'Interpol, good. You lot, bad! Blah, blah, blah, yeah yeah yeah'

I replied, exactly in the kind of way that - weirdly - the more you spoke, the more friendly and receptive to you Samuel was.

As the journey passed by, as we got closer and closer, I felt tenser by the mile. Who really ever knew what the result is going to be when sent over to another land, trying to find criminals. You're only as good as the local force that you're teamed up with and - despite hearing that initial morning about how he got the job done - as far as Samuel and his outlook towards police work, and the *unique* way that he went about it in his day, I still had a *lot* of reservations. With that in mind, it was was quite conceivable that I could well have wasted my time even coming to Scotland.

Of course, it *always* looks good when you go back to Lyon having got the job done. It's just after the first two days spent with Samuel, there wasn't much confidence that this was one of those trips that was going to be able to be filed under *successful*, on return to headquarters.

Samuel's phone went for what had to have been at least the twentieth time. I listened on.

'Aye, we're not that far away now, twenty minutes or something. Aha, right. You got eyes on him right now, though? NO, DINNAE FUCKING HUCKLE HIM, WHAT DID I ALREADY TELL YOU. Just keep following. Safe distance, no spooking him. Now dinnae fuck this up, mind. Right, right, ok, ciao ciao'

He ended the call before glancing at me and saying that Fulton was on the move.

Just hearing him say the words - given all that I said, and feared - it took an incredible amount of biting on my tongue to avoid an argument, there in the car as we now began to leave the motorway and go into the city.

'It's cool, it's cool. He's on the move but we're following him'

I hadn't said a single word back to him yet but my face must've been enough for him to try and reassure me that this operation was not now going wrong.

'Fulton slips his tail and we might lose him for good'

It was true, whether I should've just kept it to myself or not is up for debate, didn't make it none the less true.

Should've grabbed him on sight, I thought to myself but kept it at that.

'Fulton's not slipping any fucking tail, Franky. He'll be in cuffs inside the hour. Fuck, you could be eating grilled Edam sandwiches back home by tonight, all things going to plan'

I wasn't about to share Samuel's confidence, *not* until I had a visual on him myself, and him in handcuffs, sitting in the back of a police car.

A few minutes later, the phone went *again*.

'Ahoy, hoy'

Samuel answered in a pleasant way that did not match the circumstances of what we were involved in. He definitely was not like any other detective I'd ever encountered, wherever in the world I'd been. *This*, not always considered as a good thing.

'Fuck, even *better*. No, no for fuck's sake, dinnae fucking go inside. The average punter in there will smell you a mile away if you walk in. That's perfect, though. Just hang around outside and keep watch. We're not far out now so you'll see us soon enough'

'See, Frankeeeeee, fucking told you it would be sound as a British pound. Got him right where we fucking want him'

Samuel said, relaxed, as he went on to tell me that Fulton had been followed all the way to a bar and that - even judging by the average time it would take someone to have even just the one drink - we'd have arrived before he was going to leave again, and if he did, our man on the ground would let us know about it, the moment it happened.

'Do you not love that fucking feeling Franky? *This feeling*, the one you have when you're minutes away from getting your man. Literally one of the reasons that you do the job, eh?'

He asked, as we started to encounter a bit of built up traffic, and where you were now starting to see that there had been a major sporting event in the area. Lots of people in green and white colours - from the looks on their faces - walking back from the stadium having seen their team lose. Queues of cars all trying to get free of the area, while we were trying to *enter* it.

I couldn't deny him. There was *no greater* feeling than catching your man, or woman. The high it provided was, indeed, one of the reasons that we did the job, because it surely wasn't for the pay check.

'About there, my man'

He said while calling - Larkin - our man stationed on watch for Fulton hitting the street again.

'Aye, it's me. He still inside? Excellent, we're a couple of minutes away. Wait until I get there and then we'll all go in together. Good work, Larky boy, by the way. Aye, I know, I know. I'm due you a Ruby and a few beers for this, eh? Right, two minutes'

We must've been close because on hanging up, Samuel undone his seatbelt in preparation.

'We'll be coming, we'll be coming, we'll be coming down the road. When ye hear the noise of the nee naw boys we'll be coming down the road'

He sang this funny little song, with the annoying sound effect of the car letting its driver know that the seatbelt was no longer being recognised as clicked in, playing alongside.

'Literally round the corner, amigo'

Hearing this, I decided to take off my seatbelt too. From what I'd understood. Fulton was sitting tucked up inside a bar, and we had a man on the outside, so - in effect - everything was *exactly* how it should have been, to have prepared us to just sweep right in and surprise the hell out of our target, as he sat or stood there with a drink in his hand.

Simple.

Correction; *Nothing* is ever simple in the life of an Interpol Detective.

Which was why, as surprising as it was for us - to turn onto the road that the bar was situated on - to find ourselves driving down the road, the bar now in sight, and seeing the figure of someone standing with an outstretched arm, pointing a gun at someone else, it wasn't *that* surprising.

Seeing this, Samuel brought the car to an almost emergency stop, compared to the speed that - when allowed - he'd been making his way towards our destination. Letting the car crawl slowly towards the bar - so close now that I could make out that it was called The Corinthian - in a way that could give us a clearer picture of what was going on, but without us spooking the man with the gun.

For the first time - since we'd been introduced - I saw what resembled an actual serious face, and tone, to him, when it came to doing his job.

Frantically telling me that the man stood there with his hands in the air, trying to back away, was Larkin. Samuel's eyes and ears that had been on the ground keeping track, while we were making our way back from Dundee.

I'd looked at the selection of pictures of Fulton that I'd been provided with for me to have recognised him in a second. Considering Larkin had been watching over Fulton for almost a couple of hours - and that a figure like Norman Fulton would easily be associated with being likely to use a firearm - it would hardly have been out the question for Fulton to eventually notice, leading to this confrontation.

But this *wasn't* Fulton. It looked nothing like him, in fact.

'So if that's Larkin, who is that, holding the gun?'

I asked Samuel, as he brought the car to a complete stop - around fifty yards or so from the bar - and opened the door to get out.

'*That*, Francois van der Elst, is what you and I are about to find out, pal. Come on, let's go'

Chapter 33

Si

Ali versus Frazier, Evander Holyfield versus Mike Tyson, (the second one, like) fucking, Balboa versus Drago, even, I'm telling you, man. *None* of them came anywhere close to laying a glove on Ireland versus Fulton, when it came to the greatest boxing match of all time.

It had blood - *lot's* of blood - it had the sweat, and were it not for the fact that it was two of Scotland's premier radges going at it, toe to toe, then I'm quite certain that there would've been the obligatory tears to complete the set.

And there probably was no one more surprised to be sat there - *still* in that dressing room - thinking that, considering I'd written Nora off by the end of the first one. I couldn't have been the only one, in my defence. He'd been knocked down twice inside three minutes and was already blowing out his arse, and still with another eleven rounds to go.

It took him three rounds before he even started to acclimatise with things which, I'd have to grudgingly admit, only served to highlight just how solid the boy was because there couldn't have been too many people that would've been able to take nine minutes of Brett Ireland punching them at will. To reinforce this, there couldn't have been much walking the earth that could've stood up to nine *seconds* of Ireland's treatment.

Took the boy Fulton until near the end of the third before he actually looked like he'd managed to hurt Ireland, this coming through a nice wee combo. Even more amazing, this directly after Nora had been knocked down for the second time in the round, and the fourth inside the opening three.

You could tell from Ireland's coupon, though, that he'd felt it. Obviously, this seeing to it that he came right back at Nora.

Now I can't say that - as they both went into the fourth round - that from then on in for the fight that it was some ding dong affair. Like how you see in the films where both boxer stands there and trades blow for blow, barely able to stand, the both of them, neither accepting going down. If I said that, it wouldn't really be true. Of course, as had been the main issue from the opening round, only one man out of the two knew *how* to box.

Ireland put Nora on his arse so many times that - with this being some guerrilla camerawork style presentation and the viewers not being provided with the stats that you get on a proper boxing match on the telly - I eventually lost count. But that was what made it such a great fight in the first place. You had - on one side - an accomplished and knowledgable boxer, like Banjo, with an exquisite talent in hurting you repeatedly and, on the other? Someone who hadn't seen a boxing ring in their life, and who would rather die than give up on a fight with someone. To add to the intrigue, despite being a novice in the boxing ring, a unit who *still* possessed the ability to hurt you with their punches, even if half of the time they were pretty much lottery ticket punches that he was attacking with.

By about halfway through the fight, and after seeing him hit the deck for the sixth time, only to get back up and bang his gloves together and nod his head towards Banjo for them to start again, Nora had me thinking of that song that they used to have for certain skits on that programme, Jackass.

If you're gonna be dumb, you gotta be tough.

When you get knocked down, you gotta get back up.

I ain't the sharpest knife in the drawer, but I know enough to know.

If you're gonna be dumb, you gotta be tough.

This was a man, here, who had taken a couple of comments from me on an Internet forum and managed to conclude who - and where - the person behind the comments was, and had flown to another country to find them.

The jury was not even remotely out on whether Norman Fulton was dumb.

The way he kept getting up again and going right back at Ireland, occasionally catching him flush every now and again. Nora's face was an absolute bomb scare. Bruised, bleeding and all cut up, where you wouldn't have guessed - from Ireland's coupon - that the other boy in the ring had been spending his afternoon taking part in a boxing match.

Nora changing this in the sixth when - finding himself up against the ropes with Ireland pounding him punch after punch - trying to turn around a bad situation he was in, he swung a right hook that caught Ireland as good as you could ever have hoped, from a defensive position like Nora had been in.

The punch knocking him back, not quite a knockdown but enough to stop him pummelling Nora. This was hardly a five different camera angle presentation but from the angle that you were watching the fight from, you could clearly see a wee cut underneath Ireland's eye.

That alone, seeing Nora suffer another knockdown - I guess, for his impudence - before the end of the round.

I think - seeing Ireland bleeding from the cut, and some hard proof that the boy wasn't some fucking android or something - that one single moment had been enough to give Nora the strength to get himself through those last rounds.

Why is he not staying down? Actually, *How* is he fucking managing to get *up*? The dual thoughts I was left with every time Ireland put him down. He just kept coming back for more and more, though. This - at first - had appeared to annoy Ireland but - as you can often get with fighters - the longer the fight went on and the longer Nora dug in, Banjo appeared to acknowledge a bit of respect towards his opponent. Not that this meant him fucking hitting him any less, mind.

Fucking really wish there had been some ringside microphones to pick up what the two of them were saying because you could see them talking to each other all the way through it. Making each other laugh with their wideo comments. With how loud the crowd of boys surrounding the ring were, though, you were never going to pick up what the two fighters were saying to each other.

It was like a mini Easter Road - inside that room - with all those Hibs boys inside there singing their hearts out and shouting out in support of their man.

'Excuse me, can I please ask if everything is ok inside there?'

The voice from outside the dressing room enquired, as the two boxers went for a breather at the end of the tenth, sitting down on their stools.

Fucking hell, I've been sat inside here for half an hour, my immediate thought before shouting out that I was fine and would be out soon. This, enough to see them away back through to the main part of the shop again.

Fair play to, Nora. When I'd sat down to watch that stream there was *no fucking way* I'd have believed you if you'd told me that I'd still be sitting inside that dressing room thirty minutes later.

And there was still *officially* another six minutes left.

Fuck knows what personal pep talk Nora had given himself as he got his breath back - before the start of the eleventh round - but the boy quite literally came out swinging into that second last round. First of all - with a decent gap between the two of them - standing with his arms outstretched and bouncing up and down on the canvas. Now *that* was a stance that I'd seen from him shitloads of times before, *right* as he was about to steam right into someone and windmill the poor cunt. Which he went on to do with a surprised Ireland. Aye he was the only one who knew how to box out of the two of them but how the fuck are you meant to defend two windmills coming at you, from someone like Nora? Eventually Ireland - having too much to try and protect at once - let his guard down in a key area that allowed a lucky connection from Nora that buckled his legs before falling completely.

I'm not sure that this was how the script was meant to go but I'd loved to have seen someone try to tell Nora this as - while the stunned Ireland went about picking himself up from the canvas for the first time in the fight - he stood there with arms outstretched looking at some of the casuals ringside, with a face of sheer arrogance on his face. Proper statue-esque, like. Kind of like that radge bastard Mussolini and his theatrics that he'd pull, during his speeches. Standing there lapping up the hate from them all while a few tins went flying in his direction, the man not even attempting to duck them. You could only have imagined the nonsense that was in his head in that moment. The words "man possessed" would possibly not be too wide of the mark.

Obviously, Banjo Ireland wasn't chuffed about being knocked down, so late in the match. Kind of like how a keeper must feel if he lets a goal in right at the end of the game, just as he was about to bag himself a shut out. It was written all over his face as he literally couldn't get up quick enough to get himself fired back into Nora. The look of rage and fury that he had on his coupon would've probably been enough for me to just say 'Know what, Brett, mate? How about we just stop now and I just take the L now, aye?' Whatever it was that he'd had said to him, it was enough to change that moody as fuck look into a wee grin, as he threw a couple of more jabs back at the boy Fulton, the second of them taking the wind out of him big time and setting the tone for the rest of the round with Nora - despite starting the round with his first knock down - on the back foot again.

Which all brought things to the final round. Had this been an official boxing match then there's not a fucking chance we'd have got anywhere close to the twelfth. Referee - had there *been* one - would've put a stop to things, probably by the third. This fight though had been a completely different proposition to the more conventional, though. I have to admit, too. When there's credit due, then, it should be issued, no matter who it is that's earned it. I hadn't been Nora's biggest fan for more of my life than I hadn't but, even so. The fact that he came out for that last round, that he was still able to fucking *stand up* for that twelfth round? It was something that I had no choice but to grudgingly give my admiration, and respect over. So much so that, like you do with a boxing match and you've not got any money on either of the fighters, I was hoping that he could hang on for that last round and make it to the end. He'd have deserved it, for his stupidity at not taking a dive in the first round.

Last thirty seconds or so, though. With the crowd letting Ireland know that the fight was almost over, and encouraging him to finish Nora off, Banjo duly obliged. Entering into a flurry of punches that had the defensive Nora backing up, while trying to protect himself. In amongst the torrent of lefts and rights that was flying into him, a left caught the side of his head, sending him right down. No wobbly legs. No delayed reaction from punch to brain before the connection was made inside his head that he should fall to the floor. Nah, this was one of those good-fucking-night punches, where the cunt looks like he's sleeping, before he's even hit the floor. And not the kind of punch where you get up from inside the space of ten seconds.

From the crowd's roar and Banjo Ireland's reaction - inside the ring - they all knew that it was a done job, and with almost Hollywood style timing.

Once again, though. Nora hadn't read the script. I mean, the first five seconds of the count the man never even moved, just lay there on his back, motionless. I'll be honest when I say that I was more worried about his chances of being alive than I was of him making the count.

Tell me he's not fucking brown bread, I sat there with a bad feeling about things. Couldn't stand the boy but at the same time, wouldn't want him fucking dead or anything, either.

Each second - from him hitting the floor - felt to me like an hour, Just sitting there waiting on, *something*.

Would've been decent to get a closer up view of things but - from what you *could* see - when the crowd got to **EIGHT** he kind of just opened his eyes, like an alarm clock had woken him from a sleep, and automatically - but unfathomably - shot up to his feet, and with such apparent ease, it was kind of like an invisible rope had helped pull him up. He wobbled against the ropes for a second - once he'd got to his feet - but for fuck's sake, I didn't know how he wasn't either still having a wee nap, or just full scale dead. Banjo, recognising this too with his show of applauding Nora, as much as you can give someone a clap, when you're wearing things like boxing gloves around your hands.

Probably for the best, Nora - whose head *must've* been absolutely nipping - looked like he was doing his best to avoid close contact with Ireland and, instead, chose to try and see the remaining seconds out with the minimum of contact between the two of them. On principle, Banjo wasn't going to go out without trying to *take* Nora out, actually getting in a couple of proper sore ones - in the last ten seconds - into Nora's ribs and then combining this with a left uppercut that had him bouncing against the ropes, but still - unexplainable - on his feet.

When the crowd counted down to one - and the end of the match - Nora just kind of slumped into Ireland, arms around him to stop himself from falling. Banjo steadying him up again on his feet before they exchanged a few words. Due to the angle, you could only see Banjo's face as they spoke but it was unmistakable - the sincere look he had - as the two of them spoke before giving each other a proper hug. Breaking off to their own side of the ring.

Banjo with his arm in the air victorious like a boxer who has went all the way, but are confident in the work having been put in across the twelve rounds. I think the only reason that Nora wasn't trying the same was down to being so fucked that he probably couldn't raise his arm. Of course, for him to have tried to claim to anyone who had just sat and watched the fight, that *he'd* won, it would've been an exercise in working one's ticket.

There wasn't even a question who had won the fight but in my book, by lasting the distance, Nora had managed some kind of a hollow victory, even if it was only hollow. Knowing the man, though. If you'd have offered him a hollow victory - in those circumstances - he'd be ready to go twelve rounds with *you*.

The guy from before the fight in the La Mille jacket was back inside the ring again within seconds, along with a few of what looked like their young team who had stormed the ring before being told to get back out again by both Ireland and the guy in the jacket.

Getting well into things, he got Ireland and Nora stood on either side of him while holding onto their wrists. Nora - facing the camera - didn't even *look* like Nora anymore, due to taking twelve rounds of punishment, in the way that he'd just taken part in. Ireland - while, aye, by then looking like he'd been in a scrap - and *his* appearance, most definitely leaving him in the lofty position of being able to say to cunts 'Aye well, you should've seen the other guy.'

Gentleman, we go to the scorecards, sponsored by Calton Gym, fight yourself fit, www.caltonfitness.co.uk

Scottie G scored it 'Who the fuck do you think won it, for fuck's sake?'

Camper scored it 'Well, fucking Banjo, obviously. No see how many times he put the other cunt on his arse, naw?'

And Tam Stevenson scored it 'Dinnae ask fucking stupid questions, mate'

FOR THE WINNER .... BY A UNANIMOUS DECISION ... FROM LEITH, EDINBURGH, THE NEW AND INAUGURAL CHAMPION OF THE RADGE SCOTTISH BASTARD TITLE BELT .... BRETT ... BANJO ....IRELAAAAAAAAAAAAND.

Holding up Ireland's arm into the air, to the rapturous reaction to the crowd. Ireland stood there, assured. Nora? He looked like he barely even knew where the fuck he was.

After a few seconds, the crowd flooded the ring to the point that it looked like there were more inside of it than outside. Nora and Ireland disappearing into the crowd. The live stream coming to an end soon after, and abruptly.

The phone turning around so that - whoever it had been filming the fight - could show himself. A right ugly looking fucker with big nostrils and bad teeth but he also wasn't helping his case with the stupid low angle he was holding the lens at.

CCS number one - Fuck the Hertzzzz.

The stream ending on this.

Fucking WOW, I said to myself out loud, trying to truly process the insane but beautiful madness of what I'd just sat through.

What I had just sat and watched, and the reasons *behind* it? I really wished that I'd played more of an *intentional* part in it all because it would've - without any shadow of a doubt - went down as one of my finest achievements in life. It was more *accidental* than intentional, though. I couldn't take the credit, as much as I'd have liked to. Aye, I might've left a couple of comments on his videos but even so, the fact that Nora was standing almost beaten to fucking death, in some dingy Edinburgh location? *That* was fuck all to do with me and *everything* to do with the fact that Norman Fulton was an absolute moron - a dangerous one, though, mind - a sociopath, psychopath, out and out fucking radgey, whatever you'd like to call the man. Someone who had thought of themselves as superior to those around him, always thought that he knew it all when, in fact, he really was a bit of a clueless cunt, but one who no one had ever had the balls to tell him, me included in that.

Whatever happened to him over there in Edinburgh - and was possibly still to come his way - was all on him, and his stupidity. Whatever, I was sleeping soundly that night, I had absolutely no doubts on that score.

In the end, I never even bothered trying on the new pair of jeans. Instead, carrying them back out with me and handing them in at the counter. I don't think the girl - who had greeted me so friendly with when I'd come in and had possibly been smelling a sale when she'd handed me the pair to go and try on while, understandably, expecting me to emerge a few minutes later with a decision made - was too happy and I really could not have blamed her for thinking that I'd took the piss by sitting in their dressing room so long, without actually *buying* anything.

Walking out of the shop, I had already pulled my phone out to give him a call.

'Did you just fucking see *that?* What do you mean "what?" Oh, Zeek, mate. You're not even going to fucking *believe* what I'm about to tell you, in fact. You back home, the now, aye? Sound, meet me at The Dampkring in an hour's time, trust me, it'll be worth it'

Chapter 34

Detective Constable Roy van der Elst

'Now come on now, Stephen. Let's not do something that can't be undone here, pal'

Samuel showing a deeply empathetic and friendly tone that *had* to have been put on but even if it had been, sounded pretty effective, tried to talk the guy down.

This wasn't the first time I'd been part of a stand off and seen someone with a gun in their hand, and just importantly, the look that they had in their eyes. I could already see that the man - who had initially been training the gun on the Edinburgh plain clothed officer but had now added me and Samuel to his list, moving the gun from Larkin and then to us, then back again - did not have the look about him that suggested he was going to put the gun down anytime soon, and in fact, looked more likely to *do something* with it, rather than put it down.

'I'm fucking warning you, take one step closer to me and I'm pulling the trigger'

When he said this, I fully believed him. Like I said, he had that look about him.

When we'd slowly approached - after getting out of the car - we were given some kind of a debrief from Larkin, who somehow managed to combine telling us what had happened while also trying to say anything possible that would stop this man from pulling the trigger.

'The fuck's going on here, Larks?'

Samuel shouted over to him, and in doing so, announcing our presence to the gunman at the same time, who turned to us but keeping the gun pointed at Larkin.

'One step closer, ya cunts, and I'm fucking blasting'

Typical, I thought to myself. Excluding farmers there was probably only around ten guns in the whole of Scotland and - in the pursuit of picking up Fulton from the bar - we just had to run into *one* of them. Suddenly the Fulton situation was now no longer as serious as it was when we'd turned the corner, so close to the destination that my partner already had his seat belt off in preparation. Things can always change in a heartbeat, though.

Was this one of Fulton's men who had noticed something off with Larkin? Possibly we'd fucked up and had just assumed that he'd been travelling around Scotland on his own, and discounted that someone - as wanted as he was - of this kin may have had certain levels of security, looking out for his wellbeing. If this *was* the case, then you could have been sure that Fulton was aware of what was going on outside and - with that - our element of surprise now blown out of the water. Element of surprise? Depending on what this man with the gun was going to end up doing, we might not have even been presented with the chance of even *entering* the bar to arrest him.

Samuel - who was not the ideal person to be called upon for showing a bit of diplomacy - having put in the required calls to have an armed response unit rushed to the scene, attempted to play negotiator.

Larkin - who I'd have taken a good guess, from his face, that he'd never had a gun pointed at him before - was appearing to get nowhere with his frightened rabbit look while offering nothing but platitudes towards defusing the situation. From the look that the gunman had, however. Platitudes of 'put the gun down' and 'be calm' were clearly not going to do the job, he looked too far gone for *reason*. In fact, when you decide to pull out a gun on a police officer, you've pretty much already announced to everyone that quite possibly you're not that much of a reasonable man.

During the shouting back between Samuel and Larkin it had been established that, while stationed out on the street, on watch for Fulton, he had witnessed this man, in front of us in what looked like lounge wear and with a red white and blue scarf wrapped around his neck, wrap the scarf around his face before taking a gun from out of his jacket, and make towards the bar.

Larkin, in his capacity as an officer of the law, had attempted to stop him from doing so - which cannot be an easy thing to do when you're not in possession of a firearm yourself - which had now led to this scene outside of the bar, literally two metres from its front door.

As it all took place someone - from inside the bar - actually emerged with a cigarette in his mouth, just getting ready to light it before looking up and noticing that there was a man with his back to him, pointing a gun back and forward, and threatening three police officers. Due to the sheer unpredictability in moments like that where anything can happen, the smoker was lucky that he hadn't spooked the gunman and ended up suffering from the knee jerk reaction to this by taking a bullet. He dropped the cigarette from his mouth while appearing to silently say the words 'Oh, fuck' before quickly retreating back into the bar, where you could have been sure that every one inside there drinking were now going to be aware of what was taking place. This confirmed within seconds. A series of heads all began popping up, peering over the frosted effect that made up the majority of the large glass windows to the front of the bar.

'Look, tell me your name, pal. My name's Colin'

Samuel - if the gunman was at six o clock then Larkin was at twelve, which left the pair of us, while further back than Larkin, in the nine of clock position - asked the man. What scared me about him was how scared *he* was. Someone like that is completely unreadable, in a state like that. They could just as easily shoot a couple of people, as they could peacefully and amicably put the firearm down on the ground, and him closely following it.

'Nah, nah, you're not getting me on that pal, shite. You must think I'm fucking stupid'

He shouted back at Samuel while moving the gun around to point it towards the two of us, nervously holding it in the air, despite the distance between us I could see it trembling in his hand. Eventually, Samuel managed to prise a name from out of him, Stephen.

'Is that with a P or with a V?'

Samuel shouted while taking his hands and placing them palm to palm before opening them up to indicate the letter *v*. Just a simple question but - for a moment - it seemed to knock the man from his stride, just being given something a bit left field to think of. This, I'd felt, had been Samuel's intention but with him clearly not being a trained negotiator - I'd seen enough of them over the years - there was definitely an element of the spontaneous about him, as he went about trying to win the gunman's trust.

'You, just had to fuck it up, all of yous'

Stephen - with a p - shouted at us. It looked like he was in tears. Whatever it had taken, for him to be stood in this position that he was in, he *must've* known that there now was no longer going to be a suitable outcome for him. He was already going to jail for this - he must've known by this point - but if he wanted to prolong things, until the tactical response unit arrived on the scene, then he was going to be risking things taking an even worse turn for him.

'Fucking five minutes, not even that. All I fucking needed to get the job done. Why couldn't you have been sitting in Dunkin fucking Donuts or something?'

'Get. The. Job. Done'

This, in itself, sounded like he'd been hired for a hit on someone but - and maybe I was guilty of judging a book by its cover - this was *no* hitman. With me barely playing a part in things - other than just stand there with a stupid look on my face - it had given me a good chance to study him. My guess? I'm not sure that he had held a gun in his life, but when you're the one holding the weapon, you still have to be respected.

When he'd turned to point the gun at Samuel and I, he held it in a sideways position in our direction. Clearly he'd been watching too much TV because only someone who had never actually fired a gun in their life would have ever *held* one in this way. This, at the very least, gave me a degree of confidence over that if he was to go over the edge and take the decision to actually fire the gun, there was not going to be a guarantee that he'd be hitting anyone.

Still, while the target has the gun, and you don't have any ...

'I'm not a bad guy, I'm really no'

He said, now crying. It seemed hopeful, seeing this as men who are reduced to the crying stage will rarely ever pull the trigger on a gun.

'Hey, Stephen. None of us are saying that you are, pal. And you know what else would show that you're not a bad person? Putting that gun on the ground and kicking it away from you. Let's just bring this all to an end while we're all pals, and no one's been hurt eh?'

'But, that bastard ruined me and my family's life and doesn't deserve to fucking live another day of *his*'

'*Who* ruined your family?'

Samuel asked but he needn't have bothered because the guy was too far gone in letting it all out, now that he had started.

'And the fact that, after everything he's done, he gets to walk about the streets and you cunts don't even fucking lift him shames the lot of you. He ruined my dad's life, killed my mum, had ma sister desert the family and lost *me* my career. Try to tell me that's fucking FAIR'

'If you cunts had done your fucking job in the first place I wouldn't be fucking standing here. FUUUUUUCCCCCCKKK'

He ended the latest rant with a primal scream as his frustration at things appeared to boil over.

'Too busy sitting in your pervy wee speed camera vans, wanking off at cunts going over the speed limit to worry about catching *real* criminals, like fucking the Norman Fultons of this world'

I don't know? Just by mentioning the man's name, it brought a bit of steel to him, his face firming up, as the name passed from his lips. That aside, Samuel and me just turned to each other, aghast, hearing the name that the gunman had just shouted out to us.

'You *are* fucking kidding me?'

Samuel looked at me and laughed, the gunman noticing this. If it wasn't for the fact that there was still a firearm at play I'd have laughed at the thought of Samuel doing all that he could to avoid anyone else getting the collar of Fulton, while all the time there had been someone else that afternoon with plans for the man, that would have made Samuel's collar a little redundant.

'Stephen, me and this man beside me are literally here *to arrest* Fulton. We've been tracking him for days, pal. He's inside the boozer, there, and we've just arrived here to pick him up'

'Aye, I fucking *know* he's inside, why the fuck do you think *I* was going in?'

Stephen replied, not really seeing the importance of what Samuel had just said to him, or more likely, it had been taken as just some convenient lies, told in an attempt to defuse the situation. Let's face it, police *have* been known to lie in such settings. Samuel, sensing this, nudged me and told me to get out my phone and pull up the pictures of Fulton that I had as part of my electronic case file.

No way was he going to be able to see the picture on the phone screen from the distance we were stood at, however.

'Now, Stephen. My friend Franky here is going to slowly walk towards you and show you what's on his phone screen. He's going to have his other hand in the air, all nice and calm, I want to see the same from you, pal, *nice and calm*'

Samuel shouted across to him, nudging me once more.

'Oh Franky *is*, is he?'

I whispered, annoyed at Samuel's decision, that had been made - one that involved me walking towards an unpredictable man holding a gun - which had included me in a big way, but had also been taken without any input *from* me.

'Just get fucking over there, ya shitebag. He's not going to shoot you, for fuck's sake'

Samuel replied, completely nonplussed by my aversion to participate in his tactics.

Wisely doing as Samuel had advised I would. I raised one arm high in the air while holding the phone - with one of the pictures of Fulton on screen - in front of me, as far as I possibly could to ensure that he would be able to see the face on the screen, but without me being as close to him as could be avoided.

'Do you recognise the face?'

I asked, feeling I was close enough to him by then but this was not helped by his nervousness which had seen him taking a few steps backwards from me which pretty much defeated the purpose of me walking *towards* him. I was so close to the bar by now that - while standing holding out the phone - I could look up and see the eyes inside, looking over the frosted glass. Some *kind soul* looking at me and putting a pretend gun to his head and pulling the trigger. Nice.

Trying to maintain rotating the gun from Larkin to me and back again, while doing this, he stood there trying to look at the photo but never at any point allowing himself a long enough look for fear of being ambushed by Larkin, who might have seen the chance there to be taken.

'Do you see the face, Stephen? I have come from France to make sure the man is arrested. My colleague is not lying to you'

He squinted at the phone for another few seconds before - I guess - settling on that the face on my phone was the exact same person that he had come to the bar to murder.

Happy with this, I told him that I was going to slowly back away from him again, while advising him that he should let us arrest Fulton.

By the time I'd re-joined Samuel I'd noticed that the tactical response unit had now quietly arrived, with various officers - all packing - positioned, across the street, weapons pointed in the direction of our gunman.

'See, Stephen. We're not lying to you, pal. We're genuinely *here*, for Fulton. Now the way I see things, here. You've got two choices. Choice number one is that you do something extremely stupid and pull that trigger, and then one of these officers holding sub machine guns around their necks are going to take you out … *or* you could put the gun down, step aside and take the enjoyment of watching us march Fulton out of this pub, knowing that he's not going to be seeing freedom for a *very* long time, if at all. I know what I'd choose, my friend'

The gunman stood there, taking this in and weighing up the odds of it all. In that position, with all of those armed police surrounding you, knowing that one wrong sudden move and they wont hesitate to drop you, it takes a brave - not to mention extremely stupid - man to go down the road that *isn't* the one where you say 'ok, enough's enough' and decide to put the gun down, without a single bullet being fired.

'FFFFFUUUUUUUUUCCCCCCKKKKKKKK'

He screamed out in frustration, but , to me, it was a good sign.

'No fucking errors with paperwork or evidence going missing or fuck all because I know what you fucking bizzies can be like. You promise that you'll put him away, aye. I get your word on that?'

He asked Samuel, which if answered in the correct way, was looking like the pre-cursor towards him putting an end to this.

'Stephen, mate? Fulton *escaped* from jail and has been on the run for ten years. That's not really the type of evidence that can be shredded by accident. And see this guy, here?'

He pointed to me, not just Stephen but all the armed officers looking towards who Samuel was referring to.

'He's from *Interpol,* sent here to help arrest Fulton. Does that look like we're intending on letting the guy off the hook?'

'And, and what about me? What's going to happen to me?'

This, I'd felt was going to be his last question, but such a tough one to answer because there really was no lying on this one. Anyone with half of a brain would have known that they'd be seeing a spell in prison for this, and to tell them otherwise would have been stupid, possibly suicidal.

'Well, Stephen. It's like I said, it's all about choices. If you make the choice to put the gun down, you're making the choice to not be shot and killed, which is a good enough reason in my book. Apart from that, though. I'm not going to lie to you, you're going to be charged over this but trust me, it's not going to be the end of the world, unlike a bullet. Me and Franky, here, will speak up on your behalf, with the mitigating circumstances that you seem to have in connection with Fulton. That should help you, plus we'll both say that you were willing to bring an end to all of this with a peaceful conclusion, isn't that right, Franky?'

'Oh, of course' I agreed, not taking an eye off the gunman.

'The combination of how Fulton is already viewed by the authorities and all of your personal problems that he has caused you. This will *all* go in your favour, if you *please* put the gun down' I continued. This, possibly, was lies, but it sounded plausible and, at that crucial moment, that was all that was important.

'Just imagine the satisfaction, knowing that Fulton is going to be rotting in a jail cell for decades to come and, due to his past, will be in self isolation for the most part. An absolute hell for him. Shooting him would be too good for him, eh?'

Samuel backed me up, just choosing a *lot* of words that I wouldn't have elected to go with but - I guess - in that situation, whatever worked was worth saying.

He stood there, still holding the gun out around him but with much less purpose as up until that point, surveying everyone that had circled this area of the street and - more or less - penned him in.

Samuel, as unprofessional as he was when he chose to be, *was* a good Detective. Choosing to stay silent and let Stephen mull all of this over. It probably only took a minute at the very most but felt much, much longer before.

'OK, OK .. I'M GOING TO SLOWLY PUT THE GUN DOWN ON THE GROU ..'

That was all he was allowed to get out before the - frankly - overzealous armed response unit - who had clearly wanted in on the action - began to bark orders at him. Telling him - while they moved slowly inwards - to put the gun on the ground and then, following doing this, to lie face down, put his arms behind his back and lock his fingers together.

We watched the gun man comply, all the way until three officers swooping on him, pinning him there until they were able to get the handcuffs on him. His screams over how tight they were and how they were breaking his arm, the last thing Samuel and I heard from him as we breezed past, and into 'The Corinthian' to get our man.

After a few minutes of us scanning every corner of the busy - this by no means an easy task due to the combination of the patrons inside all wishing to know what had just taken place outside while some of the others, who, visibly, were not the biggest fans of the police, appeared to go out of their way to inconvenience us and dish out insults, there appeared to be one slight problem.

After all of what had just taken place outside in the street and what Samuel and me had experienced in simply trying to get ourselves *inside* the bar, and the time that it had taken.

Fulton wasn't even *there*.

Chapter 35

Nora

'Tell you what, respect, mate, and you know how much it would take for me to say that to you, of *all* people'

Tattie - the cunt who hadn't stopped banging on about the scar I'd given him in the eighties - stood over me as I sat on the battered stool, in the corner of the ring. He offered an arm to help me up, which I accepted because if he didn't offer me one then I'm not sure just how the fuck I was meant to get back up by myself.

I'd never experienced so much pain - and from so many different parts of my mind and body, all at once - in my entire puff, but then again, I'd never had a fight like *that* before in my life. Not even close.

Remove the pain part (please) and there was still the issue of how foggy and spaced out my mind was. Dizzy with a lot of flashes of light in front of my eyes which felt like Banjo had handed me a nice wee concussion. My body - rib area especially - was bruised to fuck, arms fucking hanging off from the holding up and the punches I'd been slamming into him - some even connecting - a ringing ear from a bit of a stray right hook that Ireland caught me with in the seventh - something he apologised for there and then - and a badly opened up cut under my left eye and a right eye that was so puffed up and closed that I could barely fucking see out of it. With all of that contend with, what problems would a wee concussion cause?

I was too fucked, drained and hanging on to reality to truly appreciate Tattie's words at the time but - once I'd thought back after the event - the fact that someone - with a fully legit reason for not having me on his Christmas card list - was willing to give me *any* kind of praise, was something that should not have been taken lightly. He could've kept his mouth shut and and the world would have not spun off its axis. He didn't need to say - what he said - it but the fact that he *did* spoke fucking volumes.

Being brutally honest, I was just happy to see a friendly vibe - there inside the ring - following the fight's conclusion. Having just taken part in it, there was such a gap between me and Banjo that it could not have really been considered a perfect match up, but let's just say that I *had* been from a boxing background, and had been up to the task of matching Ireland blow for blow. What if I'd knocked the cunt out in the first round and he never woke up again? Aye, I'm not so sure that there would have been much *warmth* extended my way and, in fact, the chances of me emerging from that basement would've been sitting at me not leaving again, until the pub upstairs was closed for the night, rolled up in a carpet.

There were more congratulatory sentiments handed my way - from both the younger members and the old guard - but I was too dazed to truly appreciate them. Offering them a wee half hearted smile back for their troubles.

Through the commotion, Ireland eventually made his way - through a series of cuddles, back slaps and kisses on the head, from his boys - towards me, massive smile on his face. I remember wondering what horrors were going to be found when I looked at a mirror because - despite only landing one punch on him for every fucking ten, or at least it felt like that all those rounds, he had that cut to the eye that I'd given him but, apart from that, was also showing other signs of him having recently taken part in some kind of a scuffle.

'You are a fucking warrior'

His choice of words, immediately making me think of the funny cunt on YouTube who had engineered it for me to be standing there in that boxing ring, unable to even gently move my head without a ringing pain shooting through it straight after.

'Good wee work out, there though, Nora, like. What the fuck is your *head* made out of, though? The same material as they make fucking aeroplane black boxes with or something, because I still don't know how you kept getting back up?'

Banjo said - and while my head was, admittedly a wee bit foggy - with what looked like sincerity rather than it sounding like it had been aimed as a wide comment, considering the difference between the two of them by the end of the twelfth.

'Aye, barry mate, eh. Wee bit longer than I'd anticipated, when I walked through the door of the fucking boozer, though'

We both laughed at this while he gave me another cuddle and suggesting that we maybe make this a yearly affair - aye, fuck that - and include both gyms into the mix, maybe one year in Amsterdam, the next in Edinburgh. I wasn't able to work out what the fuck I would be doing in an hour's time, never mind in a *year's*. For the sake of not complicating things I just told the boy 'aye, sound, Banjo' but in as non commitment a way as possible. Same with Ireland's plans for growing the Calton Gym - and any tips that I could help give him - and beginning to give it a bit of a more online presence, like Utility Defence.

I was in the middle of trying to tell Banjo that I might not be back in Amsterdam for a wee while - due to the obvious return journey issues that I now had - but that when I was back home we'd set up a Skype, when I wasn't feeling like I'd had my head hit with a mallet, near on constantly for half an hour, and was thinking a bit more straight, and me and Pippo would tell him all he needed to know.

'Fucking sound as a pound, lad. Be much appreciated and won't be forgotten, either. Tell you, Nora. It's funny how life can work out, eh?'

Having found myself in the basement of a pub - on a mid Saturday afternoon - that had a boxing ring inside of it, surrounded by Hibs Capital City Service, and there being a bit of a friendly vibe to things, I could not have agreed more.

Surreal was not even close to being the word for it all, but was as good as my vocabulary could stretch to.

And it was to get a *lot* more fucking surreal before it got normal.

I was leaning against the ropes - still trying to recover from the end of the twelfth round, where in actual fact it was going to take me a lot fucking longer than a wee breather there in the ring to recover from what I'd just taken myself through - chatting to a random CCS young team, when it looked like several of the boys had all started to get text messages through, all round about the very same time. And from some of the reactions that I'd been able to clock, something big had happened, or was literally taking place.

'Banjo, Banjo ... look at this'

One of the lads thrust his phone in the direction of their top boy, strangely saying it in a hushed tone, as opposed to the raucous way that everyone had been behaving from the moment that they'd all arrived down in the basement. I trailed off from the conversation as I watched for Banjo's reaction to this. His initial response being to tell everyone in the room to shut the fuck up before, also, in a hushed tone said, having made sure he had everyone's attention.

With Rangers being in town for the day, I expected something in relation to this, closely followed by all the CCS boys getting back up above ground ASAP.

'Right, some of you've already had the texts sent to you but for those that haven't. Details a bit thin on the ground at this point but while we've been down here there's been some kind of incident with some radge with a gun, holding the police hostage outside the pub. Bizzies are upstairs in the bar snooping around. Fucking international coppers, the lot'

Being anywhere in the vicinity of coppers searching for someone was not exactly that cool for me at any point but hearing the words 'international coppers' was, understandably, something that was going to have my ears pricking up.

'Did you say international coppers, pal?' I said, quietly, to Banjo. 'Because if that's the case, they're here looking for me. Got fucking Interpol chasing me, like, eh?'

'Fucking *Interpol?* Check out Carlos the fucking Jackal, here?'

Banjo laughed but - at the same time - appreciated the seriousness of things.

'We going to be safe down here, aye?'

I asked, more in hope than assisted with any kind of real confidence. The knowledge that they were literally one floor above from where I was, enough to have me starting to flap.

I'd only watched that Inglorious Basterds the year before at the Rialto up in de Pijp, and there was the exact same scenario where they were setting up a meeting, but it had been set up for below street level, and that Brad Pitt boy wasn't too cool about the meeting point *because* it was beneath street level and - paraphrasing the cunt - he was saying that it left you at a disadvantage, if things all went a bit tits up, like right now, there in The Corinthian.

'Mate, we're only as safe as which coppers are in the bar - and if they know about the basement's existence - and if there's any grasses up there who are willing to part with information, in exchange for a couple of pints'

I couldn't help but think of that old jakey from the day before who I'd sat beside in the afternoon - plying him with free drink - who had sat and told me a complete load of bollocks about 'Swanny' coming in drinking there every Hibs game.

'They catch me down here, Banjo. I'm fucked. They'll throw away the fucking key, ya cunt'

None of the fact that there were police, detectives, fucking A-Team upstairs looking for me changed the fact that I ached *all over* - moving any part of me, an ordeal .. and staying still wasn't exactly a piece of piss either - but it sure as fuck gave me an incentive to push myself through all pain barriers put in front of me.

'Stevie, Kris, get this cunt's gloves off him fucking pronto'

Ireland pro-actively sprang into action, already appearing that he had a plan in place, just without initially sharing it with me. Two of the boys immediately rushed over to me and started undoing my gloves for me, while Banjo explained to me that there was a wee "escape hatch" that was down there in the basement, and that I needed to get myself out of the boxing gear, back into my clothes and then they'd help me escape. Ominously adding, though, that the trap door leading to the basement from behind the bar could quite literally open at any moment, or it wouldn't.

'You probably don't want to take that chance, though, eh?'

Banjo asked a question he already knew the answer to.

'Walker, run and get Nora's clothes from the other room'

I was almost glad that I hadn't connected with Banjo - so many times during the fight - as, despite going twelve rounds, he was as sharp as a fucking Stanley Knife, in those following moments upon us hearing about the police upstairs above us. And thank fuck for that too.

Inside minutes they had my gloves off and I was - as fast as possible, which wasn't much, stripping there in the ring to chaotic scenes of half of the room dispensing with the Ching that they still had on them, in what looked like some group sniffing session.

'Come on tae fuck, Nora. Time is money here, lad'

Banjo tried to coax me, clearly unaware of the damage that he'd inflicted on me over those thirty minutes.

Eventually I was dressed and in some kind of a position to move, wherever that was to. At that moment I wouldn't have been too picky. Underground tunnel, panic room, invisible wall. In actual fact, it wasn't anything near as elaborate as any of those options, but it was a way out, and *that* was all that really mattered.

Through a wee - but thick looking doubled bolted, top and bottom, door - that was in the corner of the room with the boxing ring but one that I'd not clocked the whole time I'd been in there - Ireland - taking charge of things - took me over to the wee door before opening it and poking his head through, having a look, and then bringing his head back in again.

'Right, mate. It's a bit crampy, like but crawl all the way to the bottom. When you get to the end you go left and eventually you'll get to a another wee door. Might be a bit stiff, like, so you'll need to give it a good shove before you get through it but once you're through that, just head up the stairs and it'll get you up to the street again. Apologies about the rats, mice and the likely smells along the way. Fuck knows who lives or has lived inside there in the past but considering the other options you've got open to you right now…'

Banjo, offered me my directions as he sent me on my way.

'I'll fucking snap your hand off, mate'

I joked before we nodded at each other in a respectful kind of way that two people could find themselves doing after going through something of a bit of an emotional experience, like we'd just shared.

Through, into this low as fuck crawl space, the door slammed shut behind me, followed by the sound of both bolts being slid into place again.

I'm not claustrophobic by any stretch but the second I heard those locks slide shut, I instantly got the paranoid thought that maybe there *hadn't* been any coppers upstairs in the first place and that *this* was just a story to engineer me being locked up in there, never to come out. Those sick CCS bastards locking me up to starve to death, never to be found again.

Stop being fucking stupid, I told myself, and just concentrate on getting yourself out of here, and away from the bizzies. The smell *was* a cocktail of all kinds of things that amounted to me almost ralphing my way through the small journey. Proper dry boaking it as I crawled my way towards the end of this wee bit of space that, I'd assumed, was between one building and another. I felt something drop onto my crouched back, before the next noise of it hitting the ground and scurrying away in front of me.

Better not to concentrate on what that was, I wisely encouraged myself as I continued slowly moving towards the T junction, - of sorts - eventually reaching it and taking the left that Brett had told me I'd find. He hadn't been fucking joking about that other door, either. There was a moment where - after numerous attempts at barging it open and without success - I thought that it was never going to spring free. Didn't help that every fucking bone in my body was broken at the time either, mind.

Eventually I got it open, daylight streaming instantly down the wee set of stairs, blinding me from the contrast of the complete darkness that I'd just been moving through.

Happy fucking days, I said to myself as I made my way gingerly up the stairs to - hopeful - freedom. When I reached the top, I stopped to have a wee look in each direction, to see what was waiting for me up at street level, but wherever the coppers were about - and with there being an incident involving someone waving a gun around - and there would be many, they didn't seem to be in the vicinity of wherever the fuck it was that I was emerging up into, but they *had* to be close by.

As difficult as it was to walk with any real degree of freedom of movement, I just concentrated on putting as much daylight between me and The Corinthian as possible, knowing that all it was going to take would be for a police car or van to come around the corner, and it would've been curtains for moi.

Limping along the road, from the looks I was receiving, I must've looked some sight. One guy - about same age as me - visibly wincing, when he took a look at my coupon as we locked eyes before passing each other.

The second I seen a black cab it was getting hailed - with the instructions of getting me as far from Leith as fucking possible - but as is always in these scenarios, not one taxi to be seen. Always loads when you never fucking want one though, mind.

Then to my absolute salvation came a guardian angel to the rescue.

When I heard the car behind be slowing down - for fear of what was going to be behind me - I chose not to look behind me. If I can't see it, it doesn't exist, my line of deluded thinking. It kept up enough speed to then draw level with me. Some kind of black Merc that I'd have needed to have seen the rear of it for to have been able to tell you what model. It had tinted windows all round, nice looking motor, like.

The passengers side electric window slowly came down to reveal the boy in the passengers side, looking out at me.

'Quick, get in the back, pal'

The - as far as I could see - stranger urged me, nodding his head back towards the rear seats of the car.

'Who the fuck are you, like?'

I asked, not intending to reply as hostile as it might've come across as. Understandably, a lot had went on the past hour, and my head was rattled by then.

He just seemed to laugh at my tone and general attitude, rather than take it the wrong way, as could so easily have been the case.

'I'll tell you who I'm *no*. I'm not one of the squads of police that are currently combing this immediate area, looking for you, so you getting in, or are you getting caught?'

Well, when he put it that way, eh?

Looking around me - before going any further - I opened the back door and threw myself in, reaching out to grab and slam the door behind me as the car started to drive off.

'So who are you two, anyway?' I asked, looking at the boy in the passengers seat and then the one who was doing the driving.

'Couple of Banjo's boys, aye?'

The boy who had talked me into the backseat just laughed back at this.

'Don't you worry about who we are, Norman. There's someone that's wanting a word with you. Just you sit back and relax, you look like you've been through the wars, there. We'll be in Portie in no time, just enjoy the rest, you look like you fucking need one'

Portie? Oh *now* I knew what the Hampden was, and *who* it was that wanted to see me.

Chapter 36

Nora

'Norman Walker "Nora" Fulton, Fintry, Dundee'

He said, sitting on the other side of the desk, looking back at me, like I was sat at some job interview, with him looking over my CV in real time.

This was no interview for employment, though. And let's face facts, with my appearance, on arrival - the way it was - there would be *no* employer in the world - short of a boxing promoter - who would have even let me in the door.

Like I said, this was no job interview, but that didn't mean to say that this could not be classed as *an* interview. Because just exactly like how you feel, when you go in and try to nail that new job, every single minute that you're sat there you're never not aware that whatever the fuck comes out of your mouth next will help - one way or the other - determine your immediate future.

The day - trip - hadn't went to plan and - by teatime - looking back, the only parts that I could genuinely say had been worth getting out of bed for had been that panelling which I'd given that pissed up hun, - going down Leith Walk - as well as the abuse, that I'd been presented with the chance to hurl at Kirk Broadfoot at Easter Road. Everything else about the day? Painful and humiliating. A horrible combination to be on the receiving end of and no mistake.

So what made me think that the *rest* of it was going to suddenly turn around for me?

This, confirmed, by the fact that I was now sitting in a filthy Porto-cabin - that appeared to be classed as an office - with a face staring back at me and one that - while I'd have gladly been staring back at under other circumstances rather than when feeling like I'd went twelve rounds with a prize boxer, and now being flanked by a couple of tasty looking goons - I knew was going to be the cause of the day hardly going from bad to good.

'David "The Chancellor" McKenna, Edinburgh, and beyond'

I replied back, with sarcasm while also trying to let him know from the very off that, despite the whole show of having me picked up and then brought directly to him, that I wasn't as rattled by this as they'd maybe anticipated.

He just smiled back at this while looking over my shoulder towards his two men, who were standing towards the back of the cabin, which was hardly a million miles away. Smiling, he nodded at me - to them - as if he was offering an invitation to check out the wideo that was sat in front of them.

'The Chancellor? Fuck, I've not heard that in a while. Think the tabloids call me it more than anyone in the real world ever did'

'Shame, I always thought that it was a good match, as well, very dignified and respected, eh? Well, apologies for not being up on your latest nickname. I've been a bit busy the past twenty years'

He just laughed, once more, while replying that he was sure that I had been, safe in the knowledge that he knew for an absolute fact what I'd been doing for at least *ten* of those years.

It was a weird setting, sitting facing each other - knowing who one another was - and talking *like* we knew who the other was, despite having never seen each other in person before in our lives.

Seemed almost an amicable meeting of minds but - given the history between us - I wasn't fucking buying the man's opening tone of what seemed like almost friendliness to it. I wasn't sat there in front of him for a friendly chat, that was for fucking sure.

With me already having decided on this, I tailored my responses, accordingly. I'd always said that if I was left in a position that I knew I wasn't going to be walking away from, that I'd go out with my dignity intact.

'You look like you've had a day of it, Nora'

He pointed to my face, which I'd finally managed a look at via the rear view mirror inside the Mercedes, and found myself to be a couple of levels down from Elephant Man.

'Probably the *last* thing you could be doing with, sat here, with me'

On arrival at the porto-cabin there had been the farcical scene where McKenna had went full scale radge at the two goons - who had brought me inside - wrongly assuming that it had been *them* who had done the damage to me.

'What did I fucking tell you? Not a single hair on him harmed before he got here, and **LOOK AT THE CUNT?**'

I didn't have the energy for any of it but, regardless of this, still stuck up for the two of them because even after them protesting to their gaffer that they hadn't laid a finger on me, he wasn't believing either of them and it was only my intervention, saying that it had been someone else, that saved them for any more of a bollocking. One of them - despite the fact that potentially he *was* going to be laying a finger on me - gave me a wee respectful nod for sticking up for him and his mate.

'Well don't take this personally, Mr McKenna, but compared to lying in a Radox filled bath for a couple of days straight with enough whisky and fags to see me through it, having a social visit with you comes a poor second'

'But yet, here you are'

He left it hanging for a moment to assess my reaction to this - which wasn't much, I was fucking *spent* and too tired for to even be able to show much in the way of emotion, of *any* kind - before continuing.

'But, really now, Norman? Did you honestly think that you could come into *my* city, walk around telling anyone that'll listen to you in boozers what you're going to do to me, and me not find out about it? You need to be more careful who you speak to and in this case, inside this city, that means *any* cunt that you speak to. From Muirhouse to Leith and Bilston to South Queensferry. My name gets mentioned, I'm going to hear about it'

And now - for McKenna - came the part where the guy sat there and blabbered the biggest lot of shite, while begging for their life. That was how it usually went, right? Fucking *wrong*, McKenna, you fucking grassing snake.

'Well, I'm a busy man so I thought that, while I was back in Scotland for a wee while, that I thought you and me could go out for a coffee and talk about, you know? The old days, like'

While it hadn't been mentioned yet, - but you could be sure as fuck that I was going to be bringing it up before I was taken outside and thrown into the scrap metal crusher - looking at me, knowing what he'd done while also knowing that *I* knew what he'd done. If there was any kind of a man with decency in there - which I appreciate can be a difficult thing for someone with intentions of running the underworld of a major city - then the man should have felt a bit of embarrassment, even if just a tiniest of shred of it.

I wasn't looking for - or expecting - any contrition from him. Just knowing that he knew that *I* knew - in an unspoken way - was enough.

'Well, here we are, Budsy, get the man a coffee. Let's *catch up*'

He replied, arrogantly, while pointing towards the tea, coffee and drinks vending machine in the corner of the room.

'And before we even begin - considering what I already know you're going to say before you say it - you should be thanking me. From what Bud tells me, if it had been a police car rolling up behind you, instead of him and Piotr, you'd be in the cells right now'

Were it not the case that being in the police cells and in Davey McKenna's scrapyard was the equivalent of frying pans and fire, he'd possibly have had a point.

'Oh aye, proper guardian angels, them. You any idea how long I'd looked for a taxi?'

'You're some boy, Norman. Not unlike what I thought you'd be like'

'Who, me?' I laughed 'You should've caught me on a day where I hadn't been through twelve rounds of boxing. I'm a wee bit tired just now so apologies if my patter isn't exactly on key. Maybe we'll get that chat and coffee on another day, when I'm on form, just you and me, Davey, eh?'

I replied, feeling every bit of pain that my afternoon's recreational activities had produced. It was going to take a few clear couple of days before any of that stuff was going to start to disappear, and a *lot* could've happened before I reached that particular neck of the woods.

I had absolutely no right to be making veiled threats towards him, with the suggestion that there be a situation engineered that it would be just the two of us, left alone. I genuinely didn't care. This trip to Scotland had not went as planned, had made a massive cunt out of myself in doing so, been treated like a punchbag for half an hour that had felt like eternity, fucked my cover with the authorities which was going to threaten me ever getting back out of this fucking country, and to top it off I was now sitting with one of Scotland's most powerful crime bosses, who had sent for me.

Don't get me wrong, I wasn't suicidal or had decided to just throw in the towel on matters. I was simply - for that day at least and until I could get a recharge - all out of anything remotely *close* to a fuck.

'I'm afraid, like yourself, I'm also an incredibly busy man so will need to decline that offer from you but, well, you're here now. If there's anything you need to say, I'd say, now's your chance'

I didn't know whether I needed to look more into the way that he'd informed me that this was my chance. Did he mean that this was my chance, because here we were so if I wanted to say something to him then what better opportunity than when he was right there in front of me. *Or,* did he mean this was my chance, as I wasn't going to *get* another one, because I wouldn't be leaving the scrapyard again?

Thinking 'fuck it' I looked around - for show - at his two men before turning back to him and saying

'Well, respectfully, what I was wanting to talk to you about. Maybe you wouldn't want your men to know about, might be a wee bit, well, embarrassing, eh?'

'In what way?'

He replied, the first time since I'd sat down that his self assured and completely in control of things smile disappeared from his face.

'In the some of the poor form power moves that you're capable of making. Stuff that fall under the line of the unwritten rules, know what I mean, eh?'

The smile returned, then the laughter followed.

'Who? Them two?'

He pointed over me from side to side at the Scot and the Eastern European.

'Trust me, they - out of *anyone* - know what I'm capable of, they carry out the instructions for the majority of what needs done'

I looked around at the two of them again and started speaking - for their benefit, to begin with, more than McKenna's.

'The pair of you don't look old enough to have been working for this man, here, back in the early Nineties so you'll not know about this one but despite the fact that neither me or your gaffer had ever crossed paths, weren't a threat to each other and, despite being in the same industry, due to simple geography, never took food of the other's plate. And regardless of this, with one phone call ... he manages to see to it that I have ten years taken from my life, stuck in Bar L'

Whether either of them had an opinion on this, they obviously were not going to offer it. Same for any facial reaction to hearing this. I wouldn't have expected any less - knowing that while I looked at them, so would be their gaffer - from either of them. I just wanted them to know that their boss man was a grass, which I'm sure they were already aware of, and whether it was said or left unsaid. All four of us inside that porto-cabin - whatever our angle - *knew* how grasses were looked upon.

While still surveying the two of them, for any response, the laughter began again from behind me.

'Now, now, Norman. You and me know it isn't all *exactly* as you say that it is'

I didn't want to sit there arguing - as early as the subject having even been broached - but, as far as I was feeling, it exactly fucking *was* what I'd just said it was. The man got me set up and put in jail for the fucking whole of the Nineties, a decade that I'd spent the whole of the next one, hearing about how good it had been, and he had stolen that from me, just because he could.

I looked at him and just left a confused look on my coupon for him to look at, to let him know that I wasn't quite squaring with what he'd just sat and come out with, which I clearly hadn't.

'Well, is that not true, Norman?'

He said, now pushing for a reply.

Even though it hurt my face to move in any way, I afforded myself a wee sarcastic smile before replying

'You *did* have me put in jail, with the least of respect'

'Aye, aye, true true'

His reply

'*But* ... the whole remit was for to have you removed from civilisation, for a wee while. Nothing major. Just enough to get you off the streets and prevent you from making a nuisance of yourself. But, no? You had to go all fucking Black September and start taking hostages, police officers and all of that shite'

He then looked up at the two goons, asking for recognition from either of them over if any of them had remembered this story from him telling them in the past.

'Oh aye, this one here? When he found out that there was no escape he tries to take a WPC hostage'

Turning back to me and laughing at the thought of it.

'It was fucking *you* who got yourself the ten stretch - and from what I heard it was you who kept seeing to it that an early release for good behaviour continued to be a pipe dream, mainly because your behaviour wasn't any fucking *good*'

Bang to rights, there wasn't much I could really reply to any of that without reverting to getting into whataboutery - which I'd never been a fan of as I'd always felt that it had exposed someone to be lacking in any kind of debating skills - or saying that it was cause and effect stuff and that I wouldn't have *had* to react to the situation, - that got me in jail - had he not engineered it in the first fucking place.

'And then you go and *escape*, from Barlinnie, which fucked things completely for you. Don't you fucking dare come here, attempting to place the blame for any of your moronic actions at my door'

I felt chastised, sat there, while he threw my own actions back at me, and how they had impacted on my life. Pretty good gaslighting - to deflect from his own part - from McKenna, with the way that he framed it though, mind.

All those things that - once, *if,* me and him ever found ourselves face to face - I'd wanted to say to the man. Those years in Bar L - once I'd pieced things together - where I'd thought about the day Davey McKenna and me crossed paths. But here *was* that time, and I was now sat there as if I was in the school headteacher's office having been caught fighting or smoking during break.

'*But* ... You know what, Mr Fulton? For the record, I actually felt bad about setting you up, and all these years later, seeing you sat here in front of me, face to face at last, I *still* regret what I did. But I hope you understand, it was strictly business, not personal, and in my world, when someone wants to use up a favour, and for something that you can take care of, as easy as phoning a Chinkie? Well, it's a no fucking brainer, isn't it?'

I was made to sit there while McKenna took me through the ethical side to his line of work - I was not aware that there *were* any - and how anyone who ended up on the wrong side of him, had earned their place.

When I tried to interrupt him, by attempting to offer a reminder that I *hadn't*, he waved me away, saying that he'd get to that part.

'I never had anyone snuffed out or put away for a stretch that had never crossed me and deserved it, *you* were the only exception, and it never sat well with me. You have to understand, though, Norman. I wouldn't have pulled such a move for just anyone, but for Peter Duncan? Well, for him? I would've. He'd have done the same for me'

He seemed to trail off a wee bit, evidently thinking of the man that was to go on to become known to the world as *El Corazon Valiente*.

'The loyalty that the man had always shown, and the same back in return from me, when a favour is asked for, you don't turn it down, and trust me, Norman. There's not many in this world that you would see me do a favour for, unconditionally'

'Aye, well I caught up with that cunt in the end, and so did everything else, eh?' I laughed, while thinking about the last time that Duncan and me had crossed paths.

'Given what happened to you, back in the day, I don't think there's anyone who would or *could* blame you for having some bad feelings, towards those who were involved in you going away for the time that you did. We're all fiery men here, in this room, after all. I *get it*. But you coming here, to Edinburgh, *looking* for me, telling anyone who'll listen to you that you're going to take care of me? Visiting my house and frightening the breadknife? And I'll take a wild stab in the dark that it was you responsible for all the *visits* to the house the other night too. Norman? You *know* you can't go about behaving like that now, pal. Well, not without me having something done about it'

And - for a man like David McKenna - having something "done about it" was never going to be an ideal outcome for the sucker on the receiving end of things. I was guilty of all of the things that he'd just sat and accused me of, and he knew it too. Which all begged the question, *what was he going to do about it?*

The answer to this, something I could not have guessed in a decade of Sundays.

'So, like I'm telling you. This nonsense needs to stop, Norman, *now*. In this game, we leave the past in the past, if we ever want to move forward. But…. and maybe I'm going soft in my old age here, I *do* feel that you have a genuine gripe, and *that* is the only reason that has saved your fucking skin, here. I recognise that I'm possibly a wee bit responsible for it all, although, like I said, the rest of that shite is all on you, and - I think, with Hearts winning today - you've caught me in a charitable mood, so given how you know what a favour means to me, I'm going to give you a pass, as far as your past couple of day's behaviour and ask you, man to man. Is there something I can do for you, a favour, so to speak? Anything that you think will be enough for you to feel like you and me have squared up? Money, drugs you name it, you know I'll be able to arrange it for you, so long as you don't try and take the piss. Try that and things will go a bit differently for you'

I sat absolutely stunned, that I'd even been offered *any* kind of option from the man. Had literally assumed that I'd been brought into his office, just to satisfy McKenna's sick and twisted own reasons of seeing me before I was clipped. Him offering *me* a favour? Aye, ok then, mate.

I really could not have pictured a man of the stature of Davey McKenna offering favours to people, carte blanch, like this and I guess that was backed up as having a bit of truth behind it because, through my silence, he reacted, as if my lack of commitment towards what he'd just sat and offered me was an insult.

'Of course, pal. If this offer isn't for you, we're going to have to go down the *other* road and, frankly speaking, Bud and Piotr here have already smashed the hell out of their KPIs for the month and could do with a week or two of any murders or serious assaults, eh boys?'

He laughed, looking up at the two of them who nodded in agreement.

'Always room for one more though, boss. You know? To keep up the momentum, and the ratio'

The one 'Bud' said, a bit more sycophantically than I'd had him down as, even with someone like McKenna for a gaffer.

'You're a right genie in a bottle, Mr McKenna, eh. Is it not three wishes I'm meant to get though, aye?'

I attempted a joke, but it didn't transfer over as good from how it felt in my mind to then following through and actually coming out with it.

Money would've been good, money is *always* good. That said, though, what good was money going to be for me, on the run in a small country like Scotland where I was going to - eventually be caught - before I could even fucking do anything with it.

Drugs were out, too. There would've been a time where if a man like McKenna had offered me a bit of weight to take on I'd have snapped it right off him, knowing that I'd be able to turn it around into a quick profit. Those days were past though. On occasions I *took* the stuff but the selling part was consigned to the history books.

With *also* having a history of shooting myself in the foot - the current trip to Scotland that I was on being a *prime* example of this - despite McKenna sitting there and - unbelievably - offering me the world. I'd have swapped it all for five minutes alone with him, with goons away on on their break.

Pragmatically, though, I wasn't going to get what I wanted. So, instead, I felt, why not get what I *needed*.

'Well there *is* one wee thing that you might be able to help me out with. A favour, if you'd like to call it that'

I eventually conceded. A smile forming onto his face, sensing that he was going to regain some form of power in this discussion. Which was stupid anyway because he already held as much power inside of that room as was ever going to be needed.

'Go on, I'm listening'

He said, leaning forward over the desk towards me, hands interlocked with both his thumbs pressing up into his chin.

Giving him an abridged version - and most definitely leaving out the part where I'd been daft enough to think I'd identified an internet troll, only to find I'd been way off with it - of things. I explained to him that - having been on the run from Barlinnie for as long as I had - I'd travelled over to Edinburgh on a fake passport but - from the news mum and dad had given me - somehow the bizzies had tippled onto this, and I was now stranded there in Scotland. Told the cunt that if he had any connections to get me *another* fake passport, to get me out of the country - and back to The Netherlands - then he could consider that as a favour done. Also seizing the chance to remind him that if his main motivation was in getting me gone, without it being done in a more darker of ways, then what better an outcome for him than to help get me out of the country, and one that I'd probably never have the balls to try and return to, fake passport or not.

With the tentacles that the man had, and how far they reached, I'd have been astonished if he *didn't* have himself a connection in the whole forgery game.

He took a few minutes to mull this over. I'm not sure if it was to enjoy the power of it all, watching me nervously squirm as I waited on his answer. My fate - ironically - all down to whatever the man was going to say next.

Eventually that - by now - familiar smile started to appear on his face, like something had just occurred to him.

'You know what, Norman? I think I might just well be able to help you get back over the water to Europe. Don't you worry, your uncle Davey has you covered'

Chapter 37

Liam

It was *always* going to be a stupid fucking idea, to go out, *on it*, before then - and I'm talking mere hours later - going straight to work on the two day assignment, that I'd been given at the short notice that I'd been. Personally, I blamed Derrick Carter, before apportioning any in my own direction.

If it had just been a normal night - with nothing of note really going on other than your more standard low key nights that went on during the weekend in Dundee - then I'd have had no problems just sitting in the house and chilling for a wee bit, before heading out to work in the early hours the next day.

But no, Derrick Carter, from Chicago and the House Music legend was playing at Fat Sam's and - being realistic - if he was playing in Dundee you would probably be talking fucking years before you'd see him back again, if ever. Sometimes you get those wee chances in life that you either take them when they're there, or you don't and whatever your choice will be is what you have to stand by from then on, regrets held or not.

Obviously, there could be no afters for me and, in fact, once Carter brought the night to an end with his last record I'd be jumping - completely fucking wired, as well - into a taxi to take me to get my 'shift' started.

When I was getting myself ready for going out - knowing I wouldn't be home again for a few days - mum came into my room, just for a chat, like. Asking what it was I was up to and that.

Telling her that this big American DJ was playing in the town so me and the rest of the boys were all going to see him. I went with "big American DJ" for her rather than the DJ's name because it would've been wasted on her. Didn't matter that Carter was playing back when she, herself, could've been raving her tits off. Had mum been an ex raver, there's no way that she'd not have mentioned it, seeing her son go onto be the same.

'Aye, going to be some night, like'

I said enthusiastically to her, genuinely.

'I'll probably not be back home for a few days, so don't be sending out any search parties for me, eh?'

I said to her, covering the fact that I was going to be out of town on business with the very convenient facts that any big nights I went out with my mates she would then go days without me returning.

'So what else is new?'

All she really had to say on the matter because that was the beauty of things, it was the perfect cover. It would've have been *more* suspect if she'd have got up on Sunday morning and found me snoring it up in my own bed. Generally - following various visits to Fatties - beds were not something that was what you would really be seeing, for a while anyway.

Once she'd left again, I took the chance to get everything together - that I was going to be needing over the next couple of days - and packed them in Timberland rucksack. When all packed up and ready to go - and making sure that the coast was clear - I left the bag lying there, in the hall, out of mum's sight - to avoid any difficult questions over why I was taking a rucksack with me on a night out - while going through into the living room, giving her a kiss on her head while she sat there on her big chair with feet curled up, watching an episode of Luther and telling her that I'd see her in a few days time.

'Have a good night, darling and *be careful*'

I heard her say to me - a little delayed due to me walking in on a good part of the story - as I walked back out the room, grabbed the bag and left, telling her that I would try to try on the second part.

It's all you can ever really do, eh?

Chapter 38

Nora

'Port Leith, mate'

I said, jumping into the back of the black cab that was waiting outside the B&B. The driver, looking around to me, as I got into the back, wearing a look that more suggested he'd been driving all through the night, than a driver wasn't too soon into their shift for the morning.

'No bother, pal'

Me getting the obligatory question of whether 'he'd been busy tonight' out of the way, nice and early. Confirming that this *was* a man who had been grafting all through the night, while the normals were all in their bed. Telling me that he was just about to call it a morning and was making this trip down to Leith - from the city centre - his last run of the morning before he filled the car up and called it a day.

'Been on since three yesterday afternoon. That amount of driving messes with your head after a few hours, I can tell you'

He said, not exactly providing his passenger in the back seat with much in the way of security and assurance.

'Aye well just make sure you get us down there in one piece, eh?'

I barked from the back to him, no time for his pish. Fuck, I hated early rises but here I was, Sunday morning at half five in the morning, in a taxi, travelling through the city - still semi cloaked in darkness, waiting on the sun coming up for the day - on the way down to the city's port. The only other cars sharing the streets with us, other taxis and the occasional police car or van. Apart from the occasional lone wolf, walking home from whatever afters or house they'd ended up - at after the pubs and clubs had shut - the normally busy and vibrant streets were deserted.

Beggars can't be choosers, I suppose, but when McKenna said to me that he would be able to sort me out, for getting back home, I just didn't think it was going to be in the way that *he* had in mind. I had already assumed that it was going to take a day or two for him to arrange a passport for me, and until that point, I would've just had to lay low. Given the Saturday afternoon's activities in the basement of The Corinthian, laying low for a couple of days, doing fuck all but laze on a bed, watching TV and providing myself with some much needed R&R would've been something that would've easily met my approval.

McKenna's idea of, "assistance" however, had been a lot more *instant* than I'd anticipated, when asking him for help getting out of Scotland. Telling me that he had a "thing" organised for the next day that he could have killed two birds with the one stone, by letting me get on board, literally.

Understandably, he'd been deliberately vague with the details of everything involved. Issuing me with the order to be down at Port Leith - for no later than six in the morning - where I would find a boat called 'The Chipper," that would be leaving Edinburgh that morning. All the details would be handed to the captain in advance, and that I just needed to turn up on time and all my troubles would be at an end.

Had I been an actual *chooser* then aye, I'd be getting on a flight that takes fractionally just over an hour to get you from A to B. Being the beggar, however. Instead, I was taking a mode of transport - and route - that would see to it that it took over half a fucking *day*, before reaching mainland Europe. Better than a boot in the balls, though, as much of a pain in the arse it all felt at that early time of the morning, while thinking of the day ahead.

Hopefully, I can just get a good kip for the majority of it, I thought to myself - in the back of the taxi - while still deep in that 'could easily go back to bed for a few more hours' frame of mind, having only woken up half an hour before and hadn't even experienced my first cup of tea or coffee and a puff on a reek yet.

'Tell you what, she can do her walk of shame all the way to ma front door, eh?'

The driver said out loud as we drove past a young girl - clearly still wrecked from her night out and now making an attempt at getting herself home - struggling to walk in her high heels and with a skirt that was more of a belt than a piece of clothing that stretches down and around a woman's arse. I took a look at her as the car passed her. The timing just right for me to get a look at her underneath a street light, right as we passed by. If she was even eighteen years old it was only because her make up must've been on point, my guess was that she was younger than that.

'You didn't even see what she fucking looked like before saying that, ya cunt. She could've had three eyes and no septum, for all you'd known'

Fucking hated cunts like that. Decisions made on whether they'd fuck someone based on nothing more than a second's look at someone in high heels - with a decent pair of legs - and a short skirt. This made me think of that trip to Ibiza me and some of the boys went to in Eighty Seven, when Paul Levitt had made a big thing about this woman walking down the street.

'See the fucking erse on *that*?'

Levs said, while almost salivating as he kept his eyes on the rear of the woman walking along the road. The same "woman" that we bumped into at a club later on the same night, and found out that this was no woman either. I was stood next to "her" at the bar - waiting to get served - and had recognised what she was wearing. Fucking bigger pair of hands and Adam's Apple then me, like.

You can imagine the grief that Levs took for the rest of the night, after that, from the rest of us. The boy didn't take it that well, like. Just goes to show you, though. Just because a house looks decent from the rear. Decent back garden and pleasing on the eye. *That* doesn't meant to say that the front might not be a complete fucking bomb scare.

'You see how young she was?'

I'd rather the journey had been spent in silence but wasn't going to pass up the chance to dig the old cunt up on his comment. You always hear about how girls on their own don't even feel safe getting a taxi home at the end of the night, and no fucking wonder with pervy old cunts like him driving through the night. Must've been easily forty years older than her.

Either he hadn't been listening properly - to my tone - or was just completely shattered by his hours upon hours of driving, but he completely missed my point.

'The fucking perfect age, eh? What is it that all the best fitba managers always say? If they're good enough, they're old enough'

This disgusted me, the thought of him with a girl not even in her twenties. He was fucking lucky that - unlike your more informal taxis that you can find yourself in - we were separated by that perspex inside the cab otherwise there was a *very* high chance that I was going to go all Dennis Wise on the cunt. This, obviously, would not have been a good idea in any shape or form, as nice as it would've felt. No, I needed to slip out of Scotland with as minimum fuss possible, and battering fuck out of a cab driver was *not* it.

Cunts like that? That patter always catches up with them in the end. Only a matter of time before someone gives him a rap in the coupon, or he finds the council revoking his Hackney through complaints of offering rides for, *rides*.

Leave it to some cunt else and just you worry about getting gone, I told myself, while reverting back to silence again. A good taxi driver - raging pervert or not - will always be able to pick up on this from their passenger. This boy was experienced enough to see that I wasn't interested in any small talk and from that point on we travelled in relative silence for the rest of the journey down to Port Leith.

When we arrived - and considering Leith was hardly considered as one of the world's most busiest of financial hubs - I was surprised to find things much more alive than I'd have ever thought it would be at the back of five on a Sunday morning.

With McKenna being deliberately vague with me, I don't know? I had this idea that when I got down there it would be obvious what I was doing, which it wasn't.

Handing the driver a tenner - telling him to keep the change - I grabbed my bag from out of the boot before giving his roof a couple of taps to indicate he was good to go. The noise of his car - driving away from the area - still audible while I set about finding my means of escape for the morning.

Now that we were down by the water you could now see the sky starting its transformation from dark to light, the sun now preparing to appear for the day. This - in itself - a god send when it came to trying to look for names on the front of boats. Had no idea if I was travelling on a fucking dinghy, yacht or something in between. After looking at a few other boats - that had seemed to have a bit of life about them - I eventually found "The Chipper," and established that it fell into the *in between* category, and thank fuck it hadn't fallen into the dinghy one.

'This 'The Chipper,' mate aye?'

I asked someone who was standing outside the - what looked like some kind of a fishing vessel - boat, on the pier. Doing that thing where you've already spied the name on the fucking thing but - because you hardly find yourself getting on boats every day of your life - ask the obvious question, anyway.

'The very same, pal'

He replied, only giving me the briefest of glances before going back to what looked like some last minute preparations with the boat before it got ready for the off. The smell - and noise - of the engine and motors, already in operation, an indicator that it wouldn't be long before setting sail.

'Sound, sound. Davey told me to be down here for six, mate. *McKenna*, like'

This, enough for him to stop the fucking about with the anchor that he'd been doing to look back up at me again, but this time hold his gaze for longer.

Ah, the Davey McKenna effect, I thought as the boy from the boat, instantly turned a wee bit more guarded.

'Aye, he phoned and told me to expect you. What's your name, mate?'

I couldn't have blamed him for wanting to ensure that he was letting the *correct* person on board because this was some sort of Davey McKenna production and fuck knows what that actually was entailing but you didn't have to be a road man to know that if there was a boat leaving Edinburgh in the early hours of the morning - headed for mainland Europe - and McKenna was involved in things, there was definitely going to be something illegal about it all, whether that meant on the journey out, back, or both.

'Fulton, pal. He maybe called me Nora, though. Norman Fulton'

My name providing us with the 'open sesame' effect that had him abandoning what he'd been doing outside on the deck to bring me on-board, showing me the cabin that was there for me for the journey. Other than to 'keep my head down on the journey over and stay out of sight, due to the obvious,' McKenna hadn't really given me much info so I was actually a wee bit chuffed to find that I had a bed to lie down on and a wee bit of private space. Could've been crammed up front with the captain for the journey having to make small talk for all I'd known. A cabin, though? Proper wee Brucie Bonus, that.

'Listen, pal'

He said, with quite a bit of nervousness to it, as we both stood there inside the wee cabin.

'Davey told me, on the phone last night, to lock you inside the cabin, and not let you back out again until everything was sorted on the other side, when we reached dry land but I cannae even mind what year I last locked the thing, never mind *where* the bloody key for it is. Being honest, though. Looking at you, you look a bit tasty so I'm already thinking I probably wouldn't lock you in, anyway, on account of there being a pretty high chance that you'd fucking panel me, once let back out again'

I just laughed at this. He didn't know me from Adam but knew enough to know that he *would've* been on the receiving end, if he'd tried something like that.

'You'll no tell, Davey, eh? You ken what he can be like. Just make this between you and me, and if he asks you if you were locked in, just tell him that you were, call me all the names under the sun, for effect, like'

He stood there, looking like he was worrying if he'd maybe already said too much.

'Mate, I'm just glad to get a space on the boat, you'll not have any bother from me. Probably won't even know I'm on here. Your secret's safe with me. What's your name anyway?'

I assured him.

'Aww, cheers pal. You ken how it is, eh? If I'd told Davey that I didn't know where the key to the cabin was he'd have had me spending my whole Saturday hunting for it, and even then there wouldn't have been any guarantee I'd have found it. Morgan, by the way'

'Nah, you're good, Morgan'

I said, shaking his hand and giving him a knowing nod to let him know he was good.

'Right, Norman. We've got a long journey ahead of us so feel free to get a wee kip if you like. Davey said to have your cabin sorted with anything you'd need so there's a few boxes of petrol station sandwiches lying there for you, some crisps and juice as well'

He stood there and said, making sure that I was happy with everything before he left me to it, and got everything ready before we left.

There was even a wee primitive toilet in there. Oh aye, all the home comforts, like.

'Davey told me to tell you to sit tight in here and I'll give you a knock when we reach the other side, though, just so you've got the all clear. Good enough, aye?'

He passed on the info before leaving me to it.

Made me feel like one of those illegal immigrants, getting smuggled across the sea which, I kind of was, I suppose. Proper VIP immigrant though, considering I had a bed and BLT sandwiches, instead of being hidden in a fucking fake compartment in the back of a lorry where you've not got enough air, never mind Marks and Spencer scran.

Once he left, shutting the door behind him, I got myself settled. At a guess it was going to take around sixteen hours to get from Scotland to Netherlands, wherever I was getting dropped off, that was, because I'd already assumed that I wasn't going to be getting dropped off at the back of Centraal Station. If I could've eaten into those hours with a nice long kip, then all the better.

I lay there on the wee cabin bed with my eyes closed, but not sleeping. Just listening to all of the noises outside. The footsteps, sounds of plastic crates crashing, the hum of the engines and the inane whistling from the captain of the ship. Eventually, though, around about half six, I sensed actual movement as the boat began to pull out of Leith.

I wasn't even close to being out of Scottish waters but, I don't know? The feeling of being on a boat - headed for Europe - without having had to pass through any passport checks, it felt absolutely *massive*. I breathed out a big sigh of relief and allowed myself to drift off to sleep, the combination of the movement of the boat, crossed with the white noise that it was making, enough to get me back off to sleep again. The last thought that rushed through my head as I was drifting being that when I woke up again I would no longer be in the motherland and that I'd be very much on my way "home."

And so tired that I was, mixed with that wave of relief to be on my way, and all of the stresses that washed away from me the minute that boat began to depart Leith, I felt like I could've slept for the majority of that long journey, and probably *would've* done.

That fucking music, though? I was only maybe half an hour *into* the sleep when I was pulled right back out of it by the noise of knocking. Thought it was someone at the cabin door at first until - after a few seconds of coming to - I sussed that the "knock" wasn't a knock at all, and was the beat to music. A constant, non stop, monotonous beat. You could tell how fucking nippy this racket must've been for me to be able to fall asleep while a boat makes all of its noises when in operation, but couldn't at the noise. It appeared to come from the cabin next to me. Me clocking this by putting my ear to the wall to the side of me as I lay there on the bed.

Nothing fucking worse though, eh? Than you just getting yourself off to sleep, only for some cunt to wake you back up again. All those different levels of sleep that a person goes through? After half an hour I must've been approaching deep territory, and could've been out for fucking hours after that.

Fair to say, I wasn't best pleased, like.

Hoping that a few hard thuds on the connecting wall, along with my 'request' for - whoever the fuck it was next door - my neighbour to 'turn that fucking shite down,' before dishing out another couple of punches to the wall that were as much out of frustration as they were in an attempt to get them to turn the music down a bit so I could get back to sleep.

That should do it, I thought to myself, as I lay back down on the wee bed and shut my eyes again, waiting on the noise being reduced.

Put it another way, should that *not* have done it. Then the prick next door to me was going to be in for a journey that was going to feel a lot more fucking longer than the sixteen hours that I was moaning about.

Chapter 39

Liam

'I thought it was the paranoia, at first, like. Well you *would*, though, wouldn't you?'

I'd had a couple of Balmains across the night at Derrick Carter - and what a fucking set from the man, I may add but, now, sat in that wee room, still completely off my tits and - at first having found myself dancing to music that wasn't even being played - had thought

'fuck it, stick the tunes on for a bit'

I had a couple of vallies in my pocket to be deployed as and when, but I wasn't quite at that point yet. Popping on one of my go-to mixes, for that time of the morning. Reserved for whenever having been out and on it - Danny Tenaglia at Pacha, Ibiza two thousand and seven - I sat bobbing my head away to the intro of the first track of the set while I started to get the skins together for myself as the room gently rocked from side to side.

Not many things finer in life than a joint - when you've got a couple of Eckies inside you - but what is generally the biggest challenge of all, is the *making* of said spliff. I think *that's* what makes those joints so special, I suppose? That out of all the chaos going on inside your mind body and soul, you managed to find it within yourself to be able to actually fucking *make* a joint.

You know how the mind can play tricks on you, *especially* if you've been fucking with the Class A's? I thought that the noise was coming from the set, with it being played in a jumping and vibrant club like Pacha, and that. Didn't matter that I'd heard the set a hundred times before and had - up until that morning - never heard any additional sound effects to it, other than the music itself. Definitely had never clocked the Scottish accent aggressively shouting for Tenaglia to turn the music down, anyway. Obviously it didn't make sense as who the fuck would go to a club like Pacha, and then complain about how loud the tunes were?

It had been a fucking stupid idea to go to Fat Sam's anyway - before work - but this was something that I knew of in *advance* of doing, never mind it being a case of having regrets after the fact. Nah, this was the state of mind that I already knew I was going to be left in, but went ahead and done so, regardless. A victim of my own sense of free spirit, or stupidity, whichever way you wanted to look at it.

Exchanging massive hugs with the rest of the lads when we left, and me being deeply jealous of the bastards being able to now go and sit in some warm flat, listen to tunes, take more drugs and talk a lot of fucking nonsense for the next twelve hours. My metaphorical bed had been made for that morning, though, and unfortunately this was not one that you slept in.

Jumping into the taxi and - first off all - negotiating the whole problem of where my destination was and how - understandably - the driver wasn't prepared to go that distance without being paid in advance, something I'd already guessed would be the case so had already withdrawn the likely cost of the fare, ready to hand over to him so that we could get on with things.

Once he'd been paid, his suspicious attitude clearing straight away where I left him to it and with me popping my earbuds in while I sat, wired in the back of the car, he could already see that his passenger was not a talker. Which, technically, was not true as I would happily talk away with a stranger as there's *always* something to talk about, even if it's just the basics like football. When you've had a couple of pills, though, and you're around someone who *hasn't*? That's a conversation that is best skipped, for everyone concerned.

He either had the choice of driving in silence or to the soundtrack of me talking complete bollocks to him - on around a hundred different topics - that would barely make any sense, to him. It was best - for the both of us - that I just popped the buds in and listened to some music, and sit there rushing my tits off on the way to work. I probably shouldn't have had that second pill but, like I always say when the point of being able to say 'when' has well passed you by, there's no putting that toothpaste back into the tube, once it's been squeezed out. Same rules apply to when you take too much of whatever your drug of choice is. Kept it to just the one and I'd have timed it beautifully for coming down.

I was having too good a night, though, and even though I never lost sight of what was on my cards, once I left Fat Sam's, I couldn't resist that second one. And now I was still completely twisted, heading to work.

No one else's fault other than my own, so I wasn't about to start looking for who to blame. Well, other than Derrick Carter, obviously. It was the kind of stupid decision that I'd taken before and one hundred percent would take *again* at some point in the future so - despite the state of me at that time of the morning - it wasn't anything to sweat about.

This knocking noise I was hearing on the Tenaglia set, though? I think I noticed it straight away so when it stopped again I was relieved - more than anything else - as it wasn't the best of environments for me to be in, to be having any kind of a paranoia attack. Thing is - as Tenaglia set about mixing in the next track - the knocking started again, and due to the more minimal style of track - that was playing - it allowed me to hear it a lot more clearer than I'd managed the first time.

Fuck this, like, I said, a wee bit worried about things because I couldn't deny what I was hearing. I thought that maybe turning up the music to full blast would've drowned out those thoughts that I'd been having, and let me just concentrate on listening to Tenaglia.

Funnily enough, it seemed to do the trick because from the moment that the volume went up, from then all I could hear was the music.

No knocking, no muted shouting.

Drugs, man, eh? I laughed to myself as I made another attempt at getting that joint together. There was no amount of drugs that I could have possibly consumed that would have been able to imagine up what followed next, and the reason for why the knocking and shouting had suddenly stopped.

The door, without any warning, flying open and someone rushing in shouting

'I SAYS TO TURN THAT FUCKING SHITE DOWN, YOU TRYING TO TAKE THE PISS, TURNING IT FUCKING *UP?*'

He'd pretty much got his already prepared rant out, before realising *who* it was that he was lambasting. This, in itself, was fine because - due to the pills - with my double vision that I had, it took him the whole sentence before I fully clocked - and would actually *believe* - who it was, that had just stormed into my cabin, while all along I'd never considered that there would have been anyone else on-board, apart from the dude sailing the fucking thing. Morgan, the same guy that it always was.

Like father like son, I suppose, but - once we realised - we both kind of looked at each other, stunned, and then in almost perfect synchronicity, pointed at each other and - almost word for word - both asked

'What the fuck are *you* doing here?'

'Well, sit yourself down,' I jumped in before he could reply.

'I've been trying to build this joint for what feels like an hour now, if I ever get it fucking finished, we can sit and smoke it and tell each other'

He took the few short steps required to sit down beside me on the bed, with a look of sheer disbelief on his face.

Trust me, dad, I thought to myself. If you want some *real* disbelief then you should've knocked a couple of pingers down your neck before this moment.

'Wasn't fucking joking about the music though, mind. You really *do* need to turn that shite down'

He said, sitting down and giving me a smile that - at that twisted hour of the morning - I couldn't judge as sincere, sarcastic or scary.

I turned Danny down, just to make sure, like.

Chapter 40

Nora

Talk about a fucking dark horse, eh? That, Liam. *Obviously* from what I'd already picked up on, he wasn't working nine to five in some job that was making his life a misery, but was still looking like he'd been managing to get by. Didn't think that he was operating in the circles that he was and - from the wee unexpected (to say the fucking least) chin wag that we sat having in his cabin - had been for quite a few years, since fifteen.

As was often the case with a figure like Davey McKenna, you might've been doing work for him and not even *known* it was him pulling the strings. Liam recognised the name but in the five years that he'd been transporting gear from Edinburgh to Dundee on Scotrail trains and Stagecoach busses, said that he had never met the man, if he indeed worked for him. Telling me that - while over the years the faces might've changed now and again - he'd been used to meeting regulars for his collections or his drop offs, but never McKenna. Adding that if he had, then he'd kept his identity to himself.

'You know how it is, eh? Ask no questions. Get your instructions and carry them out. Makes me sound like an assassin or something like that, when I put it like that'

This cunt, eh? I sat thinking to myself, about McKenna. Gets me banged up and then years later follows that up with using my son for a bit of child exploitation. Thinking logically, there, Liam hadn't taken my second name - or a better way of putting it would be that his mum didn't fucking *give* him it - so, on the face of things, there was no actual obvious link to the two of us. You'd definitely have imagined that if McKenna had acquired a Dundonian kid to do some work on his county lines operation, with a second name of *Fulton*, you'd like to think that something like that would have been enough to ring a bell for him.

There was none of that, though. Just Liam - up to no good at an early age - who had been sent to Edinburgh to collect a package one day on an errand that - over the years - led to him being seen as, and known, for being reliable.

Those years - going from fifteen to twenty - pretty formative in a boy, like. Where they go from a daft kid and begin to evolve into a man and it was the conflation of this in the boy, while working for the type of people that he was, that saw him grow from strength to strength. This - clearly - proven in the trust shown in the boy to be put on a ship, heading to mainland, on Davey McKenna business.

Absolutely spangled out his nest, he sat there and told me it all. Told me *too* fucking much - speaking from someone who had once operated successfully in the same game - if I'm being honest because I'd been given the impression that it could've easily been someone else that he'd have sat saying the same thing to. Sitting there pie eyed on those Eckies, jaw and eyes all over the fucking shop. Some of the intel he handed out? Someone in his position, the less people knew of his hustle, the safer he'd be, but you wouldn't have known it from the way he sat there blethering away, tapping his feet to the music that had been switched off - by me - long before.

On the subject of why he was sat there, him pointing at the two bags full - and I mean *to the brim* - of notes and telling me all about what his plans were for them, once we reached Belgium.

Aye, Belgium. Better than a kick in the cunt, like but the very least somebody could've done at some point - before we'd left Leith - was to tell me that the fucking boat wasn't even *going* to The Netherlands. The boat - as always, according to my son - would be docking at Antwerp Port, and then he wouldn't be seeing it again until the next time.

'Jesus fucking Christ, son. There must be two million here, maybe even *double* that'

I said, looking up at him, having taken up his offer to check out the two bags sitting beside each other.

'I know. Mad, eh?'

He replied, with the whole general appearance of just about the very fucking *last* person, on earth, that you'd entrust with such serious amounts of bread.

'Why the fuck are you having to transport it, like this, though? McKenna not heard of international electronic transfers, no?'

It all seemed a wee bit *extra*, to have someone lugging that amount of money about. Liam, put me right on that, having asked the same question, the first time that he'd made the trip across the sea. This trip - that I'd gatecrashed - not his first time but, he admitted, it had been the first time he'd been asked to bring as much, double the amount as the other trips, apparently.

'The Belgian connect is a bit old school, although I'm not sure how much of that is enforced on them, to be honest. I was told that his brother was banged up, through being caught by some money trail from a previous bit of business and, as a result, the brother, who's still on the outside, insists on hard cash, no matter the amount. And, as you can imagine, there's not much chance I'm going to have of hopping on a plane to Antwerp with that amount of wedge on me without cunts asking questions so, hence, this long arsed journey. Good pay, though, like'

'And this boat gets *cargo* to go back to Edinburgh with, aye?'

I asked, mind racing.

'Fuck knows, I've never taken the boat back. I just give the money to the boy on the Belgian side, and then get a taxi straight to the airport to come home. Those connections are well heavy, though. Fucking practically next door to each other and yet every time coming back home I've had to do a couple of connections between Antwerp and Edinburgh. Fucking Amsterdam and *Malaga* the last time. Tell me how that's meant to make sense? Amsterdam, I get, but then onto fucking *Spain*? I've always meant to take a bit of time out and actually see what Antwerp, the city, is actually *like* but the combination of how long it took to get there and then the prospect of how long it's going to take to fly home, I've always ended up swerving the tourism side of things. And, what with me being still out of my tits on those MDMA presses I had, and how rough I'm going to feel by the time I get to Belgium, well it's not fucking happening this time around either, that's for sure'

Like I said, the boy was talkative. If there was a way for him to find ten minutes to give you a thirty second answer - that morning sat in the cabin - he would've been able to find it.

There was no way of being able to un-see that amount of money, once it had been laid eyes on. Even after zipping up the bags again and sitting back on the bed beside Liam, as he made another joint and sat speaking away to me, - whether he'd been aware of it or not, it had largely been him doing the talking but, with all he had to share, I was happy enough to stay silent, apart from ask questions here and there - while I was sitting facing him with full eye contact, I was barely taking in any of the words. The voice - my voice - that kept repeating over and over again in my head.

Two to four million quid.

'Oh, man, though. You should've heard Derrick Carter tonight. What a performance the wee man put in, like. Was really more of a musical journey, to be quite honest with you'

Liam came out with while looking like he was squinting, trying to work out which side of the Rizla had the gum on it. *Derrick* Carter? I'd much rather have watched *Get* Carter. Some set of fucking balls on Caine in that film, like. A cockney, going all the way up to Newcastle, under those circumstances, with absolutely no fucks given, like he displayed to the Geordies.

Oblivious to pretty much everything, I let him rattle on about anything that came to his mind, which was a fair bit, of nonsense. Me feigning interest and asking the occasional question - just to keep him going - while inside I was trying to formulate a plan.

Finally happy at what I'd come up with over the space of that half hour, I decided that now was the time to deploy the plan of action.

'You ever sit and think about your future, Liam?'

I probably didn't appreciate how much of a *deep* question this might've been, for someone buzzing on Ecstasy, but that was kind of my reason for choosing that exact time to ask it.
'What do you mean, like?'

He asked, taking a big toke on his sleeping bag of a joint, that he'd made before passing it to me.

'Well, exactly what I fucking said, your future. What you'll be doing with yourself and where you'll be, that type of stuff'

'Well, no, not really'

He answered back, but only after appearing to have had a right good think about it.

'And *that's* the thing, son. You're only twenty, eh? You're not really *meant* to be worrying, or thinking about stuff that's decade's away. Put it this way, if you're that age and thinking about your retirement, then you can't exactly be having the time of your life, there in your youth. But here's the thing, you've got me with the benefit of hindsight that can help guide you, proper Yoda stuff, like'

I went to take a toke of the joint and the end of it drooped right over. I just shook my head at him as we both laughed at how poorly made a joint it really was.

'Don't know whether I'm meant to smoke that or fucking sleep in it, ya cunt!'

I joked, as I put it back down into the ashtray. Trying to smoke it a waste of time, as well as an assault on your lungs.

'Anyway, it's all very paradoxical but despite the fact that present you couldn't give a flying fuck about life in forty years time, *sixty years old* you is fucking screaming at you, from the future, telling you to sort your shit out, have a plan together, and not be working until you eventually drop dead'

'Aye, that'll not be me, and anyway, I've got a good thing going with all of this work, I'll be fine, don't worry about sixty year old Liam'

He laughed, before then going on to speculate on what he would look like when he was sixty, I pulled him back in, before he could go off on one again.

'That's not going to last forever, though. The truth is, one bust - and if you're lucky it won't be you and your skinny arse carted off to jail - of someone, in connection to your organisation, and you're *out* of a fucking job. It's not like working for the council or NHS, eh? Never not precarious and, as I'm sure you're well aware by now, from week to week you never really know if you're going to be out of a job, or in the back of a police van. Look at me for a prime example of this. I was making *serious* money. Well higher up the chain from where you are, and I ended up in jail for ten years, because of one fucking phone call from someone else inside the game. The life owes you fucking Scottish Football Association, son'

For the first time since I'd stormed the cabin with intentions of hurting whoever the fuck it was that had been blaring the music, I was the talker and the wee man was the listener.

'One phone call and, well, retirement fund? Not exactly easy to build yourself a fucking nest egg, when you're stuck inside The Big Hoose for a decade. And, aye, I know I'm still a bit away from sixty myself but the point is that I'm at this part of life and, while it's been colourful, I never got the chance to get that plan hatched, for me heading out into the sunset with, once I started to get older. I don't want you to be in the same position as me'

'And, with all of this in mind, I've had this wee idea that I want to run by you'

'Fire away,' he said, picking up the sleeping bag again to re-light it. The flame touching the joint - and how loose it was - near enough burning away half of what was left of it, before he even got a chance to take a toke from it.

'We have a retirement fund sitting *right there*'

I pointed at the bags, his face - as wrecked as he was - reacting to this before I told him to just sit, listen and hear me out.

Obviously, stealing the money was a no no. He was my son, for fuck's sake. I couldn't carry out *any* kind of a hustle that I would've known would see to it that he would receive a couple of bullets in the back of the head over. It was only *because* it involved Liam that it was such a sensitive subject that had to be approached in just the right way. Not be persuasive enough and it might mean that the planting of the seed wouldn't take hold, be *too* persuasive and he'd possibly react in the wrong way that I needed him to. I'd felt that the Eckies would make him more agreeable to my idea. You, know? All of that peace and love shite that those pill heads all act like when they're rolling.

When he'd offered up a bit of resistance to all of this, on the grounds that his employers had been good to him over the years, - especially the years where his mum was out of work and *his* money had been what had kept the two of them going - I wasn't entirely displeased by this response. Showed that he was made of the right stuff, that he wasn't the type to just rip someone off, like that, in an instant. Had a fucking answer for him, though, and a good one.

'Son, why do you *think* that it was tough at times, for the both of you? Because I wasn't fucking *there* to support you. You any idea how that makes me feel, knowing the struggle the pair of you had? If I'd had my way you wouldn't have wanted for a single thing, and you wouldn't have done, had that fucking rat McKenna not had me put away'

This definitely gave him a wee bit food for thought and it was when seeing him with that suggestible face on him that I decided the best policy was to keep going.

'For the best part of twenty years, you've had to grow up without your dad, and your dad has had - one way or another - several issues that have prevented him from living in the family home, *as* your dad. And all because of one person'

I left this hanging, to see which way it would blow, before not being able to resist from adding.

'We'll *never* get that time back son, it's gone and it's a fucking tragedy that I'll never get to experience all of those important things in your life, that you'd have had growing up, but I'll tell you what, though. As much as the man stole twenty years of yours and mines collective lives, how fucking good a bit of double payback would it be, from father and son, if we were to just say fuck you and cheers for the money, and we could call it square from there, fully reimbursed'

The face that he'd pulled right at the very start - when I'd pointed at the bags and called them our retirement fund - well, that hadn't been seen on his coupon for a while now and, in fact, the more I spoke, the less it saw signs of returning.

'Fucking telling me about Derrick Carter and how if it wasn't a once in a blue moon chance to see him play you'd have not been in such a state for this trip. Imagine having the bread to be able to go see Derrick Carter, where *ever* in the world he's playing. Having the funds to never have to work again, at twenty years of age? Live where you want to?'

'But, but guys like this, who you're suggesting we tax their money, they don't fuck about, like. They'll track us down and kill us, mum too'

That the kid had even said as much had now confirmed that he was already now pretty much persuaded by me, or gaslit, depending on which way you wanted to look at things. And he was now trying to think of consequences of actions, which was smart enough a thing to be doing in such a situation.

I just looked back at him as casual as you could get and replied

'Who, McKenna, and his men? I've been on the run from fucking *Interpol* for ten years, Liam. I'm the fucking hide and seek champion two thousand to two thousand and ten. When Interpol can't find you then you're obviously doing things right. Don't you worry about that side of things. You've got me to deal with all of that, anyway. I'm not sure that I'd have fancied your chances, just deciding to do this on your own, and don't be fucking telling me that the thought hadn't crossed your mind before either ya wee cunt'

He laughed at this, evidently true. There couldn't have been many put in such a position of trust that *wouldn't* have had that thought, at some point or other. I only needed five seconds of *knowing* it was in the same room as me and I'd already started working on a plan on how it could be fucking pinched!

When I heard his next question - because once I'd managed to get under his skin with the topic, it had been all questions - this, surrounding his mum, and what would happen to her, I knew it was a done deal.

'Don't you worry about your maw, pal. We'll get her sorted, no problems'

There was no point going into any of the intricacies that involved Abigail, not at that time of the morning, anyway. When the kid was thinking a bit more clear, we'd discuss the mum situation.

Like all good salesmen, having reached the point of where I'd been looking to get to. I got things nailed down fast, before the customer has a chance to change their mind again.

'Anyway, look, we're on this boat for fuck knows how many more hours so you should get those vallies you said you had down your neck and grab a wee kip. Fucking Fulton and son, though, eh? Los fucking millionaires, my lad. You and me, eh? We'll rule the world, the pair of us'

Poor cunt probably hadn't really known what had just hit him. Sits having a wee blether with his dad and by the end of it is one to two million pound richer than he was at the start.

I wanted the blues into him pronto. The absolute *perfect* things for putting a stop to each and every thought that might have been vying for his attention. Just get the kid knocked the fuck out for a large part of the journey to Antwerp, and he won't have time for trying to persuade himself back *out of* things again.

Not that there was going to be any of that shite. He was a Fulton, after all, and he'd just made a deal with someone.

And - whether this means a good thing or a bad thing - we Fulton's *always* keep our word.

I watched him swallow the second of the two Diazepam and get himself up onto the wee bed and told him to get himself a good sleep, and that I'd check on him later on in the journey, to see how he was.

Me? Well, while I *also* could've done with a kip - and was hoping for that to be the case otherwise it was going to be a long fucking journey to endure without anything in the form of entertainment - I was absolutely fucking buzzing. In a completely different way to the Eckie head that I'd just sat speaking to, but buzzing just as hard, in my own way.

Aye, the money was the prime reason for this but it wasn't just that, it was *where* the money was coming from?

It was all simply too beautiful for words.

Chapter 41

Liam

THE BAGS, WHERE'S THE FUCKING BAGS?

The feeling of sheer and utter panic that ran through me the second I opened my eyes and - automatically - looked to the corner of the cabin, and saw nothing but wooden panels and *definitely* not two sports bags, filled with millions of pounds to buy wholesale Ching with.

It said it all, really, because when you wake up from a couple of Franky Vallies you're more sloth than cheetah, but I was out that bed like I'd woken up to find it on fire. It would be fair to say that after a couple of MDMA presses with over two hundred and fifty MG of the magic powered pressed into the fuckers - well, that was the official line, anyway, but having necked a couple, I wouldn't have argued with that - and then followed up with twenty MGs of Diazepam, you would be guilty of possibly not thinking too straight. Straight? Your thoughts resemble more of something a fucking Spirograph would come up with. When you're responsible for millions of pounds, and you see it missing, you've no other choice than to *get* thinking straight, and fast.

I bolted out the cabin - seeing daylight for the first time of the day as we made our way across the sea. It was a wee bit choppy but that really was the least of my worries, in that moment.

With dad - and that he was on the boat - popping into my head, I crashed his cabin, without any thought of whether he'd be having a kip or a wank. It was only a few seconds of panic but fuck me, they weren't half real.

With the foggy head that I had, I was questioning if I'd actually brought the bags *on* to the boat, and whether they had been left in the back of a taxi by someone who was well wired at the time. One thing for sure, leave a few - plus - million in the back of a taxi then you're absolutely positively going to be seeing those bags again. Aye, right.

It all kind of clicked into place when I opened the cabin door, saw dad lying on his bed starting to stir from the noise that I'd made, and those two black bags sharing the bed with him. That was about the same time that I then remembered *the* chat that the two of us had, on the subject of the money.

'Nice wee threesome you've got going there, sorry to interrupt, like'

I said to him, more relieved that I had fixed eyes on the money, more than anything else, *next* could come the reality of what was going to happen to it.

'Where about are we? What time is it?'

He asked, groggily, the exact way that *I* should've been waking up, as opposed to the panic merchant that had sprung into life in the cabin next door.

'I haven't got a fucking clue on either of those'

Are you ever really aware of *where* you are when you're surrounded by lots and lots of water, though? Not like there's much in the way of points of reference for you.

He checked his phone and found that we were around three hours away from Belgium. I'd had one one of those proper drug sleeps that once you slip under, you're out for almost half a day, no matter what time of day it is that you konk out.

Thank fuck I'd woken when I'd had too because - if me and dad were going to go through with what we'd discussed earlier on in the morning, and from where I was standing, it had looked like the man had made his choice, lying there in bed with all of the money - time was something that, while at the start of the journey there was too much of, was now very much required, before we arrived in Belgium.

'So you're definitely serious?'

I asked, unsure, really, whether I wanted him to say yes or no. On one hand, the thought of all that money, and what could be done with it, how can I say that the thought of it wasn't an appealing one? On the other? The thought of someone as big time as Davey McKenna, with my name on his kill list. Not much good money is when you're not alive to spend it, eh? All kind of cancels the other out.

'Never *more* serious, son'

He said this while putting an arm around the two bags almost as if it was to protect them. Like I was going to be taking them off him, as well. A tooled up mob of Honey Badgers were not going to have it in them to relieve him of those bags, never mind me.

'Me and you are due that man some serious payback, today we square things up with him'

I just stood there, thinking of the implications of what was going to follow this. Understandably, I was coming from the self preservation direction.

'And, you'll look after me, on that side, like? Until I get a plan together, because I'm fucked if I'm going to be walking around Antwerp with a couple of million on me like some fanny without a clue what he'd doing and where he's going, while dealing with a comedown?'

'Didn't I tell you that you were pulling off this heist alongside the fucking *master*. You and me will head back to Amsterdam soon as we get to dry land. Lay low for a bit, eh? All nice and cool, well, maybe take a limo from Antwerp to the Dam, like'

'I'm *joking*, ya cunt'

I thought he was actually serious. Despite the whole keeping your head down part I *did* actually like the sound of it, on the whole scale of taking the piss. Stealing someone's money and then hiring a limo as your getaway car. Fuck aye!

'I'm not going to lie to you, son. McKenna's not going to take it well, when he realises that his money has went walkabout'

I wanted to 'Well, duh' him but as little as I'd spent in the man's company, if there was one thing I'd picked up from him, it was that he wasn't one of those cunts that you said something like that to. Never a guarantee that they'd take it in the way it was meant. Really, though. Which fucking gangster *wouldn't* lose their fucking shit when they learned that they'd had their money stolen?

'I don't know what he knows or doesn't about me, and the life I've been living. And I don't have a clue of what anyone in

Edinburgh has told him, because I said and done a few crazy things when I was over in the capital city'

'Well, you were literally on the internet being watched by millions of people so there's a good chance he knows that'

That was just a cold hard fact, I wasn't wanting to argue any point but *mines* had been that you can't question what someone 'might' know about you, when you're not exactly hiding from the world, like my dad had been.

'Fucking Interpol didn't, did they?'

A decent reply because they were meant to be like some super cops or something - were they not? - and my dad had been living ten years on the outside without anyone coming close to catching him.

'Obviously, I'll be knocking the videos on the head now, anyway. Funnily enough, over this trip, I've decided that I don't really need much in the way of clicks on my videos, as a way of providing some income. Same with the gym, full stop, because I can't take the chance that either he knows about it, or someone's going to go on and tell him, once his inquest begins, because it will, and it's going to be brutal for a few unlucky cunts who are in the wrong place at the wrong time and don't have the answer to a question asked to them'

He seemed quite cool about it all, like how a major part of his life was going to just all have to suddenly stop - talking more about the gym he had than those videos which were always going to get old sooner or later, like everything else on the internet - and he was going to have to change up a lot of things in day to day life. Me on the other hand? I think - luckily - my head was bursting with so many questions, fears and thoughts that I wasn't able to concentrate on any single thing.

'What you going to do with the gym, then?'

'Still keep it, obviously. I'll just have to be an absent owner, if you know what I mean, eh? I'll get Pippo to do extra hours as the greedy wee cunt is always looking for them, get him to hire an assistant for himself if he needs one, like. Have to do it right, though. Knock up some fake ownership papers for Pippo to have in the office for the day that a delegation from Edinburgh comes calling. Get Pippo to say that I appeared back from Scotland and - in a hurry - sold him the gym, telling him that I was getting out of town fast. Couple of goons hear a story like that, it's all going to make sense, isn't it? Because someone who has just stolen money from Davey McKenna *would* be in a fucking flap, and wanting to skip town a fucking sap'

It was quite scary just how easily it all came to him, the shithousery and how carefully planned that it was. He wasn't one of those commit the crime and then think about how you're going to get away with it. Nah, he seemed like he had it all sussed out, which, to be honest, gave me a bit of confidence that was needed at that moment.

While *he* had things carefully planned, I'd walked out on, everything. Apart from my clothes and trainers, and my mates, that was about it. The clothes and trainers wouldn't exactly be able to all be replaced, but I'll tell you what? It was going to be some fucking shopping trip, the day I went out to replenish. Proper blow jobs off the sales assistant due to the commission they're going to get from you stuff.

Walking away from your mates, in that way, without saying goodbye. *That* felt as shitty as the feeling of pulling a snide move, like I undoubtedly was. Despite being from the same blood, I was given the heavy impression that dad was going through with this without one single thought for anyone else where - on my side - I couldn't help feel a degree of guilt, in more than one area.

'So it's probably time that we addressed the elephant in the room, because time is not on our side'

Dad said, looking at his phone to check what time we had left to play with. Normally when someone mentions elephant in the room, it's assumed that everyone *in* the room knows what it means. Only, inside there, dad was in on it.

'What you mean, like?'

'Your fucking maw'

He said, tapping the side of his head, looking for me to be a bit more switched on, while I wanted to ask him to cut the boy who'd been out taking Eckies the night before - and Vallies for the comedown - a bit of slack.

He wasn't wrong, though.

We sat while he took me through the reality of things, this being that my mum was no longer going to be safe, there at the flat. I had a flashback to earlier on where I'd asked him about what would happen to mum, but that was when I was fried. Had I been minus the chemicals I'd have already *known* the score, when it came to her. When I'd asked him about gran and grandad, and if they'd be in the same danger as mum was going to be, he told me that they'd be safe enough.

'You fucking *see* how old they are? Nah, trust me, McKenna is going to want to do a lot of dark and nasty things to me, you too, like, but he's old school. Neither of them will have a hair on their head touched'

Then - in a completely passing the buck way - he just started laughing and joking about how better me than him, having to make the call to my mum to tell her that she was going to have to literally decide what she was going to take with her, because once she left Dundee she was never coming back again.

Prompting me, he advised that the closer we got to the Belgian connect calling Edinburgh to say that I'd not appeared, the less time that I was giving mum to get out of town.

'You probably should give her a bell, son. Good luck, by the way. You're going to fucking need it'

He lay there laughing away, like he didn't have a care in the world. I didn't quite appreciate the way that this whole *team* that he spoke of, it clearly didn't extend towards looking after mum, she was just a bit collateral damage to him.

But I knew something - about me and mum - that he never, and I wasn't sharing either, although part of me *wanted* to, to piss on his bonfire a wee bit. Something that would remind him that mum and me were ride or die, *not* me and him. Me and my mum had spent twenty years growing together where - when it came to him and me - we'd only been in the same company twice in our lives, and the first time we met, we were trying to kill each other.

'Aye, I suppose I better go through and make the call'

I said to him before making a passive aggressive joke about him not going anywhere with those bags.

'You know me, son, always a possibility, eh?' You're safe enough there, though. Can't fucking swim, for one thing, eh'

'In a bit'

I said, leaving him there, lying back down on the bed with a smile on his face, while he said that he hoped that Abigail wasn't going to go too mental at me, laughing again and enjoying - I assumed the thoughts of how much of an inconvenience that mum was about to be hit with in a few minutes time.

What he didn't know though, was that me and mum had quite literally *planned* for this day. Not like, planned for me ripping off Davey McKenna for millions of pounds, mind. I wouldn't have ever fucking dared even dream about doing that, for it to be an actual spoken about scenario.

But we'd planned none the less.

I'd been doing the running back and forward from two thousand and five onwards, and for a couple of those years mum was out of work, and you know how fucking tight those dole cunts are, as well? It was the money that *I'd* been making through my bits of work that had literally kept us with a roof over our head, and mum obviously was aware of that. So while, as a mother, she could not have ever been thrilled about the way her son's life was going, sometimes - for the greater good - you just have to accept how things are, and not put too much of a question mark over *how* that dinner is sitting on your plate and just be thankful that it is.

Probably made it harder for her, how young I was - sixteen to eighteen - at the time. I think, because of this, her motherly instincts kicked in where if she couldn't stop me from doing the running - and, obviously, that was going to be against her own best interests, if she had - then she'd be doing what she could to make sure that the two of us were going to be safe, that's all she really had, but for a parent - I can imagine - that must be a big thing, knowing that you're doing your best to look after your own?

It was one night, the two of us were both in the house and that film - Heat - with De Niro and Pacino in it was on the telly. Wasn't even planned - especially with it being so long a fucking film - but we ended up sitting and watching it until the end. There was one bit that stuck with her, though, apparently. Because the next week she called me through to the living room and there on the coffee table was this metal Walker's Shortbread box. Telling me to sit down, she took me through things. Telling me that the film we'd watched the week before on STV had made her think about the two of us.

'That line, the one that De Niro said to Al Pacino ... about not letting yourself get attached to anything you are not willing to walk out on in thirty seconds flat, if you feel the heat around the corner'

It was a good scene in the film and that but for fuck's sake, mum. I'm only carrying drugs from A to B, I'm not a bank robber, I tried to tell her but she was insistent. Telling me that I was too young to realise it but there may come a day where I found myself - and by extension, *her* - needing to leave town, and in a hurry.

'You don't know what you're getting involved in with the drugs, or the toes that you're stepping on along the way, or what police are taking notice'

She wasn't having any protests from me, judging it all a little dramatic.

'So what's this, then?'

I'd nodded towards the metal box sitting on the table.

'This, Liam, is our "get tae fuck box" and is going to have all of the stuff that we need to leave in a hurry, should there ever be that day, and let's both hope and pray that it's not ever going to be required, eh?'

She opened it up to show that it already had some notes inside of it and telling me that it would be added to, as and when possible. There was a couple of cheap Nokia pay as you go mobiles in there too. And not just that, either. That we would be getting passports made up as soon as possible and *they'd* be getting shoved in there, too'

I just laughed at her, but humoured the craziness all the same. Went for the passport with her, even though there was zero fucking chance that her and me were ever going to be going away on our holidays and using them.

Aye, who's laughing now, mum, eh? Well, probably not even my mum - when I made the phone call - but at least she'd have been given the sense of having been right all along, with the *get tae fuck box*.

I'd fucked about - through in the cabin - and wasted time, precious time, through simply not wanting to make the call, but it had to be done.

As I went to pick up my phone I heard the scream - funny how obvious it was that someone was next door, when there was no music playing, and you weren't on a couple of pingers - from my dad, through in his cabin.

'Four fucking million point fucking two. FUCKING YAASSSS, YA CUNT'

Someone's been busy with the calculator, by the sounds, I thought to myself as I looked up mum's number - after having a wee dance around in celebration of the breaking news from dad's side of the wall - and prepared to rock her world to its foundations.

No doubt about it though. Exciting times, if sure to have their fair share of nerves, lay ahead.

That whole world being your oyster thing, that you see people say sometimes. Had never really understood the expression because, for most people, the world really *isn't* your oyster. It's one of those shitey half broken shells that's been pissed all over by a seagull, that you find on the beach, and that's if you're lucky.

That day, though, and the feeling of all the things that were now going to be possible and just how big the world could be, and with over two million pounds to help fill it.

I actually *got it*.

And it had been provided by the most unlikeliest of sources, in my dad.

'*Here we go here we go here we go, here we go here we go here we go-oh, here we go here we go here we go, here we go-oh HERE WE GO*'

Hearing him shouting and screaming with joy, next door, I couldn't help but shake my head and laugh at him, while thinking that since he'd arrived in Scotland - and me having him in my life for those few days - and how, if *that* had been anything to go by, it was probably for the best that I'd missed out on the previous twenty years with him around.

Chapter 42

Detective Constable Roy van der Elst

Detective Constable Roy van der Elst
International Serious Crimes Unit
Employee Number E420024
Interpol Headquarters
(International Criminal Police Organisation)
200 Quai
Charles de Gaulle
69006
Lyon
France

Case number - SC5635TG
P.O.I - Norman Walker Fulton
Nationality - British
Aliases - Nora

6-12-2010

On Wednesday (1st December) Head of International Serious Crime, Bert Goosens, informed me that due to an outage at AMS Schipol, their facial recognition system numerous flights' passengers were not screened. When this fault was reported and rectified it was established, that inside this window of systems being down, Norman Walker Fulton - of British, Scottish nationality - who we currently have an outstanding international arrest warrant filed for, boarded a plane to Edinburgh, Scotland.

Head Goosens advised that I was to travel the next morning to Edinburgh, where I would be connected with a detective from the Lothian and Borders police force to track down Norman Walker Fulton.

Upon arrival at Edinburgh Police HQ, however, it was made apparently clear to me - upon introduction to the partner who had been assigned to me, Detective Colin Samuel - that we, as an organisation, were wasting our time with our operation.

Never in my career have I come across an officer of the law with such blatant disregard for their role and duties, while mixed with an unflinching quest to satisfy one's own self interest.

Due to this, I attempted to steer our investigation in the right direction at all times but my assigned partner was not the type who takes kindly to being steered by anyone, which inevitably led to personality clashes between the two of us which, in my opinion, was nothing other than counter productive to my remit of catching, recovering and handing Fulton over to the Scottish authorities to deal with.

After several wasted hours on my day of arrival. Detective Samuel and I travelled to Fulton's home city of Dundee, the working assumption being that this would be the most likely of spots to recover our target.

The time spent in Dundee (2nd December) included questioning our target's parents, reconnaissance of several drinking bars, and surveillance of a professional football match at Tannadice Park. None of this produced any results or leads.

It must be also stated - at this point - that over this day. Detective Samuel had delayed our commute to Dundee - from Edinburgh - through insisting on going for an extended brunch, visit an informant, - which I'd found to be highly questionable - take the both of us further away from Dundee - to buy fish - and towards the evening began drinking on the job, leading to me driving the two of us back to Edinburgh at the end of the night.

The following day (Friday 3rd December) proved just as fruitless. I was made to wait for two hours in the Edinburgh Police HQ before Samuel appeared, where went through the same time consuming practice of going for brunch. With no leads from the previous day we travelled back to Dundee where the majority of our time was spent chasing down known acquaintances of Fulton, also without any modicum of success.

Heading into the next day (Saturday 4th December) and with still some crucial figures that had eluded us the previous day. Detective Samuel and I travelled back, again. Arriving in Dundee at a much more satisfactory time of day, my partner and I were in the process of questioning the son of Norman Walker Fulton when Detective Samuel was informed that there had been a sighting of our P.O.I, back in Edinburgh.

Spotted at an Edinburgh football stadium (Easter Road) live on television, it was my opinion that the suspect should be apprehended by officers on the ground as soon as possible. This was a position that I was adamant of, with Detective Samuel in disagreement with this, instructing his eyes on the ground to observe, but to not move in on the suspect and arrest.

This, through Detective Samuel's desire to be awarded the accolades of catching Fulton, as the arresting detective. After a heated debate between the two of us - which lasted almost the entire journey from Dundee to Edinburgh - Samuel would still not have our P.O.I arrested.

On our return back to the city of Edinburgh, we were informed that Norman Walker Fulton had been seen going into a bar, watched by in undercover officer belonging to Lothian and Borders police force, stationed outside. On our arrival at the bar - The Corinthian - we were met with the sight of a member of the public, holding a gun at the Edinburgh undercover officer.

This, - while being apparently related to our own case - delaying Detective Samuel and I from entering the bar to recover Fulton from the premises. After a brief stand off between gunman and armed police. Detective Samuel and I were able to enter The Corinthian, initially finding that there was no trace of Fulton.

Through Detective Samuel's local knowledge we were eventually taken down to what appeared to be a hidden basement to the bar where, once down there, it was discovered that a boxing ring was situated underneath the bar, and a crowd all standing around drinking. After detaining all of them for questioning, once again, there was no Norman Walker Fulton.

The working theory being that if he had been down there, in the basement, then he was gone before we'd got there, likely through the double bolted door inside the same room as the boxing ring and a door that we'd had opened for us but neither Detective Samuel or I pursued any further.

I apologise for my apparent lack of professionalism - in the heat of the moment - but given the fact that Fulton had been watched for hours before that point and had not been arrested, only to then escape police watch. My frustrations over the three days surfaced. The feeling that I was about the only person who'd really had any desire to catch Fulton.

I informed Samuel - there inside the basement - that the investigation was at an end and how I would be leaving Edinburgh on the first plane back to France and was told, in reply by my partner, that he would drive me to the airport himself before then calling me a c**t. This was not the first time he called me this over the operation.

In the following two days - since returning to Lyon - I have continued to liaise with Lothian and Borders police force on the subject of any leads they may or may not have had but at present there has not been any further sighting of Fulton, following the events of Saturday 4th December while - on The Netherlands side - AMS Schipol will continue to monitor arrivals from Edinburgh for any potential return flight.

In conclusion;

Norman Walker Fulton remains at large and should continue to be considered as extremely dangerous.

Detective Constable, Roy van der Elst
December Sixth, 2010

Also by Johnny Proctor

The Zico trilogy

Ninety

A great portrait of a seminal time for youth culture in the U.K. A nostalgic must read for those who experienced it and an exciting and intriguing read for those that didn't' Dean Cavanagh - Award winning screenwriter.

Meet Zico. 16 years old in 1990 Scotland. Still at school and preparing himself for entering the big bad world while already finding himself on the wrong side of the tracks. A teenager who, despite his young years, is already no stranger to the bad in life. A member of the notorious Dundee Utility Crew who wreak havoc across the country every Saturday on match day.

Then along comes a girl, Acid House and Ecstasy gatecrashing into his life showing him that there other paths that can be chosen. When you're on a pre set course of self destruction however. Sometimes changing direction isn't so easy. Ninety is a tale of what can happen when a teenager grows up faster than they should ever have to while finding themselves pulled into a dangerous turn of events that threatens their very own existence.

Set against the backdrop of a pivotal and defining period of time for the British working class youth when terrace culture and Acid House collided. Infectiously changing lives and attitudes along the way.

Ninety Six

Ninety Six - The second instalment of the Zico trilogy.

Six years on and following events from 'Ninety' ... When Stevie "Zico" Duncan bags a residency at one of Ibiza's most legendary clubs, marking the rising star that he is becoming in the House Music scene. Life could not appear more perfect. Zico and perfect, however, have rarely ever went together.

Set during the summer of Euro 96. Three months on an island of sun, sea and sand as well as the Ibiza nightlife and everything that comes with it. What could possibly go wrong? It's coming home but will Zico?

Noughty

Bringing a close to the most crucial and important decade of all.

Noughty - The third book from Johnny Proctor. Following the events of the infamous summer of Ninety Six in Ibiza. Three years on the effects are still being felt inside the world of Stevie 'Zico' Duncan and those closest to him. Now having relocated to Amsterdam it's all change for the soccer casual turned house deejay however, as Zico soon begins to find. The more that things change the more they seem to stay the same. Noughty signals the end of the 90's trilogy of books which celebrated the decade that changed the face, and attitudes, of UK youth culture and beyond.

Muirhouse

Living in the 'Naughty North' of Edinburgh, for some, can be difficult. For the Carson family, however? Life's never dull.

You'll give them that.

'Muirhouse' by Johnny Proctor is a story of the fortunes of Joe 'Strings' Carson.

Midfield general for infamous amateur football team 'Muirhouse Violet' on a Sunday and petty criminal every other day of the week. Above all, though. Strings is a family man and, like any self respecting husband and father, will do whatever it takes to protect his household.

A commitment and loyalty that he's about to find being put to the ultimate test.

Available through DM to help support the independents.

El Corazon Valiente; The ballad of Peter Duncan

El Corazon Valiente ; The ballad of Peter Duncan. A Zico trilogy origins story. Picking up where Noughty left off. El Corazon Valiente offers a look at how life is for Peter Duncan following events in Amsterdam, 2000. Finally find out how Stevie Duncan's father - through his own charm, ruthlessness and sense of self preservation - went from small Scottish town chancer to a vital component of a well known Colombian cartel. And how it all came crashing down around him.

The Onion Ring

Rule number one in the drug game is to always pay your debts; but what happens when you can't?

Just how far would you go to find redemption?

Something that best friends and business partners Drummond, Hammy and Hummel are faced with when their business experiences some "technical difficulties."

Leaving them to find out just how far they will go.

Available via DM at : Twitter @johnnyroc73 and Instagram @johnnyproctor90

Also available through Paninaro Publishing, Apple Books, Kindle, Amazon, Waterstones and other book shops.

Printed in Great Britain
by Amazon